The Complete Screech Owls

Volume 1

Roy MacGregor

M&S

Copyright © 2006 by Roy MacGregor

This omnibus edition published in 2006 by McClelland & Stewart

Mystery at Lake Placid copyright © 1995 by Roy MacGregor
The Night They Stole the Stanley Cup copyright © 1995 by Roy MacGregor
The Screech Owls' Northern Adventure copyright © 1996 by Roy MacGregor
Murder at Hockey Camp copyright © 1997 by Roy MacGregor

Library and Archives Canada Cataloguing in Publication

MacGregor, Roy, 1948-
    The complete Screech Owls / written by Roy MacGregor.

Contents: v. 1. Mystery at Lake Placid — The night they stole the Stanley Cup — The Screech Owls' northern adventure — Murder at hockey camp.
ISBN 0-7710-5484-X (v. 1)

    I. Title.   II. Title: Mystery at Lake Placid.   III. Title: The night they stole the Stanley Cup.   IV. The Screech Owls' northern adventure.
V. Murder at hockey camp.

PS8575.G84C64 2005   jC813'.54   C2005-903880-2

We acknowledge the financial support of the Government of Canada through the Book Publishing Industry Development Program and that of the Government of Ontario through the Ontario Media Development Corporation's Ontario Book Initiative. We further acknowledge the support of the Canada Council for the Arts and the Ontario Arts Council for our publishing program.

Typeset in Bembo by M&S, Toronto
Printed and bound in the United States of America

Cover illustration by Sue Todd

McClelland & Stewart Ltd.
75 Sherbourne Street
Toronto, Ontario
M5A 2P9
www.mcclelland.com

3 4 5 6 7   13 12 11 10 09

Contents

Mystery at Lake Placid

1

"Wedgie stop!"

Travis Lindsay could not believe his ears.

"WEDDD-GEEE stop!"

The big Ford van had been travelling nonstop since the last bathroom break — and Travis had no idea how long ago that had been. He knew only that they had finally turned off that boring four-lane highway and that, far in the distance over the trees, the high green bridge over the St. Lawrence River was now visible. Beyond lay New York State and the road to Lake Placid. Finally.

Travis had fallen asleep as they drove. He'd had the craziest series of dreams, the kind you always have when half asleep and half awake, head bobbing and eyes drifting. He had dreamed he'd finally found his father's long-lost hockey card collection, the one he searched high and low for, without success, every visit to his grandmother's old house in the country. He had dreamed he was back in grade six, that he had failed his year, and that he was failing again because someone had stolen all his workbooks from his locker. And he had dreamed he was taking a face-off in the Olympic Center in Lake Placid – the American Stars and Stripes and the Canadian Maple Leaf flying high over-head, the two anthems still echoing in the rafters, in the stands his mother and father, his teachers, his friends from school, NHL scouts, Wayne Gretzky and Bobby Orr and Gordie Howe, Alexei Yashin and Paul Kariya, Eric Lindros, the "Hockey Night in Canada" crew – and just as the referee held out the puck, Travis looked down at the circle and saw that *he had forgotten to put on his skates!*

His toes were blue! His feet were wiggling and slipping on the cold ice surface. But no one else had noticed! The referee's skates dug in, sending ice chips flying. The other centre's skates kicked in toward the circle, the skate heading toward Travis's toes with more sharp blades than a Swiss Army knife.

NNNNOOOOOOO! . . .

Travis had woken up in the van shouting, and everyone on the Screech Owls had laughed and slapped at his shoulders and the back of his head. He had refused to tell them what had scared him. Let them think whatever they wanted. It was a ridiculous dream anyway. He'd never forget his skates. Besides, he wasn't even a centre.

Mr. Dillinger had been driving since they left Tamarack and would be driving until they got there. He would have to – Mr. Dillinger was the only one in the rented twelve-seater van old enough to have a licence. Muck and the assistant coaches, the other parents who were coming, and four of the players were in other cars, some far ahead, some somewhere behind. Travis was secretly pleased that his mother and father had decided not to come, because now he got to travel with the team for once –

and delighted, too, that Mr. Dillinger was in charge of the rented van.

Travis looked ahead three seats to where Mr. Dillinger was sitting. He certainly didn't look like a kid – what kid has curly grey hair, a bald spot, and a potbelly big as a hockey bag? – but he sure did act like one. He had started the trip with a "Stupid Stop," pulling off and parking by a little variety store and then standing by its entrance handing out two-dollar bills with only one instruction: "Remember, it's a 'Stupid Stop.' I want you to spend every cent of it in one place on something cheap and useless that won't last."

Travis had bought a gummy hand that he could flip ahead two seats, past Derek Dillinger, who was reading quietly, and wrap right around the face of his best friend, Wayne Nishikawa. "Nish," the sickest mind by far on the Screech Owls, had bought a pen with a bathing beauty on it and when you turned the pen upside-down the bathing suit seemed to peel off. But you couldn't see anything.

Mr. Dillinger had tapes like "Weird Al" Yankovic singing silly songs like "Jurassic Park" and "Bedrock Anthem" and "Young, Dumb & Ugly." He had licorice, red and black, to hand back, cold pop in the cooler, and comic books – *X-Men*, *Batman*, *Superman*, even a *Mad* magazine – for them to read. He had pillows packed for anyone who, like Travis, wanted to snooze, and, best of all, he had the most outrageous sense of humour Travis or any of the other kids had ever seen in an adult. Not once had anyone whined, "Are we there yet?"

Mr. Dillinger made the perfect team manager. He even made the best jokes himself about his lack of hair, one time

showing up for a tournament with a T-shirt that said, "THAT'S
NO BALD SPOT – IT'S A SOLAR PANEL FOR A SEX MACHINE." He
was fun and funny, but serious when it mattered. Because he also
served as the team trainer, Mr. Dillinger knew first aid. Nish's
parents believed he had probably saved Nish from being crip-
pled the year before when he crashed head-first into the boards
and Mr. Dillinger refused to let the game continue until an
ambulance came. They had carried Nish off the ice on a
stretcher, treating him like a cracked egg about to spill. Then
their ice time ran out and the game had to be called with the
score still tied. Some of the other parents – mostly from the
other team, but also loud Mr. Brown, Matt's father – had been
yelling for them to get Nish off the ice so the game could continue. The two young referees had looked like they were going
to cave in, but Mr. Dillinger had angrily ordered them to clear
the ice of players so that no one could slip and fall onto Nish. It
turned out that Nish had a hairline fracture of his third verte-
brae – almost a broken neck – but thanks to Mr. Dillinger taking
charge he hadn't needed anything more than a neck brace and
a couple of months off skates and Nish was right back, better
than ever. Nish adored Mr. Dillinger.

Mr. Dillinger organized the car pools, made the telephone
calls, printed up the schedules and handed them out and
replaced those ones the players lost. He ran the fundraisers – if
Travis never saw another bottle drive he'd be happy – and he
taped the sticks and sharpened the skates. He sewed the names
on the sweaters, washed the sweaters, and even got a local computer company to sponsor the Screech Owls. The computer
company had bought the team jackets and hats and redesigned

the logo so it looked, Travis and the rest of the team thought, better than most of the NHL crests and almost as good as – Travis thought just as good as – the San Jose Sharks' and the Mighty Ducks of Anaheim's.

"Wedgie stop!

"WEDDD–GEEE stop!"

Mr. Dillinger was still shouting and laughing as he put the big van in park and hopped out onto the shoulder of the road. He ran around to the front of the van, bending over and wiggling so his big belly rippled right through his shirt, and with his hands pulling at the seat of his pants, he pretended to be yanking a huge "wedgie" of bunched-up underwear out of his rear end.

Howling with laughter, the team followed suit, a dozen young players out on the side of the road yanking at their pants to free up their underwear and wiggling their rear ends at the other cars that roared by, the drivers and passengers either staring out as if the Screech Owls should be arrested or else pretending the Screech Owls were not even there, a dozen youngsters at the side of the road, bent over, with a hand on each side of their pants, pulling wedgies.

"All 'board!" Mr. Dillinger hollered as he jumped in the van. The team scrambled back in, Nish and several others laughing so hard they had tears in their eyes.

Mr. Dillinger started up the van, then turned, his face unsmiling, voice as serious as a vice-principal's.

"The United States of America takes wedgies very seriously," he announced. "At the border they will ask you where you were born and whether or not you are having any difficulty with your underwear. If they suspect you are having problems, you will be body-searched. If they find any wedgies, you will spend the rest of your life . . ."

He paused, waiting.

Nish finished for him: ". . . in prison?"

Mr. Dillinger stared, then smiled: "In Pampers, Nish, in Pampers."

2

here had been no "wedgie check" at the American border. A guard had come out and looked in all the windows and guessed, accurately, that they were on their way to Lake Placid for a hockey tournament. He had asked where they were from and where they were born and Mr. Dillinger, organized as always, had passed over a clipboard with a photocopy of everyone's birth certificate.

Mr. Dillinger even had the passports of Fahd Noorizadeh and Dmitri Yakushev, who weren't yet full Canadian citizens. Fahd boasted he would be the first Saudi Arabian to make the NHL. Dmitri said he would be around the five-hundredth Russian and liked to joke that by the time he got there Canadians would be the exceptions in the NHL and people would be complaining that they were taking jobs from Russian boys.

Dmitri had a weird sense of humour. He was a thin, blond kid with a crooked smile and, Travis figured, the fastest skater in the league. He had started to play hockey back in Moscow and came to Canada at age nine with his parents, so he couldn't really claim to be a product of either system, the Russian or the Canadian. His uncle had once played for the Soviet Red Army team and Dmitri planned to be one of the best hockey players in the world, like him. Right now he was just one of the best hockey players in Tamarack.

But the Screech Owls were a pretty good team. Once, in the back of his Language Arts notebook on an afternoon when the class was supposed to be reading ahead, Travis had even done a scouting report on them:

GOAL

GUY BOUCHER: Quick hands, great blocker. Yells a lot while playing. Two different ways of saying both names. "Guy," or "Gee," like in Lafleur, and "Bow-cher" or "Boo-shay," depending on where he's playing. No one ever knows how his name's going to come out over the public address.

SAREEN GOUPA: Back-up. Good stick and pads, but misses high shots and can be deked pretty easily. Still, pretty good for having played only two years. Team sometimes calls her "Manon" after Manon Rhéaume, her idol.

DEFENCE

WAYNE NISHIKAWA: "Nish" is the steadiest of all the Screech Owls. Not a really fast skater, but a good shot and very good in front of his own net. Clean player, dirty mind.

LARRY ULMAR: Nish's usual partner. Slow but a good passer. Lets other team go too much. Nickname is "Data." Obsessed with "Star Trek: The Next Generation." Claims he can speak Klingon and sometimes tries. Sometimes plays like a Klingon, too.

NORBERT PHILPOTT: The team's "Captain Video" – Norbert's father owns a video rental outlet and sometimes shoots the games and they show the videos during team get-togethers. Norbert has to analyze everything. As for his own play, he's not very flashy, but he works hard and everyone on the team likes him.

WILLIE GRANGER: The team's trivia expert. Has probably 10,000 hockey cards in his collection and also has a lot of autographs – Pavel Bure, Jaromir Jagr, Pat LaFontaine, Raymond Bourque, even a Wayne Gretzky – which his uncle, a sportswriter in Toronto, gets for him. Willie is a smart player, if not particularly fast. If he had a good shot, he'd be on the power play.

WILSON KELLY: Tremendous checker. Still learning the game, but improving all the time. Always in position. Plans on becoming the first Jamaican to compete in hockey in the Winter Olympics. But for Canada, he says, not Jamaica.

ZAK ADELMAN: Quick, but not a physical presence like Wilson. Wilson can cover when Zak pinches up into the play. Quiet but funny – one of those senses of humour where you usually have to run it through your brain a second time before you realize what he's said.

FORWARDS

SARAH CUTHBERTSON: Centre and the team's best player. Mother skated for Canada in the 1976 Winter Olympics – speed skating – and she now teaches power skating. Sarah is determined to play for Canada in the 1998 Winter Olympics, the year Women's Hockey becomes an official medal sport. She's already been asked to play tournaments for the Toronto Aeros and will join that team after peewee. Best skater on the team. Great playmaker. Pretty good shot, but doesn't use it enough. Team captain.

DMITRI YAKUSHEV: First-line right wing. So fast he sometimes runs right over the puck. If Sarah hits him with a breakaway pass, Dmitri is gone. No one ever catches him and hardly anyone ever stops him. Great with his feet, which he says comes from playing soccer instead of summer hockey. Idolizes Pavel Bure.

TRAVIS LINDSAY:
Left wing, first line. Good skater, good stickhandler, fair shot. Assistant captain.

DEREK DILLINGER: Second-line centre. Good playmaker with a very good shot. Would have more points if on first line and will probably move up once Sarah moves on to the

Aeros. Because of strength is the face-off man used in tight situations. Hooked on video games. Quieter and more serious than his father.

MATT BROWN: Left wing. Great shot. Lacks speed. Doesn't like to carry the puck, but get it to him and it's in. Muck has benched him in the past for lazy back-checking.

FAHD NOORIZADEH: Third-line right wing, first-line computer expert. Produces printouts of everything from goals and assists to plus-minus and chances. Muck thinks this is ridiculous: "The only numbers that matter," Muck says, "are the two they flash up on the scoreboard." Didn't start playing until nine years old and improving all the time. Great knack for reading play.

GORDIE GRIFFITH: Third-line centre. Big and gawky. Gets noticed because of size. Most penalized player on team, the one the other parents yell at – but he isn't dirty at all. Has some shifty moves and can lift puck over net from the blueline.

JESSE HIGHBOY: Right wing. The Screech Owls' newest player, moving into town around Christmas from way up north in James Bay. His dad's a lawyer and Jesse says he's going to be one, too, and still be in the NHL as the league's first *playing* commissioner. A great team player, cheers everybody. Needs more ice time.

MARIO TERZIANO: "The Garbage Collector." Nothing fancy, hardly even noticeable – until there's a big scramble in front of the net and the puck is suddenly loose in the slot. Always has his stick down, always ready. A good-hearted guy who laughs even at himself.

The Screech Owls were even slightly famous, having been written up in the *Toronto Star* during a tournament they'd played in Mississauga. Someone must have called the paper in, because a writer and photographer arrived and talked to all the players, and the next day they were on the front page.

The story in the paper was all about how the Screech Owls represented virtually every part of the country. They had a French-Canadian goaltender. They had different religions. They had players who had come from, or whose parents or grand-parents had come from, Japan, Saudi Arabia, Russia, Lebanon, Jamaica, Italy, Great Britain, and Germany. And now this year Jesse Highboy, a Cree, had joined. And they had two girls on the team – three before Jessica Crozier had moved out to Calgary.

The story had seemed ridiculous to Travis – after all, they hadn't even made it as far as the tournament final. And the writer of the article kept referring to them as "Team United Nations," only once using their proper name, the Screech Owls. He had also described Sarah as "too pretty to be taken for a hockey player with her soft eyes and long, tumbling brown hair." But Sarah had got the writer back. The reporter had asked Sarah if it bothered her that women made up more than 50 per cent of the population but less than 10 per cent of the Screech Owls.

"Why would it?" Sarah answered. "I've been in on more than 50 per cent of the goals."

⊚

Travis began dozing off again as the big van headed up into the mountains. He heard Willie Granger, team expert on everything, spouting off facts from the *Guinness Book of Records* on how the Adirondacks didn't even compare to the really high mountains like the Rockies and Mount Everest. He heard Nish, the team pervert, giggling that two of the rounded hills off in the distance looked like "boobs." Nothing unusual there. Nish was so crazy he once said the face-off circles reminded him of two big boobs out in front of the net.

Travis placed his head against the humming window and asked himself the question he'd been asking since the first year he'd signed up for hockey: when was he ever going to start growing? He had always been small, but he hadn't started worrying about it until he turned peewee. He was twelve going on thirteen. Another school year and he would be headed into high school and − already notably small in the schoolyard of Lord Stanley Public School − he was petrified he wouldn't grow before he got there.

Growing was only one of two serious matters that deeply bothered Travis. The second was his fear of the dark − how many twelve-year-olds still needed a night light? − but most of the time his fear of the dark was something he could keep to himself and his family. But how could you hide your size?

"Hang in there," his father kept telling him. "You'll grow. I was a late grower. My brothers were late growers. You'll go to sleep one night and wake up the next morning having ripped right out of your clothes."

Travis knew what an exaggeration that was. He knew that his father meant he'd have a late growth spurt that might come over one summer, not a single night, and he knew better than to think he would ever fall asleep a peewee and wake up a bantam in a pair of torn pyjamas. But he couldn't help wishing anyway. Wouldn't it be nice if, when they got to Lake Placid, Travis stepped out of the van and his pant cuffs were up around his knees . . .

"PIT STOP!"

Travis jumped. He had been dozing again. His head felt thick, his eyes out of focus. He rubbed them as Mr. Dillinger called again from the driver's seat of the big van.

"Pit Stop! Last one before Lake Placid! Ten minutes! You go now or you go later in your pants – this means you, Nish!"

Travis could hear them giggling. His vision cleared and he saw that everyone in the van was looking back at him. Because he had fallen asleep, obviously. Well, so what? But they wouldn't stop laughing.

"What's so funny?" Travis asked Nish, who had turned around, his face looking like it was about to split.

"Mr. Dillinger. Didn't you hear him?"

It didn't make sense, but Travis let it go. He headed into the restaurant, pushed the door open, saw that everyone in there was laughing at the team coming in – what was the matter with them, never see hockey players in a van? – and decided that he'd better go to the washroom first.

Funny, there was no line-up. Nish and some of the other kids were hanging around outside the door but they didn't seem to want to go in. More like they were waiting. Travis pushed past them through the door, turned to the mirror – and saw immediately what his teammates, and all the people in the restaurant, had been giggling at:

HIS HEAD WAS COVERED IN CREAM!

It had been put on like a cone. Swirled like he was about to be dipped into chocolate at Dairy Queen. He looked like a fool. But it was so light he hadn't felt it. That's why they'd been laughing at him. It was hilariously obvious to everyone but Travis himself, who couldn't even feel it up there.

Travis grabbed a handful of the cream and threw it off his head into the sink. He reached for some paper towels and began rubbing it off. On the other side of the door, he could hear the entire team howling with laughter as they imagined his reaction.

Travis smelled his hands. Shaving cream. There was only one person in the Screech Owls van old enough to shave.

Mr. Dillinger.

3

ravis was still blotting shaving cream from his hair as the pines gave way and the van began climbing up through a twisting string of motels and motor inns, past a Burger King and McDonald's, up and over a hill and down onto the main street of Lake Placid. They were finally here. The six-hour drive was forgotten. The shaving cream was forgotten. Travis was as wide awake and alert as he would be if the team was just waiting for the Zamboni to finish flooding the ice so the game could begin.

Lake Placid was alive with cars and campers and people. It was still early spring yet it felt like an Ontario tourist town at the height of the season. Traffic barely moved. Shoppers wove through the cars as if the street were a parking lot and the stop-lights meaningless. It felt like summer to Travis, after a winter of heavy boots and thick jackets and shovelling snow.

There was a banner stretched high across the street. "WELCOME TO LAKE PLACID'S SIXTH ANNUAL INTERNATIONAL

PEEWEE HOCKEY CHAMPIONSHIP." "International" – the word made it seem impossible, more like one of his dreams than reality.

Travis had been playing hockey for six seasons – tyke, novice, atom, and now peewee – and he had got much better each year, if not much bigger. In tyke, with his dad the coach, Travis had started the season holding on to the back of a stacking chair so he wouldn't fall, and he had finished the season the best skater on the team after Sarah Cuthbertson, who had, they all joked, an unfair advantage in her mother.

He knew why: he was the one kid who skated every day – or at least every chance he got – in the open-air rink behind the school. And when he wasn't on the rink, he was in his basement, stickhandling tennis balls across the concrete and firing pucks against a big plywood board his father had bought and attached to the wall.

Travis Lindsay was hockey-crazy. His favourite team was the Detroit Red Wings. He had all the cards from the recent years – Steve Yzerman and Sergei Fedorov – but the Detroit team of his dreams played back in the 1950s, thirty years before he was even born, when "Terrible Ted" Lindsay and "Mr. Hockey," Gordie Howe, were the superstars.

Travis's grandfather had once told him that Ted Lindsay was a distant cousin, which made him an even more distant cousin of Travis's – but a cousin all the same. The same name, the same skills . . . the same size. Ted Lindsay had not been big, either, but he had ended up being known as "Terrible Ted" and was in the Hockey Hall of Fame. "Terrible Travis" didn't sound quite as good, but it was the way Travis secretly liked to think of himself.

He had been through house league. He had played on the atom competitive team for a jerk named Mr. Spratt who called them by their last names and insisted on being called "Coach." He wore a suit while he worked the bench in tournaments – even chewed ice like an NHL coach. He used to scream at the kids until they cried. With his parents' blessing, Travis had quit and gone back to house league.

And then he had tried competitive again. With Muck.

Muck Munro was so unlike "Coach" Spratt that it hardly seemed they played the same game. Muck didn't yell. He laughed at the first player who called him "Coach." He didn't wear suits during games, didn't wear matching track outfits for practices.

According to Guy Boucher's dad, Muck had been a pretty fine junior player at one time, but he had so severely broken his leg in a game that he had had to quit hockey altogether. He still walked with a slight limp.

But Travis could see the ability whenever Muck came out onto the ice with them. He had to favour his bad leg a bit, but Travis had never heard a sweeter sound in his life than when Muck went out onto the still-wet ice and took a few long strides down the rink and into the turn, his skates sizzling like bacon in a frying pan as they dug in and flicked out into the next stride.

Travis had tried to listen to his own skating, but all he could hear was the chop when his blades hit. Nothing smooth, nothing sizzling. He figured he had neither the stride nor the weight. He was too small to sound like Muck.

Muck put the team together. He was the one who got Barry Yonson and Ty Barrett to come on as assistants. Barry had played junior "B" the year before, quitting to concentrate on his school work, but Muck figured, correctly, that Barry missed his ice time and invited him out to help with the team. Barry was great: a big, curly-haired guy with a constant gap-toothed smile and the ability to slap a puck – in the air! – all the way from his own blueline over the net and against the glass at the far end.

Ty Barrett was a bit older but had also once played for Muck. He worked as an assistant manager at the Tim Horton donut shop and every time they had an early practice he would bring in a box of still-warm Timbits he had picked up on the way to the rink. Though heavy-set and a weak skater, Ty was great at organizing drills. He made them fun, always with the two sides competing against each other for first grabs at the Timbits.

It had been Muck who got Mr. Dillinger to be the team manager and trainer, and that had worked out wonderfully, as well. Mr. Dillinger kept the dressing room loose. He drove the van to the tournaments. He organized the pizza, the pop, the wedgie stops. Travis had never had so much fun playing on a team in his life.

@

"This is it!" Mr. Dillinger shouted as the van groaned up one more hill and swept into the parking lot of the Holiday Inn. It was a Holiday Inn unlike any they had seen before. Sun Spree Resort, it called itself, with a putting green out front, nature trails, a big indoor pool, a Jacuzzi hot tub, an arcade, and, straight back down the hill, the Olympic Center hockey rink. The teams could practically roll out of bed into their dressing rooms.

"Awwwww-righhhhtttt!" all twelve Screech Owls shouted. Nish pumped a fat fist out the side window.

They piled out of the van and into the hotel. Muck was already there, waiting, with his usual Diet Coke in his right hand. Spread out before him on a small table were a dozen or so white envelopes with names and numbers on them.

"Good drive?" Muck asked.

"One close shave," Mr. Dillinger answered. "Right, Travis?"

Mr. Dillinger laughed so hard two women checking in turned to stare, but he didn't care. Travis turned red.

"Check the envelopes," Muck said to the new arrivals. "You'll find your roomies and two keys per room. Soon as you find your rooms you can go on up."

Travis was in with Nish, Wilson, and Data. He couldn't have picked better roommates if the choosing had been left to him.

"One more thing," Muck announced as the players scrambled for their keys. "Don't even try to watch the adult movies on your TVs. We've had the front desk disengage the pay channels for the whole tournament. Understand, Nish?"

Nish kept them up until midnight trying, unsuccessfully, to re-wire the television so he could watch the forbidden movies. It had taken Travis a long time to fall asleep. He was just too excited about the tournament. It wasn't his fear of the dark – he'd solved that by going last to the bathroom and then "forgetting" to turn off the light, leaving the door open barely a crack. None of the other boys had complained.

By 6:30 a.m. he was wide awake again. Wide awake and anxious. He checked to see if anyone else was awake. Nish was rolled in his sheets like a tortilla, the only fragment of flesh exposed a single big toe sticking free at the bottom. Wilson, on the other hand, had nothing over him, since Nish had yanked all the blankets to his side during the night, and was rolled up in a ball like a baby. Data was snoring slightly, breathing like an old Klingon.

Travis went into the washroom and wet three washcloths with water as cold as it would run. He squeezed them out and then brought them back into the bedroom where he dropped one on each face and, in the case of Nish, over his big toe.

"Whaaaaa?" called Wilson, who bolted straight up.

"*Jach!*" shouted Data. He even dreamed in Klingon!

Nish didn't stir.

"C'mon, guys," Travis said to the others. "We got an eight o'clock practice."

"I don't have to practise any more," Wilson argued. "I can't get any better."

"Come on, Wils – you want to play in the Olympics, you better find out how slow you are on an Olympic ice surface."

Growling, Wilson threw his pillow at Travis and rolled out of bed. Data was already up and moving. Wilson and Travis jumped simultaneously onto Nish, squashing the Tortilla.

"Hey!" Nish shouted, trapped by his blankets. "Bug off!"

Nish began to twist violently, going nowhere. Wils sat on his head, lifted his arm and, with his open hand cupped under his armpit, made a loud farting noise that caused Nish to twist and scream until he bounced right off the bed onto the floor.

With Nish furiously staring up, Wils once again let one rip from his armpit, with everyone laughing at poor Nish, who'd taken the sound for something else.

"Jerk," said Nish.

"Let's go," Travis said.

4

ravis Lindsay loved dressing rooms. The smells, the sounds, the anticipation before a game and the satisfaction after: ever since he began playing Travis had loved that first feeling that came over him as he walked into a hockey dressing room.

He loved the familiarity. He loved to know he had his place and his teammates would expect him to be in it. He loved the insults, the practical jokes, the wicked, Coke-forced belches, the stupid, meaningless, harmless bragging.

Sometimes the feeling was better before a game, when everyone would be coming in at different times – Nish usually first, delivered by his parents, who knew his habits best, and then dawdling until he was the last one dressed. Matt Brown always late, his bigmouthed father in a panic and sharp with Matt as he pushed him to hurry. Fahd sometimes playing Tetris on his Game Boy until Mr. Dillinger announced the Zamboni was out on the ice, then dressing with all the precision and efficiency of a human computer. Sarah Cuthbertson arriving fully dressed but for her shoulder pads, sweater, gloves, helmet, and skates. Willie Granger with some obscure fact he'd memorized from the *Guinness Book of Records*, like the world's longest sneezing fit being 978 days or something. Travis particularly liked it when everyone would finish dressing in near-silence, everyone knowing that there was nothing now but a few words from the coach and a game to come.

Sometimes he liked it best after a game – after a victory, anyway – when he could take as much time as he wanted, sitting there grinning and sweaty, his hands in his lap, his helmet, sweater, shoulder pads, elbow pads, and gloves all off, everything else including his skates still on and tied up tight. Travis loved the feeling of a game well played, the way they would all go over the best plays and the goals and about how well Guy or Sareen had played in goal.

Players would explain missed opportunities ("I couldn't get the puck to lie down," "That ice was terrible, the puck skipped right over my stick") and they would talk about players on the other side ("Did you see his face when he got that penalty?") and hope, always, that maybe someone would say something good about the way they had played. And usually someone did. The Screech Owls were, after all, a team.

Travis had a thing about arenas. He loved the warmth and the light when the door opened for a 6:00 a.m. practice in the winter. He loved the cool and the dark when the door opened for a 6:00 p.m. practice in the early fall. He loved the smell of Dustbane when the workers were cleaning up. He loved the sound a wide broom made when it was pushed across a smooth cement floor. He loved the dry, sparking smell of the sharpening stone when it hit against a skate blade, especially if Mr. Dillinger was doing the sharpening, and he loved to watch how silently, smoothly Mr. Dillinger could work the skate holder across the shiny steel surface of the sharpener.

But more than anything else, Travis loved new ice. He liked to stand with his face against the glass while the Zamboni made its final circle. He liked to watch while the water glistened under the lights and then froze. He loved to be first onto the ice and feel the joy of new ice as he went into his first corner, coming out of it with a fine turn so he could then skate backwards to centre, watching the first marks form on the fresh surface – *his* marks.

He liked the first feel of a puck on his stick. He did not like, but could do nothing about, pucks sticking in water that had yet to freeze. Sometimes a player would be about to take a slapshot when the puck would suddenly grip on him, and player and stick would go gliding on alone, the stick swinging down on air. When other players saw that happening, they always roared with laughter. It was embarrassing, but it happened to everyone.

Travis already had superstitions. He was still a long way from Montreal Canadiens' goaltender Patrick Roy talking to his posts, but Travis had a few things he always had to do. This year he had to ring a shot off the crossbar. If he could do that in practice or in the warm-up, then he'd have a good game.

Travis had never seen a rink like this one before. Massive, white, more like an art gallery than a hockey arena. They'd walked by the hall of fame. They'd stood by the Olympic display watching the video repeat the 4–3 win over the Soviet Union that had given the Americans the 1980 Olympic gold medal. None of the Screech Owls had ever seen such a celebration – not when they won, not even when they watched the Stanley Cup playoffs and saw the Rangers or the Penguins or the Canadiens win.

The win had been called "The Miracle on Ice." And it looked like a miracle. The place had filled with thousands of blue and white balloons. The crowd had poured onto the ice. The players were in tears. Men and women – who were they? fathers? mothers? officials? – crying and hugging each other and touching players as they passed by, as if the players had some magical power that might rub off – and seeing that film it seemed as if they did. There wasn't a Screech Owl watching who didn't imagine him or herself there and part of something so special nothing else in life would ever compare.

The rink itself was huge, big as an NHL rink, with red seats and ads on the boards – Coca-Cola, Kodak, Miller Draft, milk – and the ice surface so big and square that the Screech Owls, none of whom had ever skated on an Olympic-size ice surface before, could only stare as if they were seeing a mountain or the ocean for the first time. A player could get lost out there!

The dressing rooms had shelves for the equipment, hangers and lockers for the players, and, as Nish shrieked when he saw them, "Pro Showers!" The Screech Owls' home rink didn't even have one shower. The Olympic Center had a massive shower room with stainless steel tubes running from floor to ceiling that had shower nozzles sticking out at different heights and in every direction. More like a car wash than any shower Travis had ever seen, but he could hardly wait to try them.

Before the practice, they lined up for commemorative photographs, and then, when all the pictures had been taken, Muck spoke to them. Apart from the coaches and Mr. Dillinger, whistling softly as he laid out the sweaters and socks, the players were alone in the huge dressing room, the team entirely by itself. This year Muck had put an end to parents coming in. They were "players" now, Muck had said, not "helpless infants," and the change had been profound.

Travis could still remember when the tiny dressing rooms were so crammed with parents – sometimes *both* parents – that the players could barely move. He could remember how, even after it had reached a point where their sole job was tightening the skates, the parents would stay for the coach's speech, and how some of the dads – Mr. Brown had been the worst of them – had insisted on adding their own speeches, the kids all sitting there secretly giggling and paying not the slightest attention to whatever came after the first "Listen up!"

"I want to speak to you for a minute," Muck began, his voice so soft he could have been speaking one-on-one to any of them. "This is a good tournament. We're going to have to be at the top of our game if we're going to go anywhere in it. You already know some of the teams here. We've played the Toronto Towers before. We know them and they know us. Rest assured the others are every bit as good, if not better."

Travis hated the Towers. Chippy and arrogant – the Screech Owls had played them twice before and lost once and won once. The game they won the Towers had protested, claiming Muck had stacked his team. He hadn't, of course, and the organizers had thrown the protest out. But that was the kind of team they were.

"There are teams here from New York State, Maine, Connecticut, Massachusetts, and Minnesota. We haven't seen any of them. And the first team we play – the Portland Panthers – are the top-rated team in New England."

"We'll wipe 'em," Nish said.

Muck looked up from his piece of paper and fixed his gaze on Nish, who reddened.

"You're going to be hearing there are scouts in the stands," Muck said.

Scouts! NHL scouts watching the Screech Owls? Why?

"Some of your parents have already informed me that this is so, but I want you to understand exactly what it means. They've been there before, only you never knew about it. And I certainly never would have mentioned it to your parents.

"They are *not* NHL scouts, no matter what some of your moms and dads may be thinking. They're mostly coaches, and a few general managers of bantam teams. Maybe the odd midget team. But that's all they are. This is a convenient place for some of them to see what's coming up in their own district – and remember that, you're all committed to the Central District until at least midget age – and maybe to get a sense of how the players are coming along in other hockey areas.

"That's it. It's that simple. Nobody's going to walk up to you and say, 'Sign here and you're Jeremy Roenick's left-winger for next season' . . ."

Nish let the air he'd been holding snort through his nose. Travis was surprised to find that he too had been sitting there with breath held, almost afraid to breathe. Yet Muck had been talking as calmly as if he were sitting around the dinner table, nothing more.

". . . I'm dead serious, ladies and gentlemen. I'm going to say something to you that sounds like the exact opposite of what I've been yelling at some of you now for more than four years. 'Keep your heads *down*.'"

Muck paused, letting the line sink in.

"Anyone know what I mean by that? You, Travis?"

Travis tried to speak but nothing came out. He had to clear his throat and start over. "It means we should concentrate on what's going on on the ice."

"You got it. Forget the stands. Forget thinking about what might happen five or six or seven years from now. For all you know, you might be in the same jail cell as Nish here by then."

Nish sat back as everyone laughed, shaking his head in disgust, used to Muck's cracks, enjoying the moment as much as anyone but determined never to show it.

"The Screech Owls are here to play hockey – nothing else. You've heard me say it a million times. 'Hockey is a game of mistakes.' Let's not make our first one before we even leave the dressing room. Now let's go out and make a team of ourselves. Nish, you bring the pucks."

5

"'m gonna hurl!"

Nish had turned his third colour since morning. Red-faced and angry when the other boys had jumped on him to get him up, then white and drained by the end of the practice, he was now almost grey. Travis sat beside him in the twisting, groaning van and wondered if he should try to comfort his friend, or wisely move to the seat behind so he wouldn't get splashed if Nish indeed threw up, as he was threatening.

"I'm really gonna hurl!"

Nish wasn't alone in feeling woozy. Practice had gone so well, Muck had told them when it was over and they were dressing, that he was going to take them all up Whiteface Mountain. The Screech Owls had gone in convoy, the big van followed by a half-dozen cars, and the group had snaked in such an impossible series of rises and hairpin turns that, a couple of times, those leading in the big van could look down, way down through the trees, and see one of the following cars seemingly going in the opposite direction.

Mr. Dillinger was driving, and he seemed to be enjoying it. Every hairpin turn he would shout out "I'm losing it!" and some of the players, on cue, would scream – but they all knew he was kidding, not about to crash.

They had to drive about six kilometres to rise just one, through deep woods and then pine and shrub. Every turn produced a new view, but Willie Granger, who had shut his eyes after the first rise, never saw one of them. "What's the *Guinness* record for being afraid of heights?" Wilson Kelly teased. Willie didn't let on that he'd heard.

Finally they reached the parking area near the top. They pulled up as close to the castle-shaped restaurant as they could get, parked and locked the cars, and then headed into the tunnel for the long walk to the elevator. It was dark and damp and they could hear and see water running below the walkway.

"Geez, is it ever cold!" Nish shivered.

"*toDSah!*" shouted Data, the strange word echoing. No one knew what it meant, except that it was a Klingon swear word, of which Data had dozens: *petaQ, taHqeq, yIntagh, Qovtatlh, va* . . .

"It's like a dungeon!" Sarah shuddered.

"I'm outta here!" Willie cried before they had gone ten steps. He ran back out of the tunnel.

"Wait for me!" shouted Nish.

"*va!*" barked Data, following.

"Me, too!" yelled Mario, chasing after the rest.

"Where're they going?" Travis asked, turning to watch his teammates as they flew back down the tunnel.

Mr. Dillinger was right behind him. "They'll take the stairs up," he said. "We'll take them on the way down. I can't blame them for wanting out of this."

⊙

The old cage elevator creaked and shuddered as it travelled up the inside of the mountain, the guide quietly reading a paperback as she pushed the button for the top and waited, one hand on the button, the other on her book. What a gloomy place to spend the day, thought Travis. He hoped the book had lots of action, and was set outside somewhere sunny and warm.

A few minutes later they emerged onto the observation deck, the sun like a long-lost friend when it fell on Travis's face. After a minute of feeling blinded, he got his vision back, the bright sky giving way to an unbelievable scene spreading out as far as Travis could see: blue lakes, green forest, a haze in the distance making the far hills seem almost ghostly.

There was another guide on the deck, and he pointed out the Montreal skyline far to the north, and Lake Placid and Mirror Lake and the town of Lake Placid down below, the lakes so small at this height they seemed puddles, the town all but invisible through the light haze in the air.

The players and parents broke off into little groups, most of them heading back toward the elevator, the easiest route back to the parking lot. Some wandered off on their own, taking photographs of each other and pointing out sights, before heading toward the trails and stone steps which led back down the mountain.

Travis wandered off on his own back up to the observation area. For a while he watched "Captain Video" – Norbert Philpott – and his father arguing about the correct way to film the landscape on their Camcorder. It was a ridiculous scene, the two Philpotts fighting for control of the camera. Maybe they were going to wait until they got it back home and on their television before they'd enjoy the scenery.

At the far ledge, he caught up to another group, Sarah, Dmitri, and Derek, who were pumping quarters into the big viewing machines and trying to see Montreal more clearly, some one hundred kilometres away.

"Where is the Forum?" Dmitri wanted to know.

"You can't see it," Sarah told him. "But you can see the mountain."

"I thought we were on the mountain," Dmitri said, confused.

"The Montreal mountain, Mount Royal," Sarah explained impatiently. "It's just called 'the mountain.' It's really a hill."

"Well, why don't they call it a 'hill' then?" Dmitri wanted to know.

Travis took a look, the haze so dense at such a distance he could not even tell where the mountain – or hill – was. His vision suddenly went black as time ran out and the viewfinder closed. He started fishing in his pocket for another quarter.

"Here, you kids need some change?"

They turned and Mr. Brown, grinning from ear to ear, was marching toward them with a mittful of quarters held out.

Sometimes Mr. Brown was a bit much, Travis thought. Always offering to help out with the driving or the practices or the phoning, but pushy about it. He was always the loudest in the stands. He was always the one ripping into the officials. He'd been the only parent to argue with Muck when Muck made the decision that the team no longer needed parents cluttering up the dressing room. Mr. Brown had claimed that he, and only he, could do Matt's skates the way Matt needed them done. Muck had told him Matt could do his own skates from now on, and would learn to like them. Matt not only had done his own skates fine, he seemed much happier and more talkative since his father had ceased speaking for him.

"No, we've seen enough, thanks," said Sarah.

"Okay, okay. Just trying to help."

The kids all thanked him. Mr. Brown wasn't through.

"Look, I'm glad to catch you four here alone. You're our set-up men – sorry, Sarah, set-up *players* – and if you guys are going, the whole team's going. And if Matt finally gets off his duff and scores a power-play goal, it's going to come from one of you. So I got a little proposition, just between us, okay?"

No one said anything. No one knew what to say.

Mr. Brown reached into his pocket and pulled out a massive roll of bills held together with a silver clip. Travis had never seen so much money at one time. On the outside was a twenty-dollar bill. If all the bills were that big, there must be a thousand dollars!

But they weren't. Mr. Brown eased the clip and spread the bills like a fan, the twenty covering another twenty, a fifty, and then a couple of tens, a few fives. Still more money than any of the kids could count at a glance.

"You guys play the way I know you can all play and I'm good for two dollars a point, okay?"

He looked at them all, one by one. They looked back, uncertain, not feeling right.

"We'll tabulate at the end of every match, okay? I'll keep the stats, you guys keep the cash." Mr. Brown chuckled at his little joke. No one else laughed.

"Are we on?"

Travis didn't know what to say. Dmitri would not say anything: he would wait for one of the others to take the lead. Derek was staring hard at the money. That left Sarah.

"I don't think so," said Sarah, and turned abruptly away.

Her comment so caught the group off guard that no one knew what to do next. Mr. Brown seemed flustered, angry. He held the bills out once more and shook them, trying to tempt them.

"We'd better not," said Travis. "It wouldn't be fair to the other kids on the team."

"They wouldn't want to see *goals*? C'mon –"

"We'd better not," Travis repeated. "Thanks all the same."

Red-faced, Mr. Brown slapped the bills together again and rode the clip over them, then stuffed the cash in his pocket. He was shaking his head.

"It's not like I'm offering you something for *not* scoring," he said, indignant.

"We know," said Travis. "It's just that we'd better not."

The group broke up quickly, Mr. Brown heading back into the souvenir shop, the kids off and away to the next lookout area.

But Sarah was gone. When Travis next saw her, she was in the snack shop, sitting with a Coke while Muck sat, with nothing, tapping his fingers on the surface of the table.

Muck was listening. He had a look on his face like bunched-up tape. Travis didn't need to hear to know what Sarah was telling the coach.

Travis's wristwatch said 1:57. The van was to leave at 2:00 p.m. sharp, and he knew he'd be in big trouble if he was late. He'd gone out along the rock cut and lost track of the time when he came across a friendly chipmunk so used to people that he'd scrambled up onto Travis's cupped hand, up his sleeve, over his shoulder, and down into his vest pocket. From the sound of the scolding, the chipmunk had expected the pocket to be filled with nuts. Travis had then gone off searching for pine cones for the little chipmunk, and in looking had forgotten the hour. And now he had to run.

The elevator was headed down and would take far too long to come back up, so he began to run down the stone steps, skipping and jumping to the irregular shapes. Travis had to watch himself to make sure he didn't trip, but he also had to make time, and he was practically airborne when, coming from the pines, he caught the distinct voice of Muck. An angry Muck.

Travis slowed instinctively. Slightly off the trail and through the pines he could make out Muck and another man's back. From the bald spot he knew immediately it was Mr. Brown.

"And don't you ever, *ever* let me catch you doing something like that again or you'll never come anywhere near any team I run, no matter whether your boy is on the team or not. Understand me?"

Mr. Brown was rattled, upset, uncomprehending. "C'mon, Muck. It's hardly like they're getting paid to *throw* games. Where's the harm in a tiny little reward for good play? The NHL pays bonuses, for heaven's sake."

Muck began speaking very distinctly, his words short and clipped, a sure sign, as all Screech Owls knew, that his temper was boiling over.

"The 'harm,' Mr. Brown, is that you're teaching selfishness. You pay them to score, what am I supposed to do? Pay the others to back-check? Give Boucher a five-dollar bill if he makes a save? This is a *team* sport, mister."

Now Mr. Brown was angry: "You don't have to speak to me like that."

"Fine, then!" Muck snapped, biting off his words. "I won't speak to you at all."

Muck turned, leaving Mr. Brown sputtering and fuming. Mr. Brown's hands were by his sides, furiously clenching and unclenching. "Jerk!" Mr. Brown cursed, but so quietly Muck was already out of earshot.

Travis ducked back in behind the pines and took one of the other paths leading down to the restaurant and parking lot. They hadn't seen him. And the van was still there, Mr. Dillinger at the wheel waiting for the signal from Muck to go. Travis had made it in time, thanks to the heated discussion between Muck and

Mr. Brown, but Travis couldn't find it in himself to be grateful to the two men. He hadn't liked the tone of the conversation. He hadn't liked at all the way Mr. Brown had stood there making fists and cursing as the coach walked away.

6

ravis woke with the sun on his face. He lay blinking for a while, then shifted out of the direct light of the window and lay for a while longer staring at the beam of light that seemed somehow solid and filled with hundreds of tiny, floating dust particles.

He had no idea what, if anything, could have stirred the particles up. The boys had settled down shortly after Nish gave up trying to figure out how he could re-wire the television so he could finally see an adult film – "I gotta get some tools," he kept saying, "gotta get some tools" – and all had fallen asleep quickly. Travis had even managed to be last into the bathroom, which allowed him to "forget" to turn off the light again.

There was sound in the hall. People were talking, laughing, excited. But Travis couldn't make it out. Nish rolled over, grunting, and pulled a sheet up over his head, uncovering his body. His feet wiggled for blanket warmth but could find none. He sat up.

"Wazzat?" Nish asked.

Travis's mom had often told him at breakfast his eyes were still full of sleep. But Nish's whole face was still full of sleep, as twisted as the sheets, one eye stretching open and the other stuck shut, as if he had Scotch-taped himself to sleep rather than dozed off quietly the way Travis and Wilson and Data had. Nish's stuck eye popped open so suddenly Travis expected to hear a snapping sound.

"Who's making all the noise in the hall?" Nish wanted to know.

"They woke me up!" Data called, as he, too, sat up blinking. "*jIyajbe'!*" ("I don't understand.")

"Let's get dressed and go see," Travis suggested.

It was worth getting up for; even Wilson made it in time. The recreation area downstairs was filling with guests, some of the younger ones still in pyjamas, all talking and pointing, some laughing and some very much upset. There were workers with pails and towels standing around the far corner of the pool where the Jacuzzi was completely hidden behind a huge, still growing cloud of soap bubbles. The bubbles were spreading onto the pool and beginning to drift across the water. The workers were trying to find the control button amid the suds so they could turn off the hot tub and stop the swirling that was only making more and more bubbles. They were not having much luck.

Norbert Philpott came running to tell the four roommates what was happening as they arrived. "Someone dumped laundry detergent into the Jacuzzi!" Norbert shouted. He had his father's Camcorder.

There were men in business suits running around and looking very annoyed. Several women with gold hotel badges stared at the youngsters from the hockey teams as if they'd all been in on it. The Screech Owls were one of four teams booked in the hotel. Several members of one of the teams – the Portland Panthers, Travis knew, since two of the kids had Panthers T-shirts on – were laughing and pointing, much to the fury of one of the hotel women who was scowling directly at them.

One of the workers emerged from the bubbles with three opened soap boxes, the tiny ones from the machine in the laundry room, and held them out to some of the others as evidence.

"I bet they washed off their prints," Nish said, giggling.

But none of the adults was laughing. The men in suits and one woman with a hotel badge were huddled with Muck and three other men in sweatsuits – coaches' uniforms – and all were talking very quietly, very seriously. Muck was shaking his head.

"He'll think it's me," said Nish.

"Was it?" Travis asked.

"Up yours."

Muck called the Screech Owls to the Adirondack Room for 9:30 a.m. Everyone knew what it was about. Everyone also knew that the soap storm had been caused by someone else, not one of them. Another team, perhaps. An angry hotel employee. But not the Screech Owls.

Having nothing better to do, Travis and Nish showed up early, and at the top of the escalator on the way to the Adirondack

Room, they came across a tearful Sarah Cuthbertson and Sareen Goupa being led into a corner by Muck and Mrs. Cuthbertson. Sarah's mother seemed very distraught.

The two girls had dark circles around their red eyes and looked as if they had been crying. Could it be that *they* had soaped the Jacuzzi? Sarah? Sareen? Nish and Travis could not believe it. The girls never goofed around. The idea of either of them even thinking of such a thing, let alone carrying it off, was too mind-boggling to consider. But why the tears? Why were they so upset?

The boys soon found out.

When everyone got into the room, Muck called order. Mr. Dillinger, looking just as serious as Muck, shut the big doors and the place fell eerily silent, everyone waiting for Muck to speak. He seemed to start and catch himself several times, unsure of what to say.

"First off, I don't believe it was any of our team, all right?"

"Couldn't be," Mr. Dillinger said from behind the gathering.

"I don't have to tell the Screech Owls how to behave. Doesn't matter whether it's a hotel, a motel, or you're being billeted with families, you treat where you are like it's your own home. Understand?"

No one had to answer. They had heard this line from Muck since the first time they'd headed out of town for a tournament.

"I don't know who did that stupid prank and I don't much care. I know it wasn't anyone in this room. But that being said, you have to understand you're all under suspicion because I would doubt very much that those responsible are about to own up.

"I have been informed by the manager that one more incident and every one of the teams booked in here is out, no matter who's responsible. Out in the streets.

"You understand the seriousness of the situation. It doesn't matter if any of us did it or not, we do one slightly foolish thing and we may as well have done it. So be on your very best behaviour from here on out."

There were mumbles of agreement from around the room. Travis was confused. None of this explained why Sarah and Sareen had been crying. It wasn't as if they had planned to spend the day in the Jacuzzi.

"We've got a bigger problem than that on this team," Muck said. He looked over at Sarah and Sareen, who were standing with Mrs. Cuthbertson, their heads down and backs slightly turned so no one would see their red eyes.

"These two young women say they were awake all night long. Pizza deliveries coming to the wrong door, banging on the walls, someone partying half the night."

Travis thought he saw Muck's gaze flicker sharply toward the back of the room. Travis turned. Mr. Brown and some of the other men stood there. Mr. Brown's face was red. His eyes looked little better than Sarah's. But not from crying.

"We're here to play in a hockey tournament. We're not here on vacation and we are most assuredly not here to keep young players up all night long when they need their sleep. I'd like a little more co-operation. Understand?"

Travis walked down the hill to the rink with Nish, Derek, Data, Willie, Sarah, and Sareen. The girls said they were in the south wing with parents on all sides of them; all the boys were in the west wing of the hotel, with the coaches at the end of the hall. Sarah thought there had been several parties going on, but the only parent's voice she recognized was, of course, Mr. Brown's.

"But it wasn't only him," Sareen said.

"The pizzas were worse," Sarah said. "They came three times. The last one was at 4:30 in the morning! And it wasn't Mr. Brown who ordered them. We could hear him yelling at the poor guy when he went to his door."

Maybe the yelling was part of it, Travis thought. Maybe Mr. Brown was getting back at Sarah for going to Muck about the bribes.

And maybe it *was* nothing but too much noise. It had happened before at other tournaments. But usually it was other teams' parents. The Screech Owls' parents were generally pretty quiet – for hockey parents.

Travis's group arrived at the Olympic Center at the same time as the Portland Panthers, who had come down the big hill in their very own bus – no rental for them, it even had the team name and colours painted on the side.

The Panthers' coaches and managers were dumping the equipment out onto pull carts to take into the arena. The bags all matched and sported the team logo, and each had a number on it that would match a sweater and a player. Just like the NHL. The coaches and managers wore matching blue track suits with "Panthers" in bold yellow lettering across the back. They, and all the team, had blue caps with similar lettering. They looked almost professional.

Travis always felt funny running into the players from another team. He was always amazed at how big and tough the other team seemed, always bigger, always tougher, always seeming more cocky, more sure of themselves than Travis's team. He wondered if perhaps the Screech Owls appeared the same way to the Panthers. But since he knew the Owls so well, had seen most of them cry at some time, afraid at others, he didn't see how that could be possible. How could the Screech Owls scare another team?

The Screech Owls dressed quickly, quietly, efficiently. Travis adored these moments before a big game, the way zippers sounded coming undone on bags, the way some of the players could rip shin-pad tape around their pads so quickly and loudly that it sounded like a dirt bike was coming right through the wall. He liked the sound of Mr. Dillinger filling water bottles, the sound of old tape coming off a stick and new tape going on.

Travis divided players into two groups: those who taped from the tip of the blade to the heel, and those who began at the heel and worked to the tip. Those who began at the heel, he believed, were sloppier and did bad jobs. Travis himself would never use a stick that had been taped heel to tip.

Mr. Dillinger taped tip to heel, the right way, and sticks taped by him were perfectly smooth, each wrap perfectly overlapping the next. Still, Travis preferred to do his own sticks, even if they didn't look quite as good.

Mr. Dillinger wasn't whistling. He wasn't joking. Perhaps he was upset about what had happened to Sarah and Sareen.

Perhaps it was just that he knew how important this first match would be against the powerful Panthers. He came into the room with a pair of newly sharpened skates in each hand, one pair for his son, Derek, the other for Dmitri, who had a thing about freshly sharpened skates. Dmitri had to have them done immediately before a game. If his skates had been sharpened the day before – even if they hadn't been used since – he would ask for a fresh sharp. And Travis thought his own thing about ringing a shot off the crossbar during the warm-up was weird.

Derek, on the other hand, rarely worried about his skates. Travis smiled to himself. Perhaps with this being Lake Placid and the Olympic arena and the Screech Owls' first *international* tournament, it was a case of the trainer being more nervous than the player – especially since the trainer was the player's father.

Muck began speaking, slowly, his words smooth and long, meaning he was relaxed and ready.

"You don't know this team. From what we can gather, they can put a lot of rubber in the net. The ones to watch are their big centre, number 5, and they've got a very quick little defenceman, number 4. They move the puck around well.

"We know we can sometimes panic and run around like chickens with their heads cut off. We can't have any of that against a team like this. So we stay calm out there no matter what happens.

"We get down a couple of goals I want you to forget there's even a scoreboard out there. We play our game and it's either good enough or it isn't. Understand?"

No one had to answer. They did.

"I may have to make some line changes as we go. If I change you, it doesn't mean anything except I think you'll help us more on another combination. It doesn't mean you're hurting us where you are, understand?"

No one did. No one dared to ask. Every player thought Muck was talking directly to them. Everyone thought it meant exactly what Muck had said it did not mean – that he was worried about certain players hurting the team. Travis swallowed hard and figured everyone else in the room was swallowing at the same time.

7

Ten minutes into the first period, Travis understood. Muck had been talking about someone specific: Sarah Cuthbertson, Travis's centre, the Screech Owls' leading scorer.

Sareen, her eyes still red and swollen, was sitting on the bench as the back-up goaltender who would only come into the game if Guy Boucher happened to get hurt. But Sarah, as always, had taken the opening face-off.

The game had begun terribly. Sarah had lost the face-off and the opposing centre – number 5, big, dark-haired, and menacing – had dumped it back against the boards near his left defenceman, the little number 4 that Muck had warned them to be careful around. Dmitri hadn't listened: he lunged for the puck, hoping to tip it over the defenceman's stick and into a break, but instead the quick little defender had beaten Dmitri to the puck, slammed it off the boards, past Dmitri and Sarah and perfectly onto the tape of the big centre, who had already turned and had a step on Nish. The puck reached him just as he crossed the blueline. Another few inches back or a fraction of a second slower and it would have been offside; but it wasn't, and number 5 had nothing between himself and the net but poor Guy Boucher, wiggling wildly backwards to play the angle of a long shot at the same time as he protected his crease. Guy was too slow, too late. Number 5 fired from the top of the circle, a high rising slapshot that blew past Guy as if he was flapping a wing at it. 1–0, Panthers.

Six seconds into the game and all they could think of was the score, even though Muck had told them to erase the score from their minds.

Travis couldn't remember a shorter shift. *Six seconds!* Not being involved in the play, he had hardly moved. He hadn't even shaken the butterflies from his stomach, hadn't increased his pulse or broken a sweat – and here was Muck calling them off the ice and sending out Derek's line.

They sat out three shifts, Derek's line going out twice more and the game beginning to move back onto equal footing. Once, Mr. Dillinger, in crossing toward the defensive units with a water bottle, gave Travis a gentle, encouraging pat on the arm, but Travis didn't want encouragement. He wanted Muck to call Sarah's name so they could head back out and make up for things.

"Sarah!" Muck finally barked. "And stay with your man, Dmitri."

They skated back out and Travis could hear some of the parents shouting. Dmitri looked cross, angry with Muck for seeming to put the blame on him. The face-off was to be in the Panthers' end of the ice, and Sarah was determined not to lose this one. Twice the linesman waved her around to get her to face correctly, and each time she went back to turning sideways with her bottom hand reversed, her lower grip almost at the heel of the stick, a certain sign that she was going after the puck and it was going straight back and across to Nish for the shot. Travis thought the official might wave her out altogether and he'd have to take the face-off when, suddenly, the linesman threw the puck down so hard it bounced straight back up.

Sarah was waiting for it. She clipped the puck out of mid-air on the bounce and drew it back, as Travis had known she would, to Nish, who moved in for the shot. The dark Panther centre was rushing him, though, and sliding with his pads toward the puck, so Nish, instead of hammering the puck into the pads and having it bounce out over the blueline, stepped lightly around the sliding player and rifled it around the curve of the boards so it came perfectly to Travis, who was waiting, expecting.

Travis took a moment to look. A Panther defender was rushing him and trying to poke check – a mistake – and Travis took advantage of his decision by sliding the puck between the player's outstretched stick and his skates and twisting around so he was free again, the defenceman piling shoulder-first into the boards. Travis faked a pass to Sarah at the front of the net and swung the puck back to Data, who was pinching in from the far point, and Data shot.

But the shot never came through. It hit the Panthers' little blond defenceman on the chest, bounced over Sarah's stick, and landed in empty space between the crease area and the blueline. Quick as a cat, the little defenceman gathered up the puck and sped away, with Sarah in pursuit and Travis, lost in the corner, well out of the play.

The little defenceman and the big dark centre raced down the ice, the puck moving twice between them. Dmitri, caught skating the other way, could not get back. Data, having taken the shot, had fallen trying to turn hard. He scrambled back fast but not quickly enough, and was also behind the play. Only Nish was back, his skates snaking backwards almost as quickly as the two Panthers' could stride forward.

Sarah was the only Screech Owl forward in position to get back into the play. She missed her check when the puck first went off the little defender, and tried to catch him, but by the blueline Sarah was digging deep, her head down, shoulders swinging, a tired player seeming to be wading waist-deep through water rather than scooting on this magnificent, hard ice, as the two Panthers were doing.

The big centre cut cross-ice, the little defenceman cutting so he went over the blueline just ahead of his teammate. Nish was dead centre, expecting the crisscross, playing the pass. The little defenceman looked to pass, moved his stick to pass, and Nish gambled, going down on his knees and arms to block the pass that never came. The little defenceman tucked the puck perfectly back in on his skates and kicked it niftily around the sprawling Nish, the two Panthers now home-free on Guy Boucher.

Guy, caught in an impossible two-on-none situation, had no choice but to play the shot. But to do so, he had to leave the far side of the net wide open for an easy tip-in. Number 4 faked a shot, passed quickly, and big number 5 swept it into the net effortlessly.

Panthers 2, Screech Owls 0.

Two shifts, two goals-against for Sarah, Dmitri, and Travis. They didn't even have to look for Muck's hand signal to know they were coming off. All three skated over, heads down, knowing they were in trouble.

But Muck wasn't angry. When Sarah sat down he came up behind her, placed a towel around her neck, and leaned down and whispered into the ear-hole of the helmet. Travis couldn't hear a word. He could only, out of the corner of his eye, catch Sarah choking back tears and nodding in agreement. Muck straightened up, tapped Sarah affectionately on the shoulders, and then went first to Travis and then to Dmitri.

"We're going to mix the lines. You're on with Derek for the rest of the game."

Travis felt terrible for Sarah. She was too exhausted to play. The lack of sleep and crying had worn her down. Muck had done the right thing. Sarah would play a few shifts with the other lines, but the scoring they so desperately needed now would have to come from Travis and Dmitri and Derek, who was as good a replacement as the team had for Sarah. Muck had done what he had to do, and Muck – perhaps alone – didn't think the game was lost.

Travis and Dmitri were well used to Derek. They had played together on the odd power play and in the rare situations when Sarah would get a penalty and Travis and Derek would be sent out to kill it off. They had also worked together in a tournament at Christmas time when Sarah was off with the Toronto Aeros at the Canadian Women's Nationals.

Derek wasn't as smart with the puck as Sarah, but he was

better at face-offs and had probably the team's best backhand. He couldn't pass as well as Sarah, but all that meant was that Travis and Dmitri would have to take the puck off their skates once in a while rather than feeling it click perfectly onto their tape, as was so often the situation with the magical Sarah.

The tournament games were set up in two twenty-minute periods, with a break, but no flood, in between. The score was still 2–0 at the break. The Screech Owls had yet to get a goal, but at least they were now holding their own. And no one was working harder than Derek Dillinger, who had stepped in so well for Sarah. He worked as hard coming back as going down, and several times had got back to break up Panther rushes. Other Screech Owls were working hard to pick up the slack. Mario, Zak Adelman, Jesse Highboy – all playing their hearts out. But what the team needed now were some good scoring chances.

"It's coming, it's coming," said Muck, who seemed much relieved at the break. Mr. Dillinger was busy making sure everyone had fresh water and a towel. Travis was standing, face-mask up, helmet half off, beside Derek when Mr. Dillinger came by with water, and he saw a proud Mr. Dillinger quickly reach out and gently pinch Derek's arm as he passed. Nothing more, nothing that anyone but the father and son would notice. Travis felt happy for them both.

"Derek," Muck said. Derek pulled the towel off his face, staring and waiting. "You guys have got to use the fast break more. Use Dmitri's speed on right. They're lining up across the red line. You should be able to chop one off the boards that Dmitri can catch up to on-side and be in behind them. Okay?"

"Okay."

"And another thing, Travis, I want to see the third guy coming in late for rebounds, understand?"

Travis nodded. He understood.

The second period began quite differently from the first. Derek won the face-off and sent the puck back to Nish, Nish lazily circling back into his own end to draw in the Panthers' forwards. One darted for him, and Nish bounced the puck back off his own boards so the player flew past and the puck came back out to Nish, alone. He called this play his "Ray Bourque," and much to everyone's surprise, it usually worked.

Nish used the open ice to hit Derek with a pass as Derek skated toward him at the Screech Owls' blueline, and Derek niftily dropped a pass to himself as he turned, so the puck was waiting for him when he came around and headed up-ice. Travis inhaled deeply – it was a dangerous move if a defenceman was around, but as Muck had said, the Panthers' defenders were dropping back to the red line, protecting their lead.

Derek barely looked for Dmitri. He slapped the puck so it hit the boards waist-high directly in front of the Panthers' bench. The puck jumped and lost velocity and fell near the Panthers' blueline, quickly losing speed as it crossed ahead of any players.

Dmitri already had the jump on the defence. He had come out of his own corner full-steam, and Dmitri at top speed with a puck to chase was about as fast as Travis had ever seen a peewee player. He turned the Panthers' left defenceman so fast that the defender's skates caught on each other and he went down onto one knee, Dmitri gone by the time he recovered.

The Panthers' goaltender saw the play and raced for the puck. A mistake. He had misjudged twice: first that Derek's slapper would carry down into the Panthers' end, second that Dmitri Yakushev was just another skater coming at him. By the time he realized his mistake, it was too late. The goalie sprawled and slid, waving his stick and pads to create as large an obstacle as possible, but for Dmitri, gobbling up the puck at the blueline, it was child's play. He dipped around the goaltender and, from the top of the circle in, had an empty net.

Panthers 2, Screech Owls 1.

8

ravis loved the way momentum could shift in a hockey game. Equal skills, equal number of players, equal time on the clock, and yet sometimes a game could shift so lopsidedly, first one way, then the other, that it would seem as if only one team at a time had skates on. Like in his dream.

This time the momentum was all with the Screech Owls. This time he felt as if there were no skates on his feet, but instead of a nightmare it was that joyous sensation that comes only a few times a season, when your skates are so comfortable and your skating so natural that there is no awareness of where skin ends and steel begins.

Just as the first period had belonged to the Panthers, the second, and final, was going to belong to the Screech Owls. On the line's next shift, Derek again sent Dmitri up right wing, but the Panthers were prepared this time and Dmitri wisely looped at the corner and hit Derek with a return pass as Derek came across the blueline.

Derek shot from a bad angle, but was smartly playing for a rebound, and Travis, coming in late as Muck had said he should, found the puck sliding onto his stick directly in the slot area. He rifled a shot so hard he fell with the force, the puck ringing like a bell off the crossbar and high over the glass into the seats.

There was a time when Travis Lindsay might have preferred this. There was a time – he figured every hockey player felt this way – when the finest moment possible in a game was when a puck would come back on edge and could be lofted high over the net where it would slap against the glass. Players in novice would sometimes get more excited by a good hoist than a goal. But no more. For the last year or so Travis had been able to shoot so well the concern was more in keeping it down than getting it up, and this time he had put it too high. This time he had blown it.

"Nice try," Muck said when the line came off. Travis would have none of it. He sat, his head bowed, his gloves tightly between his legs, waiting to get out there again.

Sarah was trying her best to play. She was being short-shifted by Muck to save her energy, and it was helping. She picked up a puck in her own end, played it off the boards to herself to beat a check, then hit Matt Brown at centre, just barely avoiding a two-line pass. Matt dished it off backhand to Mario Terziano, who didn't have the speed but let a rocket go as he crossed the blueline, the puck rebounding perfectly to Matt, who walked in and roofed a backhand with the Panthers' goaltender on his back, waving his glove helplessly.

Panthers 2, Screech Owls 2.

"Allllll right!"

From the bench, Travis could hear Mr. Brown's bellow above all the other shouts in the arena. He looked over and Mr. Brown, who always walked along the first row of seats, was shaking the short glass and pounding it.

"Now put it to 'em!"

Mr. Brown was red in the face and seemed more angry than happy. Travis felt sorry for Matt at a time when he should have felt happiest for him. Matt's teammates were slapping him and high-fiving him and Travis knew that Matt was hearing his father's screams above everyone else's. Too much pressure for me, Travis thought. Poor Matt.

Next shift out, Matt Brown was pulled down from behind and, with Matt out of the play, the little Panther defenceman moved up into the play and rifled home a rebound to put the Panthers up 3–2. Mr. Brown went snaky behind the glass, crawling up it and screaming at the referee.

"*Open your eyes!*"

The officials ignored Mr. Brown, who kept pounding the glass throughout the Panthers' celebrations and the face-off. Travis's line was out, and he could still hear Mr. Brown screaming.

"*Who the hell's paying you for this? You goof!*"

Just before the puck dropped, Travis saw the one official look up at the other and lightly shake his head and smile. They could hear. They knew. They understood perfectly who the "goof" was in this rink.

Nish blocked a shot beautifully from the little blond defenceman and hit Travis moving out of his own end. Travis could feel the puck on his stick and see more open ice than he'd seen all game.

He caught a flash out of the corner of his right eye: big number 5, charging at him. Travis slammed on his brakes, the big, dark centre flying past him and crashing into the boards. Travis began skating hard again, heading cross-ice, but lost his footing from a hard slash across the outside of his shin. Stumbling, he fired the puck up along the boards toward Dmitri and then felt the stick across his back, slamming him face-first down onto the ice.

The Panthers touched the puck and the whistle shrieked. Travis, still on the ice, could hear Mr. Brown screaming, swearing. He turned and he could see the big centre pointing at him with his stick turned blade down, the message clear: *I'm going to get you.*

Travis couldn't figure out what he'd done. He'd stopped and the big centre had crashed into the boards. He supposed he'd embarrassed him. Nothing more. If that was all it took to throw the Panthers' best scorer off his game, the Screech Owls had a chance.

The referee gave number 5 four minutes: two for slashing and two for cross-checking. He could have given him two for charging, as well, but the charge had missed so the referee had chosen to ignore it. Four minutes was more than enough.

Travis could feel Muck's confidence in the way he told them to stay out for the power play. Travis felt fine, not even aware of the slash or the cross-check, and he could sense time changing for him the way it always did when things were starting to go right for the Screech Owls.

It was as if everything moved in slow motion. Travis was aware of every player on the ice – even of Mr. Brown, screaming

"Gooooo with it!" from behind the glass – and he could feel himself moving as he had always dreamed he would one day move. His stride fluid, his arms steady, head up, the puck with him. Dmitri once told him the Russians called this "dancing with the puck" and he knew exactly what they meant. However he tried to move the puck, it obeyed.

Travis beat two players, one on a shoulder fake and the second with a deft slip between the player's skates. He could hear the roar from the stands. He could see Derek racing for the open ice, hear Derek's stick slapping the ice as he called for the puck.

Travis hit him beautifully, Derek not even breaking stride as he slipped past the remaining defenceman and in on net. The goalie played him to go to the backhand as Derek crossed left to right in front of the net, but Derek shot on his forehand to the short side as the goalie began to move across with him, the puck blowing the netting out like a pillow before falling, the red light flashing, Mr. Brown bellowing.

"Alllllll rrrrrrighttt!"

Panthers 3, Screech Owls 3, with two minutes to go.

The big, dark centre of the Panthers hit a goal post and Gordie Griffith almost slipped one through the Panthers' goaltender's five hole, but the game ended in a tie.

The Screech Owls raced to congratulate Guy, who ripped his mask off a red, soaked, but ecstatic, face. A tie, yes, but they had come back from being down 2–0, which in some ways was as good as a win. And against what everyone said was the best team in the tournament!

Muck and the two assistants, Barry and Ty, and Mr. Dillinger came running onto the ice to join in the celebration. There were high fives for everyone. Muck slapped the back of Travis's helmet and Sarah gave him a friendly tap on the shinpads, and Travis saw Mr. Dillinger throw a bear hug around his son. Derek deserved it. He had played brilliantly in place of Sarah.

The two teams lined up to shake hands. It was quick and almost the same as every other time – gloves tapping gloves, most players barely looking at each other, a few mumbling something like "Good game" or "Good luck" – but this time, when Travis reached number 4, the little blond defenceman of the Panthers who had played so wonderfully, he looked up.

And the little defenceman winked.

Winked, and smiled, and skated right past Travis and then off the ice, leaving Travis to skate back into the crowd of congratulating Screech Owls wondering what on earth that had been all about.

A good game? The crossbar? Sarah? The pizza deliveries? The Panthers wouldn't do something like that . . .

Or would they?

Muck made sure there would be no distractions that night. He talked to the hotel manager and was able to arrange for a separate room in the quieter west wing for the two girls. He and the coaches of the other teams staying at the hotel had the front desk cut off pizza deliveries to that wing at 10:00 p.m. He made the girls go to bed by 8:00 p.m.

Travis and several other members of the team walked down the hill and onto Main Street to see the sights. Travis, Nish, Data, Willie, Derek, Wilson, Zak, and Dmitri kept to one group and others took off in their own little groups. They were too many to stick entirely together, though some would have preferred to. Travis could never understand why some wanted to do everything as a team. He thought eight was more than enough – more than would ever be on the ice together at the same time.

Nish, of course, wanted to buy a T-shirt. He had a shirt from every tournament trip they had ever been on: Niagara Falls, Muskoka, Montreal, Ottawa, Peterborough, London – Ontario, not England. One size extra-large, and Nish was content for the rest of the trip.

His parents had given him twenty dollars to buy the shirt. It was all he had, fortunately, for if they'd given Nish a hundred he would have come back to the hotel wearing Lake Placid sweat pants, a T-shirt, wrist sweatbands, a sweatshirt with a hood, and, what he seemed to like best, a baseball cap with two big doggie doos, plastic and odourless, mercifully, perched over the brim. If something was truly disgusting, then Nish would want it.

It was cool, Main Street feeling more as if it were down in a dark basement than high in the mountains. But the sun was set now and the only light came from the streetlights. A breeze was blowing in off the lake and seeming colder every time it rippled their jackets. Travis had his Screech Owls windbreaker on and wished he had a sweater beneath. It was strange being up this high: summer in the day, winter at night.

Nish got his T-shirt at one of the trinket shops backing onto Mirror Lake. At $17.99 Travis and the others felt he'd been ripped off, but Nish was delighted with the shirt. It had the Olympic rink and the 1980 Team U.S.A. pictured on it, and "The Impossible Dream" written above "Lake Placid, N.Y." Travis told him it looked like the T-shirt was made before Nish was born, but Nish just gave him a huge raspberry, patted the bag that was holding the shirt, and headed back out the door, mission accomplished.

He stopped at a turning display tray.

"Hey! Look at that!"

Travis and the others stopped, stared, saw nothing.

"*nuq?*" Data asked. ("What?")

Nish reached out his free hand. "This!" He had a small plastic tool kit in his hands.

"You want a toy now?" Willie asked sarcastically.

"Naw. Look at it. It's perfect!"

Everyone looked. Everyone saw a child's tool kit: screwdriver, pliers, adjustable wrench. So cheap they'd probably break first turn. All in a plastic case for $3.99.

"I could fix our TV," Nish said.

"There's nothing wrong with our TV," Travis said.

Nish looked at him, shook his head in pity. "They cut off our movies, didn't they?"

"You've never even seen one," Travis countered, defensively.

"Which is why we need these tools," Nish said, plucking the package free of the case. "C'mon, a buck apiece."

"No way," said Travis.

"I got a buck," Data said.

"I got fifty cents," said Zak.

"Me, too," said Dmitri.

Nish turned to Willie. "You in?"

"It's stupid," Willie said.

"You in?" Nish repeated.

"I guess."

They pooled their money and Nish paid. Travis felt uneasy, as if they were buying cigarettes or something else they shouldn't have. But it felt weird to be uneasy over a child's tool kit.

Travis, Nish, and the others walked up and down both sides of the street. They saw the old wooden toboggan-run down by the water. They saw the little bandshell in the park. The movie theatre, the dozens of T-shirt and souvenir shops, the art galleries, the arcade, the frozen yogurt outlets not yet opened for the tourist season.

Data bought a pin and, for his mom, a silver spoon saying "Lake Placid, N.Y." for her collection. Zak Adelman bought hockey cards, but the best he could come up with was a Pavel Bure that Willie, the world's expert in everything, said was worth ten dollars, and a Martin Brodeur that was supposed to be worth eight dollars and, according to the latest *Beckett Hockey Monthly*, was "hot."

Travis bought nothing and kept walking. He didn't bother arguing with Willie, but Travis was beginning to have his doubts about trading cards. He'd collected all through novice and atom and at the beginning of peewee, but one day he had walked into a card store and suddenly just lost interest. Simple as that. Just completely lost interest.

Travis figured he'd been spending an average of three dollars a week buying cards – usually one lousy pack! – and while he did have a hardcover collection of Mario Lemieux and Wayne Gretzky (autographed!) and Adam Oates and Teemu Selanne and Sergei Fedorov and Mike Richter and Adam Graves and Pierre Turgeon and Alexei Yashin and Radek Bonk and, of course, Bure, the favourite, he had about 10,000 cards in a big box that meant nothing to him and nothing to anyone else, either.

Besides, he'd started to wonder whether or not they were really worth anything at all. Right from the start his dad had said the whole collecting thing was "a house of cards," which, according to his mother, meant it was phoney, not real, and

while Travis had periodically got testy over his father's continuing cracks about the real value of cards, he was beginning to
think his father might be right after all.

Just for fun, Travis had tried to sell about a half-dozen of his
better cards. He picked out the autographed Gretzky, a few
Donruss Ice Kings, some Ultra award winners and a Patrick Roy
and Eric Lindros from the Topps Gold Series, and took them to
a flea market where a number of dealers had tables set up.

"Would you like to buy these?" Travis had asked each one
in turn.

And each one in turn had done exactly the same thing:
taken the dozen or so cards, walked through them with their
fingers, checking, and then handed every one of them back,
including the Gretzky. "Don't need 'em," the dealers would say.
At first this made sense to Travis, but after a while he was wondering if, in fact, "Don't need 'em" meant "Don't want them,"
and that what they were really saying was that the cards weren't
worth anything to them or to him. According to the *Beckett*,
the Lindros Topps Gold was worth thirty-five to forty-five
dollars, but he couldn't even get a sniff of interest from the flea-
market dealers.

He took the same cards in to the local card store, a little store
run by a kind, elderly man who sometimes threw in a free card
or a hardcover or, once in a while, even a free monthly *Beckett*
magazine so Travis could look up the values of his cards.

"I'd like to cash these in," Travis said, handing the cards over.

The man, smiling, took the cards and examined them, just
like the men had done at the flea market. "You've got some
dandies here," he told Travis.

"They're worth a total of $86.50," Travis said. According to *Beckett*.

The man smiled. "I'm sure they are," he said. "But we're not buying right now, Travis."

Travis felt dizzy. Three years of three bucks a week – nearly five-hundred-dollars' worth of cards at home, and nobody "needs" them and nobody's "buying right now"?

"Tell you what," the man said. "I'll swap you these for this Fedorov group. Deal?"

Travis took the deal. But he also took the hint. Cards were worth cards; they weren't worth money. They had next to no value at all to anyone except for the kids foolish enough to hand over their allowance.

From that day on, he was, at best, a casual collector. He knew now what his dad had meant when he called the whole thing "a house of cards."

"*nuqDaq Derek?*" Data asked. ("Anyone see Derek?")

The group stopped at the corner, Travis about to step off the curb. He hadn't even been thinking of keeping track of every-one. But they'd been warned by Muck to stick together when they went out. And now Derek was missing.

"Maybe he went back to the hotel," Willie suggested.

"Why would he?" Nish giggled. "I have the TV tools right here."

"This isn't funny," Travis said. "We have to find him."

They backtracked and began checking the stores they'd wandered through. No Derek. Finally Wilson pointed across the street.

"There's something we missed!" he shouted. It seemed he'd forgotten Derek. He was pointing to an arcade, the lights flashing inside. The group broke into a run, Nish causing a driver to slam on his brakes and shake a fist at him. Nish shook his fist back and made like a dog barking as the car shot by.

Derek was inside. He'd seen the lights and wandered off. And when they found him, he was so deep into a game of "Mortal Combat" that he didn't even notice his teammates surrounding him to watch.

But that was Derek. Serious to a fault. Different from his father. Travis sometimes wondered if perhaps Mr. Dillinger had *too much* personality for Derek to deal with. Maybe he took up so much room that Derek had become a bit of a quiet loner in reaction. And yet they had in common their love of hockey. Derek worked so hard at it and Mr. Dillinger, obviously, was very proud of him. Mr. Dillinger was always kidding about when Derek would make the Leafs and how he would have free season's tickets to Maple Leaf Gardens.

The boys became so caught up watching Derek play they forgot they'd ever lost him. Soon Nish was bumming more money from the rest of the players so he could join in on the fun, too.

Travis had only five dollars, and he knew if he cashed it in on tokens he'd be five dollars short in about five minutes. So he held on and watched. Data had ten dollars' worth of tokens and, as usual, Nish was more than happy to borrow. They played air hockey and pool. They shot baskets. And, of course, they played video games, games so violent his mother would have marched him right out if she'd seen what they were doing to each other. At one point Nish's character hit Travis's character so hard he split in half and blood gushed all over the screen and the screen flashed, "Place token in now for extra game. Place token in now for extra game." But Nish was out of tokens.

The Screech Owls left in a group, Derek with them, and turned back down toward the hotel, prepared to call it a night. The streets were still filled with people, and Travis could tell the hockey crowd from the locals easily. The locals didn't look around. They knew where they were going. The hockey crowd was obvious: the jackets and caps, the way kids shouted across the street to each other, the way the parents awkwardly hung around in groups. Why they all felt they had to be friends when some of their children didn't even like all their own teammates baffled Travis.

He was tired and the jostling crowds were getting to him. Doors to restaurants and shops and bars were opening and closing on so many different sounds that he felt more that he was in a midway than a small town. He'd be glad to get back to his bed. He hoped Nish's cheap tools broke on the first try.

Travis was walking along only half paying attention when, suddenly, he pitched face-first out over the curb and onto the road, a car braking and squealing as the driver yanked the steering wheel hard and away from his sprawling body.

The impact knocked Travis's breath out, so he had no voice to add to what he could hear behind him.

"What the hell was that for?" Nish was shouting.

There were other voices, unfamiliar.

"Get a life, fatso!"

"C'mon, runt! Get on your feet!"

"What's the matter? Need your *girl* here to do your fighting, too?"

10

ravis felt as if he'd been punched in the heart. Data hurried to him, bending down, looking concerned. Data dug in his pocket for a Kleenex and pushed it down toward Travis's eye, and when he dabbed it off Travis could see in the thin light from the street-lamp that the Kleenex was black with blood.

But there was no pain. He couldn't breathe. He had felt this kind of pain once before when, flying in behind the opposition net, his stick had somehow become stuck in a crack in the boards and the handle had rammed up into his gut on impact. He felt like he was going to die then, felt like he was going to die now.

Nish was still shouting: "What a stupid thing to do! What the hell's wrong with you?"

The other voice again, this time a little nervous: "I never did nothin'. He tripped over his own feet; you saw it yourself."

"I saw you stick your foot out, jerk!"

Data and Wilson had Travis turned over, Data dabbing with the Kleenex, Wilson pumping Travis's legs. Why do they always do that? Travis wondered. You lose your breath from your chest, and they pump your legs. Do they think people fill up like bike tires? But, pumping or not, he was already feeling better.

"You're going to need stitches," Data said. "There's a big hunk of flesh hanging out."

Now Travis could feel his head. It was like the pain was racing from his lungs to his head and arriving twice as large as when it had left. He could feel his right eye already swelling.

"You okay, buddy?"

That voice again. Travis opened his eyes and looked up, the head peering down at him lighted from behind so it seemed black and featureless. He could not make out who it was.

"Help me up," he said.

Data kept pressure on the cut. Wilson grabbed one arm and the faceless stranger the other.

"Get your hands off him, jerk!" Nish shouted, trying to move in.

Travis felt himself yanked as the two fought over possession. Then he heard Data's high, shrill voice, bringing order.

"Shut up! Just everybody stand back! Come on, now! Stand back!"

All but Data and Wilson did. Travis stepped back up onto the curb and shook his head, Data's hand moving with the shake. He could see that a crowd had gathered. He could see his teammates – more than he had set out with – and he could see several vaguely familiar faces. The little blond defenceman who had winked at him was there, his hands jammed in his Panthers' jacket pockets, looking concerned. The big dark centre, looking scared: yes, his had been the face peering down that Travis could not make out.

"Sorry about that, buddy," the big dark centre said, his voice milky with sincerity. "Neither one of us was looking where we were going, I guess."

Nish pushed in, violently shaking his head. "That's bullroar, Trav. This yahoo stuck his foot out on purpose –"

"Did not –"

"Did so!"

"Up yours."

"Up yours, jerk."

"Quit it, now! We have to get this cut looked at, okay?" Good old Data, the high-pitched voice of reason.

Data had hold of one of Travis's arms, Wilson the other. They were trying to lead him away, but the big dark centre pushed past Nish.

"Look, buddy, I'm awfully sorry about the cut. No hard feelings?"

He had his hand stuck out to shake. Nish's face, peering from behind, looked like a twisted-up sponge. "Tell him where to stick it, Trav –"

But Travis was confused. A hand offered should be a hand taken. He reached out, realizing his own hand was already shaking, and the two players made clumsy contact. The big dark Panther centre was smiling, relieved.

"Sorry, okay?"

"What the hell's going on here?"

Travis knew this voice. It was Mr. Dillinger. He was pushing through the crowd, taking charge even before he had arrived. Travis was relieved to hear the familiar sound of someone who always knew the right thing to do.

"Travis Lindsay! What the dickens happened to you?"

Data explained the obvious: "He's got a cut forehead."

Mr. Dillinger moved right in, taking the Kleenex from Data and lifting Travis's chin and examining the cut under the weak light. "This'll need a couple," he said. "What happened?"

A dozen voices answered at once:

"We bumped into each other by accident –"

"– tripped on purpose –"

"– hit his head when he slipped –"

"– pushed –"

"– stupid curb –"

"Hold it!" Mr. Dillinger shouted, holding up both hands like a referee. "Travis, what happened?"

Travis probably knew least of all. His head was now screaming in pain. "I guess we accidentally bumped into each other," he said. "And I was the one who went down."

"Travis –" the voice of despair, disbelief, the voice of Nish.

Mr. Dillinger had no more interest in the story. "Come on," he said. "I'll take you to the hospital. Data, you come along to check the bleeding."

This night it was Travis's turn to get no sleep. The doctor at the emergency ward had frozen the area around Travis's cut, stitched it up, and, for nearly two hours, Travis hadn't felt a thing. Mr. Dillinger had stayed with him the whole time. Travis felt so grateful to him. Mr. Dillinger had been coming up from the rink when he'd noticed the commotion and gone across the street to check. Good old Mr. Dillinger, always on duty, always there when they needed him. Muck had let him handle the situation entirely, as usual. Muck ran the team on ice, Mr. Dillinger off.

Travis was fine at first. He had even gotten a kick out of watching, out of his one good eye, Nish desperately trying to remove the protective metal coupling from the back of the video box so he could plug the cable line directly into the television and, according to Nish's plan, watch all the forbidden movies for free. But the coupling wouldn't give. The cheap pliers broke. And by midnight Nish had given up in frustration and Travis had started to cry from the rising pain as the freezing left. He couldn't even turn into his pillow to hide the tears. Anything touching his forehead, even soft cotton, was like a coal jumping out of a campfire onto his skin.

Data called Mr. Dillinger, who came with some painkillers the doctor had given Travis, made him take two, and after a while Travis had dozed off into a half-sleep, half-stupor. He didn't even know, or care, if the bathroom light was still on.

He'd dreamed – imagined? – he finally met up with his long-lost "cousin," Terrible Ted Lindsay, and the two of them had compared stitches. Since these were Travis's first three, he was only about four hundred short of his hero, but Terrible Ted had smiled, half his teeth gone, half broken off, and told him hockey stitches were like military ribbons and that even if Travis only had three, he now had proof he had served and served well.

Travis was confused. Was he asleep? Awake? Did three stitches from falling – being pushed? – off a street curb in Lake Placid equal three stitches from a corner punch-up with Rocket Richard? He thought not. Terrible Ted, grinning from ear to lopsided ear, thought so. After all, it was a tough hockey opponent who had given them to Travis.

He dreamed his father came home from the office with news that the Simcoe Construction crew working on the town renovations had uncovered a variety store that had been boarded up after a fire in the 1950s and had somehow been completely forgotten. His father wanted to know if Travis was interested in going down with him to take a look at what they'd found.

Travis was certain it had happened: he and his father driving downtown and stopping outside a boarded-up front, the construction foreman welcoming the two of them with white hard hats the way they did whenever Travis went along with his father to a site, the big plywood coverings coming off the doors.

The lost store had looked so real: a metal cigarette sign over the door, tinted yellow plastic on the windows, a display of huge five-cent chocolate bars inside, and a tub of soaking wet, ice-cold tiny Cokes and ribbed Fanta orange drinks and tall Muskoka Dry ginger ale . . .

And there, tucked in under a glass cover that lifted up, three full boxes of Parkhurst Hockey Cards, 1956-57!

Travis's father, smiling, had handed the boxes over to Travis and Travis had ripped the cards open: Gordie Howe, two Terrible Teds, Boom-Boom Geoffrion, Rocket Richard, Tim Horton, Jean Béliveau, Jacques Plante, George Armstrong . . . dozens and dozens and dozens of hard-edged, mint-condition cards packed in with even harder forty-year-old gum. The Gordie Howe might be worth two thousand dollars! The Rocket Richard five hundred! The Plante a thousand! Terrible Ted? Priceless, to his cousin, Terrible Travis.

But then Travis had surfaced from this wonderful dream and gone over it carefully to see if perhaps it really had happened, and remembered that was the one season, 1956-57, when no hockey cards came out. Not only did the lost store not exist, but the cards could never have existed, even if the lost store were somehow real.

Travis felt something on his temple and brushed lightly with his hand. A tear, but from the pain of the cut or from the pain of waking up to reality, he could not tell.

All through the night he drifted in and out of weird, impossible dreams. Travis with the Stanley Cup. Travis in jail. Travis with a hippopotamus living in his back yard. Travis shot in the forehead by Nish's character from the video arcade . . .

"Rise 'n' shine, boys!"

It was Nish, first up for once. He was up and spraying them with cold water from a water pistol he'd somehow sneaked into the room. The others dove under the covers. Travis tried to dive, but his forehead hit the sheets like they were a goal post.

"Owwww . . . Owwww, owww, owwww –"

"Hey, c'mon, Nish, not Travis!" Good old Data. Last night's nurse. This morning's guardian.

"We're on the ice at ten," Nish said, packing the pistol into his pyjamas. "Let's go."

They began to get ready. Travis sat up, the pain increasing as he tried to get a grip on where he was and what had happened to him. Everything seemed fuzzy.

"Wow!" Nish shouted when he looked at Travis. "Look at you!"

Travis got up, the pain now shooting, and headed into the bathroom where he looked, blinked, and looked again, into the mirror.

The figure was somewhat out of focus, but it was him. At least it was *half* him. One side of his face looked normal, the other black and purple and swollen hideously over the eye. The eye itself was all but closed. He looked a million times worse this morning than he had last night.

"You look like Sarah," Nish called, giggling from the other room.

No way. Sarah looked in perfect shape compared to this.

11

"**M**aybe you should sit this one out."

Travis heard what Muck said but couldn't understand why his coach was saying this. Mr. Dillinger had taken one look at Travis's face at breakfast, shaken his big beard from side to side, and hurried off to consult with the coaches. Muck and his assistants had come back, stared, touched everywhere on Travis's face but where the stitches were, and looked concerned.

"If the decision were up to me," said Mr. Dillinger, "I'd say no."

Muck wasn't sure: "We'll check again just before game time."

By four o'clock the swelling had gone down considerably. Mr. Dillinger checked Travis before the rest of the players arrived and figured he'd be playing. "Couple of days from now, you won't even be able to find it," he teased.

"I want to play," Travis said.

"We need you," Mr. Dillinger said. He seemed pleased that Travis had come back so fast.

"I gotta go work on some skates," Mr. Dillinger said. "You may as well start getting dressed."

Travis was happily pulling on his underwear when Muck came in, took one long look at him and decided that Travis had better sit out the game against Duluth.

"I'm fine," Travis said. "Mr. Dillinger says the swelling will be gone in two days."

"And in two days I might need you. I won't need you tonight. But if we get into the final, I'm going to want you there. You get hit again today, even with your mask, that cut could open up again. Besides, you can barely see out of that eye."

"I can see."

"You can see well enough to watch."

Mr. Dillinger came whistling back into the room, carrying pairs of sharpened skates in each hand and under each arm. He stopped whistling when he saw Muck and Travis in deep conversation.

"Travis won't be dressing," Muck told him.

"He won't?"

"Maybe next game," Muck said, and wheeled away.

Mr. Dillinger caught Travis's eye. He shook his beard in quick disagreement. "I thought for sure you'd play, son," he said.

He seemed genuinely unhappy with the decision. Travis felt good that someone, at least, was as sure as he was that he needed to be out there if the Screech Owls were going to win.

Travis sat with the Screech Owl families and hated every second of it. When the teams came out for the warm-up he wanted to be out there ringing his good-luck shot off the crossbar. When they lined up for the opening face-off, he wanted to be out there with everyone in the building, aware that he, Travis Lindsay, number 7, was in the Screech Owls' starting line-up.

But now his place was taken by Derek Dillinger, with Sarah back at centre and Dmitri on right wing. Derek was a good winger but a better centre, and Travis wondered how he would fit in. He found himself half hoping he wouldn't, but then realized what he was thinking and shook off the thought. Travis's not playing had nothing to do with Derek, who was merely filling in where the coach told him to. And Derek, Travis knew, would be far happier knowing Travis was on the wing and he was back at centre, even if it was second-line centre.

Sarah was obviously much better rested. On the first shift, against the slower but bigger Duluth team, she picked up the puck behind her own net and skated out so fast she caught two Duluth forwards back on their heels and beat them cleanly. The Screech Owls had a four-on-three at their own blueline.

Then, in a move Travis had seen her try only in practice, Sarah did a spinnerama move past the opposing centre, turning around in a full circle at full speed as the checker went for the puck and found himself skating helplessly toward his wingers who were, like him, caught badly out of position. It was now a four-on-two, with big Nish steamrolling right up centre to join the play.

Sarah handed off to Dmitri, who dropped back to Nish, who hit Derek perfectly coming in from the side with the goaltender guarding against the other side, where Sarah was coming in backwards, looking for a tipped shot. Derek had the whole empty side to shoot at and he roofed the puck in off the crossbar, the ring announcing the Screech Owls' first goal and, by the reaction in the stands, the sweetest goal of the tournament.

Travis was caught between cheering wildly and burning with envy. If he hadn't fallen – *been tripped?* – it would have been him, not Derek, putting it in off the crossbar. Just as he always scored in his imagination. It would have been *him*, not Derek, they were all high-fiving, *his* number, not Derek's, that the scorers – and the scouts! – would be writing down on the sheets, *his* name, not Derek's, that would be bouncing around the arena walls from the public address system, *his* name, not Derek's, that they would be tying to this spectacular goal for the rest of the tournament.

Sarah Cuthbertson did not take the next shift of this line. Either Muck was juggling – and why would he juggle when the Screech Owls were so obviously superior? – or else something was wrong. Muck shifted Derek over to centre and moved Matt Brown up onto the first line.

Travis was on the opposite side of the rink, but he could see Sarah bending down, working on her skates. He saw Sarah handing her skates back to Mr. Dillinger, who left the box with them, jumped over the sideboards and hurried down the side of the rink with the dressing-room key in his mouth and entered the dressing room. Sarah, her head down, expression hidden by her helmet and face-mask, still looked forlorn as she sat and waited.

Another shift later, Mr. Dillinger returned with the skates. They had probably just needed sharpening. Sarah missed a good part of her next shift tying them up, but made it out in time to see Derek pot his second goal, a beautiful slapshot from the point set up when Nish pinched in and Derek dropped back and Nish magically tucked the puck back between his own legs to where Derek was turning at the blueline.

On her next shift, Sarah barely made it down the ice before she was hustling back to the bench clutching her sweater out from her back and screaming something through her face-mask. Again, Mr. Dillinger went to work. There now seemed to be something wrong with her shoulder pads.

She missed another shift as Mr. Dillinger worked frantically with tape to put the pads back together again. He finished, pulled her jersey down tight, and Muck sent her back out – just as the buzzer went to end the first period. The game was half over, and Sarah had one assist and, at the most, thirty seconds of ice time.

How could something so dreadful happen again to Sarah? Travis couldn't understand it. Some of the fathers were saying somebody must have cut her equipment. Mr. Brown, moving restlessly down in front of the glass, was unusually silent, studying the Screech Owls' bench for some indication of which line his son was going to be playing on for the rest of the game.

The idea that someone might have doctored Sarah's equipment seemed impossible to Travis, right up until her second shift of the second, and final, period, when Sarah came racing out from the corner, slamming her stick furiously on the ice as she headed for the bench, and Matt Brown, the sweat of double-shifting turning his sweater a different colour from Sarah's, jumped over to take the left wing while Derek moved quickly to centre again.

This time it was her pants. Mr. Dillinger tried tape, but tape wouldn't adjust, so he had to race, again, for the dressing room and come up with replacement braces.

Fortunately, the Screech Owls didn't seem to need her – or Travis, for that matter. Derek set Matt Brown up for a one-timer and, ten seconds later, sent Dmitri in on a break to put the Owls up 4–0. Derek Dillinger was well on his way to being chosen, for the second time in a row, the most valuable player of the game.

And all Travis could think was: It could have been me.

But no one else was moping for him. Travis looked around and could see that Sarah's parents were furious. The men along the back wall were angry and talking and shaking their heads. They hardly looked like parents of the winning side.

Down along the glass toward the other side, Travis could see several members of the Panthers standing watching. The little blond defenceman was there, as well as the big dark centre. The Panthers were on the ice next. The big dark centre was pointing at Mr. Dillinger struggling with Sarah's braces, and he was laughing.

Travis couldn't help but think that these laughing Panthers had something to do with what was happening. But what? And how?

@

"Someone cut it. You can see for yourself."

Mr. Dillinger was surrounded by a large crowd of parents, tournament officials, other coaches, and Screech Owl players.

He had the laces he had replaced, the shoulder pads, and the braces for the pants, all cleanly sheared for a bit, then torn.

"Whoever did it knew what they were doing," Mr. Dillinger continued. "Nothing broke while she was dressing, but as soon as enough stress was put on it on the ice, everything started snapping."

"Who had access to the equipment?" a man in a suit asked.

Muck answered. "Coaches and manager. Players if they wanted, but no players came around."

"You kept all your equipment at the rink?" the man asked.

"Everything," Muck said. "We were assigned one of the figure-skating rooms across from the dressing rooms."

"Locked?"

"Of course locked."

"And no idea who?"

"No idea at all."

Travis wondered if perhaps he should talk with Muck about the Panthers, but what would he say? That one of them had winked at him during the first game when Sarah couldn't play? That some of them were laughing during the second game when Sarah couldn't play? That one of them had made a crack about Sarah during the scuffle last night?

When Travis tried to make sense of it, he could make little, but he could see why the Panthers might want Sarah out of the way. If they had got her out of the first game then they would have had a chance to grab first place right from the start and could probably have hung onto it for the rest of the tournament.

On the final day, first and second place would play in the final, with the gold medal going to the winner and silver to the loser. Teams coming third and fourth in the standings would play off for the bronze, just like in the Olympics.

It made some twisted sense for the Panthers to get Sarah out of the Screech Owls' second game as well. If the Screech Owls had somehow lost, with only one point from their first-game tie, the Owls might well have been eliminated at that point from playing in the final. This would have meant the Panthers would end up playing one of the weaker teams for the championship. Crazy, but possible.

Travis decided he would talk to Mr. Dillinger. He had a chance when everyone else was still showering and dressing and Muck had gone off with the tournament officials to discuss what they should do about the situation.

Mr. Dillinger listened carefully while Travis stumbled through his confusing explanation about the cut equipment. He was no longer the laughing, kidding guy Travis had come to expect. Mr. Dillinger was dead serious.

"You're talking sabotage," he said when Travis was finished.

"What's that?"

"Deliberate. They'd sabotage in order to win the tournament."

"I guess."

Mr. Dillinger considered this for a long moment. "Makes some sense, Travis," he said, finally. "Makes some sense."

"What can we do about it?"

"Well," Mr. Dillinger said thoughtfully. "We've obviously got no proof and we'd need proof. Why don't you and some of the guys keep an eye out on the Panthers, particularly that guy who dumped you last night, and see if maybe they say something or do something that gives us a lead."

"Spy on them?"

Mr. Dillinger laughed, the old Mr. Dillinger back. "Not 'spy' – watch. Just watch them if you see them around the rink. And tell me or Muck if you see anything suspicious."

"Okay."

"Good."

12

he swelling around Travis's eye was going down quickly. He could see clearly again by evening, and the colour was now more like that of a bad orange than a threatening thundercloud. Even the stitched area was tightening and shrinking. It was wonderful to have stitches when they no longer hurt. He felt closer to Terrible Ted than ever.

Travis and Nish had called the players together in the afternoon to discuss what was going on with the sabotaged equipment. Later on, there was to be a parent get-together, a mid-tournament party that Mr. Dillinger had set up when he booked the rooms, and Nish and Data and Derek had already helped Mr. Dillinger carry several cases of beer from the van into the Skyroom at the back of the Holiday Inn. The players knew that the main topic of conversation for the parents would be the same one the kids were meeting to discuss.

The players met by the Jacuzzi, now clean and clear and watched periodically by a nasty-looking woman from the front desk. Nish and Travis and Data set up the pool chairs around the hot tub, which, for once, wasn't full of parents, the kids turned off the noisy bubbles, and Travis, much to his own surprise, pretty well carried the meeting.

He detailed what he knew about the Panthers. He told them everything he had already told Mr. Dillinger. The wink. The laughter. The trip. The obvious fact that Sarah stood between the Panthers and the tournament victory.

"Ridiculous," Sarah said when Travis was finished.

"No," Nish argued. "It makes sense."

"You're saying they were the ones sending the pizzas."

"Yeah."

"And the ones who cut my laces and straps."

"Yeah."

"No way. No kid would ever do something like that."

Travis butted in: "Their big centre would. He's got a mean streak."

"And what about the little defenceman?" Data added. "What'd he wink at you for?"

"Because he fell in *loooove* with Travis!" Wilson shouted. Everyone laughed.

"Who could fall for something that looks like *that*?" Sarah teased.

"*blmoHqu'!*" said Data. ("You look very ugly.")

Everybody laughed again. Travis was falling in love himself: with his stitches.

"It makes sense," said Nish.

"It only makes sense because we don't know what happened," countered Sarah.

"Well," Nish said, his back up, "you tell us what you think happened, then."

"I don't know." Sarah stopped for breath. She seemed on the verge of tears. "I just . . . want it to stop."

"So do we all," said Travis. "That's why we're talking about what to do. I think we should set up a watch."

"A watch?" Wilson asked.

"We should keep an eye on the room where the equipment's stored."

"We can't," Gordie Griffith offered. "We've got a ten o'clock curfew. They'd never let us stay up and they'd certainly never let us stay out at the rink."

"We'll tape it!" Norbert shouted.

"What?" a half-dozen of the Screech Owls asked at once.

"Tape it," Norbert said, suddenly totally assured. "My dad has his Camcorder here. I can rig it up on a timer."

"You mean set it up in the equipment room?" Nish asked.

"Sure. Then, if anything screwy happens, we'll see it when we play it back."

"Won't work," Gordie said, certain.

"Yes, it will," Norbert countered, equally sure.

"You'd need lights."

"No way. This new one takes available light. No flash, nothing. It can pick up things in the day you can't see. You shoot outside at nine o'clock at night, it looks like noon."

"That's true," Wilson said. "I've seen it."

"But how would we set it up?" Sarah asked, ever practical.

"Yeah," Nish added, suddenly giving up. "How can we get in?"

"There's still a game on," Travis said. "We can get into the rink."

"But what good does that do us?" Nish asked. "The equipment's under lock and key."

"Oh yeah," Travis said, now as disheartened as his friend.

Derek Dillinger cleared his throat. He didn't usually say anything when there were more than three or four others around. "I can get the key," he said.

"You can?" Nish asked.

"My dad's going to be running the bar at the parents' get-together. The keys will be in our room. I can get them."

The kids all looked at Derek with new respect. Finally, Travis spoke for everyone.

"Let's do it."

They decided that only some of them would go on the mission. Derek had to go because he had the key. Norbert had to go because he had the camera. Travis went, and so did Nish, Data, Willie, Sarah, and Wilson. They had no trouble getting into the rink. As players, all were wearing tournament pins that allowed them to come and go as they pleased. And no one thought anything of a bunch of kids coming into a hockey game as a group, one of them carrying a video camera.

"You fellows on a scouting mission?" the elderly gentleman at the front desk asked.

"You bet," Nish answered, giggling.

The gatekeeper waved them through. They headed into the rink area where a game was under way: the Panthers versus the Toronto Towers. Everyone had figured the Towers would be one of the dominant clubs at the tournament, but the Toronto team was already down 5–2 with time still to run in the first period. The Panthers scored again as the Screech Owl players came out into the stands at the far end. With the parents behind the Panthers' bench stomping and blowing on plastic horns, the little blond defenceman was being mobbed by his teammates at centre ice, the big dark centre high-fiving him as the others rapped his helmet and slapped his back.

"Perfect timing," announced Nish. "They're probably planning a raid right after the game."

"I still don't think it's them," said Sarah.

The Screech Owls watched to the end of the first period. Then, with the people in the stands heading for the snack bar and the teams huddling at their benches, the Owls casually walked out through the dressing-room doors, with no one paying them the slightest attention.

Data raced ahead and set up a watch. At the far doors, he signalled back with his hand for the rest to go ahead. They checked for the equipment storage room they'd been assigned on arrival – the men's figure-skating dressing room, which was not being used during the tournament. The rooms had small windows on the big orange steel doors, and from the light of the corridor they could see their logo – The Screech Owls – where Mr. Dillinger had taped it during the team's first practice.

Derek yanked the keys out of his pocket and quickly opened the door. The players slipped in.

Data flicked on the lights and they came on in stages, the room dimly taking shape, then coming brilliantly alive. It hurt Travis's black eye at first, but his pupils soon adjusted and the pain vanished.

Their room was in perfect order, just as they would expect from Mr. Dillinger. They quickly checked what they could: Sarah's straps, skate laces, sticks, the equipment of a few other key players, including Travis's, which made him glow with pride, and then decided everything was fine.

"What about the camera, though?" Nish asked. "Anybody comes in here it's the first thing they'd see."

Norbert had an answer. "We place it under the bench, low, out of sight and in the dark. Then I tilt it to catch anything near Sarah's stuff. No one will ever see it."

"Will they hear it?"

"Runs dead silent."

"What about the batteries? How long will it run?"

"Nothing to worry about," Norbert said. He pulled a small black attachment out of his windbreaker pocket. "This is an automatic activator. After I set it and we leave, it activates after a thirty-second delay. Any movement and it instantly turns the camera on − no lights, no sound. It's used for wildlife photography."

"So if anything happens," Sarah said, "the camera will catch it?"

"You got it."

Travis liked what he heard. "Set it up," he said. "We have to clear this place."

Norbert moved with an efficiency they never saw on the ice. He set the camera on a special holder and adjusted everything and checked the lens and set up the special activator. Satisfied, he stepped back.

"Perfect," he announced. "Now let's get outta here. We've got thirty seconds."

Travis first peeked out the door and down the corridor, where Data was still keeping watch. Data gave him the all-clear sign and Travis waved everyone out after him. Derek shut the door and locked it.

"How could they get in without a key?" Nish hissed.

"Maybe they have a master," said Wilson.

"Maybe some of the keys are the same," said Derek.

"Maybe they do it when Mr. Dillinger's around working," suggested Norbert.

"Maybe no one's getting in at all," said Sarah, still doubting that anything so diabolical could be happening at a simple hockey tournament.

Hers was an opinion of one. The others were absolutely certain there was something bad going on, and that, somehow, the Panthers were involved.

13

The players knew they had to get back before Muck's curfew. They wanted to be back and in their rooms, perhaps even in bed, so there would be no questions about where they had gone and what they had been up to. Nish wanted to get back to try out his newest set of pliers. He had promised that tonight would be the night when he would finally solve the wiring mystery of the blocked television channels.

The players raced out of the Olympic Center and up the hill toward the hotel, where they could slip in the side door leading out onto the tennis courts and the parking lot, undetected. Or so they thought.

As the players hurried up the grassy slope onto the paved area, they rose out of the dark into an unexpected scene. The parking lot was alive with people. And not just people, but their people. Several of the fathers. A few mothers. Muck. The assistant coaches. All standing in a circle, the tension coming off the circle in waves.

The players quickly ducked down in the dark and lay flat, their heads barely above the paved ledge where the sloping lawn ended and the parking lot began.

It was difficult to make out the faces, but there was no mistaking that one of the men, one slightly off from the circle, was Mr. Brown. He had something out – a handkerchief – and was dabbing at his nose, which appeared to be bleeding. Travis could make out Muck in the centre of the gathering.

They could hear Mr. Brown perfectly, his loud voice clearer in a parking lot on a still night than in an arena with all the echoes and other sounds. "I can damn well speak to whoever I want, whenever I want –" His voice sounded thick.

"He's drunk," Nish hissed in Travis's ear. Nish was right, Travis thought. He was glad Matt hadn't gone to the rink with them. How embarrassing it would be for him to see this. He hoped Matt was up in his room, already asleep.

Muck was speaking. It was more difficult to hear him, but they caught the tone: quiet, sure, disapproving. It was a voice they had all heard when they'd acted up on the road. But they were kids.

"It's not any of your damn business –" Mr. Brown began again.

Muck cut him off. Still soft. But completely in command. Muck's steady voice that held for no arguing back, the voice of confidence, never rising, never falling, never changing. The voice of their coach.

"You son of a – !" Mr. Brown suddenly lunged. Muck braced himself, but Mr. Brown never got through. Several of the other fathers were stepping in, blocking.

"Muck's right, you know," one of them said. Travis was certain it was Mr. Cuthbertson.

"We've all felt the same way," another said.

"You've had your say, now go to bed," said a third.

Mr. Brown seemed to shrug, then turned away toward the door. He was not walking steadily, but whether it was because of the beer or whatever had caused his nose to bleed, Travis couldn't tell. He was still muttering when he reached the door, but they could not make out much of what he said apart from the swear words.

Those in the circle waited until he was gone. One of them lighted a cigarette, the match's flare lighting his face briefly. It was Mr. Boucher. Travis considered him one of the fairest parents and knew he would help Muck if there was any trouble.

"Let's go back in," Muck said. "We've a party to wrap up."

"Good idea," Mr. Boucher agreed.

The cigarette flicked through the night toward the boys, sparking as it struck the pavement, and then skidding like a burning race car almost to the ledge.

"It's mine!" Nish hissed.

But no one else was interested. The moment the door into the Skyroom closed again Nish bolted for the smouldering cigarette and the others all asked the same question at once: "What was *that* all about?"

Travis said nothing. He thought he knew. But he wasn't sure. The players raced for the door in order to beat the parents to the rooms. Travis could hear Nish behind him, coughing violently.

Nish was first up in the morning. When Travis woke, Nish already had the television turned around backwards and was busily prying off the protective coupler that joined the cable line to the pay-TV box. He was whistling while he worked, the way Mr. Dillinger sometimes whistled when he was happily sharpening skates.

"I think I've got it," Nish said.

"Got what?" Travis wanted to know. Or maybe he didn't want to know.

"If I can get this cable off here and attach it down there, it should work directly through the TV. Won't even have to run it through the box."

Travis didn't follow. Groggily, he pulled the cover off his bed and up onto his head like a hood and wiggled to the edge of the bed to watch.

Nish had his tools laid out like a master workman. He had the protective coupling pulled back and had slid it up over the cable so it was well back and out of the way. He was twisting the connector off the pay-TV box. The television picture suddenly went, the screen filling with grey snow and the sound hissing with static.

"There," he said. "Got it."

Working quickly, he attached the connector to the back of the television. The hissing sound stopped and was replaced with silence. The screen cleared, but changed to blue, no picture.

"Didn't work," Travis concluded.

"Did too," a testy Nish countered.

"Where's your movie, then?"

"It's eight o'clock in the morning, Einstein. You think they put adult movies on at this time so little kids can watch them over their cereal?"

"There's nothing on at all," Travis said.

Nish smiled, confident: "There will be – tonight."

After breakfast, the boys went outside, thinking they would head down to the lake and check out the old wooden toboggan run.

It was a fine morning, bright and crisp with the dew ice-cold and sparkling on the green-brown grass. A thick cloud seemed to have settled over the lake, and the boys, standing in sunlight with blue sky above them, felt as if they had entered another world. Travis shivered. He could almost see the head of a Brontosaurus rising through the cloud to stare at them.

"Hey!" Nish whispered, holding up a hand to halt everyone. "Look down there."

Down past the putting green and the tilted lawn chairs and the still-leafless hedge, three men were walking and talking quietly. It was the three coaches – Muck, Barry, and Ty – and all had track suits on, though Muck's seemed more for comfort than work-out. With his limp, he could never run. Barry and Ty were cooling down from a dawn run, both young men perspiring, both wearing head sweatbands, and Barry, the fitness nut, carrying hand weights he kept pumping as he walked and talked and listened to Muck. By the movement of the others' hands, the conversation was both animated and anxious.

The three coaches were coming up over the grass to the same side entrance the players had used the night before. The men had not yet seen the boys.

"In here!" Nish hissed.

Travis looked over. Nish was signalling to the other three boys from behind the garbage dumpster, which was just off to the side of the back entrance. It was a natural hiding space. But why hide? If Muck caught them, he'd kick their butts, for Muck always said he considered sneakiness a crime equal to stealing and lying, for in its own way it was both.

But the other boys were already squeezing in behind Nish. Travis hurried to join Data and Wilson in the gap, well out of sight but well within earshot. Travis caught his breath, nearly gagging.

"Smells like you slept here, Nish," Data hissed. *"He' So'!"* ("Stinks!")

The others giggled, including Nish, who then placed his index finger over his lips to shut everyone up. If they made a sound, they would be caught. If they were caught, they would be in trouble.

They could hear the three men coming, their low conversation rising with their steps until, finally, the boys could make out what Muck was saying.

". . . not the first time, and won't be the last. But I can hardly agree with such a wild idea as you're putting out, Ty."

Ty was talking low, his voice anxious to convince. "It's not the idea that's wild. It's Brown. He's a certifiable loonie. You catch him trying to bribe the kids, he gets a few drinks inside him and suddenly he wants revenge. And what's the best way to get at you? The team, obviously. The team collapses at a tournament like this, you end up taking the rap. Maybe you even lose the team next season."

"Makes no sense at all," protested Muck. He seemed upset with what he was being told.

"Muck, just hear Ty out," said Barry. "That's what I thought at first, too."

Ty continued: "I was doing the stats Tuesday when Brown came in with a new pair of braces he wanted to fit onto Matt's pants. He showed me the package. I just nodded and let him go on in and set it up. Who's to say what he did when he was in there?"

"But the point is," said a determined Muck, "why would he do it?"

"To screw you around. You lose your top forward, our best playmaker, you lose the tournament, you lose your position."

"That's me," argued Muck. "But why Sarah?"

"The best way to get at you," said Barry.

Ty laughed, exasperated. "You're missing a big point here, Muck."

"Which is?"

"Who told on him?"

Muck sniffed, considering. Thinking about Sarah coming to talk to him at Whiteface Mountain. He shook his head violently.

Among the eavesdroppers, only Travis knew what Muck would be thinking. Even if Mr. Brown hadn't actually seen Sarah telling Muck, he might have guessed. She was the one who'd walked away from him up on the mountain, after all. Mr. Brown would want to get back at her. And would want to get Muck, too.

Muck still wasn't convinced: "He wouldn't do something like that."

"He wouldn't, eh? What about last night?"

"He was drunk."

"And this morning he's sober. But he's still a loonie, drunk or sober."

Muck said nothing in response. The three coaches were at the door. Barry had it open for the other two, and in a moment the door clicked shut.

The four boys let their breath go and hurried out from behind the dumpster to fill their lungs with fresh morning air.

"*He'So'!*" shouted Data in disgust.

"You hear all that?" asked Nish, his face alive with excitement.

"They think Matt's dad did it," said Wilson.

So, too, did Travis. But he also thought the Panthers had done it. And then he remembered why they had wanted to get up so early this morning.

"The camera!" he said.

The video camera would prove who had been sabotaging them. The Panthers. Mr. Brown. Or no one.

"Let's get Norbert up!" Nish called.

14

The Screech Owls were not scheduled to play the Toronto Towers until 2:00 p.m. in the big rink, the Olympic rink, the rink where the U.S.A. had won the Olympic gold medal in 1980, the "Rink of Dreams" according to the post cards in the souvenir shops. That gave them the morning to get the camera out and examine the videotape. They had to wait until Mr. Dillinger went up to the rink to unlock the room, and then they would have to figure out how to get the camera without him seeing.

It was simpler than they figured. The whole team knew of the camera, but only three would go up to the rink to get it. Norbert, of course, because he would be responsible in the end if they got caught or if the camera somehow got damaged. And Derek, because he had taken the keys and would also be in trouble, and because he had the most believable reason for being there, even if it was only to hit his father up for a few dollars for the arcade. And Travis should go, they decided, because he was the least suspicious of all the kids. If they sent Nish, alarms would go off in the mind of everyone who saw him. Nish, giggling, loved the idea that he was too dangerous to send.

The three boys, with Norbert carrying a shopping bag for the camera, got to the rink shortly after Mr. Dillinger had taken his keys and set off to begin preparing for the game. He was working a lot of hours for the team, sharpening skates, repairing equipment. Travis had never seen him so serious or caught up in his work. No jokes, no kidding, no pranks. He seemed to be taking the sabotage personally: as the one in charge of the equipment, he was probably blaming himself for letting it happen. But what could he have done, Travis wondered, stand guard twenty-four hours a day over the room?

Travis felt sorry for Mr. Dillinger. Here his son, Derek, was having the tournament of his life – almost entirely due to Sarah's problems – and he couldn't enjoy it. He had stopped whistling. He wasn't singing. Travis wished all this would just go away so they could have their old general manager and trainer back.

Mr. Dillinger was sharpening skates when the boys came along. The Screech Owls were, perhaps, the only peewee team in the world with their own skate-sharpening equipment, but Mr. Dillinger had suggested buying it and Muck had agreed and, after working more midnight bingos than the parents wished to remember, they had earned enough money to purchase a unit that could fold up into its own suitcase and be pulled out and set up in less than ten minutes.

Muck, who often said, "You're only as good as your equipment," was delighted. Mr. Dillinger had worked with the entire team to find out who liked what and who played best with what kind of sharp. Dmitri, the quickest, liked his blades sharpened immediately before every game and ground so deep he could stop on a pin – a dime considered too much space for him. Nish, who liked to block shots, wanted a thin edge so he could slide more easily. Travis liked sharp skates, but not sharpened too deep, because he liked to work the corners and needed the flexibility. Muck figured the sharpening machine was worth a dozen goals a year to the Screech Owls. And a dozen goals a year, he said, could be the difference between first place and last playoff spot in the league.

"Hi, Mr. Dillinger," Travis said, as the boys came along.

"Hi, there, Trav –" Mr. Dillinger looked up. He nodded at the others. "Norbie. Son."

"You need any help, Dad?" Derek asked.

"Naw, not unless one of you wants to stand here for half an hour grinding Dmitri's skates down to his knees."

The boys all laughed. They were glad to hear Mr. Dillinger joking again.

"Anything happen?" Travis asked.

Mr. Dillinger smiled. "Just as I left it."

"Good."

"Let's hope that's the end of it."

"See any of the Panthers around?" Derek asked.

Mr. Dillinger considered for a moment. "I don't think so. I don't know whether I'd recognize them if I saw them. You still think they're the ones messing with Sarah's equipment?"

"Maybe."

Mr. Dillinger went back to his sharpening. "You might be right. You might be wrong. Maybe we'll never know . . . Travis, will you run in and grab your blades for me?"

"Sure." This was the opening they needed.

"And get Sareen's, too. Muck's thinking about starting her against the Towers."

"Got ya."

Travis and Norbert went into the dressing room while Derek stayed with his father, pretending to make conversation but really making sure Mr. Dillinger didn't follow the other two. It took Norbert less time to gather up the camera and equipment than it did for Travis to root his skates out of his bag and find Sareen's. They came out just as Mr. Dillinger was finishing up Dmitri's second skate, running a thumbnail along the edge to check it. He shook his thumb, wincing at the sharpness.

"Good. Thanks, Trav." Mr. Dillinger took Travis's skates and looked down at the bag Norbert was carrying at his side. "You been shopping, Norbie?"

The boys froze. If he asked to see what Norbert had bought, he would find out about the camera. If he found out what the boys had done – taken his keys, more or less broken in, set up a camera to spy – then heaven only knew what he would do about it. And what would Muck, with all his lectures about "sneakiness," have to say?

But Norbert was quick with an answer. "My mom made me buy some sweat pants."

"Good, good – okay, see you boys later. You be here forty-five minutes before we're on, okay?"

"Okay!"

"See you later, Dad."

"See you, Son."

⊚

They gathered in the health club off the pool area. No one ever seemed to be there working out, and no one was there this time, as they had been hoping. The entire team waited as Norbert flicked on the camera and checked through the viewfinder to see if there was anything on the tape. Norbert stared, checked switches, checked the tracking count, then lowered the camera and looked up.

"We caught something."

"What?" Nish practically shouted.

"Don't know. Just know that something set off the activator. There's about thirty seconds of tape run off."

The players' excitement rose and they pushed in closer.

"There's only one viewfinder!" exclaimed Norbert. "I can't show everybody. Back off, okay?"

"Back off!" Travis repeated.

"We need a big-screen TV," said Nish. "Like they have in the sports bars."

"How would you know what they have in sports bars?" Wilson asked.

"I know."

"Biggest screen in the world was at the 1937 Paris Exposition," said Willie Granger out of nowhere. "Bigger than an Olympic ice surface."

"Just everybody back away," Sarah said impatiently. "Let Norbert check it and he'll tell us what we've got."

They backed off, waiting. Norbert raised the camera, the machine shaking from his nerves, and slowly he pressed the buttons first to rewind and then play the videotape.

"Hurry up!" shouted Nish. No one paid him any regard.

Norbert stared for what seemed like an eternity. The camera shook, the team waited.

"Someone came into the room!"

"Who?" Nish shouted for everyone.

"Can't see – only a back of someone moving across."

The team groaned as one.

"Wait, there's more!"

They waited, afraid to breathe. Finally, Norbert sighed deeply and lowered the camera. The rubber around the viewfinder had made a red circle around his eye: it looked like he'd been punched, and when he spoke, he sounded like it, too.

"It's Mr. Dillinger."

"Damn!" Again, Nish spoke for all.

Travis felt his hopes sag. Of course, Mr. Dillinger must have been up to check last night. Travis had hoped the mystery would finally be solved so the tournament could continue without incident. He had hoped, in a way, that it would turn out to be someone they hadn't even thought of. Not Mr. Brown, because that would be hard on Matt, and not the Panthers, because that would be, well, that would just not be fair. No one played hockey that way, by hurting the other team's best player.

But all the ingenious activator had caught was Mr. Dillinger going about his business, unwittingly triggering the camera as he came in to make sure the Owls' equipment had all been aired out properly.

Travis walked up to the arena with Nish and Data and Wilson. They arrived more than an hour early, eager to get a feel for the game that was coming up against the Toronto Towers. They knew they had to win to make the finals, because they were tied with the Panthers at one win, one tie each, and the Panthers were scheduled to play the relatively weak Devils later, which should mean an easy win for the Portland team.

The Towers had a win and a loss and would have to win against the Screech Owls to make the final four. Another team, from Montreal, already had two wins and a loss, so there was no avoiding the importance of the Screech Owls' next match. If the Towers beat the Screech Owls, then Toronto might advance to the finals. The first-game tie with the Panthers was going to be of little help to the Screech Owls if today they added a loss.

When Travis walked in, he saw Muck walking toward him with a serious look on his face. His first thought was that there had been more trouble. But Muck wanted to speak to him about something else entirely, something completely unexpected.

"I've already called your parents, Travis," Muck said. "And they say the decision's yours. There's an area scout from the Bantam AA's here and he's asked for permission to speak to you and a couple of the other players. All I said was I'd present his case to the parents and player. And that's all I'm doing."

"What's it mean?" Travis asked.

"Maybe nothing. Maybe something. They can draw from a wider range than us and it's one of the best teams in the province – I know the coach pretty well, he's a good man – but it's tough to make and tough on parents. Both time and money. I think they play about 120 games a year if you count tournaments and exhibitions. But they're interested in you if you're interested in them."

"I don't know."

"You want to hear what he has to say?"

"I guess so."

"The arena manager's set aside a room for him. He's there now with the others. Just down past the washrooms, first door on the left."

Travis stared at his coach, trying to read Muck, but Muck was unreadable. It was impossible to say how he felt about this. It was almost as if it was none of his business, but it was all his business. He was the coach, after all, and Travis one of his players. Still, Travis couldn't play peewee forever. And if he ever wanted to make the NHL and see his sweater hanging up there with Terrible Ted's in Joe Louis Arena, then he'd have to leave Muck at some point. Perhaps this was it.

Muck turned to go, his expression giving away nothing. Travis didn't know whether Muck thought it a good idea or a bad idea. But that was Muck: he wouldn't say. It would be the player's decision. The player's and the parents'.

Travis headed back down the corridor. Mr. Dillinger was coming the other way, singing one of his stupid songs – something about a purple people-eater – and he gave Travis a shot in the shoulder as he passed. Mr. Dillinger knew.

⟳

Travis knocked at the closed door.

"Come in," a big voice called.

Travis pushed the door open. Inside, he saw the big voice belonged to a small man who was standing up and setting down a clipboard with writing on it. On chairs pulled around him were Dmitri Yakushev, Matt Brown, and Derek Dillinger. Maybe that was why Mr. Dillinger had been singing.

Dmitri was there for obvious reasons. Skill and speed. Matt Brown, Travis supposed, would have caught their attention through sheer size and his shot. And Derek, of course, was having the tournament of his life. Even if Sarah Cuthbertson had been able to play as she could, she wouldn't have been here. Next year Sarah would be leaving for good.

"You're Travis Lindsay," the big voice boomed. He seemed to be informing Travis rather than asking.

"Yes."

"I'm Pierre LeBrun. I'm with the Crusaders, Bantam double-A. You probably know Donny Williams, who was with Muck's gang two years ago."

"A bit."

"He's with us now. We like where he comes from. We like Muck's system. We like what we've seen here from you fellows this week. Have a seat, Travis."

Travis sat, and listened. Mr. LeBrun offered information, nothing more. The Screech Owls' players fell under the recruitment area of the Crusaders. The Crusaders were, as Muck had said, one of the best organizations around. Sweaters and socks and skates supplied. Some sticks supplied. Tournaments last year in Toronto, Lake Placid, Quebec City, and Vancouver. Tentative plans for a trip to Finland this coming winter.

Finland. Travis could hardly believe what he was hearing. Finland. Home of Teemu Selanne. Home of Jari Kurri. International competition. He was already halfway to the Detroit Red Wings!

"I've already met briefly with your coaches," Mr. Lebrun told them. "And they have no problems with what I'm about to propose to you."

He waited a moment, smiling, the boys waiting.

"If you four are agreeable," Mr. LeBrun continued, "we'd like to send you invitations to attend our fall camp. I can't guarantee you you'll make the team, but from what I've seen here this week, I wouldn't want to bet that you won't."

Travis looked at the others, who were also looking around. None of them had ever heard such talk before. None of them knew what to say.

"Can I send you invites, then?" Mr. LeBrun asked.

"Sure," said Derek, his voice shaking.

"Okay," said Dmitri, his voice the same as always.

"Great," said Matt.

"Yeah," said Travis.

Yes, indeed.

15

"Sarah's sticks are missing!"

The voice was Ty Barrett's and it was coming from outside the dressing room, but everyone inside heard him. He was talking to Muck, who had just stepped outside to see how far the Zamboni had got with the ice cleaning. Muck swore – unusual for Muck, meaning he was very, very upset.

Sarah had heard as well. She had just finished tying her skates and pulling on her sweater and had her helmet, ready to strap on, in her lap, when Ty's voice burst in through the door. She didn't say a word, just shut her eyes and leaned back against the wall. Travis could hear her let her breath out slowly.

"Give us a break!" Nish shouted from behind his mask.

"How could they be 'missing'?" Jesse asked no one in particular.

The door opened and Muck came back in, his jaw working furiously but no sound coming out. He had no idea what to say himself. He signalled for Mr. Dillinger to come with him, and

Mr. Dillinger, shaking his head and blowing air out of his mouth, hurried from the dressing room to consult. The players could hear more swearing, both Muck and Mr. Dillinger.

Muck returned again, followed by Mr. Dillinger, his face now red and angry-looking.

"Someone's made off with Sarah's sticks," Muck said very matter-of-factly. "She'll have to borrow. Travis, you're a left. You have extras?"

"Two."

He turned to Sarah, her eyes now open, glistening slightly.

"You can try Travis's. If you don't like them, try some other lefts. We've got no choice."

Someone who doesn't play the game would never understand, Travis thought as the Screech Owls warmed up Sareen to start her first game of the tournament.

A hockey stick has a personality, Travis figured, and it gets the personality from the owner, the one who tapes it and bends it and handles it and feels it. Changing sticks in hockey is like a batter heading to the plate with a shovel in his hands, or a basketball player heading down the court in church shoes. It doesn't feel right, and when it doesn't feel right, it usually doesn't work right.

He had given two of his sticks over to Sarah and she had tried them but obviously was not content with them. Sarah liked to taper the top of her stick; Travis liked a big knob of tape. Sarah liked a fairly straight blade for playmaking; Travis liked as big a curve as he could get away with for roofing shots and corner-work. Sarah liked a short stick for in-close work;

Travis liked one that stood to the bottom of his chin so he could get all his weight behind a slapper.

The only player who liked his sticks like Sarah was Dmitri, but Dmitri was a right shot. She tried one of Matt's sticks and one of Jesse's, but then came back to Travis's as the best of a poor choice. She seemed sadly discouraged during the warm-up.

The game went poorly. Sareen was so nervous she let in the first shot, a long dump-in from the other side of the blueline. And Sarah could not hang onto the puck at all. This time, however, Muck refused to juggle the lines to compensate. He seemed determined to go with Sarah at ·first-line centre no matter what.

But the team was paying for her lack of stick control. With Dmitri at top speed heading in on right, she sent a pass that would normally have meant a breakaway but, thanks to the big curve, caught slightly and went behind Dmitri, throwing him offside.

And later, with Travis parked all alone at the side of the net and Sarah with the puck in the slot, the Screech Owls lost the tying goal when Sarah backhanded the puck and it went looping off the other side of the curve into the corner and out of harm's way.

The Toronto Towers, knowing they must win to have any chance of going on in the tournament, fought ferociously and were up 2–0 at the break. The first goal had been Sareen's fault, the second had been Travis's fault. He had thought Nish had control of the puck and broke over the blueline toward centre, only to have Nish checked off the puck. The Towers' defence-man pinched, picked up the puck, and hit a winger sitting on the far side of the net for a perfect one-timer. The goal light was flashing as Travis, feeling like a fool, was still on the other side of the blueline.

Finally, at the break, Muck had had enough. He put his arm around Sarah as he told her that Derek was yet again moving up onto the line and Sarah, fighting back tears, her lips trembling, had nodded that she agreed. Muck gave her a little hug as he let go.

The juggling worked again, just as it had for the first game. Sareen settled down and didn't let another goal past her. Derek played his heart out, scored once and set up Dmitri on a clean breakaway, which he cashed in. The score was tied 2–2.

Matt Brown scored the go-ahead goal on a Screech Owls power play, hammering a shot in from the point that seemed to tip in off a Toronto player's skate toe. And the Screech Owls' fourth goal was scored by Travis – but it was hardly one for the highlights.

With two minutes to go in a game the Towers had to win, they had pulled their goaltender, and Derek, stealing a puck inside his own blueline, had hit Dmitri for a second breakaway. But Dmitri, sometimes generous to a fault, had slowed down, drawn the one defender to him, and laid a perfect, soft pass to empty ice so it was sitting there, waiting, when Travis arrived at the front of the empty net. He could have scored with a bulldozer.

When they came off the ice after the handshake, Mr. LeBrun was standing to the side of the rubber mat leading to the dressing room. He congratulated each player as he or she passed, with a special tap for the four with whom he had met, and a victorious punch to the shoulder of a sheepish-looking Derek Dillinger.

Mr. Dillinger, carrying the water bottles and first-aid equipment a few steps behind, beamed as he passed Mr. LeBrun and the scout said, "You got a good one there." Mr. Dillinger knew; the whole team knew. Mr. Dillinger was glowing red when he came into the dressing room.

"All right, listen up!" Barry Yonson yelled when the clatter of falling sticks had subsided and everyone was in their seats and beginning to pull off helmets and gloves. Muck wanted to speak to them.

"You can thank your lucky stars that was Toronto and not the Panthers," Muck told them in his usual quiet voice. "Most of you played like house-league atoms out there."

The players knew it was true. Even considering what had happened to Sarah, the Screech Owls had stunk. Had it not been for Derek's inspired play when he was moved up to replace her, and Sareen shutting the Towers out in the second period, they might have been packing up to go home.

"Pick up your sticks as you go," Muck said. "Mr. Dillinger's going to lock them up in the van overnight. And Sarah, you go with Mr. Dillinger downtown. He'll take you to pick up some new ones, okay?"

Sarah smiled. She'd be able to play in the final. "Okay," she said.

"Alllll rightttt, Sarah!" Nish shouted.

"Yesss!" Derek added.

Good for Derek, Travis thought. He knows if Sarah comes back, he drops back. He knows who the real first-line centre of the Screech Owls is. He knows what a team means.

16

The Screech Owls held another meeting in the unused health club. Travis was in charge. He was surprising himself the way he was starting to take command of things so easily. But since almost everything concerned Sarah, and Sarah was the captain, it seemed better that the assistant captain represent the team. And that was exactly what Travis was beginning to do.

"We almost blew it today," Travis said. Everyone agreed.

"Muck was right about what he said. Most of us — me included — played like atom house-leaguers. We screw up tomorrow and we've lost the championship. We owe Muck better than that."

"It's hardly our fault," Data protested. "You have to consider what they've been doing to Sarah."

"That's right," agreed Gordie Griffith.

"We all know what's been happening," Travis countered. "What's happening to Sarah doesn't mean a thing on the scoreboard."

"It's true," agreed Sarah.

"Besides, Derek's been playing great hockey," said Travis. "We have to make sure we're all playing great tomorrow. So let's smarten up."

"What about Sarah?" Fahd asked.

"What about her?"

"What if they do something again?"

"The sticks are locked up in the van."

"What if they cut her straps?"

"I brought my stuff back," Sarah said. "It's safe in my room."

"You bring your skates, too?" Wilson asked.

Sarah shook her head. "They're in with everyone else's in the big footlocker, under lock and key."

"What if somebody breaks into it?" Fahd asked.

"Who'd be able to tell my skates from anyone else's?" Sarah asked.

"Maybe it doesn't matter," Fahd said suddenly. "Who's to say they won't try something else now?"

Travis didn't follow: "Like what?"

"Like what if someone takes Derek's sticks this time?"

"They're all in the van."

"Or Dmitri's skates. Or slashes Guy's pads. If they can't get at Sarah, why wouldn't they get us some other way if they're already doing what they've been doing?"

As usual, Fahd's points were dead on. If the Panthers' purpose was to cripple the Screech Owls, and if stopping Sarah was no longer possible, then it stood to reason that they would have to be thinking of some other way. If Mr. Brown's purpose – and Travis still couldn't see that he had one – was to hurt

Sarah, who had told on him, and Muck, who had humiliated him, then he would still want to get at Muck, and the only way left to him would be to go after Dmitri or Derek or Guy or Nish or, for that matter, Travis, who certainly wasn't going to have two bad games in a row.

Travis sighed, nodding. "Well, what do we do, then?"

"Bring all the equipment down to the hotel," Gordie Griffith suggested.

"Not enough room," Travis said.

"Van's already full of sticks," Nish added.

"Set up a real guard," Fahd said.

Travis didn't follow. Nor, from the expression on the faces of the others, did anyone else.

Fahd explained: "We tried the camera. It didn't work. Someone still got in. We need a real guard there."

"You mean a player?" Sarah asked.

"Yeah, someone who could stay in the room and make sure nothing happens."

"Sounds dangerous," Nish said.

Fahd considered a moment. "Maybe. But since the problem has always been equipment, all we'd need to do is know what they'd done. We'd have until 4:30 to get it repaired. If we'd known about Sarah's sticks before the game, we would have had lots of time to get her new ones."

"That's true," said Nish.

"All we need is someone to watch and see if anything's going on. Then, in the morning, either we fix it or we get Mr. Dillinger to fix it."

"We should tell our parents," Data said.

"No way!" Nish argued. "You think they'd let us stay up all night in the arena?"

"Just one of us," said Fahd.

"One?" Nish asked.

"We also want to find out who it is, don't we?" Fahd asked. "We all go up there we're just going to scare people off. Besides, if we want to win tomorrow, the rest of us are going to need our sleep."

"Okay," Nish countered. "You got all the answers, Fahd. What're we going to do?"

"There're two lockers in each one of those rooms we're using to store the equipment, right?" Fahd asked.

Derek agreed. He would know. "One for sticks," he said. "One for whatever."

"We don't have our sticks there any more," Gordie said, as if settling the point Fahd was heading for.

"Exactly," Fahd said. "It's empty. It's got air holes. It would hold a player."

"Have to be awfully small, wouldn't he?" a sceptical Nish pointed out.

"Exactly," Fahd said.

He was staring directly at Travis.

@

"Too bad, sucker. You're going to miss the show!"

Nish was in his element: giggling, surrounded by wires, the back of the television in front of him. He was teasing Travis. They had to wait for Mr. Dillinger to come back from the rink so Derek could "borrow" the keys again and, in the meantime, several of the players had come up to Nish's room to see the promised spectacle: adult movies.

Nish had the protective coupler off again and was reconnecting the cable wires. Satisfied, he swung the television around and began playing with the channel switch.

There was a light knock at the door. The boys all jumped: *had the motel figured out what Nish was doing?*

"It's Sarah," a voice called. "And Sareen."

Nish began to glow like a goal light. Travis immediately jumped up to let the girls in. Some of the other boys began giggling.

"Come on, Nish," Wilson teased. "You promised."

"Promised what?" Sarah wanted to know.

"Nothing," Nish said, a bit too quickly.

"*Nothing?*" Wilson said with astonishment.

Sarah and Sareen looked at each other, then suspiciously at Nish.

"What's going on here?" Sareen asked.

"You keeping secrets from us, Nish?" Sarah added.

Nish gave up. "I'm trying to fix the TV so we can get free movies," he admitted.

"Come on, Nish, it's more than that," Wilson said.

Nish turned on him, scowling. "Thanks a lot."

Sarah giggled. "You're trying to see a dirty movie, aren't you, Nish?"

Nish was crimson now, shaking his head. "I just wanted to see if it works," he protested.

"And does it?" Sareen asked.

Nish turned, startled. "What?"

"Can you get them?" Sarah asked.

"I don't know."

"Well," Sareen said, "why don't you show us?"

Nish seemed completely baffled. "Not with you here!"

"Why not?" Sarah wanted to know.

"You're a girl!" Nish practically shouted, pointing out the obvious.

"Why, so I am!" Sarah exclaimed, faking shock. She looked at Sareen, pretending to jump back with surprise. "Why, look, you're one, too, Sareen!"

Sareen stared, surprised, at herself. "I am? I am! How does Nish manage to pick up these things?"

For once, Nish hated being centred out. "It's not funny!" he protested.

"It is, too," Sarah scolded. "You want to watch men and women but you don't think it's right for women to watch, too. Isn't that it?"

"I just want to check. I don't really want to watch." This statement threw the rest of the room into howls of laughter.

"Put it on," Sareen told Nish. "We want to see, too."

"We're on the team, aren't we?" Sarah said, teasing Nish.

Nish seemed surprised. "You really want to watch?"

"'Check,'" Sarah corrected him.

Nish looked around the room for support. He was getting none. "Go ahead," Data said. "Everybody here but Nish already knows how we got here. He may as well finally find out." Everyone laughed. Nish shrugged his shoulders and went back to fiddling with the television, his colour fading from bright red to pink.

He flew through the channels on the manual selector, some of the regular television channels coming in instantly, some of the pay movies as well. Data tried to get them to stick with a "Star Trek" re-run, but no one else was interested. A Western flicked on. And a thriller that some of the players recognized and wanted to watch again. But Nish was determined.

His hands fiddled and, suddenly, he came upon a channel with no picture, but sound. The sound was grunting.

"That's it!" shouted Data. "*Hljol!*" ("Beam me aboard!")

Everyone laughed, Nish included, delighted that the focus was shifting off of him.

"Bring in the picture," Sarah said.

"I'm trying, I'm trying," Nish said. His chubby hands flew as they worked on the horizontal and vertical hold. He had the adjustment box open and was working every possible dial, desperately trying to pull in the picture to go with the alarming sound.

An image caught and flew by, too quick to catch. "That's it!" shouted Wilson. "Go back!"

Frantically, Nish fiddled the dial back. The picture flickered twice and then came into full, glorious colour.

A wagon train was stuck in the mud. A team of mules was braying as they pulled, hopelessly. Two young cowboys were behind the wagon, up to their waists in mud, pushing and grunting. It was another Western.

"So that's how you make babies, Nish," teased Sarah. "Now you know the big secret."

Nish's colour went back to goal-light red.

There was another quick rap on the door. Nish punched off the set, panicking.

"Who is it?" Travis called.

"Me – Derek."

He had the keys. It was time to go. Travis could feel his heart stop dead, then start up again twice as fast.

17

ravis's heart was now pounding so hard he couldn't believe the rest couldn't hear it. Derek, with his dad's keys, and a few other Screech Owls – Nish, Sarah, Dmitri, Fahd, and Travis – had come up to the rink just before curfew and just as the last game of the evening was coming to an end. Unnoticed, they had slipped down into the dressing-room area and, with Dmitri on watch, were setting up Fahd's guard.

The empty locker easily held Travis. Closed, it had enough airholes, probably for airing out figure skaters' outfits, that he could see out easily and even sit down and relax, the locker was so deep. But comfort was hardly Travis's first concern. He was petrified of what would happen when the lights went out! Petrified, and unable to tell anyone.

"I can fit here," Sarah said. "I should be the one staying. It's my stuff they've been after."

Fahd spoke for the others, Travis excepted. "You're our most valuable player," he said. "And you're still short of sleep from that first night."

Travis had wanted to beg her – anyone – to replace him, but didn't dare. No one knew about his dread of the dark, and now here he was about to be placed in a box – in a *coffin!* – and be buried alive in an arena dressing room.

"You try it, Nish," Travis suggested. "I bet even you can fit."

"No way," Nish said. "I'd get stuck in there and die."

Travis felt he was going to die himself. No one else was offering. Not Fahd, who was hardly as important to the team as Travis. Not Dmitri, whose scoring was possibly a bit more important. And certainly not Nish, who was also probably as important. He wished they'd asked little Guy Boucher to do it, or Sareen, who wasn't playing anyway but was desperate to do something, anything, to help her team.

But it was too late. Travis was assistant captain and he was expected to take responsibility. The others were completely caught up with enthusiasm for Fahd's idea and Travis had simply been carried along with them as they hurried to put the plan into action.

"You'll be all right?" Nish asked.

Travis had to lie: "Yeah."

"You're a braver man than me," said Nish. He had no idea, Travis thought.

"That's stupid talk," Fahd said. "You got some chocolate bars, an apple in this bag. There's a can over there if you need it, but you'd better use it before they shut down things or someone hanging around might get suspicious."

"What if they catch him?" Nish asked. Nish wasn't being in the least helpful.

Fahd was getting impatient with Nish raising the alarm.

"No one's going to catch anyone," he said. "Travis stays put and doesn't move."

"What if they open up the locker?" Sarah asked.

Fahd had thought of this. "Travis can bolt it from the inside with this." He had a small penknife and showed them how it would lock in the latch so no one could move it from outside. "They'll think it's locked if they try it."

"You okay, then?" Sarah asked.

Travis looked up from the locker. She was looking at him like he was the greatest friend in the world. He felt as if he was doing something important, something vital.

"Fine," he lied.

Travis thought he was going to throw up. He had settled into the locker and they had closed the door and he had tried the knife bolt and tested it, and, satisfied, they had said their farewells to him from the other side of the airholes and left.

Derek wanted to get the key back into the hotel room in case his father noticed it was gone. He would sneak the key out again first thing in the morning, and they would, they promised, have him out of there by 7:30 a.m., in time for either the first serving of breakfast or a quick cat nap, whichever Travis felt he needed more.

When they left, Fahd turned out the lights.

Total, unbelievable, suffocating, frightening, snake-filled dark!

Travis felt himself begin to panic. His heart was thundering, his chest bouncing like a parade drum. He had his eyes wide open and it seemed he could see strange lights, reds and greens and flashes of orange, and then it seemed as if he could hear sounds, movement.

Rats!

No, it was nothing. Just his imagination. Water running through the pipes. The heat coming on. Doors slamming on other rooms as the rink closed down for the night.

Travis tried to think about the games he had played and the game they would play tomorrow against the Panthers. Slowly, gradually, his heart settled and the colours seemed to leave his eyes. Instead, as his pupils slowly adjusted, he began to make out shadows and forms beyond the airholes. There were still lights on in the corridor, and some of them were making it through the narrow little window in the door and around the corner of the entrance way. *He could see!*

Well, he could see a bit. But a bit was better than nothing. He figured in a coffin he would see nothing. And breathe nothing. This was bad, this was *terrible*, but it was not death.

He waited for what seemed like hours. To pass the time he began sorting through his hockey card collection in his mind, trying to think of ways to organize cards that weren't by year or whatever company had manufactured them. He put all his cards worth over twenty dollars – well, according to the book, anyway – together. He put all his Europeans together. All his Russians. He put all his good centres together and liked that. Then all his good left-wingers, and imagined himself included.

He thought about all his autographed cards – Pavel Bure, Jaromir Jagr, Teemu Selanne, Paul Kariya, Adam Graves, Mike Modano, Gretzky – and he wondered how many times Gretzky had signed his name since the first kid asked for one. A hundred thousand? A million? He wondered how many hours, how many days, how many *months*, Gretzky had spent signing over his career.

He wondered if Wayne Gretzky had ever sat, as Travis Lindsay had sat, at the kitchen table endlessly practising a signature. A printed "T," a looping "L," a huge, exaggerated "T," an "L" that rolled off into his number "7" just as Gretzky would place that little "99" at the bottom of his name. He wondered if Wayne Gretzky's sister had ever teased him about practising his autograph the way his sister had teased him, and he wondered if a few times Gretzky, like Travis himself, had wondered if there was any sense in practising something no one wanted, at least for the moment . . .

He had fallen asleep. He was down on his haunches, slumped, his head lolling and his hands between his knees. When he woke he did not know where he was, but then it came back, not as a memory, but as a sound.

His heart pounding through his chest!

There was a sound at the door. The scratch of a key being worked in and turned, first one way, then the other, and then the pop of air as the door opened. Beyond, in the pale light from whatever light was still burning, Travis could barely make out a hulking silhouette. Form but no identity.

The lights went on. Not welcome, but blinding. Even to Travis hidden in the locker. He moved closer to the lower airholes and blinked, waiting for his vision to return. The room seemed impossibly bright. His heart seemed impossibly afraid. He was shaking, sweating. He was terrified!

The hulk moved across the room, keys jangling as they went back into a pocket. The hulk moved, opened up the latches on the skate sharpening box.

It was Mr. Dillinger!

He had come to do skates. He had his keys out and was undoing the big footlocker that held the team's skates and was rooting around for those he needed to sharpen. Good old Mr. Dillinger. Travis wanted to burst from the locker and hug him, so glad was he to see that the invader was neither a Panther nor Mr. Brown nor some unknown murderer with a grizzled beard and tobacco spit running down his chin and a long sharp knife in his boot. But he knew he couldn't call out. Knew he couldn't explain.

He also knew there was now no danger of being found in the locker. Mr. Dillinger knew better than anyone that it was empty and why it was empty. He wouldn't look in.

Travis felt a fool sitting there watching Mr. Dillinger work. It seemed so, well, sneaky of Travis to be doing this. But he couldn't help but watch. And the more he watched, the funnier he felt.

What was Mr. Dillinger doing?

M r. Dillinger had the skate sharpener open, and he had Sarah Cuthbertson's skates out. Travis could make out the little number "98" Sarah had painted in white on the heel – the number chosen to honour the year, 1998, when women's hockey would become an official Olympic sport.

But Mr. Dillinger also had a hammer out, the hammer he sometimes had to use to straighten out a crooked blade. Travis couldn't remember Sarah complaining about her blades.

Travis was unable to see Mr. Dillinger's face. He could only see his hands, and what they were doing with Sarah's skates.

Mr. Dillinger set the skates in the skate holder normally used for sharpening, but the machine was neither set up nor plugged in. He took the hammer then, and very carefully, very slowly, worked it along the blade, hammering hard at times, and then pulling the skate off and eyeing it down the blade.

It seemed he was fixing something. Perhaps, Travis wondered, Mr. Dillinger had noticed something that Sarah hadn't

mentioned. Or perhaps Muck had noticed something. Whatever, Mr. Dillinger worked over the skates for the better part of
ten minutes before he made one final check of the blade line,
seemed satisfied, and then put everything back in its place,
including Sarah's skates.

He then locked everything back up again, checked the
room one last time, never even coming near the locker, and then
went to the door, where he turned out the light, plunging Travis
back into his coffin panic, and eased silently out the door. The
key scratched quietly again, turned, and the door was once more
locked solid.

It took another ten minutes or so for Travis's heart to settle
and some of his sight to return. It seemed strange to him: Mr.
Dillinger coming up here late at night – Travis checked his
watch, the digital numbers glowing 12:45 – just to straighten
out Sarah's blades. That was dedication.

Travis was wide awake when the kids returned to let him out.
He had heard the rink attendants arrive before 7:00 a.m. and he
knew then that his ordeal was over. He had survived the dark!
He had been buried alive and was still alive! He felt prouder of
himself than if he had scored a hat-trick in the final game. Well,
maybe not quite that proud, but . . .

The key scratched again and Travis knew it would be Derek
and the others. He was already out of the locker and waiting for
them when they burst in, their faces so uncertain that he wondered if perhaps they were expecting to find a body hacked to
pieces by a chainsaw instead of their friend who had just proved
something important to himself, but couldn't tell anyone about it.

"You okay?" Sarah asked.

"Fine."

"No goblins," Nish giggled. Travis ignored him.

"Anything?" Fahd asked.

"I don't know," Travis said. "I'm not sure. Derek, you got a key on that ring for the skate box?"

Derek fiddled with the keys. "I guess so. Why?"

"I don't know. I just want to look at something."

Derek found the right key on the third try. The padlock came off, the lid up, and Travis, without explaining, reached in for the skates with number 98 painted on the heel.

"What're you doing with my skates?" Sarah demanded.

"Just checking."

Travis held the skates up to the light and turned first one, then the other, upside-down. With his eye, he traced the line of the blade and saw what he had been afraid he might see: the blades were badly curved. Deliberately bent by a hammer. Sarah wouldn't be able to skate the length of the ice on them. If she tried to turn, she'd either dig in and fall flat or slip away and crash into the boards.

"What's wrong?" Sarah asked.

Travis handed her one of the skates. The other he gave to Nish.

"They're crooked!" Sarah shouted.

"Somebody's bent them!" Nish added.

"Who would do something like that?" Derek asked.

Travis had no idea how he would tell him.

@

"I have to talk to you, Muck."

It would be wrong to suggest that Travis had never done anything so difficult before in his life. He had, barely an hour earlier.

Travis had only described what he had seen, with no suggestions, no accusations, nothing. But Derek had seen through it immediately. Derek had burst into tears in the equipment room and Sarah, also crying, had tried to comfort him, but Derek had shaken her off and, without another word, fled the room, slamming the door behind him as hard as he could pull it.

They had probably taken too much time to put the skates back and the locks on. When it came time to lock the door up again, they found they had no key – Derek had run off with it. And when they hurried outside to see if they could still catch him, he was nowhere to be seen. Nor was he back at the hotel. It seemed he had run away.

Travis had found the coach at the gift shop where Muck was buying a copy of *USA Today* and a pack of gum. Muck took him out into the sun room by the main entrance – no one there but a bellman dozing in the sun – carefully opened the gum and handed a stick to Travis and took one himself, slowly chewing as if the flavour mattered more than whatever Travis had to say to him.

"Okay," he said, "shoot. What is it?"

Travis found he could barely speak. Even with the sweet gum in his mouth, his throat was burning as if he were about to cry. But no tears came; nor, at times, would any sound. Muck waited patiently, saying nothing, slowly chewing and then snapping his own gum. Finally, Travis got it all out. The camera, the keys, the locker, what he had seen, the skates, Derek, the keys . . .

Muck took it all in without even blinking. When Travis had finished Muck sat, looking very tired, and stared for a long time at Travis, who figured he was about to get into trouble for the keys and for staying out all night.

Muck stared, shook his head, and smiled. "Hockey does strange things to people, Travis."

Travis had no idea what he meant.

19

With the championship game not scheduled until 4:30 that day, Muck and the coaches had time to meet first with Mr. Dillinger and then with the officials of the Lake Placid International. Some of the players who knew what was going on had told their parents, and those parents had told other parents, and so everyone pretty well knew what had happened. But no one knew what was going to happen next.

And they could not find Derek. Travis and some of the other players had looked for him, and the keys, without any luck. Muck said he would find Derek later. He didn't seem worried about him.

Sarah and her parents set off early for nearby Plattsburg, where there were two big malls and where they would have a larger selection of skates to choose from than the little Lake Placid sports stores could provide. Sarah seemed much relieved. Not only had the mystery been solved, but she was coming back to Lake Placid with a brand-new pair of pump CCM Tacks, and it wasn't even Christmas.

Muck posted a note on the bulletin board asking all the parents and all the players to meet in the Skyroom at one o'clock. There was no hint whatsoever of what he planned to do.

Travis sometimes got edgy before a big game, but he had never felt anything like this before. It seemed his heart was once again pounding through his chest. The parents were milling around talking in low, quick voices. Some seemed relieved, some shocked. Mr. Brown looked like he'd just won a game himself. It made no sense to Travis.

Muck came in and walked to the centre of the room. He said not a word. The murmuring stopped. Every face – players, family, coaches – turned toward him, waiting.

"Everybody knows the story," Muck said. "I don't need to go over it all again. You know what happened by now as well as I do."

He paused. The audience shuffled, coughed, waited. No one dared to speak.

"This incident has left us in a strange situation. I am informed by the tournament organizers that any such interference with another team would have been cause for immediate disqualification and expulsion of the Screech Owls from the tournament. But the organizers say since it is our own affair involving only our own people, then it is up to us to decide how we will deal with the situation."

Muck paused again, letting those in the room consider his words. Travis was sure he could hear Mr. Brown muttering under his breath, but he couldn't make out what he was saying.

Guy Boucher's father spoke for everyone: "What is the status of our manager, Muck?"

Muck breathed deeply, thinking. "Our manager, Mr. Dillinger, has resigned his post this morning."

Travis could hear Mr. Brown muttering again. Something about "charges."

Muck quickly fixed Mr. Brown with the stare his players seldom saw and, once seen, never wished to see again. The stare of a laser beam burning through steel.

Muck was looking at Mr. Brown but speaking to everyone: "I have been around this coaching business long enough to know that sometimes we can all let a simple game matter a bit too much and, before we know it, we've made fools of ourselves without even realizing what we were doing. There are some fathers – and some mothers – in this very room who know what I'm talking about. Ripping the head off some thirteen-year-old referee. Swearing at some little kid just because he happened to run into yours. Yelling at your own kid after a game because he missed a pass."

"That's hardly the same thing –" protested Mr. Brown.

Muck's stare turned into a hard drive from the point, labelled. "I've even heard of grown-ups offering bribes to children," Muck said. "You don't get much lower than that in my book."

Mr. Brown looked down at his feet.

"Now," Muck paused. "Mr. Dillinger would like to say something to us."

Mr. Dillinger! He was coming into this room? Now?

The crowd murmured with dissatisfaction. No one wanted

to see Mr. Dillinger again. Not after what he'd done. Some of them as long as they lived. Travis could see Mr. Boucher's jaw flinch. He could see Muck watching the parents' faces, not the door, which Ty Barrett was opening into the hallway.

It seemed every breath in the room was held. Not even Mr. Brown was muttering.

Mr. Dillinger came in, his head bowed, his usual bouncing walk gone. He walked slowly to the centre of the room and stood beside Muck, his eyes fixing by turn on the floor and the far wall and on Muck, but not once on any of the players or the parents.

He took a long time to compose himself. He swallowed. He coughed. He seemed on the verge of tears. He seemed about to run. But gradually he was able to speak.

"I'm sorry," he said. He swallowed again, gathering himself. No one spoke. "I am the one who bent the skates. I hid the sticks. I cut the straps."

"Would you mind telling us why?" Mr. Boucher asked. There was anger, and disgust, in his voice.

Mr. Dillinger waited a long time before continuing. It seemed he could say no more. But everyone waited, demanding more.

Mr. Dillinger's voice choked: "I guess I did it because I didn't think I was hurting anyone."

He reacted to the sharp intake of breath that came from several in the room. Mr. Brown swore, a vicious word that Travis had never before heard any of the parents use. Muck's stare was like a slap in the face; Mr. Brown looked down at his shoes, shaking his head.

"You can believe me if you want or not believe me if you want," Mr. Dillinger said. "I'd never want to hurt Sarah. You have to believe that. I love that kid like she was my own."

"That makes precious little sense," said Mr. Boucher.

"I know," Mr. Dillinger stumbled. "I know that. But when the girls weren't able to play that first game and my boy got moved up to the top line, I had this crazy thought that maybe I could help him stay there and get noticed."

"At the expense of Sarah?" Mr. Boucher asked.

"No, not the way I was thinking. She'd already made the Toronto Aeros for the fall. She'd already let us know she'd gone as far as she wanted at this level of hockey. She was the only one whose career wouldn't be hurt by something like this."

"'Career'?" Mr. Boucher said with a snort.

"That's the way I was thinking. I was all mixed up. I just wanted Derek to have a chance to be noticed. If he played with Dmitri and Travis, he'd get his points. And that's pretty well what happened . . ."

Mr. Dillinger paused a long, long time. The room grew very uncomfortable. He coughed. He wiped his eye, missed a tear that grew and then broke, sliding down his cheek as he continued to talk to them.

"What I did was wrong. It was crazy. But I just wanted Derek to have this one chance –"

Mr. Dillinger began sobbing.

"I'm sorry," he repeated. He swallowed hard once more, turned, and left. Ty Barrett held the door open for him.

Mr. Dillinger paused at the doorway.

"Muck," he said. "I owe you an apology. I disgraced you as your manager."

Then he was gone.

The room was silent. Muck still stood at the centre. He would wait for one of them to speak.

"What will happen to him?" Mr. Boucher asked. It was the question everyone wanted to know the answer to.

Muck shook his head. "I suppose that's up to us, isn't it? The tournament organizers want nothing to do with it. They say it's our affair."

"He should be kicked out of organized hockey altogether," Mr. Brown burst out.

"I suppose he would be if someone here wished to file a report with the association. I won't be. It will have to come from one or more of you."

"He betrayed a position of trust," Mr. Boucher said. He was so much calmer than Mr. Brown. And what he said made sense.

"He did," Muck said. "And I think he knows that better than any of us."

"Just so his damn kid could get ahead," Mr. Brown exploded.

Muck had had enough. "His 'kid,' Mr. Brown," Muck said with that voice that could wither a player at the far end of the bench, "is the one most betrayed here, would you not say?"

Mr. Brown, his face red as a tomato, could only shrug.

"What Mr. Dillinger did was wrong. Very wrong. He has admitted that and I, for one, respect him for doing so. But we have a saying on the Screech Owls: you're allowed one mistake."

"This is hardly the same thing as skipping a practice," Mr. Brown argued.

"I didn't say it was the same," Muck countered. "But to tell you the truth, I'm less interested in what *we* think is right or wrong than what those who matter most here think — and they are Sarah Cuthbertson and Derek Dillinger."

"They're just kids," Mr. Brown sputtered, shaking his head.

"Exactly," Muck said, and turned and left the room, his two assistants falling in behind him.

20

ravis went out into the parking lot with the other kids. The parents went off down the hotel halls in smaller groups, buzzing with concern. Mr. Brown was talking too loudly, swearing. Mr. Boucher seemed to be the one they were listening to.

Travis couldn't figure out how he felt. He had liked Mr. Dillinger so much. In a crazy way he still liked Mr. Dillinger. He felt sorry for him. Sorry that Mr. Dillinger had wanted so badly for Derek to shine that he had worked it so Derek would get a chance to shine. He felt sorriest for Derek.

"You're the hero!" Nish said, slapping Travis's back.

He didn't feel like a hero. He felt horrible. He felt as if he had ruined someone's life, for Mr. Dillinger's life was the team, the driving, the joking, the working. He was a good manager, darn it, and how could something like this ruin it?

"You can see how it happened, kind of," said Data. Data, always analyzing, always looking for explanations.

"How?" Nish laughed. "He shafted Sarah for his own kid's sake. Get a life, Data."

"He never would have done it if he hadn't known Sarah was going anyway," Data said. "It was kind of like he figured she'd understand."

"Yeah, right!" ridiculed Nish.

"Like she'd understand being kept awake all night, so long as it helped Derek," said Data.

"Derek's got nothing to do with this!" said Gordie Griffith sharply.

"Besides," added Data, "Mr. Dillinger had nothing to do with that first night. He said that was what gave him the idea."

"Who kept sending the pizzas then?" Nish asked.

"Maybe no one. Maybe it *was* a mistake."

"Mr. Dillinger admitted he'd made a mistake," Travis said.

"And that makes it all right?" Nish said with heavy sarcasm.

"No, it doesn't," said Travis. "But at least he had the guts to go in there and apologize."

"He had no choice," Nish argued. "Muck made him."

"I doubt it," Travis said. Muck would never force anyone to do anything.

Muck was coming out the door into the bright light, shading his eyes from the sun, searching. He was looking for the players. He saw the group talking and walked over.

"We have a centre to find," he said when he got there. "Any ideas?"

He was looking straight at Travis. It seemed that Travis had somehow become the team leader, the one who spoke for them all. But he had no idea what to say this time. "I don't know. Maybe down by the water."

Travis's hunch had been right. They had all started walking down the hill toward the lake, but Muck had stopped them in their tracks and sent every one of the kids back – except for Travis. He wanted Travis with him when they found Derek.

Derek was sitting on the end of the old wooden toboggan run by the park and the beach. He had climbed the fence and was sitting well out of sight, but Travis had seen a stone plunk into the water as he and Muck came walking down, and he knew immediately where it had come from and who had thrown it.

Muck seemed so casual about it all. He came and stood by the water, his hands in his pants pockets, looking out over the lake, giving not even the slightest hint that he knew Derek was sitting above him on the end of an ancient toboggan run.

"How're you doing?" Muck finally said.

Travis, who had come and stood beside his coach, knew Muck wasn't speaking to him. He said nothing himself, only waited.

Finally, Derek's voice broke. "Go away," he said. He was obviously crying.

Muck never turned to look. So Travis did not look. If Derek was crying it would be his business alone. They would not embarrass him.

"You'll want to get some lunch in you," Muck said. "You'll need energy for the game."

Derek bit off his words: "I'm not playing."

"We're on at 4:30," Muck said. "Your teammates will need you there."

Derek sniffed hard. "They won't want to see me."

"And why would that be?" Muck asked.

"After what happened," Derek snapped. As if he couldn't believe Muck's stupidity.

"And what was that?" Muck asked.

"Give me a break," Derek said angrily.

"You're not the one who needs the break, son."

No one spoke for some time. There was only the sound of sniffing and the distant gurgle of a small stream heading into the lake.

Finally, Derek spoke again. "What's that supposed to mean?"

"Your father apologized to the team," Muck said. "And to the parents. And to the players."

"Big deal."

"It's neither a big deal nor a small deal with me, son. It's just a fact. I happen to think it took some courage to do that."

"He shouldn't have done what he did," Derek snapped, angry.

"That's exactly what he said, son."

"He had no right."

"He knows that. He said that, too."

Muck said nothing after that. Derek sat and sniffled, and a couple of times choked with new crying. Travis felt terrible being there, as if he was witness to something he had no right to see. He could only wait.

Finally, Muck broke the moment with a small, short laugh.

"What's so funny?" Derek demanded.

"Nothing," Muck said. "Just that I'm beginning to wonder if anything I say to you guys ever sinks in."

"I don't follow," Derek said. Neither did Travis.

"What is it I say to you more than anything else?"

"I don't know."

"Sure you do. What is it I say at every practice and before every game and between every period. One phrase. Always the same thing."

Derek said nothing. He was sniffing again. Travis knew.

"What is it, Travis?" Muck finally asked.

"'Hockey is a game of mistakes.'"

"You got it."

Muck said nothing more after that. He stood staring out over the water and, after a while, a sniffling, red-faced Derek Dillinger climbed over the fence and dropped down onto the sand beside them. He had said nothing either. Yet it seemed to Travis as if they had somehow talked it all out, that now they could get on with the game.

"Sarah'll need her new skates sharpened soon as she gets here," Muck said. "And I'm afraid we're missing the key to the skates box."

Derek sniffed once more, then sort of giggled. "I threw it in the lake."

Muck turned and stared at Derek. But it was not the stare he had used on Mr. Brown. It was the stare he used when a play had gone particularly well. "I'd have done it myself," Muck said.

Muck then sat down in the sand and removed his shoes and socks and rolled up his pants. They could see the scar on his bad leg, red and stretching practically from knee to ankle. It must have been a terrible break.

"How far out and how deep?" he asked.

"Not far," Derek said. "Over this way, toward the dock."

"Am I all alone?" Muck asked.

Immediately, Derek and Travis started taking off their socks and rolling up their pants to join in the search. Their track pants wouldn't hold in a roll, though, so they both yanked them off and tossed them up on the sand. They were in their underwear now, their skinny legs shaking in the cold.

Muck was already headed straight out in the water, his white, white legs growing pink, and then purple, as he calmly limped back and forth, looking.

The two boys followed, the water cold as the ice bucket Mr. Dillinger always kept handy at the back of the bench. *Who would keep it today?* Muck had them all join hands and they began working back and forth on a grid, the three of them shivering and shaking as they felt across the bottom with their toes for the missing keys.

"Anybody comes along and sees us," said Muck, "I don't know you two."

Shivering, their teeth chattering, Derek and Travis began laughing at the crazy situation they were in and Muck's silly idea that they could somehow all be strangers, two of them half-dressed, all holding hands as they waded back and forth in ice-cold water.

"Got 'em!" Derek shouted. He pulled the keys up on the end of his toes.

"Thank heavens!" snorted Muck. "I can't feel my legs any more."

"Me neither," said Derek.

Muck smiled at him: "And you're going to need yours today – mine don't matter."

21

Sarah was back with her new skates. The carton they had come in was under her stall, the wrapping paper all around her, the skates, tongues flapping, on her feet as she stared down at her new equipment, delighted.

The dressing room was busy, alive. It had all come down to this one game. Panthers versus Screech Owls. For the Lake Placid Peewee International Championship. For the chance to take a victory lap on the same Olympic ice surface Team U.S.A. had skated on in 1980. For the tiny, gold-plated medals and Lake Placid tuques they were, rumour had it, going to be handing out to the victors.

And Sarah would be there to help them this time. There for the whole game, without anything to worry about for once. Travis felt wonderful inside, excited and happy and thrilled. The others were equally worked up. But Derek was dressing as if he was alone in the room, a hunched-over kid pretending to lose himself in the concerns of his hockey bag. Travis felt terrible for him, but happy that Derek was at least going to play. They would need him, too.

Muck came in and checked out Sarah's new skates. He whistled, impressed. "No allowance for ten years for you," he kidded.

"They'll need sharpening," Sarah said.

Muck strode to the centre of the room. He stopped, staring about as he always did before his pep talk. But it was too early for that. He would always do the pep talk just before they skated out onto the ice, just as the Zamboni was finishing up the flood. Never at this point, when they were just arriving to dress.

He smiled quickly at Travis, then stared long at Derek, who did not look up. Muck counted heads, satisfied.

"We're all here now. So keep it down for a minute. I have something that has to be said to you."

The players all stopped what they were doing. Even Nish. This seemed unusual to them all, not just to Travis.

"I have been talking to the tournament organizers," Muck began. "This is, as you already know, an international competition. It falls under a joint agreement between the Canadian Amateur Hockey Association and U.S.A. Hockey. A number of restrictions apply."

Nish's mouth was as open as an empty net. What was Muck going on about? The other kids were all staring up, completely silent, waiting for him to make sense.

Muck watched Derek as he spoke. "One of those restrictions is that each team must have a qualified trainer with certified first-aid training at the bench. If you don't have the proper helmet you can't play. Don't have the proper neck guard, can't play. Same thing about the proper trainer. There's only one person affiliated with the Screech Owls who has all the training necessary and all the right certification. But only one person. It isn't me. And it isn't Barry or Ty."

The whole room could sense Derek lifting his eyes from his shin pads. It was almost as if he were just now entering the room, as if up until this moment he had been missing, as if someone had been in his stall but it was not the Derek Dillinger they knew.

"Mr. Dillinger?" Fahd asked.

Muck turned, nodding. "That's correct."

"But he's off the team!" Nish blurted out.

Almost as one, the team turned and stared, Nish glowing beet-red and wincing.

Muck stared at Nish, not at all upset. "Technically, you're not quite right, Nish. He resigned from the team. We always have the option open of refusing to accept his resignation."

Derek's eyes were closed. He was covering his ears, shaking his head.

Muck continued, loud enough so Derek had to hear. "It's a simple choice. No certified trainer, we can't start the game. And it's Mr. Dillinger or it's nobody. None of the other parents has it. And I, for one, happen to consider him one of the best I've ever worked with."

Derek caught at the mention of this. His hands came down. He stared at Muck, dumbfounded.

"He's the best skate sharpener I've ever had," Sarah said.

"Me, too," added Dmitri. Dmitri was beginning to panic that he wouldn't have his fresh sharp for the game.

Muck turned to Sarah. "You're the one who should say," Muck said. "You give me the word, and I'll see if I can find him."

Everyone turned to look at Sarah. She closed her eyes a moment. Travis could see her jaw working, her teeth grinding as she thought. She opened her eyes, swallowed, and began nodding.

"I think so," she said.

On the other side of the bench, Derek's head went down, shaking.

Travis and Nish could not resist. Wearing only their long underwear, their garters, athletic supporters, shin pads, and socks, they scurried along the corridor to the bench area and sneaked out to watch.

They could see Muck climbing up through the crowd, the parents surprised to see him. They gathered tight against the wall with him when he called them over with a quick wave of the hand. They could hear nothing, but they knew Muck was giving them the same story that he had just told the players.

Travis couldn't fight the thought: *Is it really true?* Was there such a rule? Did neither Muck nor Ty nor Barry have the right training? And if there was such a rule, how did the tournament committee find out that the Screech Owls were without a proper trainer? Or did Muck go to them instead of them coming to him?

There were a million questions in Travis's mind, none of them answerable, none of them even questions he wished to share with his teammates. It was almost as if he and Muck had a special understanding now, ever since the incident with Derek down by the water. And Muck had looked at him in a certain way before beginning his speech about Mr. Dillinger.

If Muck had fixed it so they had to invite Mr. Dillinger back, why? Because Muck figured he had learned his lesson? Or because Muck figured all the parents, including, and especially, Mr. Brown, had learned a lesson that couldn't be learned by a quick punch in a parking lot? Muck was a mysterious man to the players. They liked him, they *loved* him, but they didn't pretend to understand him.

And how would Travis himself feel about Mr. Dillinger coming back? He had thought the world of Derek's father before all this. But maybe this had all happened because Mr. Dillinger got mixed up. He got far too carried away with the thoughts most parents – just look at Mr. Brown – had all the time. Only Mr. Dillinger had a way to make them happen. It was wrong, but at least he had admitted it was wrong.

Travis figured he would let whatever happened happen. He could see the parents breaking up high in the stands. He could see Mr. Boucher pointing someone out to Muck. He could see Muck walking over to the other side, where Mr. Dillinger sat by himself, his elbows on his knees and his chin in the palm of one hand.

"He's going to get him," Nish said.

"Maybe he won't come," Travis said.

"He'll come," Nish said.

Nish was right. They watched Muck talk for a while and then they saw Muck reach down and take Mr. Dillinger by the arm and pull him to his feet.

Muck then turned and began walking away, back down to the dressing room. Mr. Dillinger, it seemed, had no choice but to follow.

Everything began to happen very fast after that. Mr. Dillinger came in, looking terribly sheepish, and immediately set about doing his work, just as he always did, except there was no whistling, no singing, no kidding around.

He took Sarah's skates and sharpened them as carefully as the Screech Owls had ever seen him sharpen before. He worked for a while, came back with them, had Sarah run a thumbnail over them, but he was still not satisfied with his work. He then took the skates back and sharpened them as carefully as if they were about to go on the feet of Wayne Gretzky himself. Then he brought them back, showed Sarah that he had even cut out and taped a small "98" on each heel, slipped them on her feet and tied them. When he looked up and Sarah quickly smiled a thank you, it seemed Mr. Dillinger was going to float away.

He put new tape on the equipment box and loaded the table up with three different flavours of gum. He filled the water bottles, set the warm-up pucks in Guy Boucher's trapper, and ran for a bucket of ice from the maintenance office. Mr. Dillinger was back.

But Derek wasn't. Not yet. He would neither look at his father nor acknowledge his presence. Travis understood. It would take time, if even time could heal what had happened. It was, in a way, easier for Sarah to forgive than for Derek. Mr. Dillinger was his father.

Muck came in and stood in his usual spot as the Zamboni made its last circle. "You expect a speech?" he said when he had their attention. "I have nothing to say to you. You know who you are. You know how good you are. You know who you're playing. You know what you have to do. Now let's get out there and do it."

"Let's get 'em!" Nish shouted.

"One last thing," Muck said just as everyone was rushing to line up behind Guy. Everyone stopped in his and her tracks.

"Derek, you're going first line again," Muck said.

Derek turned, in shock.

"Take Travis's spot."

Travis never felt so happy to be demoted in his life.

22

he arena was filled to near capacity. Some of the other teams were waiting around for the awards ceremonies and most of the parents were still there as well. It was going to be the biggest crowd Travis had ever played in front of, and though he would have loved to have been lining up for the opening face-off, he was happy for Derek. Derek deserved it. Derek needed it.

They played both anthems before the opening face-off. First "O Canada," then, to a rising roar, "The Star-Spangled Banner." The roar was just like the one in Chicago, whenever the Blackhawks played on television, only here the crowd and players were smaller. But just as excited.

Travis stood along the bench for the Canadian anthem, burning with his own pride, but it was nothing to what he could see in the brimming eyes of Mr. Dillinger, who was staring at Derek as if the boy himself were the flag.

What Mr. Dillinger had done was wrong, but Travis thought he now understood what Muck had been getting at when he said, as he had been saying for as long as the boys had been playing for him, that "hockey is a game of mistakes." The kids had always thought that meant poor decisions on the ice, but they now all knew it also meant bad decisions off the ice. Muck also said mistakes are things you can always fix. You stop leaving drop passes. You take that extra split second to look before passing. You don't just fire the puck blind from the point. And, Travis guessed, you stop trying to control things when you yourself aren't out there trying to play the game. And, most important, you never hurt your own teammate to do something for yourself. Once you start doing that, there is no team.

But now the team was back, and all together. Derek was back on the ice. And Mr. Dillinger was acting like Sarah's personal valet. Still, Travis couldn't help but watch Sarah carefully as she went into her first turn. The new skates glistened and sparkled, but they held. Perfectly. And when she began striding down the ice, she skated like the Sarah Cuthbertson who had been amazing them all since she took up the game and showed everyone that a girl can not only play, a girl can star, and, in the case of the Screech Owls, a girl can be captain.

Nish, of course, was as ready for this game as any in his life. He had swiped the official scoresheet when Barry had it in the Screech Owls' dressing room to fill out, and he had figured out who the enemy was by name. The little blond defenceman was Jeremy Billings, the big dark centre Stu Yantha. Nish liked to know names, and liked to use them, too.

He went after Yantha halfway through the first period, with a face-off down in the Screech Owls' end and Travis on a line with Matt Brown and Gordie Griffith.

"Hey, Stu!" Nish called from in front of the net.

Yantha, waiting for the one linesman to bring a new puck for the other to drop, looked up, not knowing who had called his name.

Nish was grinning like he'd already scored. "I bet I know why your parents called you 'Stu' —"

Yantha just stared, baffled. Nish hit him hard and low: "'Cause they couldn't spell 'Stuuuu-pid!'"

Travis had never laughed through an entire shift before, but this time his sides were hurting when he came off. Yantha had chased Nish around the ice from the moment the puck dropped until Nish had raced off for a change. Yantha was so distracted he forgot all about the puck and had become consumed by his rage. If it hadn't been for the little defenceman, Billings, the Panthers would have been in real trouble.

Sarah was having trouble with her new skates. But it had nothing to do with sabotage. Twice during shift breaks she had loosened them and Mr. Dillinger had massaged her insteps. She was cramping up in the stiff, new Tacks. But she was not quitting. She never missed a shift.

With a minute to go in the first, Sarah intercepted a Panther pass just inside her own blueline and, on a backhand flip that might have skidded away if she'd been using Travis's stick, she hit Dmitri on the fly. Dmitri raced in alone, deked the Panthers goaltender, and sent a backhand along the ice in through the five hole.

1–0, Screech Owls.

Mr. Dillinger almost went nuts. He jumped so hard the water bottles spilled off the back shelf and onto the floor. He

whooped and cheered and, when Sarah came off, hit her immediately with a fresh towel and a full, salvaged water bottle. And
Derek hadn't even been in on the play.

With Gordie Griffith struggling, Muck told Travis to take
the next face-off, and the Panthers also changed, sending out
Yantha's line.

"Nice shiner."

Travis wasn't sure where the voice had come from. Yantha
was leaning down for the face-off, but suddenly he looked up
and Travis could see the sneer of contempt through the shield.

"You're soon going to have one for the other eye, runt."

Travis said nothing. He won the face-off on a backswipe to
Nish, but Yantha flattened Travis with a cross-check to the face
before he could turn. The referee either didn't see it or didn't
care, for there was no call.

Nish tried to hit Gordie Griffith with a cross-ice pass and
shouldn't have. The little blond defenceman had read the play
perfectly and zipped into the hole, gloved the puck down, and
dropped it onto his own stick. With Nish already beaten, he was
able to use Data as a screen and put one through Data's skates
into the short side behind Guy Boucher.

Panthers 1, Screech Owls 1.

A tie game, with the buzzer going to end the first period.

At the break, Muck told them to watch their plays. "Don't take
stupid chances," he said, without mentioning Nish's bad pass.
He didn't have to say anything directly to the big defenceman.
Nish looked like he'd just lost his home and family and television.

He was pounding his fist on his leg, desperate for a chance to make it up.

Mr. Dillinger had Sarah's skates loosened all the way. He pulled them free and Travis could hear Sarah's sharp intake of breath as she realized her feet were bleeding. Both socks were pink with blood.

Mr. Dillinger seemed very worried. "Those blisters are breaking!" he said.

"Put some ice on them," Sarah said to him.

Mr. Dillinger looked at Sarah, unsure, but the uncertainty vanished when he saw the determination in her eyes. He reached for the ice bucket, set it down, and began working handfuls of ice cubes over her feet. Sarah flinched from the pain but refused to give in, and when Mr. Dillinger pulled first one foot, then the other, down into the freezing bucket of ice and water, she actually seemed to sigh with relief.

If Sarah can do that, Travis thought, I had better do something with my good feet.

"You're better than they are," Muck said. "This game is yours if you want it."

Sarah's skating was becoming laboured. She picked up a puck behind her own net but lost it trying to pivot out. The big dark centre, Yantha, picked it up and flicked it fast, the puck hitting the back of Guy's shoulder and dropping just over the goal line. The Panthers' bench and fans let out a mighty cheer when the red light indicated what had happened. The Screech Owls' bench let out a collective groan. Travis flinched when he saw

Sarah, completely out of character, smash her stick in half over the crossbar.

Panthers 2, Screech Owls 1.

Muck put Sarah's line right back out, and his hunch paid off. She won the face-off and hit Derek, on the left, who crossed the blueline and sent a long shot ricocheting around the boards to Dmitri, racing in on the right. Dmitri neatly deflected the puck back to Sarah, coming in late, and Sarah stepped past the defence, pulled the goaltender completely out of the net, and sent a back pass to Derek, who had only to tap it in for the tying goal.

The Screech Owls' bench went nuts. As pretty a set-up as they'd ever seen the magical Sarah create.

Screech Owls 2, Panthers 2.

Travis was sent back out at centre, and again Yantha came on. This time the Panthers' big centre butt-ended Travis right off the draw, sending him spilling down.

Travis found his footing just as Yantha came back for the puck from his defence. The big centre had his head down as he picked a bad pass off his skate and did not lift it again until he reached the red line – by which time it was too late.

Travis hit him low and as hard as he could. He shut his eyes and drove as if he were going through a door, and Yantha crumpled over Travis's back, his feet flying out from under him and high up over Travis in a half-somersault where he landed hard on his back. The referee's whistle blew. He was pointing at Travis. His hand then indicated tripping.

Nish slammed his stick hard on the ice in protest. "No way! That was perfectly clean, ref!"

"Put a lid on it or you're off with him," the referee said to Nish.

The players were all milling around. Yantha was still down, moaning, so no one had to worry about him, but everyone else was looking for a partner to hang on to. The little blond defence-man, Billings, took Travis in his arms, the two of them struggling for show but uninterested in scuffling.

Billings was laughing. And he winked again. "Nice hit," he said, then released Travis.

The Screech Owls survived being a player short and, later in the final period, Yantha took a bad penalty when he went after Nish in the corner and the referee caught him for slashing.

"Stuuuuu-pid!" Nish called after Yantha as the big centre angrily headed off to the penalty box.

"One more word and you're with him," the referee told Nish. Nish wisely shut up.

Muck put out a new power-play team: Sarah, Derek, Dmitri, Nish, and, on the point, Travis. Any other time he would have been left wing on the power play, but Muck wanted to keep his first line together and bring Travis up for the advantage, so point was where he put him.

Travis, unfortunately, had never before played the point. He had no idea what Muck was up to. All he wanted to do was make sure he didn't blow it and cause the winning goal for the Panthers.

Sarah controlled the puck beautifully off the face-off. She and Dmitri began playing what they called "Russian hockey" in practice, one circling endlessly back so it seemed like the whole team was going in reverse. They kept dropping the puck to each other as they circled, controlling, waiting until one of them saw an opening to shoot through.

The Panthers, bewildered at this seeming nonsense, put two players on Sarah, who was now carrying the puck in yet another circle, and Dmitri took the opening the moment he saw it.

Sarah hit him on the tape with her pass. Dmitri crossed the Panthers' blueline and stopped in a spray of snow, circling back again but staying on-side, and hit Travis with a perfect cross-ice pass as Travis gained the blueline. Derek was on the opposite side, stick raised to shoot, and Travis dished off a quick backhand that Derek one-timed so hard it hit behind the upper inside bar and stuck, dislodging the Panthers' goalie's water bottle.

Screech Owls 3, Panthers 2.

23

here were only two minutes left. Sarah was buckled over in pain at the bench, the blisters all broken and the stiff new skates unforgiving. Muck didn't want to send her out again – didn't want to have to send her out.

He re-jigged his lines and put out his best checkers, Travis included. He told them to dump the puck when they got it and hold the line when they didn't have it. He was going for the 3–2 win.

The Panthers took out their goaltender. They sent out five forwards, including Yantha, and the little blond defenceman as the sixth player.

Travis had never in his life seen such effort. The little defenceman, Billings, led more than half a dozen rushes over those final two minutes. His last was an end-to-end race in which, with Travis almost hanging onto him, the little defence-man still managed to slip the puck through Nish's legs, danced to catch it, and rang a backhander off the crossbar and out of play before crashing into the boards with Travis.

The referee's whistle shrieked to call a break in the play. Travis could see that the referee did not have his hand raised for a penalty. He had been checking cleanly. He could hear the breathing of the little defenceman lying beside him, the little player's lungs seeming desperate for air.

Slowly they rose from the boards. The little defenceman looked at Travis, grinning, and Travis tapped him quickly on the shin pad. No one knew better than the two of them how close Billings had come to tying up the championship game.

There were only fifteen seconds to go. Muck signalled from the bench that he wanted Travis to take the face-off again, and Travis moved over and Gordie Griffith moved out. Travis could feel the fury rising from number 5, the big centre, and when the puck dropped, Travis instinctively ducked, barely missing a vicious elbow.

Number 5 hadn't even considered the puck. His intention was solely to take out Travis, and then deal with the puck. But Travis, down low, was able to snake the puck out of the big centre's skates. He rifled it off the boards back into his own end, where Nish was already back, circling.

All six Panthers rushed Nish in desperation, and he held the puck as long as he dared before looping a high backhander out that fell flat at centre ice and died immediately. Gordie Griffith picked it up and he and Travis had a two-on-one, the little defenceman instantly back, with the net empty.

Gordie tried a quick pass to Travis, but the little defenceman again anticipated perfectly, the pass intended for Travis hitting him on the shin pad and instantly up to his stick where he charged again.

But it was too late. The buzzer went. Time had run out on the Panthers.

Final score: Screech Owls 3, Panthers 2.

Sarah Cuthbertson was first over the boards, barefoot. Her feet covered in Band-aids from Mr. Dillinger's first-aid kit – and Mr. Dillinger vainly trying to stop her from jumping – she came over the boards and hit the ice and slipped and skidded and fell and whooped all the way to Guy Boucher, who was already throwing his stick and gloves into the crowd.

The rest of the Screech Owls piled on, Muck grabbing Sarah around the waist and hoisting her high off the ice so none of the skates would cut her already injured feet. They piled on Guy, who had kept the goals out. They piled on Derek, who had scored the tying and winning goals. They piled on Travis, who had set up the winner. They piled on Dmitri, who had scored the first goal. They tried to pile on Muck and Sarah, but Muck kept turning and swinging Sarah so they couldn't get them, and so they piled instead on Nish because Nish was, well, Nish. And he deserved it.

Mr. Dillinger was on the ice now and he was hugging the players as if they'd just survived a plane crash. He was dancing, shouting, slapping, hugging. Travis saw him stop when he came to Derek and Derek, still deeply troubled, gave a weak smile and took his father's offered hand. A hug would have to come over time.

Muck was Muck. He carried Sarah back to the bench and set her down until the madness stopped, and he walked around shaking the hands of his assistants and players like he had to get going somewhere. It was as if he had expected this. And he had.

They lined up for "O Canada" and the awards ceremony. The tournament officials gave out gold and silver medals – just like in the Olympics – and the Screech Owls got to do their victory lap, Nish and Gordie carrying the skateless, sore-footed Sarah, and then they lined up to shake hands with the Panthers.

Travis felt funny going through the line. These players had been regarded as the Screech Owls' mortal enemies all week, but he hardly felt any anger toward them. With their helmets off and their hair soaked with sweat and their faces so red with exertion, they no longer looked quite so big or quite so menacing. They looked like the Screech Owls. Not big, not old, but normal. And Travis wondered if perhaps, to some of them, he looked bigger than he was. He doubted it.

He came to Stu Yantha and the big dark centre stuck out his hand as if they were meeting for the first time. Not the first time since he'd tried to remove Travis's teeth with a butt end, but the first time ever. Travis didn't even feel that Yantha knew who he was. Why would he? They shook hands and said nothing.

At the end of the line, he came to Billings, who was grinning with his hand out and another hand to put on Travis's arm. They paused and, for a moment, Travis felt as if he had won the Stanley Cup and the television cameras were watching him and Billings, like Messier and Bure, as they met at centre ice. Billings knew exactly who Travis was and he knew Billings, and they had respect and admiration for each other.

"Nice game," said Billings.

"You, too," Travis said. It felt inadequate.

"Nice hit on Yantha, too."

Travis smiled, remembering.

Billings smiled back. "Clean, too."

Travis had never felt so wonderful. Mr. Dillinger had bought pop and chocolate bars for everyone. Muck had shaken each player's hand again in the dressing room. They had stared at and felt their medals – Nish said they were real gold – and tried on their Lake Placid tuques. Nish was wearing his pulled completely over his face, more like he was robbing a bank than taking off his hockey equipment.

And the Lake Placid tournament officials had come in and handed out trading cards, a pack for each player. Only they weren't the usual type of trading cards. No Gretzkys here, but Bouchers, Goupas, Nishikawas, Ulmars, Philpotts, Grangers, Kellys, Adelmans, Cuthbertsons, Yakushevs, Lindsays, Dillingers, Griffiths, Browns, Noorizadehs, Terzianos, and Highboys. That was why they had taken the players' photographs that first day. They were having trading cards printed up for each of them.

Travis spread his cards in his hand and stared at them. It was like he had opened a fresh pack of Topps and he himself had come spilling out in high gloss. There were two cards for his grandmothers. One for his parents. One for Nish, who insisted on a trade. And one for himself, forever.

Exhausted, delighted, he pulled off his skates and felt pain sear up through his leg. He looked down, baffled, and could see blood through his left sock. Not a lot, like Sarah had, but blood all the same.

He pulled off the sock, wondering. And then he saw it: his own blister, red and broken.

A blister – in old, broken-in skates?

There was only one answer: Travis Lindsay was growing out of them.

Limping slightly from the welcome blister, Travis left with Nish, the two of them examining the cards they had just traded with each other. Some of the others had already left for the hotel to check out for the long, happy ride home. Travis figured he would sleep – and dream – all the way. And the way things were going, perhaps he'd have outgrown all his clothes by the time he got back home.

"Lindsay!"

Travis turned, recognizing his name but not the voice.

It was Jeremy Billings, the Panthers' little defenceman – in Travis's opinion, the true star of this tournament. He waited. Billings walked up and pulled out his own cards.

"Neat, eh?"

"Yeah."

"You want to swap one?"

Travis looked up. Did he ever. But he had only one for himself, one forever.

He looked at his new friend, smiling, that same blond face in miniature on the card he was holding out face first. Travis looked at the card and realized, perhaps for the first time, the true value of a hockey card.

"You bet," he said.

"Sign it, too?" Billings asked.

Travis couldn't believe it. Someone was asking for his autograph!

"Yeah, sure. You got a pen?"

Billings shook his head.

"I got one," Nish said.

Nish reached inside his jacket pocket and pulled out the pen from his "Stupid Stop" – the one with the disappearing bathing suit. Billings took it and signed his name on the card he was giving Travis. He paused halfway, turning the pen so he could see if what he had thought was right. Yes, the bathing suit was peeling off the bathing beauty.

He looked at Nish, who was beet-red and shrugging. No explanation required.

Billings handed the pen and his signed card over to Travis, who pocketed the card and then signed his own: Travis Lindsay.

Big, with an exaggerated "T," a looping "L."

And the number "7" tagged on at the end.

THE END.

The Night They Stole
the Stanley Cup

1

Mats Sundin chewed his nails – just like Travis Lindsay. Mats Sundin's hands were twice as big as Travis's, but the nails were the same, bitten to the quick. It surprised Travis; he had never imagined that a National Hockey League superstar would ever have anything to worry about. Nails, like life, would be perfect. But here was the best player on the Toronto Maple Leafs, one of the best players in the NHL, and he was no different from more than half the players on the Screech Owls – nervous and fidgeting when it came to waiting around in the dressing room. Travis liked him immediately.

"Good to meet you, Travis."

Travis swallowed hard. He had imagined perhaps getting Mats Sundin's autograph on the card he had in his vest pocket, but that was supposed to involve a lot of work getting Sundin's attention. Yet here was the great Mats Sundin greeting *him* as if it were the most natural thing in the world.

"Hi," Travis said. He wondered if Mats Sundin had even heard him.

The Screech Owls had come to Toronto to play in "The Little Stanley Cup," a huge tournament that was being held over the March school break. Novice and peewee and bantam teams had been invited from Ontario and Quebec, as well as from New York and Michigan. Each team was guaranteed three games, four if they made it into the playoffs, and most were also planning to attend a Leafs game.

The Screech Owls, like the Leafs, had gone through a rebuilding season. Sarah Cuthbertson, the team captain, had moved on permanently to the Toronto Aeros after the Lake Placid tournament. There had even been a story about Sarah in the *Toronto Star* saying she was a shoo-in for the Canadian women's hockey team at the 1998 Winter Olympics.

Matt Brown and his loudmouth father were also missing. Mr. Brown had wanted Matt on another team, where he thought his son might be appreciated a bit more. Mr. Brown had, as usual, missed the point. Matt was greatly appreciated, especially his wicked shot, but Mr. Brown was not. Hockey games this season had been more enjoyable for everyone – fans as well as players. No Mr. Brown screaming at the referees. No Mr. Brown pounding the glass and shouting at them to get out there and "kick butt!"

Muck was back as coach, of course. Back and still the same. It was the Screech Owls who had changed, but not nearly as much as some of the teams they played against. Nish and Data and Willie were all still Owls, along with most of the others, but as well as Sarah and Matt, Zak and Mario were gone, as were goaltenders Guy Boucher – still hanging on as the back-up goalie for the double-A team – and Sareen Goupa, who was now the starting goalie for the town's new women's team.

With Guy and Sareen missing, the Screech Owls had taken on Jennie Staples and a new kid in town, Jeremy Weathers, who had a terrific glove hand. Derek Dillinger had moved up onto the first line to take over Sarah's spot between Travis and Dmitri Yakushev – who was *faster* this year, if anything – and the new second-line centre was Gordie Griffith, whose skating bursts were finally catching up to his growth spurts. The new third-line centre was Andy Higgins, a big, mean guy whose voice was already dropping. Travis didn't much care for Andy. He wasn't quite sure why – he just didn't like him.

The new second-line left-winger was Liz Moscovitz, a good friend of Sarah's, and the new third-line winger was Chantal Larochelle, whose family had just moved to town from Montreal. The new defenceman was Lars Johanssen, who'd been born in Sweden and had come to Canada when his father was sent over to run the chipboard factory just outside town. It was Lars's father who had arranged for the team to attend the Leafs' practice. Back in Sweden, Mr. Johanssen had worked – and once played – with Mats Sundin's father.

Mats Sundin treated Lars like a long-lost cousin and gave him a stick that had been signed by every one of the Leafs. Then he had taken the team into the actual dressing room, where some of the players were still sitting around and others were fixing up their sticks for the next game.

Travis thought he had died and gone to heaven. He could not stop staring at the players as they worked on their sticks.

One of the players had the tip of a new stick underneath the door frame and was pulling up on the handle to make a quick little curve at the very end of the blade. Travis bent down and stared, fascinated.

"You do this, too?" the man asked.

Travis looked up, startled. *It was Doug Gilmour.*

The Leafs' captain was smiling back at Travis. Travis could only shake his head, no. He couldn't talk. What could he say to Doug Gilmour? *I have your poster up in my room? I know a guy who's got your rookie card from St. Louis?*

But it didn't seem as if he had to say anything. Doug Gilmour was still smiling. Now he was pulling out the stick and trying it, leaning down hard and bending it so he could check the whip in the shaft. Then he flicked a used roll of tape and it flew hard against the wall and bounced off, straight into a garbage can.

"How come I can't do that in games?" Gilmour asked.

Travis looked around. There was no one else there. That meant Doug Gilmour had to be talking to *him*! Still, he couldn't answer.

"You a left shot?" Gilmour asked.

Travis finally spoke: "Y—yeah."

"Here, then — you give it a try."

Travis took the stick. It felt like King Arthur's sword in his hand: magical, powerful, but too big and heavy for him. Doug Gilmour threw down a fresh roll of tape. "Let's see your shot."

Travis almost fainted. Doug Gilmour was asking to see *his* shot! He stickhandled the tape back and forth a couple of times and then fired it. It hit with a dull thud against the wall, fell to the floor, and rolled away.

"Good wrister," Gilmour said.

"I've got a better slapshot," Travis said. He wasn't certain he did, but he felt he'd better explain that he wasn't quite as weak as his shot had sounded.

"Then you'd better have this stick," Doug Gilmour said. "It works better for you than me."

Travis couldn't believe it. Doug Gilmour was grinning, but not laughing at him. He was serious.

"You're giving this to me?" Travis asked.

"Only if you want it," Doug Gilmour said. "Here – let me sign it for you."

Gilmour took a Sharpie pen off the bench by the skate sharpener and signed his name and number: Doug Gilmour – 93. He handed the stick back to Travis.

"There you go. It's yours now."

The stick was alive in Travis's hands, as if it held an electric current. He could hardly believe this was happening. It all felt like a dream. He felt he was floating. He felt dizzy

"Thanks," Travis said. It didn't seem enough.

"Any time, buddy," Doug Gilmour said, and smiled. "Thanks" seemed like enough to him.

The Leafs' captain went back into the training room, where no one but the players and trainers and equipment workers were allowed, and Travis – hanging onto his stick for dear life – raced off to find the rest of the team.

They weren't in the dressing room. They weren't in the corridor. But there were bright lights shining from out in the arena, and when he got there he could see television cameramen around the bench area, where a lot of Screech Owls jacket backs could be seen.

Travis hurried over. The team was gathered in a semicircle around Mats Sundin, who was answering questions. The television camera crews were recording, and several reporters were also there, writing very quickly in small notebooks.

"Do you have another job you go to?" Fahd Noorizadeh asked.

Travis could see Nish turn to Willie Granger and roll his eyes. A typical Fahd question. What would he ask next: Do you do up your own skates?

Mats Sundin laughed good-naturedly: "This is my only job – it's more than enough to keep me busy."

"Who's your favourite player?" Gordie Griffith asked.

"Doug Gilmour, of course," Mats Sundin answered, again laughing.

Nish moved in, grinning: "What do you think of Don Cherry?"

Travis couldn't believe Nish could be so stupid. Everyone knew what Don Cherry had said on "Coach's Corner" about the Wendel Clark trade that brought Sundin to Toronto from Quebec. Everyone knew what the "Hockey Night in Canada" analyst had been saying for as long as they could remember about European players faking injuries and taking dives and never coming through in the Stanley Cup playoffs.

"I think Don Cherry is a very funny comedian," Sundin said.

"A 'comedian'?" Nish asked.

"Yes – he's very funny. But you can't take him seriously."

Fahd had another Fahd question: "Can you speak Swedish?"

Mats Sundin blinked, not believing his ears. "Here's another comedian," he laughed. "Just like Don Cherry."

Fahd didn't get it. "Can you?" he repeated.

Mats Sundin shrugged and turned to Lars Johanssen. Mats began talking very fast, in Swedish, to Lars, who giggled and said something very quickly back to Mats.

One of the reporters called out: "What're you two saying?"

Mats Sundin laughed. "I asked my good friend Lars if his team have given him a nickname yet."

"And have they?" another reporter asked.

They hadn't – until Nish jumped in.

"We call him Cherry," Nish shouted.

Everyone – including Lars – laughed. The reporters scribbled it down. The cameras turned their floodlights on Nish, who never even flinched.

"Wayne Nishikawa," he called out to the reporters.

"N–I–S–H–I . . ."

2

"Who took my underwear?"

Travis had never heard such a ridiculous question. Nish was still in his pyjamas while everyone else was dressed and ready to head off for the first game of the Little Stanley Cup. They had ten minutes to be in the hotel lobby – and Nish hadn't even brushed his teeth yet.

"Somebody took my underwear. Come on, now! This is ridiculous!"

I'll say it is, thought Travis. Ridiculous that Nish could be thirteen years old and still not know how to pack for a road trip. He had already emptied the entire contents of his suitcase out on the bed he and Travis were sharing and ploughed through his clothes like a dog rooting through garbage. Enough T-shirts to supply the team – each one proof that he had played in hockey tournaments everywhere from Lake Placid to Quebec City – pants and sweatshirts and socks and comic books and deodorant and toothpaste and toothbrush – but no underwear.

He'd only brought the pair he was wearing, and now he couldn't even find them!

"This is a SICK joke!" Nish said. He was getting upset.

"*You're* a sick joke," said Willie Granger. Willie was sharing the other bed with Data, Nish's defence partner. "You can't even pack a suitcase."

"You should have had your mom do it," said Data, who was growing a bit anxious about the deadline for being in the lobby.

Nish held up his hands. "Stop! Just sit on it, okay? We know they were here last night."

"*You* know they were here last night," corrected Willie.

"Who else was here?"

"Who *wasn't* here?" said Travis. He was right. Their room had been like a bus terminal. Everyone had run down after they checked in to see the four who'd lucked into a suite when the hotel ran out of regular rooms. There was a bedroom off a sitting room, two televisions, and a small kitchen with a refrigerator. Everyone had jealously checked out everything in the suite, but surely not Nish's underwear.

"Okay!" Nish shouted. He was beginning to panic. "We know they're here somewhere."

"I'm not touching your shorts!" Data shouted back.

"No one's asking you to *touch* them – just point when you find them!" Nish said. He was getting testy. "Travis and Data, you two do the other room and kitchen. Willie will help me do the bathroom and bedroom. Look absolutely everywhere – and *hurry*!"

They didn't like doing it, but what choice did they have? Nish had to have underwear, and he was far too big and heavy to wear anyone else's. So they began looking, Nish and Willie taking the bedroom apart bit by bit, and Travis and Data going over the sitting room and the kitchen.

"You look in the kitchen cupboards," Data said. "I'll check in here behind all the cushions."

"We didn't use the cupboards," Travis said.

"Maybe someone threw them there as a joke."

Unconvinced, Travis began looking. He checked each cupboard – nothing. He checked all the drawers – no underwear.

The only thing left to check was the refrigerator. Surely, no. He opened the door – no luck. He flicked open the freezer compartment: *there was something inside.* Whatever it was, it was crumpled up and covered with frost. He poked at it. It was as hard as a rock. Then he recognized the blue diamond pattern of Nish's boxer shorts.

"They're here!" Travis called out.

Nish came running into the room, already dropping his pyjamas. "Gimme them!"

"You'll have to chip them out," said Travis.

Nish stopped dead in his tracks, his eyes big as hockey pucks.

"What kind of a sick joke is this!" he shouted.

He pulled at the shorts and they cracked – frozen. He pulled again and they gave. He began unfolding them, the frost drifting in the air as they bent in his hands.

"Who would do this?"

"Not me."

"Wasn't me."

"I never."

It wasn't any of them, either. They all knew that. Who'd have the guts to touch Nish's shorts in the first place?

"This isn't fair," Nish wailed. "I got nothing else to wear!"

"Then you've got no choice, do you?" Data said. "We gotta roll – and quick."

The others went down to the lobby ahead of Nish. Muck was already there, checking his watch. The rest of the team and some of the parents were standing around and waiting as well.

"Where's Nishikawa?" Muck asked.

"He's coming," said Travis.

Everyone waited. Finally the elevator doors opened, and out walked Nish, his face in agony, his steps uncertain.

"What's with him?" Muck asked. "Got cold feet over the tournament?"

"Not exactly," Travis answered.

3

ravis was beginning to understand why he had such a bad feeling about the new centre, Andy Higgins. He seemed to swear a lot – much more than necessary – and he sometimes smelled of cigarette smoke. But neither of those points troubled Travis. Most of the kids swore a bit. And some of them – even Nish, his best friend – thought smoking was okay, even if they didn't do it. No, what really bothered Travis was that he believed Andy Higgins was stealing.

He'd noticed things before. Data brought his older brother's tape deck to the dressing room and said it was the Screech Owls' to keep; his brother had moved on to a CD player. They were each supposed to bring in a tape for playing before and after games. Just like the pros. Travis had saved his allowance and bought the Tragically Hip, and some of the others had brought in a variety of other tapes: Counting Crows, some rap, the Barenaked Ladies, and even, to a loud chorus of boos directed Fahd's way, Michael Jackson.

One tape apiece. Except for Andy Higgins. He'd brought in close to a dozen. All brand new, all still in their wrappers. Most were recent hits and, naturally, they got the most play, which had the effect of putting Andy in charge of the team tape recorder and making him instantly popular. But not with Travis. He'd figured out that Andy had to have spent roughly $150 to buy those particular tapes, and that hardly seemed like allowance money.

Now, in Toronto, Andy was walking around the dressing room flicking a lighter at everyone. It was brand new, with the CN Tower on it. Just like the ones Travis and Nish had seen in the hotel gift shop. But they would never have sold a lighter to a thirteen-year-old kid. He could have swiped it, however, and that's exactly what Travis thought he had done.

Travis left the dressing room and went out to clear his head. The Little Stanley Cup was being played in more than a dozen Toronto arenas, and the Screech Owls had come to play their first game in St. Michael's Arena, where so many NHLers had played their early hockey. He walked alongside the glass display case near the snack bar, looking at the old photographs under the sign "THE TRADITION LIVES ON": Red Kelly, Joe Primeau, Tim Horton, Frank Mahovlich, Dave Keon.

And then, Terrible Ted himself. Ted Lindsay, with the crooked smile and the hair that looked as if it had been parted with a protractor. Terrible Ted Lindsay smiling back at Travis Lindsay, his distant relative. Travis wondered if perhaps *he* would one day play here for St. Mike's? He imagined himself moving on to play in the NHL and being inducted into the St. Mike's Hall of Fame, right alongside Terrible Ted. Travis couldn't think of anything he wouldn't trade to get there – well, maybe except for Doug Gilmour's stick.

When Travis returned to the dressing room, everyone had started to dress. Nish was sitting wrapped in his towel. He had his shorts hanging off the blade of his stick directly in front of a hot-air vent.

"They can't still be cold!" Travis said.

"*Damp*," said Nish. "I catch the guy who did this, he's good as dead."

"The guy who did that is probably already dead from touching them!" Wilson shouted. Everyone laughed. Everyone but Nish, who just said, "Very funny."

Travis couldn't tell whether he was really annoyed or enjoying the attention. It was always difficult to say with Nish.

The Owls' assistant coach, Barry, stuck his head in the door and told them to hurry up. The room went silent as the team got down to the serious work of dressing. What Barry meant, but would never say, was that the boys should hurry so the girls – Jennie, Liz, and Chantal – could join them in time to put on their skates and get ready for Muck's pep talk.

Travis always liked these moments best. He loved dressing. He felt, at times, like a machine being assembled: underwear, protector, garter, left shin pad, right shin pad, socks, attach socks to garter, pants on loose, skates on loose, watch until Nish closes his eyes and begins rocking back and forth – Nish's way of getting ready – then tighten skates, tie pants, tighten belt on pants, shoulder pads, elbow pads, neck guard, lay sweater in lap, think, pull sweater over head and make hideous face at Nish when hidden by sweater, wait, then helmet, click on face mask, gloves, stick, and *ready*. Always the same order, always the same timing. A machine waiting only for someone to flick the switch.

Flicking the switch was Muck's job. He always said something – never too complicated, never overly critical, like a teacher's last words before an exam. In Round One of the Little Stanley Cup, the Screech Owls would be playing the Junior River Rats from Albany, New York, a peewee version of the minor pro team with the best sweater and cap logo Travis had ever seen: a snarling rat holding a hockey stick.

The three girls came in, Jennie walking stiff-legged in her goalie pads like a robot, Liz and Chantal bouncing lightly on their skates. Travis smiled quietly to himself. He had noticed the "bounce" lately, and not just from the girls, but from Nish and Dmitri too, and, he had to admit, even from himself at times. The bounce was a signal: you were a *hockey* player.

Muck came in. Muck always dressed as if he were going down to Canadian Tire to pick up some wood screws. No fancy hockey jacket with badges all over it. No tie. No clipboard filled with notes. Nothing. Just Muck. Just the way he'd always been.

"Okay," Muck said. Instantly the room went silent. Muck never had to raise his voice, that's how much respect the players had for their coach.

"This is a team we haven't seen before. I don't expect they're going to give us too much trouble, but by the same token I don't expect us to do anything but play our game. That means what, Nish?"

Nish had been staring down between his knees, concentrating.

"'Stay in position,'" Nish quoted. It was one of Muck's favourite phrases, and Nish almost sounded like the coach when he said it. Travis knew why Muck had asked Nish; everyone knew who the worst offender was if a game was too easy. Nish would suddenly think he was Paul Coffey, rushing end to end with the puck.

"That's right," agreed Muck. "*Stay in position.* No dumb moves. No 'glory hogs.'"

Nish looked up abruptly, surprised that Muck would use the same expression his teammates used when they were ragging on him. Muck stared right back, a small grin at the corners of his mouth.

"I want to see passing. I want to see you use your points. I want to see everyone – and I mean *everyone* – coming back to help out your defence and goaltender.

"Now let's go."

4

ravis did his little bounce-skip as he turned the first corner on the new ice. Just ahead of him, Nish did the same. At the next corner, he saw Liz do one too, her second thrust of her right skate digging deep, the blade sizzling as it cut into the fresh ice and left its mark. She was a beautiful skater.

Travis wished the ice could always be fresh. He loved the feel of it, but he also loved the stories in it, the way he could read how someone had shifted from forward to backward skating, the way a long, hard-driving stride threw snow.

The River Rats may have had beautiful uniforms, but they could not skate at all like the Screech Owls. Travis knew from the warm-up that it would be an easy game for the Owls – but perhaps not for him. He'd failed to hit the crossbar while taking shots at the empty net. He knew it was silly, but he liked to start each game with his good-luck sign.

The River Rats had one pure skater – one player with the little bounce-skip as he came out onto the ice – and a few big players, but little else.

Travis's line started. Derek won the face-off and put the puck back to Nish, who drew the forechecker to him and then hit Data with a perfect pass. Data put the puck off the boards so it floated in behind the River Rats' defence, and Dmitri, with an astonishing burst of speed, jetted around the turning defender, picked up the puck, and put a high slapshot in under the glove arm of the Albany goaltender.

Muck then took Travis's line off. An eleven-second shift. Muck hated to embarrass anyone, either on his own team or on any other. (Well, perhaps with the exception of Nish, who needed regular embarrassing.) The shift had been so short that from the bench Travis could actually see the play in the new ice: Dmitri's quick jump past the defence, the marks where the defence had turned too late, Dmitri's perfect trail followed by the defenceman's stumbling chase, the very point from where Dmitri had shot – all still laid out on the ice like a connect-the-dots puzzle.

At the end of the first, the Screech Owls were up 4–0 on a second breakaway by Dmitri, a good shot from the slot by Gordie Griffith, and a hard shot from the point by Lars Johanssen. At this last goal, the entire bench had erupted in shouts for "Cherry!" when everyone realized Lars had scored his first goal as a Screech Owl. It was a good thing the others were scoring, Travis thought. Even with such weak opposition, he couldn't break out of his scoring slump.

Jennie had all of two shots to handle, and one of them a long dump from centre ice. Apart from their one good skater, the River Rats were simply out of their league, outclassed and already out of the game. Muck couldn't have been more displeased.

Travis thought he knew why. Muck hated a game like this at any time – too easy, too tempting to players like Nish to start playing shinny – but he would hate it even more as the first game of an important tournament. He would say it made the Screech Owls too confident, too easy to beat in the second game, which is the game that usually decides whether a team continues on the championship side or the consolation side of the tournament. From the moment the puck had dropped in this match, Muck was probably more worried about Game Two than Game One.

Muck began giving extra ice time to the third line. But Andy, Jesse, and Chantal were still too dominant for the Albany team. Andy scored a fabulous, end-to-end goal, finishing with an unnecessary fall-to-your-knees, fist-pumping celebration that made Muck decide to yank them off as well.

Muck finally told the Screech Owls to ease up.

With a minute to go, and the Screech Owls up 7–0, the River Rats' one good player took a pass at centre. Data had been pinching up ice and was caught behind the play, leaving only Nish back between Jennie and the skater.

Nish was skating backwards as fast as possible. The ice was old now and choppy, and he dug in as best he could. But he could not cut off the swift River Rat without turning toward him and shifting from backward to forward skating.

Just as Nish made his move, the skater made his. He pushed toward Nish instead of going away from him, and as he did so he flipped the puck so it rolled high over Nish's stick and fell flat behind him. The skater simply hopped over Nish as he fell in desperation, picked up the puck, walked in, and pulled Jennie to her right before dropping an easy backhander in behind her.

The game ended 7–1. The players shook hands – Jennie congratulating the scorer on his play – and then headed for the dressing room.

Muck came in a few moments later, not at all pleased.

"What do you have to say for yourself, Nish?" Muck asked.

"What'dya mean?" Nish asked.

Muck smiled. "You got deked out of your underwear out there."

Nish shook his head in disgust. "He can have them."

5

"Y ou gotta come and see this!"

Travis had rarely seen Nish so excited. And certainly never so early in the morning. Travis had just finished showering and was getting dressed to go down for breakfast. It had been a quiet night; the team was tired from the excitement of the first game, if not the actual playing of the game, and everyone had gone to bed early.

Nish, of course, had tried to turn on the late-night sex movies, but all the television screen would say was: "ADULT MOVIES HAVE BEEN BLOCKED BY REQUEST. PLEASE CALL THE FRONT DESK FOR ACCESS." He had tried his old trick of pulling off the cable wires and re-wiring the remote box, but again it hadn't worked. Finally he had called the front desk and in a low voice pretended he was Muck giving the hotel permission for the kids to watch sex movies. That hadn't worked either.

Now here he was, flushed and on fire about something.

"You gotta come see, Trav!"

Travis pulled on his Red Wings track pants and a T-shirt and chased, barefoot, after Nish, who was already running down the hall backwards, signalling Travis to follow.

On the floor below, Nish came to a door and knocked. Not a normal knock, but three long knocks followed by two quick ones. A special code? What was this? Travis wondered.

Nish held his finger to his mouth, signalling quiet. As he hadn't been saying anything, Travis could only shake his head.

They could hear someone on the other side. Travis had the sense he was being checked out through the little spy glass in the door. Then it opened slowly. It was Data. He and Nish must have come down earlier, while Travis was in the shower. But why so secretive?

Data opened the door the rest of the way. Nish and Travis entered and Data closed the door quietly, still acting mysteriously. It was a smaller room, not a suite like Travis and the others had lucked into. Wilson and Fahd were standing at the far side of the room, staring down at something on the bed by the window. The door to the bathroom opened and out came Andy Higgins.

Andy seemed to be trying to look tough even though there was nobody there to impress. He barely looked at Travis.

Travis went over to the bed and looked. Arranged as if on display were several chocolate bars, three more CN Tower lighters, a Blue Jays mug, a brand-new Toronto Maple Leafs cap – the price tag still on it – a deck of cards still in its wrapper, and a pack of Belmont Milds cigarettes.

"Tell the world, why don't you," Andy said to Nish. He seemed both angry and proud at the same time.

Travis asked the obvious: "Where'd all this come from?"

"The lobby gift shop," Nish answered.

Nish didn't have to add that they were stolen goods. Travis knew without asking. He felt suddenly hot, prickly, like the room had only heat and no air and he had to get out. But he knew, too, that he couldn't let his panic show. He was captain. He was responsible.

"The old lady on cash is blind as a bat," offered Andy. He obviously wanted it understood that he had done the stealing.

"How'd you get the smokes?" Nish wanted to know. Nish also looked flushed. But from excitement.

"She was sorting the newspapers – I just reached over and grabbed a pack."

Nish was obviously impressed: "Shoulda grabbed one for me."

Travis looked sharply at him. *Don't encourage him*, he wanted to say. But Nish was already lost. The last time Travis had seen that look in Nish's face was when the team had been in the Maple Leafs' dressing room. Nish was star-struck – with a shoplifter!

Travis felt like a clothes dryer: standing still but spinning inside. He knew he couldn't show his nervousness or they would laugh at him. He knew they would never listen to him if he told Andy to put the stuff back. But he was captain – he had some responsibility to the Screech Owls. And he knew if some of the team got in trouble, Muck would want to know where his team captain had been and whether he had known what was going on. No matter the outcome, Travis already felt he was going to be in the wrong.

Finally, he steeled himself: "You shouldn't have done that to her, Andy."

Andy just laughed. Nish laughed with him, not even knowing why.

"It's not *hers*," Andy sneered. "You think a big hotel chain like this is going to miss a few lighters? What kind of a wimp are you anyway, Lindsay?"

Travis could see he wasn't going to get any support. Nish was all but sneering himself. Data was playing with one of the lighters.

"Take one," Andy said to Data.

Data seemed surprised, pleased. "You mean it?"

"Sure," Andy said. "Plenty more where that one came from."

The boys all laughed at the joke.

Everyone, that is, but Travis Lindsay, team captain . . . wimp.

Mr. Dillinger, the team manager, had done a wonderful job of organizing the team's time in Toronto. They'd been to the Leafs' practice, and they were going to see the game against the Blackhawks. It wasn't the Red Wings, but it was still an Original Six team, and Chicago had two of Travis's favourite players: Jeremy Roenick and Ed Belfour.

Mr. Dillinger had also laid out a full program of sightseeing for both the players and those parents who had come on the trip. Parents and players weren't always interested in the same things. This morning the players were going to walk down Yonge Street on their way to the CN Tower, and they were all going up to the top – even Nish, who hated heights.

Travis should have been more excited, but all he could think about was what to do about Andy Higgins. No one else seemed bothered by it, or maybe they just wouldn't say. Who wanted to be called a wimp by their teammates?

It was a beautiful early spring day for the walk. Since they could see the CN Tower from the hotel and there was no chance of anyone getting lost, Muck and Mr. Dillinger said the players could walk on their own, so long as they stayed in groups. Andy joined Travis's bunch, which both surprised Travis and bothered him.

They had barely gone a block when Andy stopped, took a cigarette out of his shirt pocket, and made a big show of lighting it.

"Muck better not see you," Travis said. He thought he sounded like his mother.

Andy blew smoke out and waved it away as if he'd like to wave Travis away too.

"'*Muck better not see you*,'" Andy whined, impersonating Travis. The others laughed. "Muck's the *coach*, not my *mother*."

Travis half-felt like walking away, but he couldn't. He knew he had to stay with the group. He had to.

"You guys?" Andy said, holding the stolen cigarettes out and raising his eyebrows as he offered them around. Nish helped himself – "For later," he added sheepishly – but no one else reached for one. Travis wouldn't even acknowledge the offer.

"Suit yourselves," Andy said. "Which way're we going?"

"I'm checking out the Zanzibar," Nish announced.

"What's the Zanzibar?" Data asked. Travis had no idea either.

"Just the biggest strip joint in the world, that's all," Nish said, as if it were common knowledge.

"Yeah, I heard about it," said Andy.

Travis knew he was lying.

"My cousin told me about it," Nish said. "A hundred bare-naked women."

Travis closed his eyes. Nish was, as usual, out of control. Mr. Markle had told their class this year that puberty would be coming on soon for some of them. He talked about shaving and voices dropping and moods – but he had never said anything about Nish being committed to a psychiatric hospital.

"And how do you expect to get in?" Travis asked.

"I'll worry about that when I get there," Nish said.

They walked on down Toronto's busiest street, the sights and sounds and smells almost too much for a head to hold at once. The hint of good weather had brought out the sidewalk vendors: hot dogs, jewellery, T-shirts, sunglasses. There were kids not much older than himself with green hair and safety pins through their cheeks. There was a man reading aloud from the Bible and another screaming in a strange language at everyone who passed by.

"Isn't this fantastic?" Nish shouted.

Travis didn't know if that was quite the right word for it, but it was *something* – fascinating and frightening at the same time.

"*There it is!*" Nish shouted again, pointing ahead of them. They could see the sign, "ZANZIBAR," and they could see a rough-looking crowd milling around the photographs of the dancers on the front of the building. Loud rock music burst out every time the door opened and closed. Travis felt alarmed – but also curious. He hadn't the nerve to walk up and look in.

But Nish did. He elbowed his way through the crowd and stood, hands in pockets, staring at the photographs as if he were shopping for something and knew exactly what he wanted. Andy joined him, his cigarette now burned down near the filter. He stomped it out on the sidewalk and spat. The two of them looked ridiculous, Travis thought.

Travis, Gordie, Fahd, and Data hurried on past the bar and stood waiting nervously.

Finally Andy came along, putting a fresh cigarette in his mouth. He stopped to light it, acting as if nothing at all was happening, when he knew perfectly well that the others were almost in full panic about Nish's whereabouts.

"Where is he?" Gordie shouted. Andy raised his eyebrows as if he hadn't heard. But of course he had.

"What'd you do with him?" Data asked, smiling.

"He's probably on stage by now," Andy chuckled.

"*He is?*" Gordie and Data said at the same time. Andy nodded, drawing deep on his cigarette, then choking. *Good*, Travis thought.

Before they had time to ask anything else, the crowd behind them parted as if a mad dog were coming through, and out from the middle burst Nish in full flight, a huge, angry man close behind him shaking his fist. He swung at Nish but missed, Nish's thick legs churning on down the street and past the other boys.

At top speed, Nish turned the first corner he came to, but his hip caught the edge of a vendor's table, flipping it as he tore by. The table, covered with sunglasses, spilled out onto the street, blocking the man from the Zanzibar, who came to a halt and between gasps for air screamed after Nish.

"And don't you ever . . . try that again, punk!"

The vendor was tempted to take up the chase but turned instead to his more-immediate problem: a street covered with sunglasses. After looking twice in the direction Nish had run, he cursed and bent down to pick up his spilled goods. People in the street, including the boys, came to help, and soon the table was back up and the vendor was trying to pop a lens back into a pair of glasses.

"Thanks," the man said. He didn't look too pleased.

The boys hurried on down the street, the CN Tower periodically looming high to their right when the skyscrapers gave way to open space. They knew they would eventually come across Nish again. At least they hoped they would. If someone didn't kill him first.

"*Hey!*"

They looked across the street. It was Nish, waving. They crossed at the light and joined him. He was red as the stoplight and puffing hard. He must have crossed and doubled back. He kept looking back up the street for his assailant, but he was grinning.

"What happened?" said Data.

"Did you get in?" Gordie asked.

"'Course I got in," Nish said angrily. Travis knew Nish too well not to know the truth. He hadn't even come close.

"What'dya see?" Data asked.

"More'n you can imagine, sunshine."

Travis knew it was really just as much as *Nish* could imagine. Some people could look at a cloud and see things; Nish could look at an empty blue sky and see anything he wanted.

"You'll probably need these after that eyeful," Andy said.

He was handing Nish a brand-new pair of sunglasses. He'd swiped them when they were helping the street vendor clean up.

"Where'd you get these?" Nish asked, impressed.

"Found 'em on the street," Andy said.

Everyone laughed.

Everyone but Travis. This wasn't some rich hotel that "would never miss" a few lighters and chocolate bars; this was a real person trying to make a living. Travis was furious that Andy would do something like that to the vendor – who had *thanked* them, for heaven's sake.

Nish put the glasses on and checked himself out in a store window.

"Cool," he said. "Thanks."

Andy and Nish began walking down the street together, leaving the other three behind them.

Data and Gordie moved to catch up, swept up in the adventure, the fun, the *daring*.

Travis followed along, furious at himself for being there, for saying nothing.

He was a failure as a captain.

7

Travis wondered how airplanes could fly. Not how they actually did it, but how they could land and take off in a wind like this. The tour guide said it was usually like this at the top of the CN Tower. It felt as if the wind was whipping the tower like the aerial on a car going through a car wash.

Nish had come up in the elevator, but he wasn't going back down that way. Halfway up the outside of the thin structure, he had made an announcement that almost panicked everyone packed into the glassed-in elevator.

"*I think I'm going to hurl!*"

But he didn't. He just turned a bit green and closed his eyes behind his stolen sunglasses and held his breath. When the elevator reached the top he went to the washroom and sat for a long time. Not sick, just gathering his courage.

Travis couldn't understand Nish's fear of heights. He remembered the time they went up White Mountain at Lake

Placid and Nish had reacted the same way. Nish would block a shot with his teeth if he thought it would win the Screech Owls a hockey game, but he wouldn't climb up on a garage roof even if he thought it would get him drafted into the NHL. He'd only stepped into the elevator because he couldn't stand the idea of them calling him a chicken.

Travis loved it. He loved the way he could look down and see the SkyDome and the way he could look out over Lake Ontario all the way to the United States. A small commuter plane was coming in to land at the Island Airport, and already it was well below where Travis stood.

It had been Derek and Lars who'd come running from the far side of the circular observation deck to tell the rest of them about the wind. Standing where they were, they had been protected and hadn't felt the full force of the blow. But Lars – "Cherry" – had walked around and come upon it, gone back for his new friend Derek, and now the two of them had already mastered one of the greatest sensations Travis had ever felt: they could stand facing the wind, hold their arms out like an airplane, and fall forward – but never hit the ground.

The wind was cold this high up, but it didn't seem to bother them. It held them at a forty-five-degree angle, floating in outer space but for the contact of their shoes on the deck. It was fantastic: the wind pushing and falling, their bodies moving with the flow like weeds in a river. Only in their case, the flow was pushing them back up instead of ahead and down. It felt as if they had beaten gravity.

"*Amazing!*" Fahd shouted. They could barely hear him.

"*Get Nish!*" Gordie Griffith shouted.

Travis found Nish staring out through one of the coin-operated binoculars. It seemed he was more interested in having something to hang on to than to look through. Though it was cold up here, Nish was sweating heavily.

"You gotta see this," Travis said.

"I've seen enough," Nish answered. "I'm going back down."

"But you said you'd never get back on the elevator."

Nish looked desperate. "I'm going down the stairs."

"Stairs?"

"Yeah – over there."

Travis looked over toward an exit.

"I asked," Nish said. "People do it all the time. Willie says there's 1,760 steps, 138 separate landings."

"We haven't got time."

"Sure we do. Game's not till five-thirty."

Travis looked at his good friend. He could sense the terror in Nish's eyes. This was no time to push him further. If Nish saw what the wind was doing to his teammates on the other side of the deck, he'd pass out. He needed Travis now, and this was one time the captain wasn't going to let a teammate down.

"I'll see if anyone else wants to go."

@

They all thought it was a great idea. Travis presented the suggestion as a team project, something that would bring them all together. They'd "floated" together; now they could all say they'd walked down every step of the CN Tower together, all 1,760 of them. It would be like a souvenir.

They found Nish waiting at the stairway. He, too, was pretending there was more to this than merely giving him a way to avoid the glass elevator. He had his watch off and was holding it in his hand. He was setting up the stopwatch to time them.

"Everybody throws in a couple of bucks," said Nish. "First one to hit the bottom gets it all. No jumping allowed."

Everyone laughed at Nish's little joke. Nish seemed relieved. Relieved to be leaving the tower. Relieved not to be on the elevator. Relieved to have the company.

Travis had a sudden thought that, as captain, he probably should have told Muck or his father that they were walking down. But what would it matter? They were all supposed to meet at the entrance at one o'clock and then go for lunch. Everyone had to get down somehow.

"I'm in!" shouted Data.

"Me too," agreed Liz.

"And me."

"Travis'll hold the money," Nish said.

Travis found his hand filling with loonies and two-dollar bills. He took it all, counted it, and announced: "Thirty-four bucks." A lot of money to the winner. His first hope was that he would win himself, but that didn't seem fair since he was holding it. He was captain: he shouldn't win.

"Okay," Nish announced. "Wait'll I count down!"

They waited, pushing toward the door, each one jockeying for a better position.

"Three! . . . Two! . . . One! . . . Go!" Nish yelled.

They took off in a scramble, pushing, jostling, almost as if they were all atoms again, fighting for the puck in the same corner of the rink. Travis's first thought was that they'd made a mistake; someone was going to get hurt. But by the fourth turn in the staircase they had spread out, and all he could hear from above and below was shrieks of pleasure. What a great idea!

For a long time Travis kept count. By the mid-fifties, however, he was beginning to lose track of how many flights of stairs they had pounded down, whirling around each time to begin another. Fifty-three? Or was this fifty-four? What did it matter?

Somewhere in the eighties – he *thought* – Travis began to feel it. He had passed a number of players – Fahd, Liz, Willie – who had started fast but were now walking. Their legs were killing them. So were his. He felt as if his legs were another part of him, a borrowed part that might buckle any minute.

But he kept going. By the time he had passed maybe the hundredth flight, it had been some time since he had heard any shrieks of joy. There was the odd moan and yelp of pain, but no longer any sign of fun.

He knew he was nearing the bottom and kept going. He could hear voices – then a scream!

"Ooowwwwwwwwwwwwww!!"

He could hear more voices – all filled with concern. Travis hurried down three more flights and turned to find several of his teammates gathered around Nish, who was lying crumpled in the corner of the stairwell. Nish was moaning.

"What happened?" Travis called.

"He fell from the top step," Andy said. "I was right behind him."

Travis's first thought was: Did Andy push Nish? Were they racing? Of course they were racing – and Travis had the prize-money in his pocket to prove it!

He pushed through and knelt by Nish, who had tears in his eyes and was holding his leg.

"You okay?"

"I–think–I–broke–my–ankle," Nish answered through gritted teeth. He was in real pain.

"We're only four flights from the bottom," Wilson said.

"You better go down and tell somebody," Travis said. "We'll wait here – we better not move him."

"What're you going to do?" Nish asked nervously.

"They'll bring a stretcher up," said Travis. "You'll have to go to the hospital."

Nish's face seemed to take on a new agony.

"*I can't!*"

"What do you mean, '*can't*'? You'll have to if that's what they decide."

"But I can't, Trav," Nish said, looking around, lowering his voice to a whisper, "I haven't got any underwear on!"

Travis stared into the terrified face of his best friend. No underwear? He'd come with only the one pair and given up on them after the freezer incident. And he still hadn't gone shopping for some new ones.

"Nothing I can do about it," said Travis. Except, he felt like adding, *laugh*.

Nish's ankle wasn't broken, but it was twisted and swollen. They had taken him over to the Sick Children's Hospital on University Avenue. The X-Rays showed nothing was broken, but they'd wrapped the foot and outfitted him with crutches and given him instructions about icing. No one said anything to him about his lack of underwear.

Nish took it all very well. At least he was off the dreaded Tower. No one claimed the prize money, and Travis made sure everyone got their two dollars back. It now seemed like a dumb idea for them to have raced down.

Travis had watched while Barry, the assistant coach, broke the news to Muck, and he had noted how the coach listened and nodded and bounced on the balls of his feet as he did so – always a sure sign to the Screech Owls that Muck was upset. The quieter Muck went, the more it bothered them. Muck's silence was worse than if he'd lined them up at centre ice and screamed at them. Muck's silences didn't bother the ears – but they sure hurt.

8

ravis felt as if he had overstretched elastics in his legs instead of muscles. He could barely walk. He wasn't able to walk at all down stairs. Nor could any other of the Screech Owls – especially Nish, who wasn't even capable of hobbling in a straight line. Yet here they were, lining up for the face-off in Game Two of the Little Stanley Cup.

They needed to win this game. The Montreal Vedettes were one of the top teams in their division, and Muck and the coaches had expected it would be either the Vedettes or the Screech Owls in the final against the powerful Toronto Towers. The Owls' defence might have been a bit better than the Vedettes' – but better because of Nish, who was no longer able to play.

Travis knew they were in trouble long before the opening face-off. Muck had no speech for them – his silence still saying it all – and Mr. Dillinger had been quiet and frowning, which was most unusual for him. Nish had come in on his new crutches and sat in the dressing room to inspire the team, but it had inspired no one. All they could think about was how much they needed him and how sore their legs were from their foolish race down the CN Tower.

The puck dropped, and the big Vedettes centre took it easily from Derek and sent it back to his right defenceman. It was Travis's job to cut him off and take away the pass, if possible, but when he dug in to spring toward the defender, his legs felt like rubber.

The Vedettes' defenceman fired the puck across ice to his far winger, and when Travis turned, too late, the defender hit him with an elbow. It caught Travis on the side of the helmet and, with his legs already weakened, put him down instantly. He could hear the crowd yelling and his bench yelling, but there was no whistle. He couldn't get up, and the next thing he heard was the crowd cheering a Vedettes goal.

Travis got to his feet slowly, feeling terrible. First game, his line had scored immediately; second game, it had happened to them, with Travis lying face down on the ice at the time. He pushed his aching legs toward the bench, afraid even to look at his teammates. He could have sworn he heard the word "wimp" – from a teammate with a deep voice – but he wasn't sure. He pretended he hadn't heard it.

But Travis wasn't alone. By the time all three lines had had their first shifts, it was obvious to everyone that no one on the Screech Owls had any jump. Not even Dmitri, whose entire game was his quick acceleration and speed. It was as if the Screech Owls were playing a player short – two players at times – the entire game.

At the end of the first period, they were down only 2–0 thanks to Jeremy Weathers' fine goaltending. Dmitri finally did get a break in the second and scored to make it 2–1, but the Vedettes scored on an excellent two-on-one against Willie, who was filling in for Nish. Travis couldn't help but think that if it had been Nish back there, he would have had the pass.

In the third period, Travis could feel his legs beginning to come back. Dmitri had more jump as well. The Vedettes were just dumping the puck in, trying to kill off the clock, and Travis, feeling finally that he was in the game, raced back to pick the puck up behind his own net. He hit Derek as he curled back with a pass at the blueline and, without even looking, Derek fed the puck between his own legs to Dmitri, who was already in full flight.

Dmitri blew past the defenceman who should have been watching him. He kept to the boards, hoping to sweep in across net – his favourite play – and get the goaltender moving just before he put it on the short side. But the opposite defenceman came hurling toward Dmitri, completely ignoring the open ice on the other side.

Travis saw his chance and shot for it as fast as his weakened legs would take him. Normally, he would have already been up with Dmitri, but he was still in the centre-ice zone when Dmitri flicked the puck back. It was a beautiful play, one that only Dmitri, or Sarah Cuthbertson last year, could have made. The puck floated through the air and then landed flat, slowing instantly. A location pass, placed perfectly where a player is going to be rather than where a player is at the moment of the pass.

Travis drove hard toward the net and picked up the puck as it lay there waiting for him, just inside the blueline. He came in alone, the defenceman committed to Dmitri and now entirely out of the play. Travis dropped his shoulder and the Vedettes' goaltender went down on the fake. Travis went to his backhand and hoisted as high as he could. The puck pinged off the crossbar and went high over the glass into the crowd. What he couldn't do in the warm-up he had done in the game. But now it meant nothing. There was no time left for the Screech Owls.

"We'll walk back to the hotel, okay?" Muck said after the game. The team groaned as one.

"All except Nish, who'll ride with Barry. The rest of you can use the exercise. Fortunately for you, it's mostly downhill."

Downhill!

Muck never even smiled – but he knew, he knew.

verybody's legs felt better the following morning. Even Nish's injured ankle. He hobbled to the bathroom, no crutches, and even tried putting his weight down on it. But it still hurt. He was pushing it too soon.

Travis was first dressed and out the door for breakfast, and first, therefore, to notice the Eaton's bag hanging off the outside of the doorhandle. He took it off and looked inside: three brand-new pairs of youth underwear, large, still in their package.

Travis turned and fired the bag at Nish, who was sitting on the side of the bed. Nish caught it, opened it, and pulled out the package of new underwear as if he held the winning ticket in a draw.

"Good old Mr. Dillinger!" he shouted.

"How do you know it was him?" Travis asked.

"He was with me in emergency – he was there when they cut away my jeans."

Data stared, unbelieving. "They cut off your pants?"

"Yeah, of course – they could hardly pull them off over my foot, could they?"

"Who was 'they'?" Data wanted to know.

"A nurse. Who else?"

"She cut your jeans off and you had nothing on underneath?"

Nish was turning red. "I had a towel Mr. Dillinger gave me."

"*A towel?*" Willie screeched.

"Yeah – so what?"

"Maybe she thought you were a dancer from the Zanzibar," said Data.

Everyone laughed. Everyone except Nish, who was struggling with the plastic to get the bag opened and the new underwear on.

Mr. Dillinger had arranged for the entire team to visit the Hockey Hall of Fame. The visit, even more than the tournament, had been the talk of the Screech Owls since they began their bottle drives and bingo games and sponsorship search to fund their trip. Many of the parents were also going, and were just as excited as the players.

The Hall of Fame staff were expecting them, and had even laid on a wheelchair for Nish, who sat down on it as if he were royalty taking the throne. He even snapped his fingers for Travis to start pushing, which Travis did while everyone cheered and laughed.

Most of them shot right through the historical stuff and headed for the broadcast area, where they'd be able to broadcast their own games into microphones. Travis had to push Nish and so he was slowed down, and very soon glad that he had been, for the history section was wonderful.

There were old sweaters and old skates, sticks made of a single piece of wood, and wonderful old photographs that seemed to say that everything imaginable has changed about this wonderful game, but also that nothing whatsoever has changed.

Together, Travis and Nish looked at all the glass cases containing the stories of the truly great. Howie Morenz. Aurel Joliat. King Clancy. Jean Béliveau. Gordie Howe. Bobby Orr.

"Look at this!" Nish shouted.

He had wheeled himself over to the Maurice "Rocket" Richard exhibit and was pointing to Richard's stick as if it were the biggest joke in the world.

"'*Love & Bennett Limited'!*" Nish laughed. "*That's* a stick manufacturer? He used a Love & Bennett instead of an Easton or a Sherwood – I don't believe it. And just look at it: absolutely perfectly straight. How the heck could you even take a shot with it?"

Travis stood staring at the Richard exhibit for a long time. Richard had once scored fifty goals in fifty games. He had often heard his grandfather say that half the goals from the old days could never be scored these days because no one in hockey knew how to take a backhander any more. He claimed it was physically impossible to take a proper backhander with a curved blade.

"Ah, now *there's* a hockey stick!" Nish announced.

He was pointing to one of Bobby Hull's. It didn't even resemble a stick. It was so curved it looked like the letter "J."

"That can't be real," said Travis.

"Sure – you could do anything you wanted before they made them illegal," said Nish. He shook his head in admiration. "Those were the good old days."

The two boys moved on. Past the international hockey stuff, past the broadcast zone, where they could hear Data and Fahd high above them screeching out play-by-play into a microphone, past the minivan with dummies in the seats and hockey equipment stashed in the back, past the display of goaltender masks.

They stopped at the Coca-Cola rink, where several of the Screech Owls were taking shots and having their speed measured by radar. Wilson was just about to shoot.

"It doesn't give minus signs!" Nish yelled out.

Wilson stopped, laughing. "You're throwing me off!" he shouted.

"The only way they'd ever time your shot is with a sun dial!" Nish shot back. He had returned to form. Travis could only laugh and push on.

In the replica of the Montreal Canadiens' dressing room, they found Jennie and Jeremy sitting beside a pair of goaltender pads and a big sweater on a hanger: No. 29, Ken Dryden's.

"You think if you sit there long enough something might rub off?" Nish asked.

"We think if we sit here long enough you might go away," said Jennie.

"Let's get outta here," Nish ordered. He snapped his fingers and pointed toward the exit. Travis, his servant, pushed on, trying not to laugh out loud.

"I want to see the Stanley Cup," Nish said.

"I think it's upstairs."

"That's your problem, not mine."

10

ravis would have to find an elevator.

There was no other way to get Nish up to the next floor to the Great Hall where they kept all the NHL trophies, including the Stanley Cup.

He asked one of the custodians for directions. There was an elevator at the rear, she told him. It was for the staff to come and go from their offices on the third and fourth floors, but it was also available for the use of anyone in need – and his friend in the wheelchair was certainly in need.

Travis pushed Nish down a long corridor, at the end of which were sliding doors and a single button. Travis pushed the button and the doors opened on an empty elevator.

"Lingerie, please." Nish announced, as if he were addressing an elevator operator in a department store.

"You're sick," Travis said.

Nish grinned: "And proud of it."

They rose to the second floor and the doors began to open.

Suddenly, both were blinded by a flash of light!

At first Travis couldn't see, but as the flash faded from his eyes he could make out two bulky figures, one with a camera half-hidden in his opened coat.

The men seemed caught off guard. The man taking the pictures – dark, surly, with a scar down the side of his face as if he'd run into a skate – seemed to be trying to hide the camera. The other – tall, balding, but with a ponytail tied behind his head – seemed nervous.

"How ya doin', boys?" the tall man asked.

"Okay," Travis answered, unsure.

"We're just taking some shots for a few renovations," the man explained.

Travis pushed Nish past. It didn't make any sense. The Hockey Hall of Fame was almost brand new. Why would it need fixing up already?

"What the heck's with them?" Nish asked as they moved further down the corridor.

"I have no idea," said Travis.

When they got to the Great Hall where the trophies were – a dazzle of lights on silver and glass, the Norris, the Calder, the Lady Byng, the Hart, the Vezina – several of the Screech Owls were already positioned in the designated area for taking their own photographs.

The scene made Travis even more suspicious of the men. If they had come in here with a camera, surely it was for this. Why would they want to take a picture of an elevator?

"*There's the Stanley Cup!*" Nish shouted, pointing.

Derek and Willie were already there. The cup looked glorious. So shining, so rich, so remarkably *familiar*, even though none of them had ever seen it in real life before this moment.

"This isn't the real one," said Willie, who knew everything.

"Whadya mean?" Nish scowled, disbelieving.

Willie pointed back over his shoulder. "The real one, the original one that Lord Stanley gave back in 1893, is back over there in the vault. This building used to be a bank, you know. They keep it back there because it's considered too fragile to present to the players, so they present this one – which in a way makes this one the real Stanley Cup as well."

Travis looked to see what Willie was talking about. He could see another room back behind huge steel doors – "LORD STANLEY'S VAULT," the sign overhead said. There were more lights in there and what appeared to be another, smaller trophy.

And the two men were there, too!

The shorter, dark one had his camera out again. He was flashing pictures as fast as he could. But not of the cup, of everything else: the walls, the vault doors, the base the trophy stood on.

What were they up to?

"Wait here," Travis said to Nish.

Nish turned back, hardly caring. He could get Data to push him if necessary. But anyway he wasn't much interested in leaving the cup he was planning to carry around Maple Leaf Gardens.

Travis circled wide around the other trophies so he could come up on the entrance to the smaller room without being seen.

There was no one in the vault but the two men, still taking photographs. It made no sense.

Travis kept close to the wall and edged to the doorway. He could hear the taller man talking.

"It's perfect," he kept saying. "Perfect."

"No one can see from any of the other areas. There's only the one surveillance camera, the main alarm, and a secondary alarm on the display case. We plan it right and we can be in and out of here in less than thirty minutes."

The man with the camera stopped and turned, scowling.

"Keep it down. You wanna tell the whole country?"

The tall one laughed. "The whole country will know soon enough – and they'll pay whatever it takes to get this baby back, believe me."

Travis could feel his legs shaking, and it wasn't from the CN Tower run.

11

ravis hurried back to the group around the other Stanley Cup. They were taking so many pictures and talking so loudly that he couldn't get a word in edgewise. But even if he could, what would he say? That there were two men over there plotting to steal the real Stanley Cup? What if someone pointed? What if the men called him a liar? What if he ended up in trouble just trying to alert someone? He would tell Muck; Muck would know what to do.

The custodians of the trophy room asked the Screech Owls if they would mind moving on to let some of the other visitors closer. Travis was happy to leave – it would give him a chance to get to Muck before the two thieves left the building. Muck would tell the security people and they'd know how to stop them.

"Let's go back down to the souvenir shop," Travis suggested.

"Yeah, let's," Derek agreed.

They had all seen the store as they'd come in, and all had vowed to get back in time to buy something to remember their visit by.

"I need a T-shirt," Nish said. He always had to have a souvenir T-shirt from every tournament. Always.

"Maybe they sell Hall of Fame underwear," Willie suggested, to great laughter from the rest.

"Very funny," said Nish. "Now push."

Travis saw Muck as the coach came out of the Hall of Fame's store. He and Nish had just dropped off the wheelchair, thanked the workers for it, and Travis was helping Nish, who was back on his crutches, out through the turnstiles. He could tell from a distance that Muck was not at all pleased.

Muck was standing with two of the Hall of Fame's security guards and a man in a suit who looked like he ran the place. They were all deep in conversation. One of the security people had her arms full of merchandise.

They drew closer, and Nish saw Andy over by the cash register. He looked shaken. He was with Lars and Jesse and Liz, and they all looked upset.

"What's up?" Nish said as he hobbled up to them.

"Something to do with Data and Wilson and Fahd," said Liz. "They've got them back in that office there."

Travis could just make out Data's head through the window in the office door. He looked as if he was crying.

"They got caught lifting," said Andy.

Travis turned. "*What?*"

"They had some T-shirts stuffed into their windbreakers."

Travis couldn't believe what he was hearing. *Caught stealing?* Data? Wilson? Fahd? They wouldn't steal – *would they?*

"You gotta be kidding," said Nish.

"I'm not," said Andy. "I was right here when they got picked up."

Yeah, Travis wanted to say, right here leading them on.

"Why would they do it?" Nish asked.

Andy had no answer. Because he knew? Travis wondered. Or because there was no answer?

"There must be some mistake," Travis said. "They wouldn't steal."

Andy gave Travis his sarcastic lifted-eyebrow look. "Yeah, right," he said.

They *had* been stealing. The cameras had caught it all, and they were found with the goods stuffed into their windbreakers. That was what the security woman had been holding.

Muck and Mr. Dillinger and Travis's dad had then met alone with the man in the suit. After a long time, the three men came over to where Data, Fahd, and Wilson had gone to wait with the assistant coaches. Muck and Mr. Lindsay did the talking. Fahd was wiping away more tears. Wilson was sniffing.

The three boys got up and left with Mr. Lindsay and Barry. Muck came over, limping slightly from his old hockey injury. He signalled the rest of the team to follow him to a quiet corner.

"Sit down," Muck said. They sat. Some on benches. Some on the floor.

Muck took his time. Whether it was for effect or because he didn't know what to say, Travis didn't know, but Muck had a look that he had seen only a few times in the past. And Travis didn't like it.

"You're not stupid people," Muck said. "Though some of you, it seems, can still act stupid. I don't need to tell you what happened."

He paused again.

"The manager had some good advice for our three team-mates," he continued. "He recommended they go home and tell their parents what they've done and what they think about what they've done. He said if they promised him that they would do this, he wouldn't be pressing charges. The three young men are on their way home as we speak. Mr. Lindsay is driving them.

"They are no longer members of the Screech Owls."

Nish couldn't help himself: "*Forever?*"

"For as long as it takes," Muck answered.

No one had a clue what he meant. And no one had the nerve to ask.

"Let's go back to the hotel now," Muck said, and he turned to go.

Travis didn't know what to do. How could he now chase after Muck with a story that two men were planning to steal the Stanley Cup? Why would Muck believe him or anyone else on the Screech Owls after what had happened? Nothing like this ever happened when Sarah had been captain.

And now he couldn't even tell his father, who had left without a word to take the three disgraced players home. Given the distance, he probably wouldn't be back.

"Give me a hand, eh?" Nish said, trying to get up. Travis helped his friend to his feet and bent down for his crutches. As he stood up and handed them to Nish, he saw the two men come up the stairs from the Hall of Fame and out the door.

They were *leaving*. Heading off, Travis was certain, to put the finishing touches to their plan.

12

Travis had never felt so young and insignificant in all his life. He had gone to the hotel payphones and, with two quarters, made two calls. The first was to the Hockey Hall of Fame, the second to the police.

"Two men are going to steal the Stanley Cup," he'd said, wishing his voice didn't sound so young.

"Is that right?" a man at the Hall of Fame had said.

"Yes."

"Well, we watch it pretty closely," the man said. "What's your name, son?"

He couldn't give it. The last thing Travis wanted was the police and the Hall of Fame security people racing to the hotel to talk to Muck about what a Screech Owl knew about some plot to steal the Stanley Cup. That would be the last straw for Muck. He might pull the entire team out of the Little Stanley Cup. And Travis, as captain, would never be forgiven by his teammates for such a thing. So far, he hadn't even told Nish what he knew – or at least suspected. Nish could never keep his mouth shut, and Travis didn't want the whole team knowing. Not until he'd figured out what to do.

"They *really* are!" Travis insisted. He knew he sounded like a silly fool. "I heard them plotting to do it."

"Yes," the man said. He sounded bored, as if he handled several such calls a day. "Well, if we don't know who you are, then we don't know whether to believe you, do we?"

Travis had hung up. Both times. His call to the police was almost exactly the same. Both were utter failures. They thought he was a kid pulling a prank.

Travis gave up. If the Stanley Cup was stolen, so be it – he had tried his best. At least he told himself it was his best.

But he knew it wasn't.

To no one's surprise, Muck cancelled the trip to the Leafs game that night. A once-in-a-lifetime opportunity lost because three of the team got caught shoplifting. There were bad feelings all round. Most were angry with the three boys for costing them a chance to see a real NHL game at Maple Leaf Gardens. Travis was angry with Andy Higgins, even though he had no proof that Andy had been involved or had put the three up to stealing. He just knew Andy was in there somewhere.

Muck put a 9:30 curfew on the team and did room checks to make sure everyone was where they should be and ready for bed. With Data now back home, Travis moved over into the other bed with Willie so Nish and his injured ankle could have a bed to themselves.

At 8:00 a.m. the Screech Owls were scheduled to play the Muskoka Wildlife – an all-star team made up of players from the three towns in the Ontario resort area – and the winner of the game would have an outside chance of making the final. It all depended on what happened in the Toronto Towers' next game against the Sudbury Nickel Belts, a team both the Owls and Towers had beaten several times. If somehow Sudbury could beat the Towers, then the Owls would still have an outside chance.

Nish said his ankle was feeling much better. He used only one crutch to go down for breakfast, and by the time they got to the arena he was claiming he was good enough to play.

Muck didn't think so. But he was three defencemen short, with Nish's ankle and Data and Willie sent home. Gordie Griffith had already been told to play defence, with Liz moving over to centre the second line and Travis double-shifted to cover the shortage at left wing. Muck said Nish could go out for the warm-up, but he wouldn't make any decision until they were ready to start the game.

Travis felt great. His legs were back. He hit the crossbar with his very first warm-up shot. His skates were sharp and he had no sense of them being on his feet – the best possible feeling for a good skater. He was sure he was finally going to have a good game and glad that he would be getting extra ice time.

Nish tried, but couldn't do it. He could barely take his corners.

"Not this game," Muck told him. "You'd better get undressed."

"Can't I just sit on the bench?" Nish asked.

Muck stared at him, then nodded. Nish would at least make it *look* as if the Screech Owls had enough players.

The Muskoka Wildlife were good. They had excellent skaters, good shooters, and big players. Travis and some of the other Owls found them intimidating just to watch in the warm-up, but Muck said something just before the face-off that made them think they might have a chance.

He called them all around the bench while the Wildlife were down in their own end going through their team yell.

"All-star teams are rarely good teams," Muck said, seeming to contradict himself. "You put three stars together, you don't necessarily have a line. You have a situation where everyone is chasing glory, you won't have anyone chasing the puck. Understand?"

They all shouted that they did, but Travis wasn't so sure any of them followed Muck when he talked this way. He knew the reason his line worked was because Dmitri had the speed, Derek could make the passes, and he, Travis, could come up with the puck. A line of three Dmitris might look sensational, but who was going to dig out the puck for them?

Five minutes into the game, the Muskoka Wildlife were up 2–0 on the Screech Owls. Muck's little speech was starting to ring a bit hollow, but he wasn't letting up. "Two goals on two individual rushes," he told them. "You stop the individual, you stop this whole team."

Muck changed the game plan so that there were two Screech Owls going in to forecheck instead of the Owls' usual plan of having one go in and the other two forwards holding back. Muck's hunch was that the Wildlife would be weakest on passing because each all-star player would always be trying to make the big play.

He was right. The first time Travis and Dmitri pressed in on a defender, he tried to step around them. He got past Dmitri, but Travis took the body, forcing the defenceman to panic and dump the puck out blind. Derek snared it at the blueline with his glove, dropped the puck, and hit Dmitri as he circled the Muskoka net. Dmitri waited for the goaltender to make his move – and he did, going down – and then roofed a forehand into the top of the net. The Owls were back in the game.

Not long into the second period "Cherry" Johanssen hit Liz Moscovitz with a breakaway pass and Liz was home free from centre ice in, the Owls all standing at the bench, petrified she would blow it. Liz had speed, but bad luck in scoring. "Stone hands," she said herself. But this time it seemed she had Dmitri's hands, deking out the Muskoka goaltender and dropping a light backhand in behind him. Tie game.

Once the game had been tied, Muck's words came true. The Muskoka Wildlife gave up even pretending to pass and work as a team and turned instead to an endless series of individual efforts. All the Owls had to do was concentrate on the puck carrier and there would be a turnover and the Screech Owls could counterattack.

Cherry Johanssen used his speed to pick up a dropped puck and rushed down the ice with Derek and Travis. They crossed the blueline on a three-on-one, Cherry slipped it under the defenceman's stick to Derek, and Derek dropped it back to

Travis, who faked a shot and slid the puck over to Cherry, who had the wide open net to score.

The Screech Owls had a 3–2 lead. The Wildlife tried frantically to come back, but Jennie never even let a rebound out. The Owls had won the game they had to win.

When the horn blew, the Screech Owls bolted over the boards and the entire team spilled over the ice toward Jennie as if they'd been dumped from a pail. Nish, of course, was right in the middle of it all. The only player on the team who hadn't broken a sweat.

They lined up for the naming of the Player of the Game. When the announcer began, "Most Valuable Player, Screech Owls . . . ," Nish pushed out from the blueline to the centre of the ice and did a little twirl. The Muskoka Wildlife, who weren't paying full attention, rapped their sticks on the ice to congratulate him while his own team booed. ". . . is the goaltender, *Jennie Staples!*"

Now the Owls could cheer and slam their sticks. Jennie skated out and collected her prize, a tournament T-shirt. As she skated back she rolled it up and tossed it at Nish, who caught it, delighted.

"Take it," she said. "You earned it."

"How so?" Nish asked.

"First game you ever dressed for when you haven't screened me," Jennie laughed.

"It's not 'screening,' " he protested, "it's *blocking.*"

"Whatever," Jennie said. "It's still your big ugly butt in my face."

13

"Y ou come with me," Nish said to Travis.

Nish had come up to him in the hotel lobby and told him he had been thinking about the sunglasses and what to do with them.

"You should have taken them back right when Andy handed them to you."

"I didn't, okay. And I can't give them back now."

Travis didn't suppose Nish could. How would it look: Nish, nearly two days later, handing over something and saying it must have landed in his pocket when he dumped the vendor's table?

"But I can *put* them back," Nish said, smiling.

"What do you mean?"

"If Andy can lift them, I can lift them back, don't you think? I'll just have to make sure I don't get caught."

"You're going to sneak them back?"

"Reverse shoplifting. Like a film running backwards. C'mon!"

The two of them, alone, started off down Yonge Street. The springlike weather was holding. Nish wanted to try walking without the crutches, and he seemed fine except for a slight limp.

They walked down the other side this time until they were past the Zanzibar strip club – Nish had good reason to steer clear of it – and then, a half-block below, they crossed back over.

Nish had the stolen sunglasses in his pocket. When they reached the vendor's table he began trying on various glasses and twice asked the vendor for the little hand-held mirror so he could see what they looked like. They all looked ridiculous.

Travis moved on down the street to wait. He was uncomfortable standing there and knew that two young kids would make the vendor suspicious, especially if they weren't buying anything.

As he was waiting, two familiar faces cut through the crowd outside the Zanzibar. He knew them both immediately – one tall and balding with a ponytail, the other dark with a nasty scar on the face. It was the two crooks from the Hockey Hall of Fame!

They came to a stop right beside Travis, not because they recognized him, but because they were hungry. When Travis turned his back so they wouldn't recognize him, he saw he was standing right next to a hot-dog vendor, and that was where the two plotters had been headed. They ordered bratwurst and Cokes, and while they were waiting for the vendor to finish cooking the big sausages, they talked.

"You're certain we can trust him?" the short dark one asked.

"For five thousand dollars you can trust anyone."

"He leaves the fire exit open – that's what he said, eh – after six p.m.?"

"That's when they close today. There'll be just the two security guards after that – and one of them's one of us." The one with the ponytail laughed, enjoying his little secret.

The two plotters finished their food and drinks and were off down Yonge Street. Travis shifted carefully as they passed, always keeping his face out of sight, and when they were gone he let out his breath as if he were letting a balloon go.

Nish came running up.

"Done! He never even noticed."

"Good," said Travis. "But now we've got another problem."

14

Most of the Screech Owls were gathered in the lobby when Travis and Nish returned from their mission to return the stolen sunglasses. Liz raced toward them with the news.

"The Towers lost!"

"*What?*" Nish couldn't believe what he was hearing.

"You're kidding," Travis said.

"No, I'm not. They ran into a really hot goaltender and lost 3–2. It came down to total goals – and we're in!"

"*Fan–tas–tic!!*" shouted Nish.

The rest of the team – what was left of it, anyway – came running over to tell Nish and Travis, even though they obviously already knew. Travis could feel the excitement in his teammates, Gordie, Jennie, Willie, Jesse, all of them shouting his and Nish's name. Then he caught sight of Andy Higgins along the far wall, just staring. Travis couldn't tell what Andy's stare meant. Resentment over the excitement everyone else was showing toward Travis and Nish? Jealousy? Or just that he didn't feel a full part of the Screech Owls yet?

Travis saw Muck and the assistants coming in through the hotel's revolving doors and went over. Muck showed no emotion.

"Well," he said. "I guess we got in the back door."

Travis was startled at the contrast between his teammates and his coaches. The team had all been celebrating; the coaches, particularly Muck, looked as if they'd just come from a funeral.

Travis didn't have to have it spelled out for him. Muck had been embarrassed and humiliated by the incident at the Hockey Hall of Fame. It didn't matter that Muck himself had nothing to do with what had happened – in the coach's eyes he had everything to do with it. A team wasn't made up of individuals, just as he'd said when they played the Muskoka Wildlife; if the Screech Owls were a real team, then what some of them did affected them all. And whatever the team did, both on and off the ice, reflected on the coach.

Travis felt just as disappointed himself. He didn't feel excited like his teammates. He felt empty.

The final was scheduled for the next day at 11:00 a.m. Muck put them through an afternoon practice, and they all worked hard. Nish skated and even played a little scrimmage, but still wasn't fully recovered. The rest were sharp and eager, which seemed to please Muck. He didn't cancel the planned visit to the Ontario Science Centre as he had the Leafs game.

It was a difficult afternoon for Travis. He did laugh once, when the Science Centre guide selected Nish to stand on a rubber mat and put his hand on a silver globe while they shot a charge of static electricity through him. Nish's hair looked like it was trying to run away from him! But there was a big difference between laughing at a little moment and feeling good about their whole time in Toronto.

They went to the Science Centre cafeteria for a snack at the end, and Muck asked Travis to come and sit with him. Muck had two Cokes, one for each of them.

Travis felt his stomach churning. He didn't know what Muck wanted. He didn't know what to say. Maybe he'd get a chance to talk about the two plotters.

Muck took a long drink of his Coke, swallowed, and stared hard at Travis.

"Did you know anything about the stealing?" he asked.

Travis shook his head. He knew Muck was talking about the Hockey Hall of Fame, and he had known nothing about it. But he did know about the other stealing, only it had involved others, not the three who were sent home, and Travis couldn't tell on Andy and Nish. He couldn't squeal. Certainly not on his best friend.

Technically, he was right to shake his head. But he was wrong, too. Either way, he was behaving like a wimp. A wimp if he squealed. A wimp by letting Muck think something was true when it wasn't exactly true.

"A good captain has to lead by example, Travis," Muck said. "I wanted you as captain for precisely that reason."

Travis swallowed hard. "Yes, sir."

Surprisingly, Muck gave a slight grin. "Think we can win with half a bench?"

Travis was relieved at the change of topic. "I hope so," he said.

Muck took another swallow, nodding.

"We don't deserve to," he said.

Muck gave them a free evening. He set the rules when they got back to the hotel lobby: "Stay in groups of a minimum of three. Stay off the streets, except for those who plan to go shopping at the Eaton Centre. Be in your rooms, lights out, by nine-thirty. I'll be checking."

Some of the Owls were going shopping with their parents. Some wanted to stay around the pool.

Travis was in the elevator when he decided to act. He and Nish were headed up to their rooms to change into their swimsuits, not knowing what else to do. Travis figured that, as captain and assistant captain, it was clear what their duty was.

All he could think about was Muck's enormous disappointment in the team and how a captain was expected to lead by example. Perhaps if he could prevent one of the thefts – a much bigger one than the lighters or sunglasses or T-shirts – he could be a good example, at least in his own eyes. That might be a start, anyway.

The elevator was just coming to a halt on their floor.

"Let's go back to the Hall of Fame," he said.

"Been there, done that," said Nish, unimpressed.

Travis made the decision he'd been avoiding. He had to tell Nish.

"We have to go back."

"What d'ya mean?"

"There's two guys planning to steal the Stanley Cup tonight."

Nish turned, staring. If his hair could have shot straight up without static electricity, it would have.

Good old Nish. Once Travis had explained, he was all for it, almost like a player who's been sitting on the bench all along and finally gets a chance to play. He understood why Travis had been unable to tell Muck. He was outraged that the police, as well as the Hall of Fame, had dismissed Travis as a childish prankster when he'd called. He saw this as a marvellous opportunity for them, supposedly the team leaders, to right a few wrongs. He had put back the sunglasses, and now he'd make sure the Stanley Cup never got lifted by anyone who wasn't on a winning team.

They prepared carefully. Nish had his little backpack, and they had apples and chocolate bars and drinking boxes to put in it.

"I hate those stupid boxes," said Nish.

"So do I, but pop cans make noise."

"Right."

"Do you have any shin-pad tape?" Travis asked.

"A couple rolls."

"Get them. You never know, they might come in handy."

"How'll we get there?" Nish asked.

"I've got subway tokens. It'll take us twenty minutes, tops."

Nish suddenly frowned: "We can't go."

"What do you mean?"

"Muck says we have to stick in threes."

Nish was right. They were already risking enough trouble just in going. But they might not even get out the front door of the hotel if they were on their own. More important, even if they did manage to slip away unnoticed, they were still only two peewee hockey players against two grown crooks. They could use at least a third person – if only to serve as lookout.

"We'd better find someone," Nish said.

"Data would be perfect."

"Data's probably been sent to his room until the end of the next century."

"Derek?"

Nish shook his head. "Went to the movies."

They were stuck. Willie, their roommate, was down in the pool. Besides, they needed Willie here if they blew curfew. They'd left a note on Willie's pillow telling him they might be a bit late and to answer for them if Muck happened to knock on the door.

They went down to the lobby, looking and checking around. Everyone was either gone or else tied up with plans.

All except one.

"Andy," Nish said. "He's not with anybody."

"Take a thief to catch a thief?" Travis asked, incredulous.

"Why not?" Nish grinned. "He already thinks like them."

Andy was sulking around the lobby. Since the three shop-lifters had been sent home, he'd been more or less frozen out by the rest of the team.

Travis shrugged.

Nish headed toward Andy and Travis followed, feeling he really had no choice. Andy saw them coming. He was sitting on one of the big lobby chesterfields and had a plastic shopping bag on his lap. He shifted uncomfortably.

"What're you doing?" Nish asked, plunking down beside Andy.

"Nothin'," Andy replied. He seemed nervous.

"What's in the bag?" Nish asked. Good old Nish. Never shy about things.

"Nothin'."

"C'mon, let me see."

Nish grabbed the bag out of Andy's hands and dumped the contents out. The CN Tower lighters and the Blue Jays mug and the deck of cards came spilling out, as well as several loonies. As quick as he had dumped them out, Nish scooped everything back into the bag and threw it in Andy's lap.

Travis's first thought was that Andy had been stealing again from the shop. But why the loonies?

"I was trying to figure out how to get it back," Andy said.

"What's the money for?"

"To pay for the cigarettes, I guess. Whatever."

Nish was grinning: "Why the change of heart?"

"It's my fault they got caught, obviously." He stared hard at Travis. "You don't have to pretend everyone isn't blaming me for what happened."

Travis said nothing. What was there to say to Andy?

"I'll put it back for you," Nish said.

Andy looked at Nish, not understanding.

"I am the world's leading expert at returning stolen merchandise," Nish announced with pride. "Just give it to me."

Andy handed over the bag. Without a word, Nish got up and walked straight over into the gift shop. As casual as could be, Nish began talking with the old woman at the cash register and pointing to a cap clipped to a rack high above the front window. She nodded, got a short stool and a stick with a hook on it, and began reaching for the cap.

With the woman's back turned, Nish simply leaned over and stuffed the bag in one of the low shelves full of candy. She'd find it soon enough, but never figure it out.

She lowered the cap and handed it to an angelic-looking Nish, who tried it on, looked at his reflection in the window, and then, seeming disappointed, handed it back to the old woman. She nodded and turned to replace the cap. Nish walked out.

When he got back to where the others were waiting, he said, looking at Andy, "Travis, I think we've got our third man."

Travis found himself nodding.

15

They took the subway down and, with their car fairly empty, explained all to Andy along the way. Travis couldn't believe the change in Andy. No longer surly, no longer staring at Travis as if there were some mysterious grudge between them. He seemed as keen as Nish to stop the heist of the Stanley Cup. He seemed proud to be part of the team that was setting out to save the cup.

Travis tried to figure it out. Maybe it all had to do with wanting to fit in instead of being different. Andy wasn't a good enough player that he'd make an impression on the other Screech Owls by his play alone. The team automatically loved Dmitri because he scored the goals, but for third-line players like Andy, it was different.

Andy had brought attention to himself with the shoplifting. He'd even been, momentarily, popular because of it. But now three of the players had been sent home for stealing and Andy had become a virtual outcast from the team.

They paid to go in. "We close in less than an hour," the young woman taking their money had said, but they had nodded and thanked her and happily paid the admission.

Travis kept looking at the various security guards, wondering which one was on the take for the five thousand dollars. The crooked security guard made it impossible for the boys to go to one of them and say that there was about to be a break-in. If they happened to pick the wrong one – and there weren't many to choose from – they would either blow their plan or, even worse, end up being taken hostage.

There was nothing to do but wait.

Travis felt a deep, deep shiver go through his body when the announcement came that the Hockey Hall of Fame was closing at 6:00 p.m. and visitors were to begin to leave. He knew now that it was just a matter of minutes. He also knew that in many ways these were the most crucial minutes. If they got kicked out, they wouldn't be able to do anything to prevent the theft.

The boys were concerned that the Hall of Fame might have taken a body count of all those entering and leaving. But Nish had already thought of this and, just for safety, had triggered the exit turnstiles three times as Travis was paying. If there was a counter, then the three boys would be cancelled out the moment they entered.

Travis couldn't believe the change in Andy. He'd suddenly come to life. Travis's idea had been for them to hide in the washroom while they closed the building. They could shut the doors and stand on the toilet seats and no one would see them.

"But they'd see closed doors and wonder," Andy cautioned. He was right.

And after they looked around, Andy had a better idea.

"Come on over here," he whispered just before the final closing announcement came.

They followed Andy to the minivan that was supposed to show a typical suburban hockey family of the 1990s. In the back was a hockey bag as high as the window, sticks stuffed in every which way, and in the seats up front the "family" was happily driving: dummy dad, dummy mom, dummy kids.

"Data's dad has one exactly the same," said Nish. "Right down to the little dummy in the back."

"We could crawl in here and wait them out," Andy said.

An excellent idea. Good for Andy, Travis thought, even though he shuddered slightly at the idea that he'd be in the pitch dark. No night light for him here. But this was much better than hoping to pass unnoticed in the washrooms. How would someone react, pushing open a door and seeing Nish standing on the lid?

Nish hurried over and carefully tried the latch. It clicked and gave. He quickly checked to see if any of the custodians were watching, but there was no one. He lifted up the tailgate.

"Hey, Data," Nish said to the closest dummy kid. "Looking good, man. Looking good."

The boys scrambled in underneath the hockey equipment. Andy pulled down the tailgate so the roof light inside went out but the lock didn't catch. Getting back out would be a simple matter of pushing out from the bottom.

They settled down and everything went quiet. Travis could see out of the tinted glass even if he was at the far side of the trunk. He was pretty sure no one could see in.

"How long do we have to wait?" Andy asked.

"Not long," said Travis. "The security guard's supposed to rig the fire exit for them so they can come in without setting off the alarm."

"What if I have to go to the can?" Nish asked.

"Tough," said Travis. Then he giggled: "You should have brought extra underwear."

"Very funny," Nish said.

16

ravis checked his watch: 6:44 p.m. The Hockey Hall of Fame was dark but hardly pitch black. He was grateful for the dim glow of the security lights. It was so silent he thought he could hear his heart beating.

They'd eaten their food and drunk the fruit juice. And then they had waited.

"*Ssshhhh!*"

It was Andy, who'd been on lookout. He ducked down below the windows. "Someone's coming with a flashlight!"

Travis stretched up, careful not to put his face too close to the tinted glass. He barely peeked out – he felt like a frog in water, with just his eyeballs showing – and could see the swinging wash of a flashlight along the hallway.

The beam turned full into the large room where the minivan sat. Travis instinctively ducked as it swept over the van. The light moved closer. Travis could sense Nish bobbing up to see, and he put his hand on his head and pushed down.

The beam turned and washed back over the robber with the ponytail.

"The elevator's over this way!" said another voice. It was like a hiss. But Travis could still recognize it. The smaller, darker one with the scar.

"Hold your horses," the ponytail told him. "We've all the time in the world."

They moved on, past the stairs and toward the elevator. Travis knew why they weren't taking the stairs; the steps were visible from the front entrance. The elevator, on the other hand, was well hidden.

"Where's the security guard?" Andy whispered. Travis hadn't realized that his head had popped up and he was watching. Travis's hand was still on Nish's head, holding him down. But now Nish was pushing up again.

"I don't know," said Travis.

"Maybe already up there," Nish said. "Maybe he went ahead to disconnect another alarm system."

"We'll wait one minute," Travis said, "then go."

It was a long minute. Travis could feel the tension. Usually, when he felt like this, he'd be chewing a fingernail. But now he didn't even feel the urge.

"Let's go!"

Andy pushed up on the tailgate and it swung silently out and up. The three of them scrambled out. Nish set the gate back down, careful not to let it close all the way.

They began moving very quietly down the hallway when Travis thought he heard a thumping. *Was it his heart coming right through his chest?* He signalled for them all to stop, and listened. There it was again.

"Let's check this out first," he said, turning.

The three Screech Owls headed back down the hall, and the thumping grew louder. Further on, they could see a door almost closed. The thumping continued, then stopped.

"Let's get outta here!" said Nish.

Travis forced himself to tip-toe closer.

He crept up to the door and peered into the small room. *There were two security guards inside, both tied up and gagged!* One of them must have been pounding his feet on the floor.

Travis's first instinct was to untie them, but then he realized that one of them had to be the guard who'd let the robbers in.

Had they double-crossed him? Or what if he'd been tied up as part of the plan? So no one would suspect him? Maybe he was still with the robbers?

And which one was he?

Travis raced back to Andy and Nish.

"What is it?" Nish hissed.

"They tied up two guards," Travis told him.

"Shouldn't we untie them?" asked Andy.

"Maybe one of them's working with the robbers – we can't take the chance."

Andy and Nish thought about it for a second and then realized the dilemma.

"We're going to have to pull this off ourselves," Travis said.

17

ravis's first inclination was to head for the elevator, the same way he and Nish had gone when they first bumped into the robbers. But elevators make noise. Besides, it was already up a floor, having taken the two thieves up.

"We've got to use the stairs," Travis whispered.

Neither questioned him. In the dim security lights, he could see both Nish and Andy nod.

"Keep your heads down and go fast, and not a sound," Travis said.

Travis went first, low and scrambling up along the side of the stairs. From the top he could see the Great Hall where the trophies were. The elevator was to his right, down the short corridor where they had first encountered the robbers.

Nish came up, then Andy, each crouching low. He could hear them breathing. Travis had them all wait a moment until they calmed down.

They could hear noise from the vault area. The big doors were still open, and the robbers were talking.

"You think somebody's really going to pay a million bucks ransom for a piece of old tin like this?" It was the darker one with the scar.

"This hockey-mad country?" the ponytail said. "You could get whatever you asked."

"Can't you hurry it up?"

"Just relax, okay. We move too fast, we trigger the secondary alarms. It's gonna take twenty minutes to do this right."

A power tool started up. A saw? A drill? It was difficult to say. Travis turned and looked at Andy and Nish. They looked back at him, waiting for instructions.

Travis felt a strange sensation. He thought he might actually know what to do.

"Follow me," he whispered, and ducked back down the stairs.

At the bottom they caught their breath again. Nish and Andy waited for Travis to talk.

"We're going to block the elevator," said Travis.

"How? It's already up there," said Nish.

"We'll block it with a hockey stick," Travis said. "Get a good straight one out of a display case. You can handle that part, Nish. Bring the stick over and call down the elevator – I don't think they'll hear it with all the noise they're making – and then jam the door open."

"What good will that do?"

"If the door can't close, they won't be able to call it up again and they'll have to use the stairs."

Both Nish and Andy thought about it a moment, then nodded.

"Get going," Travis said, and Nish ducked away, still staying low to the ground.

"C'mon with me," Travis said to Andy.

He scooted in the same direction Nish had gone, with Andy right behind him. When they came to the minivan, Travis stopped.

"Very quietly open the doors – we're taking Mom and Dad."

Andy glanced at him, not understanding, but said nothing. Travis seemed to know what he was doing and Travis was in charge.

The dummies were strapped in, but pulled out fairly easily, and Travis, with Mom over his shoulder, turned and scurried back toward the stairs. Andy, carrying Dad, hurried along behind.

At the bottom of the stairs, Travis stopped and listened. He could still hear the whir of power tools. He looked over toward the elevator and saw Nish, with a hockey stick in one hand, pushing the button to call the elevator.

"Bring Dad over here," Travis said.

Andy dumped him beside Mom.

"Can you bring both kids now?" Travis asked.

He nodded and hurried away, back to the van.

Travis sat down, breathing hard.

What now?

18

Before Andy came back with the two smaller dummies, Travis was well into his plan. He'd taken one of the rolls of shin-pad tape out of Nish's bag and was putting it across the stairs about three-quarters of the way down and low to the ground. The cloudy tape did not show up in the dim light from the distant entrance way.

"It's done," whispered Nish, who came back just as Andy emerged from the darkness with the two kid dummies and plunked them down beside their parents.

Nish gave Travis a puzzled look.

"You'll see," said Travis. "You think you could get jackets and caps from the security guards? Maybe flashlights?"

Nish swallowed hard. "Alone?"

Travis looked at him, waiting.

Nish swallowed again. "I'll try."

He hurried off, past the minivan, past the Richard exhibit where he'd found the perfectly straight Love & Bennett stick,

and on to the partially closed door to the room where they had
found the guards.

He stopped to gather his courage. He breathed in twice,
deeply, then gritted his teeth, stepped up to the door, and pulled
it open.

The two security guards were sitting on the floor. Their feet
and hands were tied and tape was plastered over their mouths.
All he could see was their eyes: wondering, frightened, puzzled,
anxious.

He couldn't help himself. "Sorry, boys – looking for the Tie
Domi exhibit."

The two security guards looked at him as if he'd just
dropped in from outer space. They had just started their evening
snack when the robbers had come in. Luckily for Nish, both
had removed their uniform jackets and placed them over the
backs of folding chairs. One hat was hanging up, the other on
the floor. He grabbed the hats and jackets and looked around
for flashlights.

There was a small cupboard at the back of the room. He
opened it. Inside were several big, silver flashlights and a bullhorn, just like the ones used on television for armed stand-
offs. Perfect.

It was hard to carry everything. He had to put one cap on
his head, then he looped the jackets over one shoulder and gathered up two flashlights and the bullhorn. The only way he could
carry the second cap was to put the hard plastic peak in his
mouth and bite down.

He pulled the cap out of his mouth for a moment. "I'll try
not to slobber," he told the guards, who were still looking at him

as if he were crazy. He bit down again, and with his arms and hands and mouth full, waddled quickly back to where Travis and Andy were finishing up the tape job on the stairs. When the other boys saw what Nish was bringing, they grinned. "Perfect," said Andy.

Travis looked around. The angle was just right; anything seen from the stairs would have the dim light in the corridor behind it and only show up as a silhouette.

"Get the jackets and caps on Mom and Dad," Travis said.

The two other boys struggled to put the jackets on, then the caps. Nish had to pound one cap down onto Dad. "Fathead," he whispered.

They moved Mom and Dad, now "Police" Officers Mom and Dad, out into the light of the corridor. Then Travis took the two kid dummies – whom they had named Data and Sister – and placed them behind a low exhibit on the opposite side. Again, with dim light behind them and nothing but a sweeping flashlight in front, they might appear to be crouching officers, waiting. Travis hoped so.

"Nish," Travis said, "you and I'll have to work the dummies. Andy – we want your deepest voice for the loudspeaker."

Andy looked shocked. "What'll I say?"

"You'll know. Just make it convincing."

19

The whining of the power tool came to an abrupt stop. The silence was overwhelming – more frightening than anything Travis had experienced this scary evening.

The boys waited for several minutes, breathless, but there was nothing. No sound. No movement.

Travis could not understand what was happening. Were the robbers already gone? Was there another way out? He hadn't considered that possibility. The boys' whole plan depended on the crooks having to come back down the stairs when they discovered the elevator wasn't working.

"*Pssst!*" Travis called to Nish, and signalled for him to follow.

The two Screech Owls stepped carefully over the tape and ran quickly to the top of the stairs, where they crouched, waiting.

Travis thought he could hear something! A rustle. A grunt. The boys edged silently closer until they could peek into the vault.

Nish let out a slight gasp.

The robbers had only just got the Stanley Cup off its stand. The ponytail was holding a sack open and the smaller robber was lowering it in. They'd be leaving any moment!

Travis and Nish hurried back down the stairs, careful to step over the shin-pad tape once more. Travis gave Andy the thumbs-up to let him know everything was okay and to get ready. Nish scooted back to his post.

The robbers were moving along the upper hall now. The boys went silent. Nish held onto the dad dummy for dear life for fear the figure would fall and the flashlight clatter across the floor. Travis was afraid to breathe.

They could hear the robbers, angry.

"What the hell's going on?"

They had obviously pushed the elevator button and nothing had happened. Travis could hear the propped-open elevator door bouncing lightly back and forth as it tried to close, but the stick was holding it. The elevator was going nowhere.

"C'mon, we'll use the stairs."

Good, Travis thought, *exactly what we want.*

Travis's heart could have accompanied a rock band. It was pounding so hard he thought it might be echoing off the walls. He thought maybe he could hear Nish's heart as well. And Andy's.

In fact Nish was so afraid of making a sound his heart wasn't even beating. He was hugging the dad dummy and holding onto the flashlight, and he had shut his eyes so tight he swore he could hear his eyelids squeak. He imagined the robbers suddenly coming to a halt, one of them holding up his hand and saying to the other: *"Did you hear that? Sounded like a kid's eyelid, didn't it?"*

Andy was crouched down behind an exhibit, his thumb about to flick the switch on the bullhorn. He was praying the robbers would knock themselves out on the stairs after they hit the tape – anything so long as he didn't have to go through with Travis's plan. He imagined flicking the switch and standing up and nothing whatsoever coming out of his mouth. Either nothing at all or some high-pitched squeak as if he were still in kindergarten: *"Put your hands up, Mr. Bad Guy, or I'll tell the teacher on you!"*

But there was no more time for wild imaginings. The robbers were on the stairs. The big one, the one with the pony-tail, had the bulging sack over his back. The little one with the scar had a black bag – the power tools.

They came down quicker than Travis expected. A quarter of the way. Half way. Three quarters of the way, and they hit the tape together.

"Aaaaarrrrghhhhhhhhhh!!!" the ponytail shouted.

"Geeeez!!" screamed the scar-face.

20

The sound was like an explosion. Travis forgot all about his heart. He jumped up as the two robbers hit the tape. They fell face-first, the power tools clattering, the Stanley Cup ringing as it hit the hard floor of the lower hall.

The robbers rolled a couple of times before settling in a heap at the bottom. Both seemed out cold – for a moment. Then they started swearing – worse than Travis had ever heard on a hockey rink – and began moving.

"FACE DOWN ON THE FLOOR!" a huge voice boomed. "NNNNOOOOWWW!!"

Travis spun around, thinking for a moment that the police actually had come. But it was Andy – his voice as deep and powerful and commanding as Travis had ever heard in his life. He almost hit the floor face-first himself.

A big beam of impossibly bright light swept over the two bewildered, swearing robbers. It blinded them, then bounced about the room, sweeping quickly over the two kid dummies so it appeared, just for a fraction of a second, that there were more "cops" present than just the two standing in the entrance hall.

Nish was very effective with his flashlight. He used it to make it seem that there was movement and to show that there were people there, but never let it linger. Every time he bounced it away from the robbers he turned it quickly back on them again, straight into their eyes, so all they could see was what must have looked like one big car headlight coming at them. Travis started to do the same with his light.

"I SAID ON YOUR FACE. MOVE IT!!"

Both robbers did exactly as they were told. They rolled, groaning and swearing, over onto their stomachs, faces down toward the floor but still straining to look up.

All they saw was the blinding flashlights.

"BEND YOUR FEET UP!! HANDS BEHIND THE BACK!! RIGHT NOW, MISTER! MOVE!"

This was Travis's signal. His heart skipped as he moved out from the shadow of the stairs and approached the robbers from behind.

"FACES DOWN!!" Andy shouted in his deepest voice. His voice was filling the room. It frightened even Travis, who knew where it was coming from.

"DIG YOUR NOSES INTO THE FLOOR, AND NOWWW!!"

The robbers, still cursing, did as they were told. Travis, careful to stay directly behind them so they couldn't see, quickly taped their hands and feet together with a roll of shin-pad tape. He went through two rolls before the ponytailed one turned and caught a glimpse of him.

"What the hell?! It's a kid!!"

The scar-face also twisted to see, his eyes bulging. "Ehhh?! What the . . . ?"

When they realized the person doing the tying-up was Travis Lindsay, captain of the Screech Owls, not Chief of the Metropolitan Toronto Police Force, they began twisting like fish at the bottom of a boat. Neither could move his hands or feet, but they could still scream.

"You little . . ."

"You take this tape off right now, you little jerk – or else!!"

Nish came running up now, suddenly brave. He had the security officer's cap on and was waving the flashlight. He had Dad over his shoulder. He tossed him toward the robbers.

"Stay with them, Officer Dummy!" Nish ordered.

When the two robbers saw they had been fooled by a dummy, they began twisting and cursing even more.

Andy came running out from his hiding place holding the loudspeaker.

"NO SWEARING!" Andy ordered. That only made them curse all the more.

"Such mouths!" Nish said, shaking his head in a disapproving manner.

"Trav," he called. "You got any of that tape left?"

Travis nodded, pulled half-a-roll out of his pocket, and tossed it to Nish. Nish put down the flashlight and went over to the ponytail. Standing behind him, he pulled out a length of the tape and tried to fit it over the robber's screaming mouth.

"Now, now, now," Nish said in his best teacher's voice. "This is for your own good."

It took him several tries, but finally he hit the robber's mouth and the screaming and swearing was partly muffled. He continued to loop the tape around the robber's head, careful not to cover his nose, and soon he was silent, but still furiously squirming.

Nish moved over and did the same to the scar-face. Soon there was only the sound of the tape coming off the roll. The sound, Travis thought, of a hockey dressing room. How appropriate!

The two robbers were trussed and ready for pick-up. All they needed was the police to come – but Nish wasn't through. He was scrambling after the sack. He picked up his big flashlight and threw it to Travis.

"Work the spotlight!" he shouted.

Travis hadn't a clue what Nish meant.

Nish reached into the sack and pulled out the Stanley Cup. He checked it. A new dent, perhaps, but nothing more. He lifted it up and kissed it, just like the victorious NHL players do.

He then hoisted the Stanley Cup high over his head and began pretending he was skating about the hall with it. "My spotlight!" he yelled out. Travis turned on the flashlight and shone it on Nish. It *was* just like a spotlight!

Nish completed a circuit of the hall, blowing kisses into the stands, blowing kisses at the two squirming robbers, bowing, kissing the Stanley Cup.

He then took the cup and, very carefully, set it on the step behind the taped-up robbers. He kissed it one more time.

"Let's get outta here!" Nish said.

Travis had two more things to do. With Nish's flashlight, they went back down the hall to where the two security officers were still tied up and taped silent. They stared and made muffled sounds as the boys came in, but the three had no intention of loosening them, even if one was totally innocent.

Travis rooted around the room until he found a piece of cardboard and a black felt pen. Then he made a quick sign:

ONE OF THESE GUARDS WAS
WORKING FOR THE ROBBERS.

He turned and showed it to the guards. One looked fiercely at him, the other looked surprised at the other guard. Travis was pretty sure he knew which one was guilty, but he still couldn't take a chance. He propped up the sign on a chair and they left the room.

At the exit the guard had opened for the two robbers, Travis found a fire alarm and set it off. The security alarms were probably all disengaged, but the fire alarm still worked. It began to ring throughout the Hockey Hall of Fame and it would be ringing at the nearest fire hall. In a few moments fire trucks would begin arriving.

"Let's go," he said.

21

From the sound of the cheering, Travis could tell that the Toronto Towers were already on the ice. They were the home team, and their parents and fans had filled up the lower seats of Maple Leaf Gardens. This was to be the highlight of the Little Stanley Cup, and even a camera crew from TSN was here. Player introductions and floods between periods. The real thing.

And yet it couldn't compare to what Travis already felt inside. Travis and Nish and Andy had made it back before curfew. They had told Willie, who didn't believe them until Nish found the news channel and there was a brief report on a foiled break-in at the Hockey Hall of Fame. They made him swear he wouldn't tell anyone.

In the morning the attempted robbery was front-page news – complete with a composite sketch of the three youngsters who had apparently been involved somehow but had slipped away into the night. The descriptions had been given by one of

the tied-up security guards – Travis presumed the innocent one
– but the sketch of Travis looked nothing like him whatsoever.
Nor did the drawing of Andy. Nish, on the other hand, was . . .
well, Nish was Nish.

Muck had been reading the paper when they came down.
He had the story laid out on his lap and he kept looking at the
drawings and looking up at Nish. But Nish never let on. "Sleep
good, Coach?" he asked as he passed by.

If Muck suspected anything, he wasn't letting on. He didn't
speak to them until just before the game, when he pulled a piece
of paper out of his jacket pocket and announced, "I have a letter
to read to you."

Dear Screech Owls,

Please accept our sincere apologies for what we did to
you all. We are very sorry about what happened.

What we did was wrong and we know it. We don't really
know why we did it, just that it happened and we were very,
very lucky to be given another chance by the manager of
the Hockey Hall of Fame.

We hurt a lot of people by our actions. We hurt ourselves
by betraying those who trusted us: our parents, our coaches,
and our teammates. We hurt the Screech Owls by causing
the team to be short players when you were all counting on
us. We cost you all a chance to see the Leafs play.

We know we can't bring back the game, but we are all
going to try to earn this trust back. We hope one day you

will have us all back on the team, because that is where we want to be, more than anywhere else in the world. We love being Screech Owls and we're proud to be Screech Owls.

Thank you for listening to us.

Yours sincerely,

Larry Ulmar (Data)
Fahd Noorizadeh
Wilson Kelly

P.S. Beat those Towers!

Muck folded the letter, put it in his pocket, and walked out of the room without another word.

Travis pulled his sweater over his head, making the worst possible face at Nish as he was momentarily hidden from view. He pulled on his helmet and picked up his gloves.

"Let's go!" the captain of the Screech Owls shouted as he stood up.

22

Travis figured it was an impossible task. The Toronto Towers were ahead 3–1 by the end of the first period. The Screech Owls simply didn't have the depth on the bench. Nish was playing, and giving everything he had, but he was slowed down by his bad ankle and had been on for two of the Toronto goals.

Muck didn't seem alarmed. At the break he simply went over the forechecking plan on his little blackboard. "It's coming," Muck said. "It's coming."

In the second period a pass hit Travis on the shin pad. The puck bounced ahead and over the defenceman's sweeping stick, but the defender was quick enough to wrap an arm around Travis, blocking him from the puck.

No matter – Dmitri had it. He flew down the ice, faked a pass to Derek coming in from the left, and fired a shot along the ice that went in under the goaltender's stick. 3–2, Toronto Towers.

It remained 3–2 into the third. Travis looked toward Nish at the far end of the bench. He was bent over, holding his ankle, and there were tears falling off his cheek. He was in terrible pain but had said nothing. And Muck, standing behind him, hadn't noticed. When Muck touched the back of Nish's sweater, he jumped right over the boards. He was going to give everything he had.

Nish tried a rush and made it to centre. A Tower hit him and the puck lay, untouched, at centre ice, where Liz picked it up and made a magnificent (was it accidental?) spinnerama move that took her around a check and created a two-on-one with Andy Higgins.

Liz hit Andy inside the blueline and Andy tried the big slap shot that usually caused Muck to roll his eyes. But for once the stick connected perfectly. The puck blew right through the Towers' goaltender's glove. 3–3 – *tied*.

23

uck had one time-out and he called it the moment the Screech Owls tied the score. The players all gathered around him, waiting. Muck just stared at them.

"Just keep it up," Muck said.

That was all, *Just keep it up*. Why would he call a time-out? Travis wondered. Just to make the Towers think he had a master plan? Just to put them off? Travis had long ago given up trying to figure out Muck.

The referee's whistle blew. Travis's line was to take the face-off. Nish was on, wincing as he stood waiting for the puck to drop. Travis looked back at him and had never been so proud of his crazy friend.

Derek won the face-off and blocked off the Toronto centre. Travis was able to get his stick on the puck and slide it back to Nish, who fired low and hard, but not at the net. Instead, the puck flew at Dmitri, who simply turned his stick blade down and let the puck hit it and glance straight into the open net.

4–3, Screech Owls!

The Owls pounced on Dmitri, and also Nish, who had made the play.

"Watch it!" Nish kept shouting, to no avail. He didn't want anyone dumping him on his bad ankle. He shouldn't have been scurrying around the night before at the Hockey Hall of Fame, Travis thought. He should have been in bed, resting, just as Muck wanted.

The Owls held the lead until the final minute, when the Toronto Towers pulled their goaltender for a face-off in the Owls' end.

"Don't Panic!" Muck hollered from the bench. He had his hands over his mouth to make a megaphone. He sounded like Andy on the portable loudspeaker.

But they did. Derek lost the face-off, the puck went out to the point, Travis tried to block the shot and the defender simply stepped around him as Travis slid out past the blueline. It was now six-on-four for the Towers. The defenceman shot, the puck fell in a scramble of players, and a Toronto player put it in on the backhand.

4–4, tie game.

Dmitri had one more chance before the horn went, but lost the puck on the deke. The Towers were halfway back down the ice when time ran out.

Overtime.

24

can't!" Nish said, his voice cracking.

Muck was leaning over his best defenceman. He had just asked Nish if he could take another shift. Muck had now seen the pain Nish was in, and he wouldn't make him. He patted his back while Nish buried his head below the boards.

Derek and Travis and Dmitri started the overtime, with Willie and Lars on defence. They didn't have Nish anymore. They didn't have Data. They didn't have Wilson. They didn't have Fahd.

The puck had barely dropped when it was over. Derek poked the puck ahead, but the Towers' best defenceman picked it up, stepped around Derek and pounded the puck off the boards so it floated in behind Willie, who turned too slowly to catch the swift winger breaking in. It was a design play, a plan, and the Towers had pulled it off perfectly.

The winger came flying in on Jennie, who in desperation lunged toward him, swinging her stick to poke-check him as she went down. But he had too much reach and too good an angle, and in a flash he was in behind her, dropping the puck in the net as if it were the easiest task in the world.

Maple Leaf Gardens went crazy! The Towers' bench emptied and the team piled on their scorer and their goaltender. Coaches, managers, parents leapt over the boards – the scene was as crazy as when a team wins the Stanley Cup.

The Screech Owls were crushed. They came and comforted Jennie, who could only shrug. No one blamed her, of course. It was a *team* loss. Muck wrapped a big arm around her neck and hugged her, face-mask and all. With her mask still on, no one could tell if she was crying.

But you could tell with Nish. He was limping on the ice, his ankle stiff and useless. Tears were rolling down his face and dropping onto his sweater. He couldn't help it. He didn't even bother wiping the tears away.

The Little Stanley Cup was on the ice, and Doug Gilmour – the Leafs' captain! – was coming on to present it. Travis looked at Doug Gilmour, who caught his eye and gave him a wink and a thumbs-up sign. *He had recognized him.*

They handed the Little Stanley Cup to Doug Gilmour, and he presented it to the Toronto Towers' captain, who lifted it over his head to the roar of the crowd. Triumphant, he began skating with it around the rink.

Travis felt a little tap on his shoulder. He turned. It was Nish, still crying, but now smiling through the tears as they both watched the Towers' captain hoisting the Little Stanley Cup.

"I prefer the original, myself," said Nish.

Travis couldn't help himself. He began to laugh. Andy Higgins, standing close by, began laughing as well.

THE END

The Screech Owls'
Northern Adventure

1

"'m gonna hurl!"

Five rows away, Travis Lindsay could hear Nish moaning into a pillow. He could hear him over the tinny pound of the Walkman hanging loosely off Data's bent ears as he dozed in the next seat. He could hear him over the clatter of the serving cart and the shouting coming from Derek and Dmitri as they played a game of hearts in the row behind. He could even hear Nish over the unbelievable roar of the engines.

How could anyone sleep at a time like this? Travis wondered, glancing at Data. This was the first time Travis had flown, and it hadn't been at all what he had imagined. This was no ten-minute helicopter lift at the fall fair; nor was it like the big, smooth passenger jet his father took once a month to business meetings in Montreal. This was three solid hours of howling engines, air pockets, and broken cloud. They were headed, it seemed, for the North Pole. They had all driven to Val d'Or, Quebec, the day before, and from there it was 1,500 kilometres further north by air to their final destination: Waskaganish, a native village on the shore of James Bay.

They were on a Dash 8, an aircraft that Data – who knew everything about computers and National Hockey League statistics, but nothing whatsoever about life – claimed could take off and land in the palm of your hand. This was an exaggeration, of course, but Travis had felt it wasn't far off when the cramped fifty-seat plane taxied out onto the runway, revved the engines hard once, and seemed to shoot straight off the ground into the low clouds.

Travis had barely taken a second breath by the time the plane rose through the clouds and into the sunshine hidden beyond. It was as if the cabin of the plane were being painted with melted gold. Blinded by the sudden light, Data lowered the window-shade, but Travis had reached across and raised it again. He wanted to see everything.

The pilot had come on the intercom and warned them that the flight might be bumpy and that he'd be leaving the seatbelt sign on. The flight attendant would have to wait before bringing out the breakfast cart.

The coaches and several parents, Travis's included, were sitting toward the back of the plane. Data's and Wilson's and Fahd's parents were all there. Perhaps they wanted to make sure nothing went wrong this time the way it had in Toronto.

The three boys hadn't missed a game or practice since Muck let them come back at the end of a month-long suspension over the unfortunate shoplifting incident at the Hockey Hall of Fame. They'd apologized to the team and they'd missed a key tournament, and eventually Muck figured they'd learned their lesson. Travis knew they had. He'd talked to Data on the telephone almost every night during his suspension, and he knew that several times Data had been in tears.

Jesse Highboy was sitting directly across from Travis. Beside him were his father and mother and his Aunt Theresa, the Chief of Waskaganish. No one called her Theresa or even Mrs. Ottereyes – they all called her "Chief." She had come down to Val d'Or to welcome the Screech Owls, and now she was bringing them all to Northern Quebec for the First Nations Pee Wee Hockey Tournament, which would feature, for the first time, a non-native peewee hockey team: the Screech Owls.

Jesse's father had set it up. He had met with the team and parents and talked to them about the chance of a lifetime. The hockey would be a part of the trip, he had stressed, but the real reward would come in getting to experience the North and the native culture. All they had to do was get there. The people of Waskaganish were so pleased with the idea that they'd offered to put everyone up, players and parents, free of charge. No wonder so many hands had gone up when Mr. Highboy asked for a show of interest.

The Owls had held bottle drives and organized car washes, and the parents had worked so many bingos that Mr. Lindsay celebrated the end of them by burying his smoke-filled "bingo clothes" in a deep hole behind the garage. The team had read up on the North and were excited about what they had learned: the northern lights, caribou, traplines, the midnight sun.

"It's *spring*, not summer!" Willie Granger, the team trivia expert, had pointed out to those Owls, like Nish, who figured they'd never have to go to bed and could stay up all night long.

"Day and night are just about equal this time of year – same as where we live." But no one expected anything else to be the same. No one.

Perhaps, Travis wondered, this was why Nish had been acting so oddly. In the weeks leading up to the trip, Nish had kidded Jesse mercilessly.

"Should I bring a bow and arrow?" Nish had asked. "Will we be living in teepees?"

Some of it had been pretty funny, Travis had to admit, but it left him feeling a bit uneasy. Travis knew that the general rule of a hockey dressing room was "anything goes," and certainly Jesse had handled Nish's cracks easily, laughing and shooting back insults, but Travis still found it intriguing that no one other than Nish took such shots.

No one expected teepees. But beyond that they didn't really know what to expect.

Chief Ottereyes and Air Creebec, the airline that set up the charter, had put on a special breakfast for the Owls. Once the turbulence had settled enough, the flight attendant handed out a breakfast the likes of which no Screech Owl, Jesse Highboy excepted, had ever seen. There were tiny things like tea biscuits that Chief Ottereyes explained were "bannock – just like we cook up out on the trapline." And there was fish, but not cooked like anything Travis had ever seen at a fish-and-chip shop. This fish was dry and broke apart easily. At first Travis wasn't too sure, but when he tasted it he thought it was more like *candy* than fish. "Smoked whitefish," Chief Ottereyes said. "Smoked and cured with sugar."

"I got no knife and fork!" Nish had shouted from his seat.

Chief Ottereyes laughed: "You've got hands, haven't you?"

"Yeah."

"Clamp 'em over your mouth, then!" Wilson had called from the other side of the plane.

"This is traditional Cree food!" Chief Ottereyes had leaned forward and told Nish.

"I'll take a traditional Egg McMuffin, thank you!" Nish called back.

He wouldn't try the food. Instead, he'd dug down into the carry-on bag he had stuffed beneath his seat and hauled out three chocolate bars and sat stuffing his face with one hand while he used the other to hold his nose as though he couldn't stand the smell of the smoked fish.

They had just been finishing up this unusual breakfast when the plane rattled as if it had just hit a pothole. The "fasten your seatbelt" light flashed and the pilot had come on the intercom to tell the attendant to stop picking up the trays and hang on, they were about the enter some more choppy air.

"I'M GONNA HURL!"

With the plane starting to buck, the attendant was unable to move forward to help Nish in case he was, in fact, going to be sick. Instead, she passed ahead a couple of Gravol air-sickness pills, a juice to wash them down, and a barf bag in case the worst happened. Nish took the pills and soon began moaning.

After a while, when the plane began to settle again, Nish called out, "Can I get a blanket?"

Travis thought Nish was acting like a baby. The attendant handed over a blanket, and the players behind Nish tossed theirs over, too. He wrapped himself tight and pressed his face into the pillow, then closed his eyes and continued to moan.

The pilot took the plane to a higher altitude, and the flight once again smoothed out. Derek and Dmitri's card game started up again, the attendant completed her collection of the breakfast trays, and Nish moaned on.

Data stood up in the aisle. "I think he needs a few more blankets!" he called out, grinning mischievously. "I can still hear him."

Blankets and pillows by the dozen headed in Data's direction. Even Muck, shaking his head in mock disgust, handed his over. Data, now helped by Wilson, stacked them on poor Nish until he could be neither seen nor heard.

"There," Data announced. "That ought to hold him."

Nish never budged. Travis figured he must have gone to sleep. He hoped he was able to breathe all right through the blankets, but it was nice not to have to listen to him any longer. Travis turned toward the window and thought about the tournament and how he would play. He felt great these days. Hockey was a funny game: sometimes when you didn't feel well but played anyway, you had the most wonderful game; sometimes when you felt fantastic, you played terribly.

He tried to imagine himself playing in Waskaganish, but he couldn't. He couldn't picture the rink. He couldn't imagine the village. He could not, for the first time in his life, even imagine the players on the other side. Would they be good players? Rough? Smart? Would they have different rules up here? No, they couldn't have. He was getting tired, too tired to think . . .

"*. . . put your seats in the upright position, fasten your tables back, and ensure that all carry-on luggage is safely stowed under the seat in front of you. Thank you.*"

The announcement and the sudden sense that something was happening woke Travis with a start. He could hear seats being moved, tables being fastened, excitement rising.

"I can see the village!" Derek shouted from behind.

Travis leaned toward the window. He could see James Bay stretching away like an ocean, the ice along the shore giving way to water that was steel grey and then silver where the sun bounced on the waves.

The plane was beginning to rock again. The plane came down low over the water, then began to bank back toward the village. Travis could see a hundred or more houses. He could see a church, and a large yellow building like a huge machine shed. The rink? He could see the landing strip on the right: one long stretch of ploughed ground.

Just then, they hit a huge air pocket. The plane banked sharply and seemed to slide through the air sideways before righting itself with a second tremendous jolt.

"HELP MEEEEEEEE!!"

Travis could hear Nish screaming over the roar of the engines and the landing gear grinding down into position. No one could go to him. They were landing.

"I'M DYINNNGGG!" Nish screamed from beneath his blankets.

The big plane came down and hammered into the ground, bounced twice, and settled, the engines roaring as the pilot immediately began to brake. The howl was extraordinary.

Nish moaned and cried until the plane slowed and turned abruptly off the landing strip toward an overgrown shed that had a sign, WASKAGANISH, over the doorway. There was a big crowd gathered. It seemed the whole town was out to greet the Screech Owls.

"HELP MEEEE!!" Nish moaned. Travis had never heard such a pathetic sound.

Finally, as the plane came to a halt, the attendant got up and began pulling off Nish's blankets, digging him out, until his big, red-eyed face was blinking up at her in surprise.

"I thought we'd crashed," he said, "and I was the only survivor." Everyone on the plane broke up.

The attendant just shook her head. Travis couldn't tell if she was amused or disgusted.

"You wouldn't want to survive," the Chief told him. "You'd never make it out of the bush alive, my friend."

Nish looked up, blinking. "I *wouldn't*?"

"Of course not," she said, then reached over and pinched Nish's big cheek.

"The Trickster eats fat little boys like you!"

Nish looked blank. What *was* she talking about?

2

ravis felt the difference as soon as the door of the Dash 8 opened. It was like walking into a rink on a hot day in August. The unexpected cold was shocking. The Screech Owls had started the journey in spring-like weather, but it seemed now they had travelled all they way back into winter.

Quickly pulling on their team jackets, the Owls spilled out of the plane and down the steps, where they were met by a greeting party the likes of which none of them had ever imagined. People stood in the backs of pick-up trucks, banging their fists on the cab roofs while those inside the cabs honked their horns. Young men and women revved their snowmobile engines. Some two hundred villagers stood about in thick winter clothing, stomping their feet to keep warm and applauding, the laughter and shouts of the people of Waskaganish hanging above their heads in quick clouds of winter breath.

A gang of youngsters moved toward the Screech Owls. They had to be a hockey team, Travis figured; they wore matching jackets with an animal face on it. But it was an animal he had never seen before. It looked a bit like a bear, a bit like a wolf, a bit like a skunk. The letters underneath the face (if they even were letters) meant nothing to him.

Giggling, the Cree team moved to one side to reveal one shorter player carrying a huge boom box. He hit a button and the air filled with the pounding lyrics of the rock group Queen:

We will,
We will,
ROCK YOU!

Everyone laughed – everyone but the Screech Owls, who didn't know what to make of this. It seemed a great joke to all the locals, including Chief Ottereyes, who made her way to the front of the gathering and held up her right hand. Instantly, the boom box was switched off.

"What I'd give for that kind of authority," Muck muttered just behind Travis. He could hear some of the parents laughing, but they obviously didn't know Muck, Travis thought. When Muck had a certain look in his eyes, he didn't even need to raise his hand to bring the Screech Owls' dressing room to full attention.

The Chief turned to address the Screech Owls. She seemed to be smiling right at Travis.

"The people of Waskaganish welcome the Screech Owls to our village. Please consider our home your home for the next five days."

The villagers applauded in agreement. Even the team was clapping, Travis noticed. Perhaps they weren't so bad, after all.

The Chief then spoke in Cree. It was a language Travis had never heard before, and every so often the villagers laughed as if it were some great inside joke.

Nish, too, was laughing.

"What's she saying, Data?" he whispered.

"How the heck would I know?"

"You're the only one on the team who speaks Klingon, aren't you?"

Chief Ottereyes returned to English. "Could we have the Screech Owls' captains come forward, please?"

Travis felt a slight nudge at his back. It was Muck, gently encouraging. Travis stepped forward and signalled for his assistant captains, Derek and Nish, to follow him. Nish seemed extremely reluctant, shaking his head and giggling nervously as he pushed through the protection of the Screech Owls crowd.

"And the captains of the Wolverines . . . ?" the Chief added.

Wolverines? Was *that* the animal on their jackets? Travis had never seen a wolverine.

A lanky young man shrugged and moved forward. On the arm of his jacket was the number 7, the same number Travis wore. On the other arm the name "Jimmy" was stitched.

Behind the Wolverines' captain came the three assistants. Travis studied them quickly. One, a big, thick kid with a bit of a scowl. The second, a skinny kid with a Toronto Maple Leafs cap on backwards, and, underneath the cap, fur earmuffs. And the third . . . a *girl!* Travis hadn't noticed her. He was surprised, but he knew he shouldn't be. The Screech Owls' previous captain had been Sarah Cuthbertson, and she had been their best player. And they'd had Sareen in goal back then, and now they had Liz and Chantal and Jennie. But still, he hadn't expected to find a girl on a team up here in the North. He thought it would be more like when his dad played and his mother had never even learned how to hold a hockey stick. He didn't know why he thought it would be that way here. He just did.

"Travis Lindsay and Jimmy Whiskeyjack are the two team captains," Chief Ottereyes announced. "And Jimmy has a gift for Travis."

Travis didn't know how to react. A gift? He hadn't brought anything to give in return.

Jimmy Whiskeyjack reached inside his pocket, withdrew a small flat blue box, and handed it to Travis. Travis took it, and then took Jimmy's free hand, which was also extended. Travis shook, wondering if his grip was strong enough.

Travis looked up at Chief Ottereyes. She was smiling encouragement. "Go ahead," she said. "Open it up so we can all see."

Travis knew everyone was looking at him. He lifted the lid and stared at the object inside. He hadn't a clue what it was: a twig tied in a circle containing a loose web of string, and feathers tied to the side.

He looked up at the Chief. "Go ahead, Travis. Take it out," she told him.

Travis removed the strange object and held it up. Some of the Screech Owls' parents *oooh*ed and *ahhh*ed. It was beautiful. The sun danced in the colours of the feathers.

"It's a dream catcher," Jimmy Whiskeyjack said.

Chief Ottereyes explained. "It's an Ojibway dream catcher. There's an old legend that says one of these will catch all your dreams. The good ones pass through into your future. The bad ones are caught, and when the sun comes out in the morning, it destroys them."

"*Looks like a goldfish net*," Nish hissed to Derek. Travis heard, and hoped no one else did. He wished Nish was still buried in blankets.

"It was made by Rachel Highboy," the Chief announced, "the Wolverines' assistant captain."

Everyone applauded the slim girl who had stepped out with Jimmy Whiskeyjack. She blushed and looked at Travis, who was still holding up the dream catcher for all to see. Travis felt funny inside. The effects of the plane ride maybe. He hoped he wouldn't have to say anything.

He didn't. On a cue from Chief Ottereyes, Jimmy Whiskeyjack stepped forward and shook Travis's hand again. Jimmy then stepped past him and shook hands with Derek and Nish. The other assistants from the Wolverines came to shake hands as well.

Travis took Rachel Highboy's hand and was surprised by how small it felt in his. No way could she be a player, Travis thought. She held on.

Travis looked up. She had large dark eyes and her long black hair was whipping in the wind. She smiled, and Travis felt like he was still in the plane, with the bottom dropping out of it.

3

ravis had heard about getting your sea legs –
when you could finally stand on the deck of
a ship and roll with the waves instead of hang-
ing weak-kneed and sick over the railing – but after the plane
ride he had to wonder if Nish was having trouble getting back
his *land* legs.

They had been on the ground for more than three hours,
but Nish was still wobbly. That was fine when they had just been
getting set up with their billets – Travis and Nish were placed
with the Wolverines' captain, Jimmy Whiskeyjack, and his
family – but it was quite another matter now that they were all
out on the ice, about to play their first game of the First Nations
Pee Wee Hockey Tournament.

The Screech Owls had drawn the Moose Factory Mighty
Geese as their first opponents. The Owls would have an easy
time of it, Jimmy had predicted as he helped Travis carry his
equipment over to the rink. The Mighty Geese didn't have
much of a team; they didn't even have a proper rink to practice

or play in. Instead they played outside, and the last time the Wolverines had gone to Moose Factory, they had been forced to cancel the third period on account of the wind. It was knocking players over.

None of the teams over on the Ontario side of James Bay were all that good, Jimmy continued. They were all Cree, but the Ontario Cree were very poor and didn't have much to spend on hockey. The Quebec Cree were better off. It was on the Quebec side, through land owned by the Quebec Cree and Inuit, that the big rivers flowed into James Bay and where the huge hydro-electric dams had been built. They had opposed the projects, he explained, but when they realized they couldn't stop them, they made a deal with the governments that had given them things like airstrips and new houses and a school and a brand-new hockey rink. They had *two* Zambonis, just like Maple Leaf Gardens!

"If one breaks down," Jimmy had explained, "you can't just drive a new one in through the bush."

The ice was terrific. As usual, Travis let the Owls' two goaltenders – Jenny Staples and Jeremy Weathers – lead the team out onto the ice, but he made sure he was next. And while Jenny and Jeremy both skated straight to the near net to place their water bottles, Travis burst for centre ice, his head down so he could see the marks his skates left as they dug in deep. Good old Mr. Dillinger: another perfect sharpening job, with the blades sharp enough that when he cornered on new ice they made a sound like bacon frying.

The other Screech Owls came out behind him. Dmitri Yakushev, the Owls' best skater, dug down deep and flew around the new ice. Derek, Gordie, Data, big Andy Higgins, Liz, who was fast becoming one of the team's smoothest skaters, Lars – all leaned deep into their turns to produce that sweet clean cut and spray that is possible only on fresh-flooded ice.

After looking around at the others, Travis found Nish, flat on his back in the Owls' far corner. He dug in and raced around, stopping in a one-skate spray.

Nish just lay there, staring straight up.

"What the heck are you doing?" Travis asked.

Nish blinked once. "*Stretching,*" he said.

Out by the red line at centre ice, Travis began his own stretches, alone and quiet, the way he liked it. While he stretched, he studied the Moose Factory team. Their sweaters were all right, with a laughing goose on the front that looked a bit like Daffy Duck. But no matching socks. And the equipment! Travis had never seen a team so poorly outfitted. The Mighty Geese were lined up at the blueline to take shots, and two of the players were sharing a stick, one of them waiting until the other had shot and then throwing the stick to him when he raced back.

The referee called for the two captains, and Travis skated over. When the captain of the Mighty Geese joined him, Travis saw he was one of the players who had been sharing the stick.

"Shake hands, boys," the referee said. "Let's have a good, clean game, okay?"

The Mighty Geese captain stared as Travis slapped his stick, not his hand, into his opponent's outstretched palm.

Travis had done it without even thinking. He had brought three sticks with him, all brand new, but he didn't need all three.

"You're short a stick," Travis said. "Take this. I brought extras."

The other captain stared at it, tried it once (he shot left, the same as Travis), then nodded. He took Travis's hand and shook hard.

"Thanks a lot."

"Just don't score too many goals," Travis said, and grinned.

The captain smiled back. He had two broken front teeth. Travis wanted to ask what had happened. Was it a puck? A stick? Not likely – everyone here wore a full face-mask. It had to be from something other than hockey. A fall? . . . A fist?

Muck seemed concerned. Before the actual face-off, he called the Owls over for a quick huddle by the bench. He usually did this only when they had a big game, a championship, to decide, but this time he seemed every bit as serious.

"No fancy stuff, now," he said. "I want to see a team out there, not fifteen individual superstars."

By the end of his first shift, Travis knew exactly what Muck meant. The Screech Owls were badly outclassing the Mighty Geese. The Owls were better skaters, better positional players, better passers and shooters, and they had three good lines, whereas the Geese only had the one, centred by the captain with Travis's stick.

Nish couldn't resist. You put Nish on the ice against a weak lineup, and it was as if he'd had too much sugar on his cereal. Wobbly-legged or not, he couldn't help himself. He picked up the puck at the blueline and skated, *backwards*, into his own end and around the net past Jennie, who'd been given the first start. He then slipped it through the other captain's skates, and came hard down the ice, with Dmitri on one side charging fast.

Nish turned backwards as he reached the last Mighty Geese defenceman and attempted the "spinnerama," a move Nish claimed had come to him in a daydream during music class but which Willie Granger said had been used in the NHL by everyone from Bobby Orr to Denis Savard before Nish was even born.

It didn't matter to Nish. He believed he had invented it, and he had certainly invented this version of it. He spun directly in front of the defender, lost his footing, and crashed, butt first, into the backing-up defenceman. Both went down. Travis heard the scream of the poor defenceman as Nish's full weight landed on his chest and they slid in a pile past the puck, left sitting there for Travis as if it were glued to the ice.

Dmitri gave one quick rap on the ice with the heel of his stick and Travis cuffed the puck quickly across. Dmitri one-timed his shot into the open side of the Mighty Geese's net to the shriek of the referee's whistle.

First shift, 1–0 Screech Owls!

Travis threw his arms around Dmitri as Dmitri spun around behind the net, his arms raised in triumph. They smashed into the boards together and felt the crush of their teammates hitting them. Travis could hear, and feel, Nish, and there was no mistaking the whine in his voice.

"They better give me an assist on that one – I set it up!"

Travis could see the referee out of the corner of his eye, and he didn't like what he saw. The ref's arms were crossing back and forth down low, the sign of a goal being waved off. And now he was raising one hand and pointing with the other at the crush of Owls in the corner. The whistle blew again.

"*No goal?*" Travis called out. The scrum of players broke, all turning to look at the referee.

"*You're outta here, Number 4!*" the referee shouted as he closed in on the celebrating Screech Owls. "*Two minutes for interference!*"

"*What the h–?*"

The curse was barely out of Nish's mouth when up went the arm again, and again the whistle blew.

"*And two more for unsportsmanlike conduct!*"

Travis looked at Nish. His face was scrunched up like a game's worth of used shinpad tape, but at least his big mouth was shut.

Nish got into the penalty box, and the Mighty Geese went ahead when a shot from the point took a funny bounce off their captain's stick – the stick Travis had given to him – the puck dribbling in behind a flopping, scrambling Jennie.

Nish got out on the goal. He skated over as if he were dragging the Zamboni behind him, and never even lifted his head to see what Muck was thinking. He knew. He was in the doghouse. Without being told he moved down the bench and took a place on the very end.

Travis got a tap on the back of his shoulder and leapt over the boards onto the ice with Dmitri and Derek. They knew what to do. Travis won the face-off back to Data, Data clipped it off the boards to a breaking Dmitri – and Dmitri swept around the Mighty Geese defenceman so fast the defenceman fell straight backwards as his feet tangled. Dmitri went in and deked twice, sending the goaltender down and entirely out of the net, and then he roofed the puck so high he broke the goalie's water battle open. It was like a fountain bursting behind the empty net.

Wolverines 1, Screech Owls 1.

Next shift out for Travis, Dmitri's speed caught the Mighty Geese on a bad line change, and the Screech Owls went ahead to stay. They went on to win 5–2, and when the two teams shook hands at the end, the captain slammed his stick into Travis's shin pads, a salute of thanks for the stick. Travis couldn't help but note again that several Mighty Geese had no gloves on. They had to be sharing gloves. No wonder the Owls had caught them short on line changes.

Travis could hear the crowd applauding them as they skated off. He looked up and saw the Wolverines' assistant standing on a bench, clapping. *Rachel*. He yanked his helmet off, then began pushing his hair down. It was wet, and he worried that it was sticking up where it shouldn't be.

4

That night there was a banquet to celebrate the start of the First Nations Pee Wee Hockey Tournament. The Screech Owls, all in team jackets, white turtlenecks, and dark pants, were seated at one long table to the side. Muck, the assistant coaches, and Mr. Dillinger, the team manager, sat at the end nearest the head table, and Travis, Data, Jesse, and Nish were at the far end. But it still wasn't far enough away for Travis.

Nish had brought some of his candy stash with him, and laid it out on his plate: a Caramilk bar, a couple of green licorice twists, a Twinkie, a pair of Reese peanut-butter cups.

"A balanced diet," he announced as he laid it all out and pointed deliberately to the licorice. "Right down to my greens."

What had got into Nish?

Chief Ottereyes had announced that a traditional Cree feast would be held at the community hall. There were Cree drummers pounding as the eight teams playing in the tournament had entered: the Screech Owls, the Wolverines, the Mighty Geese, the Northern Lights, the Caribou, the Trappers, the Belugas, and the Maple Leafs. (Jesse Highboy had pointed out that there were no maple trees this far north, but they picked up the Toronto Maple Leaf broadcasts by satellite.) The Screech Owls were the only non-native team. The Mighty Geese were the only group without team jackets.

The banquet opened with a long Cree prayer recited by an elder, then Chief Ottereyes talked a bit about life along James Bay. It was a speech clearly meant for the visitors from the South. She talked about the history of the area, a history that white people like to date from 1611, when the British explorer Henry Hudson sailed into this bay and anchored at the mouth of the Rupert River, "which you can see for yourself if you just step outside the front door here," she added. The Crees, however, preferred to say that 1611 was the year they discovered the white man.

The Chief told them the Crees had had to learn to accept other languages and other religions and customs, and that the visitors should feel free to ask any questions they might have about how the Cree lived in the North. "Tonight," she said, "you will be eating traditional Cree food. This is the diet we have lived on for centuries – and we're still here, so enjoy."

She sat down to great applause, no one clapping louder than the Screech Owls. They began serving the meal immediately, starting with bannock. Nish, however, would have nothing to do with it.

"You can't eat just junk," Travis warned.

"You'll make yourself sick again," Jesse added.

"I'll make myself sick if I have to watch you people eat," Nish snapped back.

The feast proceeded: huge bowls of boiled potatoes, moose stew, caribou steaks, cheese, smoked whitefish, fried trout. At one point, a large bowl was carried past the Screech Owls that seemed, at first glance, to have a small hand sticking up from it.

"GROSS!" Nish shouted before Travis could even point it out to Jesse.

"*What is it?*" Travis hissed at Jesse.

Jesse Highboy was laughing. He stood up and excused himself as he picked up the bowl from the next table. Inside was, indeed, a small hand sticking up. An arm and a wrist and a . . . *paw*.

"Beaver," Jesse said, matter-of-factly.

"BEAVER?" Nish howled. "WHAT'S NEXT . . . SKUNK?"

Travis cringed. People were staring. Some were laughing at Nish. Some, like Rachel Highboy, were definitely not impressed.

Jesse handled it perfectly. "Beaver is a very special food here," he said.

"I thought you trapped beaver for fur," Data said.

"We do. But even if no one in the world wore fur coats, we'd still trap beaver. It's our food up here, same as cattle and chickens are your food down south. You think the original natives went after beaver so they could wear fancy fur coats?"

Data had clearly never thought about this. Neither had Travis. He had presumed trapping was wrong because it hurt. But as Jesse had once said, did he think that cows and chickens *volunteered* for McDonald's?

"I'm gonna hurl!" Nish said, opening up his Caramilk and laughing a bit too loudly. Travis glanced down the table. He could see Muck was watching. He did not look happy.

Jesse tried another approach. "Look, Nish, do you like crackle?

"Crackle?"

"Yeah, you know, the hard outside when your mom cooks a pork roast."

"Oh, that. Yeah, you bet, I *love* it!"

Jesse signalled to a woman who was carrying a tray to the head table. She stopped and smiled as Jesse stood, checked the tray, then helped himself to a plate piled high with what seemed like slices of bacon that were all fat and no meat.

Jesse took a fork and placed a slice carefully on Nish's plate right beside the licorice twists – Nish's *greens*. He stood back: "See what you think of ours."

Nish sniffed, then nodded happily. "*This* I can relate to," he said.

He picked up his knife and fork, cut a piece off, placed it in his mouth, and chewed happily.

"First rate," Nish pronounced. "My compliments to the chef."

"What about to the hunter?" Jesse asked.

Nish opened his eyes, blinking. "You *hunt* pigs up here?"

"Who said it was pig?"

"You did – pork crackle."

"Call it crackle if you like," Jesse said, "but it isn't pork."

Nish stopped chewing. "What is it then?"

Jesse turned to the woman carrying the tray. "Tell him," he said. "He won't believe me."

The woman smiled at Nish. "Moose nostrils," she said. "Would you like some more?"

Nish looked as if he was about to pass out.

"*I'm gonna hurl*," he repeated, spitting his food out onto his plate.

Muck had seen enough. He got up and walked straight down the aisle toward Nish, who winced when he saw him coming.

"Outta here, Nishikawa," Muck ordered.

There could be no fooling. When Muck used that tone, you jumped. When Muck used last names, you jumped twice as fast. Nish scrambled to his feet and, with Muck at his elbow, was escorted out of the banquet room.

5

Travis had never seen Nish so quiet. They had all returned to their billets, and the Whiskeyjacks had put out hot chocolate and cookies for the boys, but Nish was hardly even sipping his.

Travis had no idea what Muck had said to Nish, but he knew Muck wouldn't have minced his words. Nish was clearly out of sorts. As they'd washed up in the bathroom, he'd told Travis he wished he'd never come. "If there was a road outta here," he said, "I'd hitchhike."

"You haven't even given it a chance," Travis said.

"It sucks."

"It's just different."

"Gimme a break. No movie theatres, no McDonald's, no corner stores, no buses, no cable TV, no video arcade, not even a pathetic T-shirt for me to buy."

"There's more to going different places than getting a T-shirt."

Nish made a big face. "This is *backwards*, man. Open your eyes. We're in the Stone Age here – the Ice Age by the feel of it."

There was no point in arguing. They went out and sat with Jimmy Whiskeyjack and his big family – father, mother, grandmother, two sisters, and three younger brothers – and drank hot chocolate and talked while Nish kept looking at the TV in the corner as if he wished he could turn it on just by staring at it.

Normally, that's what Travis would have been doing, too, but the Whiskeyjacks showed no inclination whatsoever to turn to the TV. Instead of sitting in a half circle around it, they sat in a full circle around the kitchen table. The younger kids played and listened, and Travis and Jimmy – but not Nish – talked a bit about the hockey tournament. Most of the talk, however, came from the grandmother, translated either by Jimmy's mother or father.

In this house, the grandmother was like the TV. They all stared at her and listened as if she were some special program they'd been allowed to stay up and watch.

It was fascinating. She and her husband had both trapped, and six of her nine children had been born in the bush, as she had been before them. Through her daughter, Jimmy's mother, she told how two of them had died and how they had buried the babies in the bush and marked the graves, and how they would go back to visit them every year, right up until 1979.

The old woman took a long, long pause. Travis couldn't help but ask: "Why 1979?"

Jimmy's mother answered. There were tears in her eyes. "That's when they flooded my parents' trapline."

"Flooded?"

"The dams," Jimmy explained. "The hydro dams. The graves are under sixty feet of water."

"Didn't anybody tell them there were graves there?"

Travis's question made Jimmy's parents laugh. They translated this to the grandmother, and she shook her head angrily.

"We tried," explained Jimmy's father. "But they didn't even tell us they were going to do it."

The old woman clearly did not want to dwell on this part of her story. She launched into a tale that soon had everyone laughing again, but as Jimmy's father translated, Travis realized it was really about her family almost starving to death.

The grandmother told how, one year, the beaver had all but vanished from their trapline, and her husband had left her alone with the children while he followed the trail of the caribou herd, hoping to return with food before the little they had left ran out.

He did not come back in time. The food was just about gone. Christmas was coming and she had nothing to give the children – usually she would have bought some sweets at the Hudson's Bay store and hidden them until Christmas Day.

Christmas Eve it had snowed. And when they woke the next morning, the sun was bright and the new snow sparkled like white gold, so bright they had to squint when they turned back the flap of the tent. The old woman told her children that it had snowed sugar during the night: a Christmas present for them. She made them line up at the doorway, and then she took a spoon, went out into the snow, and very carefully scooped some up. She brought it back and told the oldest child to close his eyes. He did, and when she gave him his present he licked his lips, saying it was the most delicious snow he had ever tasted.

She then did the same thing for each of the younger ones, who were already waiting with mouths open and eyes closed.

"It really tasted just like sugar," said Jimmy's mother. "I can still taste it today."

Later in the day her husband returned with his sled piled high with caribou meat. They would make it through the winter. And none of them would ever forget the Christmas it snowed sugar in the bush.

Travis had never heard such a wonderful story. He was fighting back tears. His throat hurt. He looked at Nish, who was still staring longingly at the TV set as if he wished he were someplace else.

They talked a while, and Nish surprised Travis by suddenly turning and asking a question.

"What's a Trickster?"

Jimmy's mother looked at him, surprised. She glanced at her husband, then back at Nish.

"Where did you hear about the Trickster?"

"The Chief," Nish said. "She said if I got lost in the bush up here it would eat me."

Jimmy's parents laughed. The old woman fiercely worked her jaw.

"It's just an old story," Jimmy's mother said. "Like a fairytale."

The old woman said something sharp. Everyone turned to listen, even Travis and Nish, who couldn't understand a word.

Finally, Jimmy's mother explained. "My mother says the Trickster is real, no matter whether you can actually touch it or just feel it in your head. She says her own father said he saw it, that the Trickster came and punished a family that was being too selfish one winter and wouldn't share a caribou they had killed."

"What happened?" asked Jimmy.

His mother answered, but she didn't seem to believe. "The Trickster came and killed them and ate them."

"The Trickster is legend," Jimmy's father explained to Travis and Nish. "Many tribes have it in their myths. It's a monster that comes at night and either eats its victims or drives them insane. Myself, I think it probably grew out of tough times, people actually going mad in the bush and needing something to blame it on. People getting attacked by bears maybe and someone saying it was cannibalism."

Again the grandmother said something sharp. Jimmy's father answered her in an apologetic tone. Then he addressed the boys: "She says Cree hunters don't make things up."

"What's it look like?" Nish asked.

"No one knows," said Jimmy's mother. "There are lots of drawings, of course. Sometimes a monster with three heads. Sometimes with just one. But always with a head like a wolf and eyes like hot coals in a fire."

Jimmy's father checked his watch. "It's eleven o'clock, boys. We stay up all night, you'll be in no shape for your game tomorrow. Let's get to bed."

Travis and Nish were in bunk beds in Jimmy's room down in the basement. The three of them lay awake for a long time, talking quietly.

"You ever see this thing?" Nish asked.

"Of course not," answered Jimmy. "They used to warn us that he'd come and take us away if we weren't good."

"Like the bogeyman," said Travis.

"I guess," said Jimmy.

"Sounds stupid to me," said Nish. Then, after a long pause, he thought to add: "Sorry, Jimmy."

"Sounds stupid to me, too," Jimmy said. But he didn't sound particularly convincing.

6

They were awakened at dawn the next morning by Jimmy Whiskeyjack's father shouting down at them from the top of the stairs. They had an eight o'clock game against the Belugas, a team from a community called Great Whale, another hour north by air. But he wasn't calling to get them up for the game.

"Come and see the geese!" he shouted. "They're back!"

Jimmy kicked off his covers and was dressed in an instant, already scrambling up the stairs as Travis and Nish stood in their underwear trying to rub the sleep out of their eyes.

"Didn't we just play them?" Nish asked in a sleepy voice.

"That was the Mighty Geese," Travis said. "These are *real* geese."

"You expect me to run outside to see a stupid goose?"

"You can do whatever you want," Travis told him. He was tired of putting up with his friend's complaining. "I'm going out with Jimmy."

Travis bolted up the stairs and out the front door, which

had been left wide open as the entire family came out to see what all the fuss was about. Travis couldn't believe his ears: the honking sounded like something between a traffic jam and a schoolyard at recess.

The sky was filled with geese. There must have been half a dozen different V formations. One had only five geese in it, another, much higher, must have had two hundred. And the noise wasn't coming just from the sky; almost everyone standing in the roadways held their fists up to their mouths, honking back at the geese as if to say hello.

Travis went and stood by Jimmy, who kept pointing to new formations coming in from the south. "The spring goose-hunt is on now," he said. "Our hockey tournament just lost half its spectators."

"How come they all come at once?" Travis asked.

Jimmy laughed. "They don't. This is just the start. They'll be flying in for the next three weeks. It'll look like this every morning – some mornings there'll be twice this many. Aren't they beautiful?"

Travis agreed that they were. He had never seen such grace. He loved the way they seemed to be barely moving their wings. He loved the perfect distance they kept from each other, and the arrow-straight wedge they formed as they flew, the one in front sometimes dropping back so another could take the lead.

He looked back toward the house. Nish had come out and was standing on the porch steps, blinking as he looked up. He was shaking his head. He didn't seem impressed.

@

The Belugas were already on the ice when the Screech Owls skated out. Travis bolted past the goalies and made a wide circle at centre ice, pretending not even to notice the other team. He would have preferred to be out first, to be first on the fresh ice, but it was still clean and he could feel – and, even better, *hear* – his skates dig in with a perfect sharp. Dmitri and Derek had caught up to him and the three of them, in perfect unison, swept behind the net and came out in a perfect V as they headed fast down the ice, their strides smooth and evenly matched, their speed constant.

Just like the geese, Travis thought. He wondered if anyone else was thinking the same thing. Certainly not Nish, who was stretching by the boards. Nish had a look that said he was thinking only about hockey. Muck had plainly got to him.

They lined up for the face-off, and, for the first time, Travis took his measure of the opposition. The Great Whale team had beautiful sweaters, with an Inuit drawing of a big, white beluga whale on the front. And they were laughing, something Travis had never seen a team do before the puck dropped. They were speaking in Cree and pointing at Nish.

"Hey," one of them called in English, "*Moose Nostrils!*"

Travis turned quickly and glanced at his friend on the blue-line. If Nish had heard, he was giving no indication of it. He looked as if the Stanley Cup final was about to begin.

The puck dropped, and Travis swept it back to Nish, who skated all the way back to his own end. Oh no, Travis thought, he's going to try to go coast-to-coast. Nish the Superstar.

But nothing of the sort. Nish deftly got one of the Belugas' wingers to race at him and left him behind the net as he burst out the other side. He hit Data with a perfect pass and Data played the give-and-go, feeding Nish the puck back at the blue-line. Nish hit Derek at the red line, and Derek put a beautiful pass to Dmitri just as he hit the Belugas' blueline. Dmitri cut to the centre, dropped the puck, and took out his checker with a shoulder brush, leaving Travis to walk in alone, pull the goal-tender down, and then send the puck back to Derek, who had the wide-open net to score in. *Tic-tac-tic-tac-toe.*

They lined up as the goal was announced: "Derek Dillinger from Travis Lindsay and Dmitri Yakushev." Not even a mention of Nish's name, but everyone knew who had set up the play in the first place, including the Belugas.

"Hey, Moose Nostrils!" they called at him. "You hungry, Moose Nostrils?"

But Nish paid no attention. He was dead serious. He had come to play.

And a good thing too, for the Belugas were a good team, fast and tough, but lacking a strong third line like the Screech Owls'. Andy Higgins and Chantal Larochelle both scored, Lars (Cherry) Johanssen scored from the blueline on a screen, and the glove hand of Jeremy Weathers simply proved too fast for the Belugas' snipers.

The Screech Owls won easily, 4–1, and lined up quickly to shake hands with this excellent team. Nish was first in line, ready for what was coming as the other team filed by:

"Good game, Moose Nostrils!"

"Thank you very much."

"Moose Nostrils . . ."

"Thank you very much."

"Moose Nostrils . . ."

"Thank you very much."

                              ⊙

Jesse Highboy was as excited out in the lobby as he'd been when the final buzzer sounded and they'd pounced on poor Jeremy to congratulate him.

He came straight over to Travis. "My dad says we can go out to the goose camp and stay overnight. He'll let us take the Ski-Doos."

Travis was taken aback. Ever since he'd arrived in Waskaganish he'd been hoping for a ride on one of the snow machines. But only a ride – he'd never considered driving. But then, he was from down South.

"All by ourselves?" Travis asked, a bit uneasily.

"My grandparents have been there for two weeks already. They'll be starting to hunt today. You gotta see it, Travis. It's a fantastic experience."

"It's all right with your grandparents?"

"My dad talked to them this morning. They saw the geese too."

"They have a telephone out there?"

Jesse laughed. "No way. A radio. We radioed them."

"I don't know," Travis said. He was suddenly unsure.

"My dad already asked your dad. There's no problem. I know the way. And my cousin Rachel's coming too. You know Rachel."

She was coming too?

"She's bringing Liz from your team. Liz is staying with Rachel, and they've become good friends."

"How long does it take to get there?"

"Two hours. C'mon, let's clear it with Muck."

Muck listened carefully and then excused himself to go off and talk to Jesse's father. The two of them then spoke to Travis's and Liz's parents. The boys could see them talking, and were happy that heads were nodding in agreement. It seemed, however, to be taking an awfully long time.

Muck came back and said they could all go – on two conditions.

"What are they?" Travis asked.

"One, you get back here first thing in the morning. We play tomorrow at five p.m. I don't need tired players."

"We'll be back," Jesse promised.

"And two," Muck said, "you take Nishikawa with you."

Travis didn't understand. Or maybe he did. He looked at Muck, and Muck looked at both boys.

"He needs to open his eyes up here," Muck said. "And if he won't do it, we'll just have to do it for him."

7

Travis had never felt anything like it! It was as if he were surging right through his skin and leaving his body behind.

G-force. He only knew what it was because Data, the *Star Trek* freak, always talked about things like G-force and warp factor. You felt G-force in jet fighters and helicopters, and, Travis now knew, on very fast Ski-Doos.

Jesse's older brother, Isaac, had brought them out to show how to operate the machines they'd be taking to the goose camp. There were three: two larger machines pulling toboggans, and one smaller but quicker one.

Nish had reacted with what seemed like shock at the news that he was going. He obviously didn't want to seem *afraid* to go, but he didn't mind letting Travis know he was *reluctant*. He'd said he couldn't possibly go without his parents' permission, and when Muck had countered that by saying he had already called them from the band office and they thought it was a wonderful opportunity, he gave in and said he *guessed* he'd go. He was treating it like an extra practice Muck had scheduled.

Travis, on the other hand, could hardly wait. He was most excited by the chance to drive one of the Ski-Doos, and had eagerly taken up Isaac's offer to show him how. They had gone down on the bay to practice. It was flat and safe from trees and banks, and Isaac, sitting directly behind him, had called out, "*Open her up!*" and Travis had squeezed the accelerator.

The machine leapt from the ground. Travis felt airborne, his neck snapping back into the massive snowmobile helmet. The machine screamed down the shoreline, on a well-worn racing course that turned into a long, gentle curve. Travis tried to take the turn, but the machine skipped over the slight bank and began heading straight out into the bay, the pitch-black terror of open water far out in front. He let go of the accelerator, the machine slowed, and he could hear Isaac laughing.

"You have to *lean* into your turns!" Isaac told him. Then, with Travis now hanging on behind, Isaac drove the Ski-Doo back into the same curve, only this time leaning into the turn, with the machine following his coaxing. Travis took it for the run back, leaning just as Isaac had shown him, and the heavy slapping on his back from his passenger told him he'd done well. Travis felt great.

Jesse's father had spent the morning getting them ready to go. Five kids, three snow machines, two toboggans. The covered toboggans were filled with things like sleeping bags for the kids and extra supplies for the camp. As soon as the hockey tournament was over, the Highboys would be heading out for a two week stay at the camp.

"Bring your stick and skates!" Jesse called to Travis and Nish as they went to pack. "There's sometimes good ice out by the goose blinds. If it's clear, we'll play some shinny."

"Sounds good!" Travis called back.

"Sounds stupid," Nish said as they continued toward the Whiskeyjack home to get their stuff.

"What do you mean, 'Sounds stupid'?" asked Travis.

"Where'll we dress? What'll we use for boards? Nets? Who's going to play? Us against the *girl*?"

What *was* it with Nish? From the moment they'd left Val d'Or, he had been in a sour mood. He hadn't said anything about Liz coming, and *she* was a girl. It was hardly like Nish to dump on someone just because they happened to be female. He wouldn't even use Rachel's name.

Nish didn't seem to like it that Travis and Rachel were getting along so well. The other night when they'd been lying in bed and Travis had been asking Jimmy Whiskeyjack some perfectly reasonable questions – like how old Rachel was, and in what grade, and what kind of music she liked – Nish had given a huge sigh and then made a big thing out of turning his back on them.

"Why don't you guys shut up so I can get some sleep?" he'd said angrily.

They got away by noon. Plenty of time, Mr. Highboy told them, to get there in good light and get settled in. Travis's and Liz's parents came down and took photographs of the expedition setting out. Travis's mother seemed worried, and he suddenly felt a little uneasy. But it was silly to fret, he told himself. They had three machines, so it would hardly matter if one broke down. They were dressed warmly and had big mittens and padded helmets. Jesse's father was a fanatic about taking all the right precautions, and there was going to be no fooling around.

Muck was there, too, and he took the three of them aside for a moment. "You stick together," he said to Nish and Travis and Liz. "And you do what Jesse and Rachel tell you, understand?" Nish clearly did not. He was, after all, an assistant captain, and Jesse was a third-liner. But having already fallen out once with Muck, he wasn't about to make a second mistake. Nish nodded.

Travis got to drive right away, with Nish as his passenger. They followed Jesse and Liz, who took the lead, and Rachel brought up the rear with the single snow machine.

They left the shoreline and headed into the woods, where the trail began to bounce and roll with a rhythm that reminded Travis of riding a horse. It was never like this in a car. He could feel everything, and he loved it. A light squeeze of the accelerator and the big machine responded instantly.

They rolled over the countryside for the better part of an hour. They passed over frozen lakes and swamps and through short, dark stands of black spruce – and every once in a while they would catch a glimpse of the bay itself, the dark, menacing water far out from the shoreline.

They stopped to share a couple of oranges, and Nish complained to Jesse that he wasn't getting a chance to drive. Jesse immediately offered him the single machine, moving Rachel up to ride with Travis.

"Do you want to drive?" Travis asked when she moved over.

"You drive," Rachel said. "I can do it any time. You're only here until Sunday."

She smiled at him so nicely that, when she sat down behind him, Travis had trouble catching his breath. And when they moved on again and she placed her mittened hands on his hips to steady herself, he wondered if his heart would stop.

There was no use talking. With the helmets and the roar of the engine, they wouldn't hear each other. And anyway, that was just as well; Travis didn't have a clue what to talk about. Much-Music? Whether Rachel owned a compact-disc player? What did they talk about in the North?

They moved down a gentle slope and back to the shoreline of the big bay, the ice thick and covered with hard-packed snow, the trail perfect. In front, Jesse opened his machine up a bit and pulled ahead. Travis squeezed the accelerator and felt Rachel grip a little tighter. He felt wonderful. He had never in his entire life enjoyed anything as much as this.

Travis saw Nish before he heard him. His helmet blocked the sound and the engines of the three machines were all screaming together as Nish left the trail and flew past them with a wave of his hand.

Travis couldn't believe how fast Nish was going. Nish turned the machine so it jumped across the trail in front of Jesse and then continued on the other side, leaving them far behind.

"HE DOESN'T EVEN KNOW WHERE HE'S GOING!" Travis shouted. It was useless.

Nish let up on his accelerator until he had fallen back with them. Maybe he scared himself, thought Travis. But a moment later he was off the trail and flying away again, far out onto the frozen surface of the bay, the black, open water in the distance beyond him.

Travis couldn't help himself. "DON'T GO OUT THERE!"

He felt Rachel's grip tighten. Perhaps she was yelling too. But they couldn't even hear each other, so how would Nish ever hear them?

Jesse turned his machine off the trail and started out onto the bay, where Nish was in the middle of a long loop. Then Jesse came to a stop, jumped off, and began waving frantically to Nish. Travis stopped his machine.

The four of them – Jesse, Liz, Travis, and Rachel – all began waving at Nish. Travis thought that Nish must have been trying to turn back, but he wasn't leaning out the way Isaac had taught them, and the machine wasn't responding. Nish smashed into a drift and for a moment was airborne, the snowmobile almost turning sideways before he righted it and bounced into a landing that almost threw him off. Travis didn't need to be there to know that Nish had just scared himself half to death.

And then Nish vanished!

"Nooooooo!!"

Travis was aware of the scream before he realized that it was him doing the screaming. He instinctively yanked his helmet free and started running, only to find he was going nowhere; someone had hold of him.

"YOU'LL GO THROUGH, TOO!" Rachel was shouting at him.

It was all too much for Travis. The screaming. The cold wind whipping in off the bay into his face. And a great dark hole where a moment before had been his best friend.

Travis panicked. He started to cry. He could feel tears burning. He looked at Liz. She was screaming.

Something bobbed in the water! Something surfacing. A head. An arm, flailing!

It was Nish!

Travis tried to move forward again, but Rachel was still holding him tight. He tried to shake her off, but Jesse grabbed him too.

"Cool it, okay?" Jesse shouted. "We panic, we're all going down with him. We do this right, okay? We do it right!"

Travis had never heard Jesse like this. He was so sure of himself. He stopped struggling.

Nish's helmet must have come off when the machine broke through the ice, because his head was bare – and he was *swimming*. Or at least trying to swim. With his heavy jacket and mitts, he could hardly move. But he managed to reach the unbroken ice and clung on.

"HELLLLLP MEEEE!!" he screamed.

Travis could feel his tears hardening on his cheek. They were freezing! It was that cold – and the wind was stronger now.

"Spread out!" Jesse ordered. "Spread out and walk slowly toward him! If we go in a single line we'll break through!"

Jesse got them into position, and they began walking in a wedge, Jesse in the lead, toward Nish, who was desperately hanging on.

"PULL ME OUT! PULLL MEEE OUTTT!!"

Rachel broke away and ran back. Travis couldn't look at her. She must have been afraid. He couldn't blame her – so was he. But before they were halfway to where Nish was still scrambling, she was back. She was carrying hockey sticks and skates. *What the heck's with her?* Travis wondered. *Nish is drowning and she wants to play hockey?*

"Good idea, Rach," Jesse said.

Travis couldn't believe the calm in Jesse's voice. What "good idea"?

"HELLLLLP MEEEE!!" Nish called again.

They were close enough to see his face when Jesse held up his hand for them all to stop. Travis could see the terror in Nish's eyes. He knew just from looking that Nish believed he was going to die, drown before their eyes while they stood there, watching helplessly.

There was desperation and anger in Nish's voice. "HELP MEEEE!!"

Nish tried to scramble onto the ice, but it shattered in front of him, plunging him down in a splash of ice-water. He bobbed back up, his hair plastered to his head. "PLEASE, HELP ME, TRAVIS!!"

"Hang on, Nish!" Jesse called. "We're gonna get you outta there! Just hold on and don't try to pull yourself up! You're breaking the ice!"

"HELLLLLP MEEEE!! I'M GONNA DIE!"

Signalling them to stay back, Jesse tested the ice by stepping ahead gently, then pressing down, waiting, and bringing the other foot forward and setting it down in the same careful way far to one side. He was slowly working his way as close to the hole as he dared get.

Travis looked around, desperate for something to do to help. Rachel was sitting on the ice with the hockey sticks placed together. She was unlacing one of the skates as quickly as possible.

She looked up, her face calm but determined. "Do the other ones," she commanded.

"Huh?"

"The other skates. We need the laces."

Travis and Liz began furiously unlacing the other skates. By the time they handed the laces to Rachel, she had already tied two hockey sticks together. She took Travis's lace and began tying another knot higher up for added support. Liz jumped over and began doing the same thing with her lace. Liz knew what to do. Travis could only stare uselessly.

Nish screamed the most terrible, pitiful scream. It was bloodcurdling. Travis shivered. He was still crying. He could feel his cheeks burning. He couldn't even see straight. His best friend was drowning and he couldn't do anything about it.

"Hold onto my legs!" Jesse shouted at Travis.

"What?"

"Hold onto my legs!" He repeated. He sounded angry.

Jesse lay down on his stomach and wiggled forward toward Nish. He looked back impatiently. Travis grabbed Jesse's legs, and when Jesse wiggled ahead again Travis moved with him.

Nish was still trying to pull himself up. He was breaking through and falling back.

"Stay still!" Jesse ordered Nish. "You might break right through to us!"

There was so much command in his voice that, finally, Nish stopped struggling.

Jesse looked back at Rachel, who was ready. She handed the sticks forward to him. Jesse swung them carefully out in front. He was at least one hockey stick short of Nish.

"We're gonna have to get closer!"

Travis didn't know if they could. He was afraid of breaking through. His heart was pounding so hard it seemed to be shaking his whole body. He could imagine his parents finding out that they'd all vanished on the bay, with nothing remaining but two snowmobiles and a big black hole. They wouldn't even know how it had happened, that Nish had been such a dummy.

He felt someone grab his own legs. He looked back. It was Rachel, and behind her Liz was down with her arms around Rachel's legs.

"Go on!" Rachel shouted ahead to Jesse. "We can hold you!"

Jesse wiggled forward. Travis wriggled. The girls wriggled. They moved ahead like a slow snake, the blade of the farthest stick coming ever closer to Nish.

"Grab it and hold!" Jesse shouted to Nish. "Don't pull! We'll do all the pulling! You just hold on and try to slide out, okay?"

Nish was no longer screaming. He was scared. He was placing all his hope in Jesse.

"O-k-kay!" Nish said. He was crying openly. Travis couldn't blame him. He was crying too.

Jesse wiggled ahead one more time. Nish reached out with one mitt and took hold of the blade. He had a good grip.

"Let go of the ice!" Jesse called.

"I CAN'T!" Nish shouted. There was pure terror in his voice.

"You have to!"

"I'M AFRAID TO LET GO!"

Suddenly, from behind Travis, Rachel shouted, "LET GO, NISH! YOU'LL BE ALL RIGHT!"

There was a brief pause, and then Nish let go of the ice and took the blade with both hands.

"Hang on!" Jesse shouted. Then, to Travis and the others, "Slowly, now. Pull back slowly!"

They began to inch backwards.

Nish pushed at the ice. It cracked loudly and gave under him, sending him back down.

"JUST RIDE RIGHT OVER THE ICE!" Jesse yelled. "DON'T DO A THING BUT HANG ON AND SLIDE!"

They pulled again, and Nish came out part way. The ice gave a mighty crack and Travis closed his eyes – but nothing happened. It was holding.

They pulled again. Nish came up a bit more. His upper body was out and resting on the ice. His face was twisted into a scream, but no sound was coming out.

"ONE MORE!" Jesse called. "ONE MORE AND HE'S OUT!"

Travis felt a tremendous yank on his legs. He couldn't believe the strength of the two girls behind him. He pulled as hard as he could. He could feel Jesse pulling.

"HE'S OUT!"

Jesse turned over on his back, gasping for air. Nish was fully out of the water and on the ice. He was wiggling toward them, still holding the stick.

They worked Nish back. As soon as he was able, Jesse reached out, grabbed Nish's hands, and pulled him quickly to them.

"Spread out again!" Jesse ordered. "We don't want to break through!"

Travis moved away quickly. Nish tried to get to his feet. He was gasping, choking, and shaking violently. Jesse stayed with him, got him standing, and slowly they all began retreating from the hole.

Nish was bawling. He couldn't stop. He was sobbing and blubbering and couldn't seem to get his breath. But he was alive!

Though how long could he last before he froze to death? Travis wondered.

9

ravis had never felt so helpless. If he had been in charge, Nish and he would have turned to ice on the banks of James Bay, their frozen tears proof that they had been bawling like newborn babies right to the bitter end.

Fortunately, Travis wasn't in charge – Jesse and Rachel Highboy were. Jesse opened up the lead toboggan and removed one of the sleeping bags, which he quickly unrolled and wrapped around the shaking, whimpering Nish.

"We've got to get out of the wind," Jesse said. There was no panic in his voice, just grim determination.

Jesse wasted no time. He got Nish onto the lead Ski-Doo with him, Rachel and Liz took the other one, and Travis straddled the toboggan. Jesse quickly found a trail up from the shore, and as Rachel followed, Travis took one last look behind him. The bay was quickly vanishing from view, but above it he could see a huge, threatening cloud the colour of a bad bruise. He hoped it was going away from them.

The two machines entered a thick stand of spruce, and Travis could see Jesse standing up as he drove, his helmeted head turning this way and that, until finally he came to a clearing surrounded by trees. He stopped his machine, and Rachel pulled hers up directly behind.

"Keep Nish warm!" Jesse shouted to Travis as he began opening up the two toboggans.

Travis could see his friend was shaking right through the sleeping bag. What was he supposed to do? Turn up the thermostat?

"*Rub him!*" Jesse shouted. He already had an axe out, and was throwing other things onto the ground. Out came a big orange plastic sheet, another axe, a shovel. Rachel took the shovel and began to make a bank of snow around a small area within the clearing.

Travis and Liz felt stupid and useless. Travis shrugged at Liz, wrapped his arms around Nish, and began rubbing him through the covers. He could feel his best friend shaking – no, *rattling* – like a machine that was about to burst apart. Travis was scared. Liz moved in to wrap her arms around Nish, too.

"LEMME BREATHE!" Nish shouted. It was like music to Travis's ears. At least Nish was still Nish. Frozen, maybe, but still Nish.

While Liz and Travis rubbed the freezing Nish, Rachel continued banking up the snow. Then she snapped off dead branches from the spruce trees and set about making a fire. She carefully laid down the dry wood, crisscrossing the branches, then returned to the spruce for some live boughs with needles still on them.

With what seemed like a dozen quick chops with the axe, Jesse had felled one of the spruce trees. He lopped off some of the branches, then pulled a small Swedesaw from the toboggan and quickly set to work cutting up the trunk. Travis could see the sweat pouring off Jesse's forehead.

When he had cut three good-sized pieces, Jesse knelt down in the snow and chopped at each one until he had dozens of long, curling chips that were only half cut away from the logs. Travis had no idea what he was doing.

Rachel started the fire. The dry branches caught easily, and then the needles ignited, the fire roaring and snapping almost as if she had poured gasoline on it. As soon as it was really going, Jesse piled on his three logs, and Travis saw now why he had cut them the way he had. The long, curling chips sticking out from the logs caught fire easily, and not only did they help the fire grow stronger, they kept the logs apart so the flames could lick up in between. Jesse had no time to admire his work: he was right back sawing more logs from the downed spruce.

Rachel had the other axe and was cutting down smaller trees. The axe was so sharp, some fell with one or two blows, until Rachel had nearly a dozen down and was busy hacking off the branches. It looked to Travis as if she was making fishing poles.

"I-I-I th-th-th-ink I-I'm dyyy-inggg!" Nish suddenly howled. He sounded like a sick dog.

"Don't be ridiculous!" Liz snapped at him.

She, too, seemed suddenly in control. In fact, everyone appeared to know what to do but Nish, who thought he was dying, and Travis, who thought he was useless.

Rachel was working the poles into the snow to one side of the fire. "Travis!" she called. "Can you help me for a minute?"

Travis had hold of Nish and was afraid to let go. But Liz pushed him off and hugged Nish closer. Travis hurried over.

"Help me get these up!" Rachel told him. "They'll have to hold against the wind."

Travis followed Rachel's instructions exactly. They pounded the poles down like fenceposts in a semi-circle, and then built up more snow around them. Rachel had planned her structure so it included three live spruce, their roots holding them far more solid than anything Travis and Rachel could manage by pounding. She cleared off their branches with the axe so that the standing spruce fit perfectly in line, one on each end and one in the middle.

Travis still had no idea what she was doing.

"Help us with the tarp!" she called. She and Jesse were already unrolling the big orange plastic sheet. The three of them hoisted the tarp up and, using bungee cords, carefully attached it flat against the spruce posts. Rachel and Jesse took special care to secure it to the three spruce trees that still had their roots. When they were done, they had built a wall that curved in a semi-circle, which not only cut off the wind but also caught the heat of the fire. Travis could feel the heat blasting at him. It felt wonderful.

Neither Rachel nor Jesse had spoken a word to each other during the whole procedure. They had called out instructions to Travis and Liz, but nothing whatsoever to each other. Had they practised this in case some idiot fell through the ice? Travis wondered.

But there was no time for foolish questions.

Jesse remained in control, though he still looked concerned. "Get that sleeping bag off Nish!" he commanded, coming over to help. Nish whimpered and held tight to his covers.

Jesse was almost angry. "You *will* die if we don't get you dried out!" he said in a very firm voice. "Now let go!"

Once Nish was out of the sleeping bags, Travis could see how much his friend was shaking – and it scared him. His jacket, his pants, everything was absolutely soaking.

"Off with the clothes!" Jesse commanded.

"I-I-I'll freeeeze!"

"You'll freeze if you don't. C'mon. This is no time for modesty. Get 'em off."

With Jesse's help, Nish began taking off his stuff. As each item was removed, Rachel gathered the wet clothing up and carefully hung it to dry on spruce branches she had arranged around the fire.

Travis was shocked at the sight of his friend. They were in the middle of nowhere, in freezing cold, with an Arctic wind, and Nish stood there naked like a beached whale, almost a blur he shook so badly. Jesse got a dry sleeping bag from the toboggan and gave it to Nish to wrap around himself.

"Travis," Jesse called, "break into his pack. Get us some dry clothes."

Travis was thankful he finally had something to do. He hurried to the second toboggan and pulled out Nish's pack. He quickly undid the straps and untied the cord. Then he stopped, blinking in astonishment.

The pack was filled with candy! Mars bars and Caramilk and

Snickers and licorice and bubble gum and Gummi bears and Reeses and Smarties and a six-pack of Coke. All Travis could find for Nish to wear was a fresh pair of boxer shorts and a sweatshirt.

Travis took the clothes back, holding them out as if he had failed. "This is all he brought."

"I-I thought w-we were st-staying only th-the one night!" said Nish.

Then why bring enough candy for a month? Travis wanted to say, but bit his tongue.

Jesse shook his head in disgust. "Okay, put 'em on!"

"P-put what on?"

"Put 'em on!" Jesse ordered again. There was no mistaking what he meant; he was holding out the boxer shorts. He wasn't taking no for an answer.

Whimpering, Nish started to change. He pulled the dry sleeping bag tight and stepped out of his wet shorts, kicking them aside with an alarmingly white foot. *Was it frozen?*

"Travis 'n' me are too small," Jesse said. "Have you got anything he can wear, Liz?"

"I'll check," Liz said, and hurried to her own pack.

Nish howled like a dog who'd just had his tail run over. He was halfway up with his dry underwear and the sleeping bag slipped off.

"*I can't wear girls' clothes!*"

"Right," Jesse said. "Then they can all say, 'Good ol' Nish — he froze to death like a *real* man.'"

"How's this?" Liz said. She was holding a thick pink sweater, a pair of black tights, some thick socks, and a pair of blue jeans with some beadwork on the back pockets.

"*T-t-tights!*" Nish wailed.

"Put them on," Rachel said. Even she was losing her patience. "Put them on or freeze your buns off."

Nish accepted the bundle. He began to dress, whimpering still; but whether it was because he thought he was going to die from freezing or from embarrassment, Travis could not say.

Jesse returned to the job of cutting up wood, and Travis went to help him. They cut more logs and stacked them, and Travis gathered more dry branches. The fire was going well.

"You look lovely!" Rachel said as Nish emerged from his sleeping bag.

Liz's clothes didn't fit quite perfectly, but at least Nish could wear them. The pink sweater was okay, but the pants he couldn't quite do up, and they could see the tights through the zipper. The beads sparkled in the firelight as Nish warmed his behind.

Jesse and Rachel still weren't finished. They pulled another plastic tarp out of the toboggan and used it to make a partial roof over the shelter. On the enclosed side it was now so warm Travis could hardly believe it. Rachel cut down some soft spruce boughs and spread them around so they could sit and not get wet or cold from the snow.

Nish was no longer shaking. His clothes were steaming beside the fire. The wind was higher now, and rippling loudly along the outside of the plastic tarp.

"We're in for a storm," said Jesse, very quietly.

"I think so," answered Rachel.

Travis didn't like their near-whispers. It was almost as if they were warning each other, but didn't want the rest to know. He stared toward the bay. He could see nothing but a blur. It was snowing, hard – and coming their way.

Jesse shook his head, seemingly angry with himself. "If only I'd packed some food."

"There's nothing?" Rachel asked.

Jesse shook his head. "I figured we'd get there easily before dark. They'd already have geese."

"We've got something," Travis said.

All heads turned toward him, including Nish, who couldn't contain a look of alarm.

"Nish brought his candy," Travis said.

Nish stared at him with a look that said: *How could you betray your best friend?*

"Let's have a look," said Liz.

Travis hauled out the bag and opened it. Rachel giggled when she saw the enormous cache of sweets. Jesse just shook his head.

"Stuff like that attracts bears, you know, Nish," he said.

"There's no bears around here, are there?"

"You better hope not."

10

They had a three-course supper. Licorice as an appetizer, Mars bars and Snickers for the main course, bubble gum for dessert. And all washed down with Coke.

"We'll open two cans and share," said Jesse.

"I'm not touching it after someone else," protested Nish.

"Suit yourself," said Jesse. "But we have no idea how long we'll be here."

"We can eat snow," Nish suggested.

"People die eating snow. You have to melt it first – so save the cans."

Travis had never seen this side of Jesse. Usually Jesse hardly said a word; he always let others take the lead and simply followed along. But now he was in charge. Captain, sort of, of the lost team.

They kept the fire going and talked. Travis asked about Jesse kneeling when he chopped with the axe, and Jesse explained to him that all the Cree did this. "You live in the bush, you can't take a chance on cutting your foot," he said. "You'd never get to help in time."

Nish was warm finally, and most of his clothes were dry. He wrapped himself up again in the sleeping bag, changed back into his own clothes, and sheepishly handed Liz hers back with an awkward "Thanks."

"Any time, cross-dresser," said Liz.

Nish squinted and frowned at the same time. "Not one word of this to the others, okay?"

"Of course not."

"Good."

"How could *one* word describe you?"

They all laughed, until a great burst of wind suddenly hit the shelter and snapped the plastic, bending the poles.

"It's really gonna blow," said Jesse.

"They'll be wondering where we are," said Liz.

"They'll know where we are," said Jesse. He seemed certain.

Later, Jesse and Rachel got up to arrange the snowmobiles and toboggans so that they gave more shelter as the kids huddled into the best corner of the wall they had built. They were fairly comfortable – out of the wind and snow, each one wrapped in an Arctic sleeping bag, lying on soft boughs over the snow – but they were also miserable, and badly frightened.

Travis had never seen such a storm. It seemed to howl and pounce like an animal, the air growing eerily quiet and then suddenly rising and punching the tarp so they felt it would rip off and come down on them. But Rachel had done a good job; the tarp held. And Jesse had cut and stacked enough wood for the fire to burn forever.

But they were still cold. Cold and hungry, despite the chocolate bars and licorice. Travis felt ill from all the sugar. Nish was making funny gurgling noises. Travis realized he was crying, very softly, to himself.

"What's wrong?" he asked.

"I lost the Ski-Doo," Nish said.

"It's not important," Jesse said.

"It's my fault," Nish said.

"That's right," Jesse said. Travis had the sense that this wasn't what Nish was hoping to hear. "But it would have been my fault if we'd lost you."

"And mine," Rachel added.

"How?" Nish moaned.

"We're responsible for you," said Jesse.

"Our grandparents would say you are guests in their home," said Rachel. "So if something does go wrong, it's up to us to fix it."

"But we're not in their home, we're in the middle of the bush," corrected Travis.

"*This*," she said, "is our grandparents' home."

11

Muck and Mr. Lindsay were in the band office with Mr. Highboy and Chief Ottereyes. The storm had come up very suddenly – "It happens sometimes," said the Chief. They had radioed the Highboy goose camp, but the grandparents had seen no sign of the five youngsters yet.

Both the Chief and Mr. Highboy said not to worry, and didn't seem particularly worried themselves, but Muck and Mr. Lindsay were definitely worried.

"Jesse knows what to do," Mr. Highboy kept saying. "Jesse and Rachel know the bush."

Abraham and Hilda Highboy had known the storm was on its way since shortly after noon. Abraham had heard the wind in the high trees and knew. They considered radioing the village to let them know, but it was Rachel and Jesse coming out. They'd be okay.

Hilda had been in the cooking tent since morning. She had a huge fire going and she had four geese trussed and hanging from the main poles out over the centre, where they were spinning on their tie lines and sizzling in the waves of rising heat. Every once in a while she would take a bowl and catch the grease drippings. Perfect for bannock, she said to herself. The kids would be hungry when they arrived.

Abraham had skinned a beaver he had trapped the day before and had stretched the pelt for curing outside. The beaver meat was cooking in a slow pot held high over the main campfire. The entire camp smelled of food. But it was not the cooking smells that were making Abraham's nose twitch. He did not like the smell of the wind bearing down on them, gusting direct from the north, the temperature dropping.

Even the dogs were uneasy. Abraham was one of the last Waskaganish trappers still working with sled dogs. He could have bought a Ski-Doo, but he stuck with the dogs because he had always loved working with them, and, besides, what could a snow machine ever tell you? The dogs were letting him know the storm was a bad one. They were nervous, and selfish. He had noticed them fighting over the meat; a storm like this made everyone, man or dog, think survival. The only thing good about the temperature going down further was that soon it would be too cold to snow. Soon, he figured, he would be able to see enough to travel in the dark. If he had to.

Nish was sure he'd heard something. And it wasn't just Jesse up again to stoke the fire: this sound had come from outside the shelter.

He hadn't been able to sleep. He could hear Travis snoring. He could make out the girls huddled against each other. He could see Jesse closer to the fire, his face turned toward it.

The fire was crackling. Rachel had explained that it was caused by the resin in the spruce. It was spitting and sizzling and snapping . . . *snapping?*

No, the snapping was coming from outside! Nish held his breath.

Snap!

Something was moving through the trees!

Nish could feel his heart pounding. The wind kicked the sides of the plastic tarp and it rattled and rippled the entire length.

Snap!

"*Trav!*" Nish hissed.

No answer.

"*Jesse!*"

No answer.

"*Rachel! . . . Liz!*"

Nothing.

Nish didn't know what to do. He didn't want to shout for fear of alerting whatever it was on the other side of the tarp. He also had to go to the bathroom – *bad*. Too much Coke.

Quietly, barely daring to breathe, Nish waited. He counted to a hundred, then to two hundred. He was desperate, now, to go to the bathroom. Three hundred. Four hundred. *He had to go!*

Satisfied that whatever it was had moved along, he quickly pulled himself out of the sleeping bag. It was freezing cold – particularly for a twelve-year-old about to unbuckle his pants!

Nish stepped around the edge of the shelter. He'd go so quick, he figured, the hole in the snow would be like a bullet had passed through. But he never even got to try.

Something was breathing nearby . . . something big!

Nish was shaking. He could see nothing but pitch black around him. The trees were like huge shadows, with darker shadows below them. *And one of the shadows was moving!* He could hear growling, and snarling!

"*Uhhhhhh!*" Nish started. He didn't dare move.

He could see eyes! At first he wasn't sure, then he saw them again, yellow, *shining*.

The thing lunged. He could hear the intake of breath, the growl. It hit him dead centre in the chest. Nish went down, gasping. He could smell the animal. Sharp, rancid, disgusting. He could smell its panting breath – hot, and fouler than anything he had ever smelled. Nish thought he was going to throw up.

He still couldn't see. He was down and the beast was striking him with its paws, the claws ripping into his arms and sides and tearing out his insides. He began to scream.

He screamed and gurgled, sure that it was blood rising in his throat. There was no pain . . . *yet*. But he knew he was badly injured, probably dying. All he could see was the burning eyes, all he could feel was harsh, thick fur, all he could smell was the foul, dead, disgusting smell.

Nish tried to move and could not. If his legs and arms were broken, he couldn't feel them. He could feel a terrible warmth on his stomach, a sickening warm sensation that could only be his own blood pouring out.

"*I'm dying!*"

He tried to warn the others, but they wouldn't wake. He could hear the tarp tearing as the beast ripped through it. He could hear snorting and ripping. He turned, barely, the warm liquid of his own insides cooling now. *So this*, he decided, *is what it feels like to die.*

He could see the beast dragging something. *It was Travis!* It had torn Travis out of his sleeping bag and was dragging him off.

"TRAAAAVIS!!!"

13

Nish! . . . Nish!"

"C'mon, Nish. Wake up!"

Nish twisted, tried to open his eyes. He thought he must be in heaven, but it didn't make sense; God wouldn't call him by his nickname. He must be in a hospital. Somehow he must have been saved.

"*Nish, wake up!*"

That was . . . Travis's voice. Nish shook his head violently. A good sign: it didn't fall off. At least the beast hadn't ripped out his throat. But he couldn't tell if he could feel his legs, and the pool of blood on his stomach was freezing cold now.

"WAKE UP!"

Nish opened his eyes. Travis was leaning over him, shaking his shoulders. So Travis hadn't been eaten! Behind Travis, Nish could make out the others, all looking at him, concerned. And behind them – what *was* that? The *beast*? He could see something big, and dark, and covered with fur.

"Travis," Nish said, "you're okay?"

Travis laughed. "Of course I'm okay. It's you we're worried about. Jesse's grandfather is here! We're saved, Nish!"

Saved? How could they be saved when a minute ago they were being eaten by a wild animal? He shifted so he could see creature. *It was an old man!* An old man with thick eyebrows and long greying hair, wearing a big fur coat. The old man looked more like a bear than . . . Jesse's grandfather. But that's who it was.

Nish could feel his legs now. And his arms. But he could still feel the wet where the beast had ripped out his guts.

Oh oh!

Nish closed his eyes. He knew.

He had gone to the bathroom last night all right. But he had never left his sleeping bag.

@

When the old trapper found them, the fire had gone down to nothing. Cree hunters had frozen to death in the past in a good shelter with a fire going: sleep had tricked them. When he first got there, with his dogs barking and nobody waking up, he had become quite worried.

As he told them later, with Jesse translating, he had tried to shake one kid awake. He pointed to Nish, laughing. Nish, he said, had started screaming at him. And then he had fainted. The old trapper said something and laughed to himself, shaking his head.

"My grandfather says you saw the Trickster," said Jesse.

"I saw an animal," Nish protested. "I think it was a wolverine."

"You wouldn't know a wolverine from a skunk," said Rachel, laughing.

"Get a life," Nish snapped.

"Get a diaper," said Rachel.

Nish shut up. What could he say? He'd made a complete ass of himself. They thought he was a scaredy-cat, a baby. And he'd done nothing to make them think otherwise. He'd lost the Ski-Doo through the ice; he'd almost drowned; he couldn't do a thing to help when they built the camp; and he'd peed his bed.

They all helped themselves to the meat that Jesse and Rachel's grandfather had brought. It was black and greasy – "Mostly goose, some beaver," Jesse had said – and it smelled . . . well, delicious, Nish thought. He took a nibble of what Jesse swore was goose, and it tasted wonderful. He took a second piece. It tasted even better.

They rode quickly to the goose camp. The wind was down, and the morning was, unbelievably, as beautiful as the day before when they had started out from the village. They looked like a gang out for a casual ride in the forest: two snow machines and a dog sled, nothing to show that they had nearly drowned, or frozen to death, or, for that matter, been attacked by the dreaded Trickster.

Travis got to ride on the dog sled with the grandfather. It was wonderful, if a bit slower than the Ski-Doos. The dogs barked and pulled, more with a series of yanks than with the steady drive of the machines, but it felt better. He could sense them surging, he could feel their joy as they got onto an open stretch of the bay. The sun was fully out now, and glistening where the ice had been swept clear of snow by the winds. There was no open water around here.

Travis thought about what had happened to them and how incredibly lucky they were. Lucky that Jesse and Rachel knew how to get someone out of the water and build a fire and a shelter. Lucky that the old man had found them.

Nish was still acting as if the dream was real, not something he had dreamt at all. Travis couldn't believe that Nish could have gone to the bathroom in his sleeping bag; he must have been truly terrified. He wondered why he hadn't had a bad dream himself. And then he remembered. *The dream catcher.* Rachel's present was in his pack. It was working!

The dogs began yelping and howling as they came closer to the island where the camp was. The snow machines had already arrived, and Jesse, Rachel, and Liz were hurrying about, checking out the camp.

Jesse and Rachel's grandmother had all sorts of food laid out for them: bannock, caribou, goose, and big fat oatmeal cookies baked with the goose drippings she'd been collecting.

"I'm *starving*!" shouted Nish, and he began digging in. He winked at Travis.

Jesse radioed back to the village, and Travis, standing beside him, was sure he could hear whoops coming from someone who sounded a lot like Muck. He had never heard Muck whoop before, but he was still pretty sure it was him.

"We've all missed games," Jesse said when he turned off the radio. "Rachel's team won this morning."

"*All right!*" shouted Rachel. "*Go Wolverines!*"

"We can't get back in time for our game against the Northern Lights," said Jesse. "My dad and some others are coming, but they can't be here until at least two o'clock."

"What'll we do?" asked Nish.

"Play hockey," Jesse said.

"Yeah!" agreed Rachel.

"Whadya mean?" Nish thought they were still making fun of him.

"Didn't you see the ice on the way out here?" Rachel asked. "It's better than Maple Leaf Gardens!"

"And a hundred times as big!" Jesse added.

14

Travis liked to think of himself as a bit of an expert on ice conditions and hockey rinks, but he had never seen, or felt, anything quite like this.

Until now, he had always believed he liked the ice at the beginning of a game best, when it seemed a puck might slide forever. He liked the way he could kick his ankles out on a corner and shoot up a quick spray of ice with nothing more than a flick of his skate blade.

But now he liked new ice in an arena second best. *This*, he told himself, was special. The howling wind of the night before had cleared the narrows between the island and the shore. The surface was smooth as polished marble.

It was the hardness that delighted Travis the most. Once he put on his skates and set out, he found the noise of his blades astonishing. It was as if someone had turned up the volume.

There was a light wind and, when he went with it, it seemed he was flying even faster than Dmitri. With the skates making a sharp rasp on the ice, he could turn in an instant, the ice so hard and the skates so sharp that there was simply no play in the two at all. Instant response.

They were all out there now. All in their team jackets, different coloured toques, pants, gloves. They threw down a puck and began rapping it back and forth, the sound much louder than in an enclosed arena. It sounded like music to Travis.

"*Let's have a game!*" Jesse shouted.

"*Uneven numbers!*" Travis called back.

There were five of them out on the ice: Jesse, Travis, Liz, Rachel, Nish. They'd have to go three-on-two.

"Where'll we play?" Nish asked. The others all laughed, but he shook his head violently. "No, I'm serious – where?"

"*Wherever we want!*" Liz shouted.

"I'll get some posts," Rachel said.

Rachel skated back toward the camp. Travis could see the grandparents outside, down by the shoreline. They were piling a toboggan high with a variety of goose decoys, some of them the modern plastic kind from the South, most of them original Cree style, made from tamarack twigs tied together to fashion a head, long neck, and plump body.

Jesse and Rachel came back, each carrying two of the large plastic geese. Rachel dumped hers close to the other kids, while Jesse skated farther down the ice with his two.

"Goal posts," she announced as she began setting them upright.

"We've still got uneven numbers," said Travis.

"Grandpa's going to play. It's North against South."

Nish couldn't believe it. "Your *grandfather?*"

Rachel smiled. "It's *his* rink!"

Travis had never even imagined a game like this. No boards, the ice going on forever, goose decoys for goalposts, a switch at half-time because of the wind, *and a goaltender with a shovel!*

There was nothing else for the old man to play with. He didn't seem to mind. He dropped it off his shoulder and plonked it down onto the ice. Then he shoved it hard into Travis's stick and dislodged the puck. The old man laughed. "Hockey," he said.

"Hey!" Nish shouted to Jesse. "Your grandfather can speak English!"

"He can't," said Jesse, laughing. "There's just no Cree word for the game."

They split up into teams, and Travis, Liz, and Nish went down to their own goal, carrying the puck. They gathered for a moment.

"Go easy on them," Travis said. "We don't want the old man falling down or anything."

"Let's go!" shouted Nish.

Travis lugged the puck out a way, then dropped it back to Nish. Nish tried to hit Travis as he broke, but the puck was behind him and shot away, nearly all the way to the island.

"Go get it!" Rachel laughed. "You missed it."

"Now you're finding out why Crees always complete their passes," Jesse called after him.

Travis couldn't believe how far the puck had travelled. Maybe Jesse was right: play here every day and you'd never take a stupid chance. And come to think of it, Jesse's one great strength was the accuracy of his passing.

Travis brought the puck back and lobbed a long pass to Liz, who skated easily with it and then dropped it back to Nish. With Rachel chasing him, Nish dumped the puck out to the middle, where Travis picked it up in full flight. He took Jesse with him toward the island, then let a soft backhand go for Liz, who went in on the old man, *only to have him poke-check her perfectly with the shovel!*

"No fair!" Nish called from behind.

"Whadya mean, 'No fair'?" Jesse demanded.

"How are we supposed to get by a shovel?"

"Wait till you see him rush with the puck!" Rachel laughed.

"Huh?" Nish said, then realized she was kidding.

Jesse carried the puck up, skating easily by Liz. He then passed to Rachel, who was coming up Travis's side. This was the first Travis had seen her skate. She was fast, very fast.

He cut her off, and when she tried to tuck the puck in under his stick, he used his skate to catch it and move it up onto his own stick. He was clear. Nothing between him and the Stanley Cup but an old man with a shovel.

Travis came down on the goal not knowing what to do. He couldn't get too close or the shovel would come out. He couldn't hoist – that would hardly be fair. And he couldn't just shoot a quick one along the ice: the shovel pretty well covered the whole net.

Travis decided to try the amazing move he'd been working on in practice but never dared try in a game, the one Muck kept shaking his head over. He came in, and Jesse's grandfather, laughing, went to the poke check. But just as the shovel moved toward the puck, Travis dropped the puck back so it clicked off first his right blade and then his left, and then, on an unsuspected angle, past the shovel and out the other side. Travis jumped over the shovel, home free, and tapped the puck between the geese.

He turned back and dropped instantly to his knees, spinning as he glided down the ice. He flipped his stick over, pretended to clean the shaft like a sword, and then made a motion as if he were sheathing his trusty blade.

"*Hot dog!*" Jesse shouted, laughing.

"*Muck should be here!*" Liz called. "*The famous move finally worked!*"

"Yeah," Rachel added, "on an old man with a shovel and no skates!"

Travis couldn't tell whether she was kidding him or insulting him. He had to admit it was a bit much. He didn't really know why he'd done it – the big turn, the drop to the knees, the stupid sword thing – but he had. He wanted Rachel to appreciate his terrific move. He wanted her to know what a good hockey player he was. Maybe he didn't know much about the bush, but he sure knew the game of hockey.

They played with no sense of score or time. They raced from end to end, the sounds of their skates as loud as their shouting, the ice flying, the skate blades flashing in the sun, the old man laughing as he stood his ground at the Cree net with his shovel and big hunting boots.

They played until they dropped, and then they went back to the camp, where the grandmother had another meal laid out. Only this time it wasn't goose. It was moose.

"Sorry, Nish," said Rachel as they sat down. "No nostrils, I'm afraid."

Nish scowled and held his plate out. He was too hungry to waste his breath taking shots at anyone. He took extra bannock.

"You haven't got any of that candy left, have you, Nish?" Jesse asked after they had eaten their fill. "We could do with some dessert."

Nish shook his head. "You guys ate it all."

"Come on outside," Rachel said, holding up a clean spoon. They looked at her like she was crazy. "Come on," she repeated. "Everybody."

The sun was still high, and they came out blinking in the strong light. They could see and hear the rescue mission from the village as the snowmobiles appeared along the far shore. They would be here in a few minutes.

Rachel went over to the closest snowbank. It was perfectly white, perfectly clean. She reached out and took a spoonful, blowing some of the fine powder off before turning to Travis.

"You want to try first?" she asked.

Travis didn't know what to say. Rachel had obviously heard the story about Christmas in the bush, but Travis didn't know whether she was making a fool of him or whether he was being given a great honour. When he saw the way she was smiling, he could only nod his head.

"Close your eyes," she said.

Travis closed his eyes.

"Open your mouth."

He opened his mouth.

The spoon rattled on his lower teeth. He could feel the cold of the metal. He closed his mouth over the soft, frozen snow and took it off the spoon. It seemed to explode on his tongue, the cold so sharp, tickling the roof of his mouth, the instant ice and water so refreshing. And almost . . . yes, he had to admit it, almost *sweet*. Just like Jimmy Whiskeyjack's grandmother had said.

"Well?" he heard Rachel ask.

Travis opened his eyes, blinking in the brightness, surprised by how close she was to him. He could smell her, and she, too, smelled bright and sweet as the open air.

"Good," he said.

"You want to try, Liz?"

"Sure."

The grandparents were out, watching and laughing as if they knew the story, perhaps had done it themselves for their own children. Clapping her hands as if she'd just remembered something, the grandmother turned and hurried back into the camp.

Liz smacked her lips.

"Can I have seconds?" she laughed.

Rachel shook her head. "It's a once-in-a-lifetime experience. Nish?"

Nish shook his head. "No way."

"C'mon, Nish!" they called out. The grandmother came back out, giggling to herself.

"C'mon! Give it a try," Liz said.

Rachel nudged him: "It's good – you'll like it."

Nish shook his head, his mouth tightly clenched.

The old woman laughed and took the spoon from Rachel. She grasped Nish by the hand and led him to another bank, where the angle of the sun was now turning the snow the colour of gold. She reached out and took an enormous spoonful. She held it up, smiling.

Nish didn't know what to do. He couldn't say no; she didn't even speak his language. He couldn't be rude.

The grandmother began speaking Cree, almost as if she was singing. She reached up with her other hand and placed it over his eyes, so he would shut them tight.

Nish closed his eyes. He made a quick face and then opened his mouth wide.

Travis barely saw it happen. At first he wasn't sure what she had done, but it seemed the spoon with the snow in it had disappeared into the old woman's pocket and another spoon was suddenly in her hand. Only this one had been dipped in water and then into a sugar jar. It was covered in sugar crystals. She quickly passed the spoon over the snowbank to cover the sugar with a layer of snow.

Then she placed the spoon in Nish's mouth. He bit down, sucked a moment, then opened his eyes wide. Nish looked in total shock.

"Well?" said Rachel.

"I can't believe it," Nish said, his eyes big and black as hockey pucks. "*I can-not be-lieve it.*"

15

ll the way back to the village, and even after they'd arrived, Nish kept repeating, "I can't believe it. I can not believe it."

Travis was amazed at the reception when they got back, the way the entire village once again turned out to greet them, including, this time, the rest of the Screech Owls, their parents, and the coaches.

The first figure they saw when they came within sight of Waskaganish was Muck. Growing impatient, he had walked out to meet them. He hugged them all, even Nish, and Muck never hugged anyone. Not even when they won the championship at Lake Placid.

Data and Andy and Chantal and Derek and Dmitri and Cherry and Gordie and all the rest of the Owls had been standing high on the snowbanks so they would see the snowmobiles come into view, and most of them ran down and out over the frozen bay to meet the lost Screech Owls as soon as they appeared, jogging alongside and cheering their return.

Nish sat like Santa Claus on the last float of the parade, waving to each side. Travis wondered if it had occurred to Nish that this whole thing was taking place because of him.

"*We're in the final!*" Derek called as Travis's ride passed by him.

The Screech Owls had won their game against the Northern Lights, even without their best defenceman, their captain, and Jesse Highboy. And after all the wins and losses had been added up, and all the goals for and against accounted for, it was announced that the First Nations Pee Wee Hockey Tournament final would be played that evening: Screech Owls versus the Waskaganish Wolverines.

"*We made the final!*" Rachel shouted when she got the news. She pointed at Travis and Nish. "*We're* going to play *you* for the championship!"

"You won't have a prayer," Nish said.

"Why not?"

"Shovels are illegal."

Travis was out of sorts. He had dressed carefully for the final game, but he still didn't feel right. Mr. Dillinger had sharpened his skates perfectly. "Good gosh," he'd said when he looked along one of the blades, "what on earth were you doing with these, whittling wood?" Travis told Mr. Dillinger about the hard ice of the bay, and Mr. Dillinger had just shaken his head and gone to work. Now the skates were back the way Travis liked them, even at his most fussy.

He hadn't cut any corners. He had his lucky underwear on. He had tied his right skate first, and then his left. He had wrapped his ankles in shinpad tape. He had kissed the inside of his sweater as he yanked it over his head. He had placed his hand on the "C" stitched over his heart. "C" for captain.

But it still wasn't right. He had only one stick. He liked to have two, minimum, each one as new as possible. Each with the same curve – a "Russian curve," he called it, with a slight flick at the end – and each freshly taped with black tape on the blade and white tape on the handle. Muck had taught him that. "Black tape will rot out the palms of your gloves," he had said, "white tape won't."

But *one* stick – he had only *one* stick. He had brought three up, all brand-new. One he'd given to the captain of the Mighty Geese, the first team they had played. The other he had taken to the camp and stupidly left there. Now he was down to one stick, and if something happened to that one, then he didn't know what he would do.

Muck seemed happy. He had no plays to go over, no hockey to discuss, but he did insist on making a speech.

"This is the icing on the cake," he told them. "You kids have had one of the greatest experiences of your lives up here, and you should be thinking about that when you're out there on the ice.

"We're playing our hosts. If not for them, you wouldn't be here. That doesn't mean you give them the victory – a win that comes that way is really a defeat – but it does mean you play with courtesy. No cheap stuff. No showing off. Listening, Nishikawa?

Nothing but a mature approach and good hockey. Understand?"

No one said a word. No one ever had to say a word after Muck had spoken.

Travis was captain. He knew his job. This was his cue. He leapt to his feet.

"*Let's go, Screech Owls!*"

Nish jumped up after him.

"*Screech Owls, Screech Owls . . . GO, SCREECH OWLS!*"

16

he atmosphere at the Waskaganish Community Arena was electric. The little rink was packed so tight, there wasn't an empty seat to be found. The entire village was there. And all the other teams. It felt like Hockey Night in Canada, not Hockey Night in Waskaganish. He could hear the cheers, the boos, the thundering clap of the public address system as the Wolverines' came onto the ice.

We will,
We will,
ROCK YOU!

Travis rounded the net and did his sweet little hop. He skipped slightly, shrugging his shoulders. He felt good. But he couldn't help thinking about his missing stick. What if he broke his last one?

The Owls warmed up Chantal, who was getting the start on the basis of her play in the game Travis and Nish and Jesse had missed. Travis hit the crossbar – the good luck sign he needed.

The warm-up over, the Screech Owls gathered at the net to charge themselves up. They rapped Chantal's pads. They tapped each other's shins. Travis knocked helmets with Chantal, then his linemates, Dmitri and Derek, then Nish. He usually stopped there, but he found himself going to Jesse and tapping him, helmet to helmet. Travis led the team cheer: "*Screech Owls, Screech Owls . . . GO, SCREECH OWLS!*"

Travis skated out to take the face-off. He looked into the stands and saw Chief Ottereyes sitting with Jesse and Rachel's grandparents. They had come in from the camp to see the game.

He scanned the crowd and found his parents, waving to him. He saw where the Moose Factory Mighty Geese were all sitting.

Travis was facing off against Jimmy Whiskeyjack, his host and the Wolverines' captain. Jimmy winked and tapped Travis's pads with his stick. Travis returned the tap. The big, surly assistant captain was on defence, already scowling at him. Rachel wasn't on the ice. He checked the Wolverines' bench. She was sitting, waiting. He could see the "A" on her sweater.

When the puck dropped, he wasn't paying full attention. The Wolverines' captain swept it away easily, sending it back to the big defenceman. Travis and Dmitri both gave chase (Muck usually wanted only one to forecheck), and the defenceman waited until the last possible second before flipping the puck up to the left winger. Travis and Dmitri turned into each other, catching up in each other's sticks and legs. Travis went down.

The winger hit Jimmy Whiskeyjack as he made the blue-line. The Wolverines' captain deftly flipped the puck over Data's stick and then was all alone, bearing down on Chantal.

Until Nish hit him. Nish simply threw his body at Jimmy, cutting him off and knocking the puck off the stick before, spinning like a top, he tore the legs out from under him. The puck dribbled away harmlessly into the pads of Chantal, who covered up.

"*Alrriigght, Nish!*" Travis shouted. Good old Nish – he had saved the day.

They lined up for the face-off. The big defenceman moved up tight, hoping for a quick shot. Nish took note and shifted.

"*Hey, Moose Nostrils!*" the big defenceman called.

"*Whadya say, Bear Butt?*" Nish called back.

Travis laughed. He knew Nish was here to play. It was going to be a game.

Travis won this face-off. He dropped it back to Nish, who circled his net and hit Dmitri along the boards by the hash marks. Dmitri chopped the puck out into centre, where Derek picked it up and headed for the blueline, the big defenceman backpedalling at full speed.

Derek carried the puck over the line, then left it there while he and the defenceman came together in what looked like, but certainly was not, an accidental collision. The puck sat waiting for Travis, who scooped it up, danced past the defenceman, and put a nifty pass over to Dmitri, who one-timed it off the crossbar.

"OHHH NO!" Travis shouted.

Back on the bench, Muck patted their shoulders. He liked what he was seeing, even though they had no goal to show for it. Travis couldn't stop his legs from jumping with nervous energy. He sat, anxious to get right back out.

Liz's line was on now against Rachel Highboy's. Rachel had the speed, and she also had a big centre with good reach. The centre beat Andy Higgins to a puck and swept it away. Wilson missed it and Rachel flew past him, picking it up and moving in, one-on-one, on Chantal. Rachel deked once and went to her backhand, and roofed a beauty as she pulled around the net.

Wolverines 1, Screech Owls 0.

They flooded the ice between periods. Just like the NHL. Floods, stop time, announcements, goal judges. In the dressing room, Muck seemed content with the way things were going, even though the Owls had failed to score and were now behind in the game.

"Just keep doing what you're doing," Muck said. "It'll come."

He walked to the centre of the room and paused. "Nishi-kawa," he said.

Nish, who had been bending down, catching his breath, looked up, wincing.

Muck almost smiled. "That's hockey you're playing, son."

Travis knew what he meant. Nish was playing the game of his life. He was being double-shifted by Muck and never seemed to stop moving out there. No stupid rushes, no foolish pinches, just Nish at his best: steady, dependable, good on the rush and absolutely perfect on defence.

"You're playing great, man," Travis said as they walked down the corridor to start the next period.

"I have to."

Nish said nothing more. He moved ahead of Travis when they hit the ice, sticking to himself.

Travis's line was starting again. He won this face-off and got the puck back to Nish, who kept it long enough to draw his check. Nish then flipped the puck back to Travis, who headed down-ice, slowly looping when he made the blueline so he could see where Dmitri and Derek were going to be.

Travis hadn't even been looking at his stick or the puck when the big defenceman slashed him. All he felt was the jolt.

The whistle blew. And then, when he looked down, he saw his stick was broken. He threw down what was left of it. Good, at least the big guy was going to get a penalty.

"*Number 7!*" the referee shouted. "*Let's go!*"

Number 7? Travis turned and looked at the defenceman, now skating away. He was wearing number 22. Number 7 was Travis Lindsay.

The referee was glaring at him and pointing to the penalty box. "*Let's go!*"

Travis couldn't believe his ears. "What for?"

"Two minutes for playing with a broken stick! Now let's go! Or it's two minutes more for unsportsmanlike conduct!"

Travis couldn't believe it, but he knew better than to argue. He skated to the penalty box, where the door was already swinging open.

He could hear the cheers. He could hear the odd boo from the Screech Owls' supporters, but it wasn't very loud or very serious. Everyone knew Travis had made a mistake.

Derek skated across with a new stick. He handed it over the boards to Travis.

"You haven't got any left," Derek said. "This one's Liz's. They're almost the same."

Travis took it. They *were* almost the same, but there was still a world of difference. He felt the stick. A left lie, but Liz never put a Russian curve in hers. Neither did she tape the handle the same way. He stood in the penalty box and flexed it, but it didn't feel at all right.

The Owls were shorthanded now with Travis in the penalty box, although it didn't seem that way. The Wolverines were a good team – they moved the puck well, and they shot well from the point, particularly the big defenceman who'd broken Travis's stick – but Travis couldn't believe the way Nish was playing. He was diving in front of pucks. He was ragging the puck and breaking up rushes, and once he even took the puck up-ice and had an excellent shot himself, only to have it tick off the post. When Nish went to the bench at the end of his shift, every fan in the building rose in tribute to him. Nish never even looked up. He sat on the bench, his head down between his legs, gasping for air. From the penalty box on the far side of the rink, Travis could see Muck lay a hand on Nish's neck as he passed behind him. He knew Nish would feel it. He knew Nish would know whose hand it was and what it meant.

"*Hey, Travis!*"

Travis turned, not recognizing the voice.

The captain of the Moose Factory Mighty Geese was standing behind him. He was holding up Travis's stick, the one Travis had given him.

"Looks like you need this back, pal."

Travis took it, flexed it on the floor of the penalty box. It felt great! Perfect! He looked back at his new friend and smiled.

"Thanks," he said.

"Get a goal for me," said the captain of the Mighty Geese.

17

wo Wolverines, the captain and the big defence-man, came down, two-on-one, on Nish. Nish waited, then lunged, brilliantly poking the puck free and up to Derek. Derek turned immediately and hit Travis, who was circling just outside the blueline. The puck felt right on his blade. It was good to have his old stick back.

Travis hit Dmitri right at the opposition blueline. Dmitri swept past the one remaining defenceman and shot, the slapper catching the Wolverines' goaltender on the chest and bouncing back out toward the blueline, where Nish cradled it in his glove and dropped it onto the blade of his stick.

Nish pivoted beautifully, hit Jesse Highboy, coming on in a quick change, with a beautifully feathered pass, and Jesse rifled a shot high in under the crossbar.

Wolverines 1, Screech Owls 1.

The crowd went wild. A goal by the visitors, yes, but a goal by a *Highboy*. They stood and cheered, and cheered again when the announcement was made. Travis skated back to the bench, where Nish was already sitting, trying to catch his breath.

"Great poke check," Travis told him.

Nish looked up, grinning. "An old man taught it to me."

At the next intermission, Muck had nothing to say. He seemed satisfied. Travis had already spoken to him in the corridor, and now Muck stood in the middle of the room and signalled to Travis that it was time for him to speak.

"Your captain has something to say," Muck said.

Travis stood up and cleared his throat.

"We've had a great time here," he said, "no matter whether we win or lose. You all saw that first team we played. No equipment. No gloves. Players had to share equipment. What do you say we leave behind some stuff for them?"

No one said anything. Perhaps they weren't listening. But then Nish began to tap his stick on the cement floor, and soon everyone was tapping their sticks. The answer was yes.

The Screech Owls then played what they would later call their best period ever.

They couldn't get by the big defenceman, and they couldn't get the puck past the Wolverines' goaltender, but it was the same for the opposition. They attacked, especially Jimmy Whiskeyjack and the big defenceman and Rachel, but they couldn't get past Nish. He seemed to be everywhere. Travis looked at his friend and knew that he had found his "zone." He was playing a game that should have been impossible. And if he had wanted to prove a point, he was proving it. No one was calling him Moose Nostrils any more.

Nish broke up another play and sent Dmitri away with the puck. One of the defencemen had been caught pinching in, and the other fell when Dmitri's startling speed caught him off guard. The only Wolverine to make it back was the assistant captain, Rachel Highboy. Dmitri tried to take her off into the corner, but she wouldn't go for the move, so he looped at the blueline and hit Travis coming in.

It was perfect. If Nish had found his "zone," then Travis had found his, too. Everything felt absolutely right: the skates like part of his feet, the stick like an extension of his arms. *He would try his new play!*

He came as close to Rachel as he dared, and then, just as she was about to poke out, he dropped the puck back into his skates. It hit the left one perfectly. The puck bounced with his stride, heading for the right skate – but it never arrived!

He dug in, falling as he turned. Rachel Highboy, with the puck, was moving fast up the ice. She hit Jimmy Whiskeyjack at the blueline, and Jimmy fed it back to her along the boards. She put a pass back, and he one-timed the shot, the puck just clearing a falling, desperate Nish and passing under the blocker arm of Chantal.

Wolverines 2, Screech Owls 1.

In the dying minutes, Nish gave everything he had. He rushed the puck. He shot. He set up plays. He broke up plays. After Muck pulled Chantal for an extra attacker in the final minute, he even stopped a couple of sure goals. But he couldn't do enough.

The Screech Owls had lost.

The horn blew, and the place went wild. It wasn't just the cheering, which was deafening – standing and cheering was not enough. The stands emptied! The crowd poured onto the ice and lifted Rachel and Jimmy Whiskeyjack and the big defenceman and the goaltender onto their shoulders. They sang and cheered and the loudspeakers rumbled with the Wolverines' theme song.

We will,
We will,
ROCK YOU!

Travis couldn't feel bad. The Owls had played well. He had made a mistake, but, as Muck often said, "Hockey is a game of mistakes." And Rachel Highboy had turned his dumb play to her advantage. The hometown team had won, and Travis knew how much that meant.

They lined up to shake hands. Travis congratulated everyone, and when he came to Rachel, she laughed and smiled.

"You shouldn't have showed me that move on the bay," she said.

Travis felt foolish. "I guess not."

She smiled again. "You're a wonderful player."

And then she was gone. Travis hurried through the line, feeling as if he'd just won the Stanley Cup. He had never felt so fantastic in his life!

They lined up at the bluelines. Chief Ottereyes said a few words into a microphone that were lost completely in the echo, but no one was much interested in speeches anyway.

Then the Chief announced the Most Valuable Players from each team. Now everyone paid attention, and when it turned out to be the cousins, Rachel and Jesse Highboy, both sides cheered.

They gave Jesse a new hockey stick, and he immediately skated over to the boards where his family was sitting and handed it to his grandfather, who took it with a smile. The people cheered. But maybe only Travis knew what Jesse meant by giving his prize to his grandfather. He had taught Jesse the secrets of the bush that had saved them. And he had found them in the wilderness. What would have happened if he hadn't come along? Besides, Jesse's grandfather needed a stick. He couldn't go on playing forever with a shovel.

The Chief then announced that there was also a prize for the defensive player of the game. Both sides went quiet so they could hear, but there was never any doubt who would win it.

"Wayne Nishikawa," Chief Ottereyes announced.

Everyone cheered. Both teams slammed their sticks on the ice in appreciation. Nish skated out, saluting the crowd, and took his prize from the Chief.

It was an Ojibway dream catcher.

When Rachel Highboy saw, she yelled, "*From what I've seen, you could really use one!*"

"*Moose Nostrils thanks you!*" he called back. She laughed, along with several other Wolverines who heard him over the din.

Back in the dressing room, Muck shook everyone's hand. He did this only on rare occasions, and this was indeed a rare occasion. No one talked about losing. No one felt as if they had lost.

"This pile in the centre," Travis announced, tossing down his stick. "This is what we give to the Mighty Geese."

One by one, the Screech Owls tossed in their sticks. Barry, the assistant coach, grabbed the entire rack of extras and dumped them into the growing pile in the centre of the room.

"They need gloves, too," said Nish, and tossed his in.

Travis couldn't believe it. What would Nish's mother say? He decided his friend had the right idea, though, and pulled his own gloves off and tossed them onto the pile. Several others followed suit.

Mr. Dillinger walked over with a handful of the skates he carried in the equipment box for emergencies and dumped them all down without a word.

Nish then threw his own skates in, the ice still glistening on the blades.

Not bad, Travis thought, for a guy who wanted to leave the second he got here.

18

Travis didn't want it to come to an end. But it was time to go. The sun was out, the sky as blue as the Maple Leafs' away jerseys, and the entire village had once again come out to the airstrip – on snowmobiles, in pick-ups, and by foot – to see the Screech Owls. Only this time the Owls were going home.

There were actually more people there to see them off than had seen them arrive. The Moose Factory Mighty Geese were out in force. The captain had brought Travis's stick to get it autographed by all the Owls.

"We're going to keep this as our good-luck stick," the captain said.

"Then you should have taken one of mine," Nish said.

No one had changed as much as Nish. He was friendly now. He and the Wolverines' big defenceman had struck up a friendship at the final-night banquet – where the menu had featured burgers and fries and pizza – and Nish had even promised to come up and visit again. Even more startling, they had brought in some moose nostrils, and, to great cheering, Nish had had his photograph taken eating some.

"I guess I won't see you for a while."

It was Rachel. She was alone, smiling, but she did not look happy.

"We're already talking about inviting the Wolverines down for a return match," said Travis.

"That would be nice."

They stood staring at each other for a few seconds. It struck Travis that he might not see her again.

"I'll send you whatever Mr. Dillinger writes up for the paper," he said.

"Thanks."

Travis cleared his throat. He didn't know what to say.

"I really like that dream catcher," he said.

"Use it," Rachel said. "It's specially for you."

"Yeah, well . . . see you."

Rachel said nothing. She reached out and touched his lips with the tip of her mitten – then she was gone.

"ALLL ABBBOARRRDD!" Mr. Dillinger called out.

They began climbing the steps to the Dash 8. Travis turned just before the door and looked back. Rachel was standing at the back of the crowd, on a snowbank, alone. She waved.

Travis turned back and bumped into Nish, who had also stopped at the door to look back.

"She waved at me," Nish said.

Travis started to open his mouth to correct him when Nish gave him a big wink. Chuckling to himself, Nish moved ahead down the aisle and found a seat. Travis joined him. Still laughing to himself, Nish bent down and began removing goodies from his pack: bannock, and wild meat. Travis could see the MVP award, the dream catcher, carefully placed in Nish's pack.

Out over the water, the plane hit the first turbulence. It bucked, settled, then bucked again wildly as the pilot tried to rise into smoother air. But all he found was more pockets as the north wind struck the shore of James Bay and rose right over the village. The plane bucked, fell, jacked sideways, and bucked again.

"I'M GONNA HURL!"

THE END

Murder at Hockey Camp

1

ravis Lindsay shuddered. He couldn't help himself. He had never seen – or felt – anything quite so frightening, so powerful, so absolutely raw.

The storm had broken over the lake. The boys in cabin 4 – which was known as "Osprey" – had seen it coming all afternoon: big bruised fists of cloud heading straight for the camp, the sky dark as night even before the dinner-bell rang. They had gathered on the steps of the cabin to listen to the growling and rumbling as the storm approached, and watch the far shore flicker from time to time under distant lightning.

There was a flash, and Nish began counting off the distance: "One steamboat . . . two steamboat . . . three steamboat . . . four steamboat . . ." A clap of thunder cut him off, the sound growing as it reached them. "Four miles," Nish announced matter-of-factly. Nish the expert. Nish the Great Outdoorsman ever since the Screech Owls' trip up North, when he nearly froze to death because of his own stupidity.

Then came the first overhead burst, and not even Nish dared speak. Directly above them, the sky simply split. It broke apart and emptied, the rain instantly thick and hard as water from a fire hose. The boys scrambled for the safety of the cabin and the comforting slam of the screen door. Travis had his hands over his ears, but it was useless. The second crack, even closer, was like a cannon going off beside them. The air sizzled as if the thunder clap had caused the rain to boil, and the walls of the little cabin bounced in the sudden, brilliant flashes of light that accompanied the explosion.

Not even a half steamboat, Nish, Travis thought to himself. Not even a *row*boat between flash and thunder. The storm was right on top of them!

The six boys in "Osprey" moved to the window. Wayne Nishikawa in front, then Gordie Griffith, Larry "Data" Ulmar, Andy Higgins, Lars "Cherry" Johanssen, and, behind them all, Travis Lindsay, the Screech Owls' captain. They could barely see in the sudden dark of the storm, but then lightning flashed again, and instantly their world was as bright as if a strobe light had gone off. The streak of lightning seemed to freeze momentarily, like a great fiery crack in the dark windshield of the sky. Again they heard the sizzle of fire. And again thunder struck immediately, the walls bouncing, Travis shaking. He felt cold and frightened.

Another flash, and they could see, perfectly, as if in a painting, the girls' camp across the water. Travis wondered if Sarah was watching. Sarah Cuthbertson had been captain of the Owls before Travis, and her new team, the Toronto Junior Aeros, were

in six cabins out on the nearest island, along with the three girls
– Jennie, Liz, and Chantal – who played for the Owls.

In the long weeks leading up to the end of the school year
and the start of summer hockey camp, Travis thought he had
anticipated every part of the upcoming adventure. Swimming . . .
swinging off the rope into the lake . . . diving from the cliffs
. . . waterskiing and fishing and campfires . . . even the mosquitoes. But he hadn't imagined anything like this.

The storm held over them, the explosions now coming so
fast it was impossible to tell which clap of thunder belonged to
which flash of lightning. It seemed the world was ending. The
light over the lake flickered like a lamp with a short circuit.
The rain pounded on the roof. The door rattled in the wind.
And Travis shook as if he were standing naked outdoors in
winter instead of indoors, in a track suit, in July.

It wasn't the cold so much as the feeling of helplessness, the
insignificance. Being afraid of the dark was nothing compared
to this. He'd gladly trade this unearthly light for pitch black and
a thousand snakes and rats and black widow spiders and slimy
one-eyed monsters lurking at the foot of his bed back home,
where there had never, ever, been a storm like this one . . .

KKKKKKRRRRRAAAAACKKKKKKKKK!!

They saw a flash and heard a snap of thunder – but the
sound that followed was new! It was a cracking, followed by a
rushing sound, then a crash that made the cabin jump and the
boys fall, screaming, to their knees.

"*What the hell?*" shouted Nish.

"*The roof blew off!*" yelled Data.

But it wasn't the roof! They were still dry! Andy Higgins, who was the tallest, was the first to stretch up and look out to see what had happened.

"Look at that!"

Now they were all up to see.

"What happened?"

"Lemme see!"

Travis looked out through the rain-dimpled window. One pane of glass was broken, and wind and water were coming in on their faces. Outside, the lawn had vanished. Across the grass, lying right between their cabin and "Loon," the next cabin over – where Willie Granger and Wilson Kelly and Fahd Noorizadeh and Jesse Highboy were staying – was a huge, shattered hemlock, its trunk split and its wood as white as skin where the bark had been ripped away.

It had missed both cabins by a matter of inches.

Travis began to shake even harder.

2

"They're coming to murder us!"

Travis woke sharply to two screams, one coming from Nish, the other coming from a chainsaw right outside the door. Travis must have slept while the storm had passed. Nish was sitting straight up in bed, his sleeping bag pulled over his head, his arms wrapped around his pillow, and he was still yelling about murder. Travis shook his head: his friend had watched too many bad horror movies for his own good.

"They're cutting up the tree!" Travis shouted over the din.

Slowly, Nish pulled off his sleeping bag. He blinked in the bright morning light, then smiled sheepishly.

"I knew that."

It was amazing what a few hours had done. The rain and wind and clouds had all vanished. Sunlight was dancing in the wet grass, and the air smelled new and full of fresh-cut wood.

Two men, wearing hardhats and safety glasses and orange plastic earmuffs, were cutting up the big hemlock. Their chainsaws roared into the wood, the chips flying in a rooster's tail straight into their chests. The men were beginning to look as if they'd been coated in wet sawdust.

There were some spectators gathered off to the side. Travis could see Muck, the only one not in shorts. No one had ever seen Muck in shorts. He had a bad leg, with a long scar that Travis and Derek Dillinger had seen the time the three of them had gone wading after the keys that Derek had thrown away during the trip to Lake Placid.

Travis had trouble imagining Muck in shorts – in fact he had trouble getting used to seeing him in summer at all. Coach Muck Munro went with wintertime. He was at the rink when hockey season began, at the rink when hockey season came to an end. The players rarely, if ever, saw him in the months between.

It was almost as if Muck was something they pulled out of the equipment box in September and stored away again in April with the sweaters – all washed and folded, in his team jacket, baggy sweatpants, hockey gloves, skates, and whistle.

Muck was having words with a man standing on the other side of a thick branch of the fallen tree: it was Buddy O'Reilly, who ran the Muskoka Summer Hockey School, which included both the girls' camp on the island and boys' camp on the mainland. Willie Granger, the Owls' trivia expert, said Buddy had played three NHL games for the Philadelphia Flyers – "No goals, no assists, no points, thirty-two minutes in penalties" – but he carried himself as if he'd won three Stanley Cups. Buddy had on shorts, a tank top, and thongs. He was also wearing neon-purple wraparound sunglasses. And he was chewing gum, fast, using just his front teeth. He was holding a cellular telephone in his right hand, as if waiting for an important call, and had a whistle around his neck. His tank top had the logo of the hockey camp on the back and one word, *Coach*, stitched over his heart. He seemed to be laughing at Muck.

Suddenly, both chainsaws quit at once. A red squirrel seemed to be razzing them from the hemlocks that still stood. The workers laid the chainsaws down so they could twist a large branch. In the lull, the conversation between Muck and Buddy drifted through the cabin's screen door.

". . . irresponsible," Muck was saying.

"Nobody got hurt, big guy," Buddy O'Reilly said through the thin opening between his teeth. He popped his gum. "Nobody got hurt."

Muck stared fiercely, trying to find Buddy's eyes behind the mirror shades. He was very upset. Travis knew Muck would be furious at being called "big guy."

"Look at the core of that tree," Muck said. "It's rotted right out."

"And it's down now," Buddy replied impatiently. "It's down and nobody got hurt."

"Lucky for you."

"Relax, big guy. It's summer-vacation time, okay?"

Muck said nothing. He continued to stare, frustrated by the ridiculous sunglasses.

Buddy ignored Muck completely. He poked a finger hard into the numbers of his cellphone, then waited impatiently while the number rang.

"*Morley!*" Buddy shouted when his call was finally answered. Morley was the gentle, white-haired manager of the girls' camp. "*Morley! Get your butt over here! And find that lazy goof, Roger! We got a tree down between 'Osprey' and 'Loon.' He'll have to clear out these branches!*"

Shaking his head in disgust, Muck finally turned away as the workmen took up their chainsaws. He glanced over at the boys' cabin.

"*What are you staring at, Nishikawa?*"

"Nothin'," replied Nish. He wasn't convincing.

"Dry-land training at eight-fifteen," Muck said, and turned away.

The workers both pulled their chainsaw starting-cords, then gave the smoking engines full throttle. The roar made any more talk impossible.

The boys hurried to dress for breakfast.

@

The girls paddled over from the island camp for the dry-land training session. When they reached the mainland, they carried their canoes up from the beach and turned them over, stuffing paddles and life-preservers underneath. It was a wonderful way to start the day, thought Travis. Sarah paddled as well as she skated: smooth and elegant and strong. It was great to be all back together again.

Travis had been looking forward to this ever since Mr. Cuthbertson, Sarah's father, had approached Muck Munro with the idea of the two teams, the Owls and the Aeros, all coming to the Muskoka Summer Hockey School for a week. The camp covered an area the size of three schoolyards, the land falling away from the boys' cabins to the beach and dock, where they could swim and dive from a tower. A large boathouse at the far end of the beach held a speedboat and equipment for tubing, kneeboarding, and waterskiing. There were also sailboats and paddle boats.

The girls were on the larger of the two islands nearest the shore, and they were allowed to swim or paddle out to the smaller island, where they could hold marshmallow roasts. And best of all, at week's end, they were going to have a one-game, winner-take-all, Owls-against-Aeros Summer Hockey Camp World Peewee Championship.

Muck had never been too keen on the idea of summer hockey – "Ever seen a frozen pond in July?" he'd ask – but was finally talked into it by the other parents and the enthusiasm of the kids on both teams. Besides, the hockey school was just outside Muck's old home town, and he said he had a score to settle with a thirty-pound pike that was still lurking some-where in the narrows that led out of the lake toward the town of Huntsville.

"This guy's a jerk," Sarah whispered to Travis when the boys and girls were assembled together on the training field.

She didn't need to explain. Travis knew she was talking about Buddy O'Reilly, who was indeed acting like a jerk. He had a new shirt on now – candy-apple red with the sleeves cut away at the shoulders to show off his muscles and a tattoo of the Tasmanian Devil chomping a hockey stick in half – and he was blowing his whistle and barking out orders. He had placed his clipboard beside him on the grass, and on top of the clipboard was the ever-present cellphone. No matter what the situation, Buddy wanted everyone to know exactly who was in charge.

"BEND! C'MON, BEND WHEN I SAY 'BEND'!"

Buddy had them doing warm-ups in unison: neck twists, shoulder rotations, leg stretches. Next he ordered everyone to do bends from the waist, and then, bent double, to roll their heads from one side of the knees to the other.

Nish fell over, face forward, which made everyone laugh . . . with one predictable exception.

"WHATSAMATTER, FAT BOY? THAT BIG GUT OF YOURS THROW YOU OFF BALANCE?" Buddy screamed at Nish. And though he wasn't laughing, he was smiling – delighted, it seemed, to have someone to pick on. Nish flushed the colour of Buddy's muscle-shirt.

Travis winced. *Fat Boy!* All Nish had meant to do was put a little humour in the situation. Travis had seen him do dumb things like that before, and even believed that Muck kind of liked Nish's hi-jinks, although Muck would never let on.

Travis looked around for Muck. He was standing off to one side, staring. Muck was the only coach the Screech Owls had at the camp – Barry and Ty, the Owls' two assistant coaches, couldn't take the time off work – and he seemed terribly alone here. Muck didn't have the camp personality. He just didn't fit in. He didn't allow any of the players to call him "coach" ("I don't call you 'forward,' or 'defence,' or 'goaltender,'" he once explained), and he didn't wear wraparound sunglasses, and he sure as heck didn't have any T-shirts with the sleeves ripped off them.

"KNEES UP! KNEES UP!"

Sweat was already pouring down Buddy's face. If this was warming up, Travis wondered, what was working out going to feel like? He could hear Nish puffing and chugging behind him. Travis didn't have to turn around to know that Nish's face would still be shining red. Only by now it would be from anger, not embarrassment. *Fat Boy!* What was with this guy?

At least Travis didn't have to worry about Nish fooling around any more. Usually, if Nish was standing behind you where you couldn't see him, you were in just about the worst place on earth. Just when you least expected it, Nish would be likely to reach out, grab the sides of your shorts, and yank down, showing the world your boxer shorts.

Data was so wary of Nish and his stupid pranks during gym class that he once took the precaution of joining his gym shorts and boxers together with safety pins. But the idea backfired. When Nish snuck up behind Data and yanked, the pins held all right – but Data's shorts and boxers *both* came down!

No, Nish wouldn't be risking another "*Fat Boy!*" insult. If anything, Travis thought, he would be plotting his revenge. And Nish was very, very good at revenge.

As the Screech Owls and Aeros worked out, a work crew moved the chainsawed logs from the cabin area over toward the tool shed. Travis could see a white-haired man struggling with one of the wheelbarrows. It was Morley Clifford, the manager of the island camp. Sarah and the other girls said he was a nice old guy, and Travis couldn't understand how he had ever got involved with Buddy in this summer hockey-school deal.

When the players had finished their field work-out, they ran cross-country around the camp: twice around the playing field, then up along the nature trail, down along the rock trail to the beach, and back, finally, to the main camp building where they ate their meals.

Travis ran with Sarah, and as they ran he wondered what it was that Sarah had been born with that allowed her to be so good at everything she did: skate, paddle, run. Sarah could even talk as she ran: "Word has it that Nish is planning the World's Biggest Skinny Dip."

"H-how d-did you hear that?" Travis panted.

"Data told me yesterday at lunch. It's all over the island."

"H-He's just k-kidding. You know N-Nish."

"He's nuts."

"T-tell me about it."

3

"ssshhhhhhhhhhhh!"

Andy Higgins had his finger raised to his lips as Travis and Lars came back from the afternoon swim. He met them at the door, carefully holding the screen so it wouldn't slam behind them.

"What's up?" Lars demanded.

"Just don't say a word. Come on in."

The three boys entered the cabin silently, Andy carefully setting the screen door so it closed soundlessly.

Nish was lying on his bunk, flat on his back with his eyes wide open. His eyes were rolling around and didn't seem to be focusing on anything. Was something wrong?

"*Shhhhhh*," Andy hissed very quietly.

Travis drew closer to Nish's bunk. His eyes were still rolling; he seemed to be searching for something. In his right hand he clutched the microphone from Data's boom box. Data had brought along the tape recorder and the microphone so he and the others could make up a camp song about the Screech Owls, but so far no one else had shown much interest in it.

What was Nish doing?

Andy signalled for Lars and Travis to freeze. Nish had raised the microphone and was holding it next to his face. Travis could hear a very quiet buzzing whine, and then realized that Nish's rolling eyes were following a mosquito circling around his head.

Nish hated mosquitoes. *What on earth was he up to?* Nish let the intruder land on the side of his neck, and, instead of raising a hand to crush the dreaded insect, he slowly moved the microphone closer. The mosquito rose, circled, whined, and landed a second time. Nish moved the microphone near again, causing the mosquito to take off once more. This time, when it landed, Nish's other hand came down like a hammer.

"BINGO!" Nish yelled, and rolled out of the bunk bed looking delighted.

"Did you get it?" Andy asked.

"I don't know," Nish answered. "I'm not sure."

"It's right on your hand," Travis pointed out. "You squashed it – look at the blood!"

Nish and Andy looked at Travis as if he came from another planet.

"Not the *mosquito*, dummy," Nish said, "the *sound*."

Andy and Nish settled over Data's boom box to rewind the tape. Then Nish pushed the *play* button and cranked up the volume.

Travis and Lars couldn't believe the effect. It seemed as if the cabin was filled with mosquitoes. The squeal of the insect was unbelievable. They could hear it circling, landing, circling again, landing, circling a third time and – *slap!*

"That's gotta go!" Nish said. Andy nodded.

"What's gotta go?" asked Travis, confused.

Nish looked at Travis, unimpressed. "The *slap*, of course."

"Why?" Lars wanted to know.

"You'll see, my friend. You'll see."

C-RACKKKKK!

Nish was first to jump up: "*What the . . . ?*"

"What was *that*?" Travis asked, running to the screen door. His first thought was that it was another round of thunder – or maybe another tree coming down – but the sky was clear and blue.

C-RACKKKKK!

"*It's coming from over there!*" Andy shouted, pointing in the direction of the shed where the lawnmowers and chainsaws were stored.

The boys began running toward the shed. They were joined by others heading in the same direction; the gang from "Loon"; Dmitri Yakushev from "Raven" cabin; Jeremy Weathers and Derek Dillinger from "Kingfisher."

Nish stopped in his tracks, his mouth falling open in shock.

There, behind the shed, Buddy O'Reilly was wrestling with a man holding a rifle! Buddy seemed to have jumped him from behind. The man, in greasy green coveralls, was trying to twist away. Travis thought he recognized the man, but couldn't quite remember where he'd seen him.

Others were running up now: Morley Clifford from the island camp, the lines in his face dark with concern; Muck from the cabins.

"What the hell's going on here?" Muck demanded in a low, cool, commanding voice.

Buddy now had the rifle free. He turned, triumphant, holding the gun away from the man, who scowled. Buddy held up the gun as if it were a trophy he'd just been awarded.

Muck moved faster than the Screech Owls had ever seen him move before. He ripped the rifle out of Buddy's hands, and worked the bolt back and forth to empty out the rest of the bullets – *one, two, three, four, five*, the bullets flew, spinning and glittering in the sunlight – and then he stomped them into the ground. Travis couldn't believe how smoothly Muck handled a gun.

"*Explain*," commanded Muck.

"Just keep your nose out of it, okay?" said Buddy. He seemed very angry.

"You fire a rifle around my kids, you answer to me," Muck said. "What's the meaning of this?"

The man who had been shooting spoke. He had bad teeth. "You wouldn't want a rabid fox around your kids, either, would you, mister?"

Buddy winced, and gave the man a look that said, *Why can't you keep your mouth shut?* Suddenly his manner changed, from nasty to nice.

"Roger here *thinks* we might have a small wildlife problem . . ."

Travis remembered where he'd heard the name. *Roger* – of course, the caretaker Buddy had called to clean up the fallen tree.

"Whatdya mean '*thinks*'?" Roger snarled. "You know as well as me there's rabies around."

"That true?" Muck asked, staring directly at Buddy.

Buddy smiled, but the smile seemed forced. "There *was*, but way back in the spring."

"A fox don't walk in here in plain daylight lest he's sick," Roger argued. "No matter what the season."

"Is that what you were shooting at?" Muck asked him. "A fox?"

"And I'd'a got him, too, if this lunkhead hadn't grabbed me."

"Easy now, Roger," Morley Clifford said soothingly. Roger seemed to respect Mr. Clifford, and nodded quickly, as if to say he knew he'd better cool down before he really upset Buddy.

But Buddy was acting sheepish, almost sweet. "C'mon, Roger. We can't have guns going off at a summer camp when there's kids all over the place, now, can we? Lucky for you they were having rest time in the cabins."

Roger spat. Travis could hear Nish beside him: "*Yuk!*" Roger obviously chewed tobacco.

"I think I know the difference between a rabid fox and a damn kid," Roger said.

"And I know the difference between a properly run camp and a joke," Muck said to Buddy O'Reilly. "You didn't think we needed to know there was rabies about?"

Buddy smiled, trying to win someone onto his side. "The Ministry said it was all cleared up."

"Not that I heard," said Roger.

Travis knew instantly that Roger was telling the truth and that Buddy was lying. There was something about Buddy's overly sincere look that told you not one word this man said could ever be believed.

"And you didn't think there was anything wrong with firing a gun with kids around?" Muck asked Roger.

Buddy gasped, shaking his head in disbelief. "You forget – *I'm* the one who tried to stop him from shooting!"

"It would all be over now if you'd just let me alone," muttered Roger.

Muck had heard enough: "Well, gentlemen – it *is* over now. I want the rest of those bullets."

Muck held out his hand. There was no mistaking the order. Roger looked at Morley Clifford – not at Buddy – and Mr. Clifford closed his eyes and nodded once. Roger seemed about to argue, but instead dug into the pocket of his filthy coveralls and pulled out a small box, which he slapped into Muck's open palm.

Muck pocketed the bullets.

"And I want a Ministry official out here to talk to the kids about rabies," Muck added in a firm voice. "Understand?"

"No problem," Buddy answered. He was smiling, but he didn't look pleased.

Muck looked at the rifle, now cradled in his elbow and disarmed. "I'll be hanging on to this until the end of our stay."

4

The ministry sent two park rangers out in the evening. Both groups, the boys from Arrowhead Camp and the girls from Algonquin, gathered in the dining hall to listen to the talk on rabies. They learned what it was: a disease that causes wild animals to stop drinking water and eventually makes them go mad, often attacking other larger animals and sometimes even humans.

"You've all heard about the foaming at the mouth," the older ranger told them. "But that's when the disease is far advanced. There are few signs in the early stages – although the animal often shows up somewhere it wouldn't normally be. Like in your backyard, or walking directly toward you."

"Sometimes people get bitten and we can't find the animal to see if it really has rabies," said the younger ranger. "And unfortunately that generally means the person has to be treated, just in case rabies was present. That's a series of shots. Big needles, too, and they hurt – believe me, I've had them."

The kids shuddered.

The rangers quickly added that it was unlikely there were any sick animals around the camp. There had been a small outbreak in spring, but nothing lately. Even so, they said, the kids should avoid approaching any wild animal that appeared disoriented and not afraid of them, no matter how harmless and cute that animal might seem. They should be particularly wary, the rangers said, of foxes and, especially, skunks.

At the mention of skunks, everyone turned and looked at Nish, who had a reputation for making long road trips unbearable. Nish shook his head and rolled his eyes so he looked insane. He took a quick bite in Andy's direction and Andy jumped, which made the whole room break up.

Even Muck smiled. The Owls needed something to break the tension. This week at camp wasn't going at all as planned.

Nish had his own plans.

The boys returned to "Osprey" after the Ministry rangers had left and everyone had enjoyed a late-evening snack of hot chocolate and huge oatmeal cookies. Usually, Nish could be expected to beg or scrounge a second or even a third cookie, but this time he and Andy took off for the cabin as soon as the cookies were served. They said they were wiped out and wanted to turn in early.

The others – Travis, Gordie, Data, and Lars – came in later, and already the lights were out. Andy was lying in his bunk, still awake, but Nish was already snoring like one of the chainsaws cutting up the big fallen hemlock. Andy raised a finger to his lips: "*Shhhhh.*"

The boys came in quietly, undressed quickly, and slipped into their sleeping bags. Out on the lake, a loon called. Travis smiled; he loved its strange, laughing cry. The moon was out, and enough light was spilling in through the cabin window for Travis to make out the bunks. He liked the moon coming in like that. No need for a night-light.

Travis could tell that Lars had fallen asleep. Data was also dead to the world; he was breathing deeply and, from time to time, mumbling to himself, but Travis couldn't quite make out what Data was saying. Perhaps he was speaking Klingon, as he sometimes did. Andy was still moving about. Lars was trying to get away from a mosquito. And Nish was still out cold. Or so it seemed.

Nish giggled.

Travis had been sure Nish was sound asleep. But no, he was moving in his sleeping bag, getting up. Had he forgotten to go to the bathroom?

Now Andy was getting up, too.

"What's up?" Travis whispered.

"*Shhhhh,*" said Nish. "Just watch this."

Nish and Andy tiptoed over to the bunk where Data lay mumbling in a deep sleep. Nish kept giggling, and Travis and Lars crept up to see. Travis had no idea what was going on.

Nish pulled Data's boom box out from under his bunk. He hoisted it up and set it beside Data's head. "*Shhhhhhhh,*" he repeated. It was hardly necessary, but Nish was now into heavy dramatics.

Andy balanced the boom box carefully and, on Nish's signal, turned it on.

Instantly, the room filled with the sound of a circling, angry mosquito. It sounded, Travis thought, as much like a siren as an insect, but Nish and Andy seemed to want it loud.

Nish pulled a white gull feather out from under Data's mattress, and as soon as the mosquito's whining stopped for a moment, which meant it had landed, Nish very lightly tickled Data's nose with the feather.

Data stirred, and Nish giggled softly, delighted with the results.

The mosquito on the tape recording took off again, the sound rising as it circled closer and closer. This time, when it landed, Nish ran the feather very lightly along Data's ear. Data's right hand came up and brushed away the tickle, but he didn't wake.

Nish signalled to Andy. Andy hit the *stop* button and then pushed *rewind*.

Nish reached under Data's bunk bed again and this time pulled out an aerosol can of shaving cream. Very carefully, he began to fill Data's right hand with foam. When he had built up a nice big mound, he capped the can and slipped it back under the bunk.

Nish gave Andy the thumbs-up. Andy pushed the *play* button and the mosquito took off again. Andy turned up the volume and moved the tape recorder even closer. Data stirred, mumbling.

The taped mosquito landed. Andy pulled the boom box away. Nish leaned over and poked the feather just under Data's nose, then ran it down over his mouth and onto his chin.

Slap! Data's right hand came up and smacked into the imaginary mosquito, sending shaving cream spattering into his face and pillow. Data mumbled, but didn't wake up.

"*Perfect*," hissed Nish, backing away from the bunk.

"Better than we thought," whispered Andy.

"Why Data?" Travis asked.

"Test case," said Nish. "Nothing personal."

"What do you mean, 'test case'?"

"If it worked this well on Data," grinned Nish, "think how great it'll look on our good friend, Buddy O'Reilly."

"Fat Boy" was going to have his revenge.

5

Travis woke before the morning bell. It was going to be a glorious day. He lay in bed, staring out the window and listening to the birds. He wished he knew birds better. He wished he could say things like "white-throated sparrow" instead of just "bird." He decided he would become an expert on birds some day. He'd even find out what an osprey was.

Data was sitting up in bed. He was rubbing his eyes with the back of his hands, but still hadn't noticed the dried shaving cream all over his face. He hadn't even noticed it on his hand. Perhaps it was too early in the morning for him.

"You feeling okay?" Nish asked with utmost sincerity.

Data blinked. "Yeah . . . why?"

"You don't look so good, you better go look in the mirror."

Data still hadn't caught on. Puzzled, he slipped out of his sleeping bag and peered into the mirror over the sink.

"*What the – ?*" Data shouted.

"You're foaming at the mouth, pal," Nish told him. "Looks like rabies to me."

◎

"In-your-face hockey!

"You understand me – you, Fat Boy? You understand what I'm getting at here?"

They were at the arena in the tourist town just down the road from the camp. Buddy O'Reilly was standing at centre ice, sweat pouring off his face. Nish lay flat on his back in front of Buddy, moaning as he gasped and twisted on the ice.

Buddy had just flattened Nish with one of the hardest and meanest checks Travis had ever seen, and the hardest, by far, he had ever seen at a "practice." The hit had caught everyone off guard, but none more so than Nish himself, who had had his head down as he moved up toward centre on a simple five-on-four power-play drill. Nish knew his job: pick up the puck behind the net, then lug the puck up past the blueline and hit Sarah as she cut across centre ice. He'd timed it perfectly, slipping a nifty little pass in under Buddy's outstretched stick and sending Sarah and Travis and Dmitri in toward the opposition blueline.

Then Buddy had struck. He hit Nish full on, his hands and stick coming up hard into Nish's helmet, and Nish had dropped instantly.

Buddy stepped back to demonstrate.

"You see what I mean by in-your-face hockey? This is what I want to see from you guys – I don't give a damn whether it's for the Stanley

Cup or summer-camp practice. You take your man out. Understand? You okay, Fat Boy?"

Buddy was laughing – that strange, front-of-teeth, chewing-gum snicker – as he reached down and helped Nish get to his feet. Travis couldn't help noticing that Buddy seemed a little concerned; perhaps he realized he had hit Nish just a bit too hard. Nish skated away, trying to get the air back in his lungs. He was bent over, his face almost on his knees. His skates wobbled and he almost went down again.

Nish's face was twisted up and red. He was hurting, fighting back tears.

"You hit, you follow through. Understand? Hit high, follow through like I showed you, with your forearms – it's perfectly legal. You take him out, okay? You saw what happened. They came out on a power play, I hit Tubby here, and suddenly it's even-up again, four-on-four, with Fat Boy wobbling off to the bench. Understand now? Huh?"

Buddy looked around, pulling nods of agreement out of some of the shocked Owls and Aeros. Others just stared, waiting to see what Buddy would do next. He had been screaming since the on-ice drills began, and he had skated them until Nish, predictably, had called out, *"I'm gonna hurl!"*

"Then hurl!" Buddy screamed back at him.

It seemed to Travis that Buddy was particularly hard on Nish. Calling him "Fat Boy" and "Tubby," and now almost knocking him cold. What had Nish done to deserve this?

Muck had waited until the warm-ups were through before coming out. He had put on his skates and had his stick and gloves – his plain windbreaker a sharp contrast to Buddy's neon-red tracksuit – and he had stayed out of it, at first. This was Buddy's hockey camp, after all.

But after the hit on Nish, Muck came forward, pushing through the shocked players and speaking, very softly, to Buddy.

"Can I see you for a moment?"

Buddy looked irritated, as if his train of thought had been broken.

"How's after practice?" Buddy asked.

"Only if it ends right now."

Reluctantly, Buddy skated away with Muck. They left the ice entirely, leaving the remaining drills up to the two young junior players, Simon and Jason, who were helping out for the summer.

"I'm gonna get that guy!"

Travis turned quickly. It was Nish. He had skated up behind Travis and was still bent over as he worked on getting his breath back.

"I'll get him – I promise you that."

With Buddy out of the way, practice became fun again. Simon and Jason ran a couple of passing drills and then decided to turn the last ten minutes over to a game of shinny – A-to-Ls versus M-to-Zs. That put Sarah and Travis on the same team, just like the old days, and against Nish, who slapped the blade of his stick on the ice and announced for all to hear that neither Sarah nor Travis would score while he was on the ice.

Travis hadn't played with Sarah since the Lake Placid tournament. And he hadn't played left wing since he'd replaced her at centre. Derek Dillinger joined them on the right wing for the opening face-off.

Sarah faced off against Liz Moscovitz, who'd joined the Owls after Sarah had left for the Aeros. Liz, who usually played wing, had no idea what kind of tricks Sarah could pull in a hockey game. Simon dropped the puck, but it never even hit the ice: Sarah plucked it out of midair, knocking it baseball-style over to Travis.

"That's *illegal!*" Liz shouted. No one paid her the slightest attention.

Travis had the puck, and he turned back quickly, skating behind his own defencemen and dropping the puck to Beth, a member of the Aeros, as he moved back across the blueline. She read the give-and-go perfectly, waiting until Travis had beaten Liz before flipping the puck ahead to him. He hit Derek across ice, and Sarah broke fast toward the opposing blueline.

Derek sent the pass to her – hard and accurate.

But it never got there. A big blur slid across the ice and snared the breakaway pass before it could snap onto Sarah's tape. It was Nish! He knew Sarah's renowned speed, and he had guessed – correctly.

Travis could hear Nish's giggle as he passed while still down on one knee. Nish hit Liz, who was coming back across centre, and Liz, without seeming to look, fired a hard backhand pass up to Dmitri, who was breaking down the right-wing boards. Dmitri was in alone on net, did his shoulder fake, and fired the puck high in off the crossbar.

Nish, the hero, lay flat on his back, pumping arms and legs into the air as if he'd just won the Stanley Cup, in overtime.

"He's never going to grow up, is he?" Sarah said to Travis as she looped past him.

"Not if he can help it," said Travis.

He could see Sarah smiling through her mask. She didn't seem in the least upset that Nish had outsmarted them. "Watch this," she said.

Sarah won a second face-off from Liz and moved the puck back fast to Beth, who waited just long enough to trap the wingers before flipping the puck high and over centre ice. It was obviously a play they'd worked on with the Aeros. So long as the puck went across centre before Sarah, she wouldn't be offside, and she was so fast she could follow the lobbing puck and almost catch it on her stick when it fell.

The play worked perfectly. Sarah snared the puck on her stick and skated toward the net as Nish backed up, ready.

Sarah skated toward Nish, then cut sharply in a quick circle that let her drop her left shoulder. Nish went for the shoulder drop and lunged with a poke check – but Sarah's stick and the puck were gone. She had scooped the puck onto the end of her stick blade as if it were a small pizza she was about to place in a hot oven.

Sarah flipped the puck high over Nish's head and flailing glove as he lost his balance and fell. Then she skipped over him and walked in on net, pulling Jeremy Weathers far to the right before sending a remarkable pass back through her own skates and straight onto Travis's stick. Travis merely tapped it in.

Travis rode his stick like a horse to the blueline. He yanked the stick from between his legs and turned it on its end, pretending to sheathe it at his side, as if it were a sword and he a triumphant knight returning from the battlefield.

Then he heard Sarah scream.

6

ravis turned in mid-celebration, suddenly embarrassed that he had made such a show of a totally meaningless goal. Sarah's scream had come from the corner where she had turned after her cute set-up. She was crumpled on the ice, and Nish was skating away backwards, pointing at her with the blade of his stick.

Jason's whistle shrieked as he and Simon raced toward Sarah. Travis skated over quickly as well, passing Nish on the way. He glanced with dismay at Nish, but he couldn't read Nish's look. Anger? Surprise? Shock?

Simon loosened the strap on Sarah's helmet, and Travis was able to get close enough to see that she was crying before Simon chased everyone away.

"*Give her some air! C'mon, back off!*"

Travis and the others skated back toward the blueline. Everyone looked shocked.

"What happened?" Travis asked Dmitri.

"Nish took her out. He hit her from behind when she wasn't looking."

"Nish?"

"I saw him."

It had to be true. Jason was ripping into Nish over by the penalty box. Even in the hollow arena, the rest of the players could make out every shouted word.

"*You stupid idiot!*" Jason was screaming. "*You coulda broken her neck. You can't hit someone like that when they're not expecting it!*"

Nish's answers were harder to make out, but Travis knew his friend's voice well enough to get the drift.

"I thought we were supposed to 'take out our man,'" he said to Simon.

"Who told you that?"

"*Buddy*. That's exactly what he said when he creamed me. Remember? Or don't I count?"

"He didn't mean like *that*, you stupid jerk. You never, *ever*, *ever* hit from behind like that again. Now get off the ice before we throw you off! *Get outta here!*"

Nish swore and slammed his stick on the boards so hard it shattered. As he left, he pulled the gate behind him hard, so the noise exploded in the hollow rink.

Travis didn't need to follow to know what Nish would do next. Kick the dressing-room door. Kick every bag and piece of equipment between the doorway and his locker. Throw his broken stick against the wall. Yank off his skates and throw them against the wall – better yet, strike the blades so Mr. Dillinger has to grind them down and rocker them again before a new sharpening. Throw his sweater on the floor. Throw his shoulder pads in the garbage. Throw his socks. Throw his shinguards. Sit and slump and sulk in his underwear until everyone comes in and sees how badly life is treating poor Wayne Nishikawa.

Travis knew Nish well enough to be almost certain he regretted his check on Sarah the moment he realized what he had done. The problem with Nish was that he couldn't put the brakes on even when he knew he should – even when he *wanted* to. Having made the dumb hit, he had to follow through, knowing that only he would lose in the end. He was like fireworks. Once the fuse had been lit, there was no way to prevent the explosion. You couldn't change direction, delay, or stop. You could only wait for it to go off and eventually die down on its own.

Sarah was still lying motionless on the ice. Simon had done the right thing by not taking off her helmet or attempting in any way to move her. They were asking her about her limbs – "Your left foot? . . . Your right arm? . . . Wiggle your fingers for us" – and Sarah was able to do as they requested.

"I think I'm all right," she said. Her voice sounded weak and frightened.

"We have to be sure," Simon told her. "Jason's calling an ambulance. You just stay exactly where you are and don't move."

Simon rose from his knee and turned toward the rest of the players.

"Practice is over for today!" he called. "Off with your gear and shower. We're headed back to the camp at ten-thirty sharp. Get a move on!"

Nish was exactly as Travis had pictured him: slumped against the wall, the results of his personal tornado all about him. He seemed distraught and angry at the same time. He was shaking his head and mumbling to himself. Travis figured it was just as well they couldn't make out what he was saying.

Everyone gave Nish a wide berth. Apart from Andy Higgins, hardly anyone even looked in his direction.

"That was a dumb thing to do," Andy said directly to Nish.

Travis was surprised Andy would be so blunt. But good for Andy – he was speaking for them all.

Nish made an empty-hands gesture to show his own surprise. "Fine," he said, his voice cracking. "It's a big joke when 'Fat Boy' gets creamed by 'Buddy Boy,' but it's a criminal act when 'Fat Boy' does the same thing to someone else."

"Don't be stupid, Nish," said Andy. "You didn't get hit from behind. And besides, nobody thought it was a big joke when that ass creamed you."

"I was just finishing my check," said Nish. He looked around, desperate for an ally, begging for anyone to agree with him, or even nod in sympathy.

"You may have finished Sarah," said Travis.

Nish turned quickly, hurt and anger flashing in his eyes. He hadn't figured Travis, his best friend, would turn on him.

"It was an accident."

"No it wasn't," said Dmitri. "It was just stupid."

Nish answered by picking up the one piece of equipment still within reach, a dropped glove, and hurling it hard against the ceiling. The glove popped back down and bounced off the top of the door to the washroom stall – up, over, and *splash*, directly into the toilet boil.

The sound was so unexpected, the bounce such a fluke, that everyone in the room began to giggle. Nish had accidentally released the tension that had built throughout this disastrous practice, and the giggles became laughs, and the laughs became howls of derision, all aimed his way.

Nish slumped deeper into the bench, his arms folded defiantly, his eyes closed, and, it seemed, small tears squeaking out on each side.

The fireworks were over.

7

fter they had dressed, the Screech Owls and the Aeros gathered at the edge of the parking lot to watch the ambulance come and take Sarah away. They stood in silence, not knowing what to say, not wanting to say anything, only hoping that everything would be all right.

Travis stood outside with Data and Wilson and Derek and Lars, the five of them with their hands in their pockets, kicking at loose stones with their sandals. They stared as the ambulance drew up, lights flashing. It backed through the Zamboni entrance and into the arena, right onto the ice and over to the corner where Sarah was still flat on her back, not moving a muscle.

Travis noticed Nish in the parking lot at the far end of the arena. He was leaning into the wall. He seemed lost. As Nish's best friend, Travis knew that now, only now, he should go to him. And if Nish felt like talking, they would talk. If he didn't, they would say nothing. Travis didn't have to hear the words to know how his friend felt.

He broke away from the waiting crowd and walked toward Nish. He came up behind him quietly, but not quietly enough. Just as Travis cleared his throat to speak, Nish raised his hand behind him in a warning to be quiet. He turned quickly, finger raised: "*Shhhhhhh . . .*"

Travis tucked in tight to the wall. "*What's up?*" he whispered.

"*Take a look — but don't let them see you.*"

Travis poked his head out just far enough that he could see around the corner and into the arena's main parking lot. Beyond the two buses that would take the players back to camp was a flashy red-and-black 4x4: Buddy O'Reilly's truck, with his name on the side. Beyond the truck stood Buddy and Muck, toe to toe, arguing about something.

"*What're they saying?*" Travis asked Nish.

"I can only make out a few things. Muck told him if he ever so much as touches one of us again, he'll come after him."

Buddy was swearing now, very loudly. The words cut across the parking lot. Muck would not take well to this. He himself hardly ever swore. He threw kids off the ice if they swore. He made parents leave the stands when they swore at referees. Buddy was insulting Muck in a way they could never have imagined.

". . . *washed-up old fart!*" Buddy screamed.

He swore and yelled at Muck worse than he'd yelled at Nish. "*The game has passed you by!*" he shouted. The disgust in Buddy's voice was cruel. ". . . *a bunch of losers coached by a loser!*"

Muck took a step forward and slapped Buddy's face. The slap was so hard, Travis could hear it as plainly as he heard Nish's stick when he had slammed it into the boards.

"*Did you see that?*" Nish asked. His voice was shaking with admiration for Muck.

"*See* it?" Travis said. "Did you *hear* it?"

Buddy recoiled in shock. He put his hand to his mouth and looked for blood, then threw his wraparound sunglasses in on the seat of his 4x4 and attacked. He lunged at Muck, but never got there. The Zamboni driver and Jason, the junior coach, had come running out into the parking lot and were trying to break the fight up before it started. Jason had Buddy pushed back toward his truck, and the Zamboni driver had his arms circled around Muck, who was putting up no resistance. Muck had made his point.

Buddy was another matter. He was struggling, but not too much. He seemed to be desperate to get back at Muck but unable to break free of Jason's hold. Travis had seen this a hundred times before in NHL games. The fighters made it look as if they were trying to get through the linesman, but in fact they were grateful the linesman was there and that the fight was over. You struggled for show. You made it seem like you'd kill the guy if you could only get there – a huge, hulking hockey player in full equipment, held back by a smaller, older linesman wearing hardly any protective equipment at all.

Travis wondered whether professional hockey fighters had any idea how silly this looked.

That's how Buddy O'Reilly looked now. He was much bigger and stronger than Jason, but he was acting as if he couldn't get through him. Travis and Nish knew why. "*He's afraid of Muck*," said Nish. "*The bully's a big chicken.*"

Buddy wouldn't throw a punch, but he was sure throwing insults.

"*You stay the hell out of my way!*"

The boys had to strain to hear Muck. "No, mister," Muck was saying in his steady, firm, almost quiet voice, "you stay out of mine if you know what's good for you."

Nish was giggling: "Good ol' Muck."

"Buddy O'Reilly's a nut," said Travis. "This thing isn't over yet."

@

Sarah Cuthbertson was fine. As she lay on the ice, they had locked her head into place with a special brace, then worked a stretcher under her and whisked her away to the Huntsville hospital. She'd been checked over, X-rayed, given a couple of Tylenol, and then sent back to camp with instructions that she was to rest and be woken up every two hours to make sure there had been no concussion. She'd be able to go back on the ice the moment she felt like it.

When word went around the camp, it was as if school had been let out for the summer. The Screech Owls, most of whom had been resting in their cabins, ran around high-fiving each other and cheering. The girls from the island camp paddled over, and they all spent the rest of the afternoon swimming and skiing and kneeboarding and wakeriding behind the camp's outboard, with Simon driving and Jason acting as spotter.

The star of the skiing contest was, much to everyone's surprise, Lars "Cherry" Johanssen. He could not only slalom but could take off on the one ski. Cherry was also the best on the camp's new wakeboard, turning 360s as he took the wake, and twice trying a full flip, once successfully and once landing smack on his head, which brought a great round of applause from the dock.

"How'd you ever learn to do that in Sweden?" Data asked when Lars swam back in after his fall.

"You think we don't have summer and water and fast boats in Sweden?" Lars asked.

"Do you?" said Data.

"Of course we do. But I didn't learn it there. I learned those tricks in winter."

Wilson bit: "*How?*"

"Snowboarding, dummy. You ever hear of it?"

"You do that there, too?"

"There's a lot more to winter than hockey, you know."

Wilson tried the wakeboard but couldn't even get up. Travis tried it and got up, but he couldn't stay up long. Nish insisted on being next.

"You can't even ski on snow," called Travis from the water.

"If the Swede can do it, anybody can do it," Nish announced. He was back in form. No one, Travis knew, was more relieved than Nish at the good news about Sarah.

Nish put on a life-jacket and sat down on the edge of the dock. He called to Travis to push the board in to him.

"*You're not going from the dock?*" Data shouted.

"Why not? Cherry did."

"But he's an expert!"

"He can do it, I can do it."

Nish got the board onto his feet with some struggle, then picked up the rope and gave the thumbs-up for the boat to head out. Simon put the outboard in gear and slowly took up the slack, then he gave full throttle.

The rope tightened, and Nish closed his eyes, and hopped off the edge of the dock. The board submarined, then surfaced, and up went Nish, to a huge cheer from the crowd, led by Lars. *He had done it! Nish was up and away!*

Travis stood cheering with the rest of them. He hadn't expected this of Nish, who usually frowned upon any activity other than hockey or trying to rig up motel TVs so the Owls could watch restricted movies. He was doing a pretty good job of it, too, leaning his body just as he had seen Lars lean, digging in just as Lars had done. Only Nish, being so much heavier, was throwing up twice the spray.

Nish turned sharp so that a thick curtain of water rose between him and the cheering spectators on the dock – then it seemed the water behind the spray simply exploded.

"*He's down!*" Gordie Griffith called out.

"*Nish fell!*" Data shouted.

"*Whale!*" Andy yelled.

With everyone laughing, Nish surfaced, lake water spurting from his mouth. He did indeed look like a whale coming up for air.

Simon turned the boat and brought it around. He and Jason were laughing as well.

"*You want to go again?*" Jason shouted at Nish.

"*See if you can get up from the water!*" Simon yelled.

"*I'll try!*" Nish called, choking. He began struggling with the board, but it was impossible. It kept slipping off and popping to the surface. Finally he shook his head. He couldn't do it.

"I'll swim in!" he called to the boat. Jason began pulling in the tow rope, looping it neatly around his forearm as he did so.

Nish began coming in, the life-jacket making it difficult to swim with much grace.

"THE TURTLE!" someone screamed.

Travis turned. It was Liz Moscovitz. She was pointing off the dock, toward Nish.

"THE BIG SNAPPER!" Jennie Staples shouted.

Travis couldn't see it, but it had been there earlier. The area under the dock was home to Snappy, a huge snapping turtle, its shell as big as a truck hubcap. Sometimes on a sunny day it would crawl up on a log. It was grey and green and had a huge head and jaws. Someone said a previous camper had once tried to knock it off with a paddle and that the turtle had snapped the paddle clean in half before slowly dropping into the water and down under the big boathouse where the boats and sails and life-jackets were stored.

"*It's coming right at you, Nish!*" Chantal Larochelle screamed. She seemed really frightened, genuinely afraid for Nish.

Nish panicked. He began pounding the water as he tried to swim faster, but the life-jacket slowed him down.

"HELLLPPPPPP!!!!"

Simon heard him and gunned the boat toward Nish, who was now churning up the water as he tried to reach the boat.

"*Look out, Nish! Look out!*" several of the girls screamed at once.

Travis was running along the side of the dock trying to find the turtle, but he couldn't see a thing. Liz was on the diving platform, so she had a better view, and she seemed to be tracking the beast.

"*He's right under you, Nish!*" Liz screeched.

Nish howled: "AAAAYYYYYYHHHHHHHHHHHH!!!!"

Travis couldn't believe what he was seeing. Nish seemed to rise up out of the water, almost like a whale breaching, and straight into the outstretched arms of Jason, who hauled him into the boat, stomach first. Nish spilled onto the floor of the boat while his feet kicked wildly in the air. They could see him run his fleshy hands along his toes. *Was he actually counting them?*

Simon and Jason leaned over the side of the boat and peered down into the clear lake water. They were squinting and shaking their heads.

"He's gone!" said Jason.

"Can't see a thing," said Simon.

Liz leapt from the diving platform and splashed into the lake almost precisely where she had been pointing. How could she do that? Travis wondered. How could she jump into the exact spot where old Snappy had been seen?

Chantal jumped off the dock as well. Then Jennie, Sareen, Beth – all the girls from the island camp. And when they surfaced, they all were laughing.

There had been no turtle sighting at all. They were just getting a little revenge for their friend Sarah.

arah was at supper. She seemed fine. She'd slept in the afternoon, and probably should have stayed in bed in the evening, but she didn't want to miss out on any fun. After they ate, there was to be a singsong down by the beach.

Nish stayed away from the gang gathering around Sarah's table. He was obviously still embarrassed about the snapping-turtle false alarm. But it wasn't just that: it seemed to Travis that Nish didn't know how to tell Sarah how bad he felt. He was acting as if the whole thing would eventually go away if he just waited long enough.

Travis was sitting with Sarah when the others went to line up for cookies. Jennie said she'd get one for Sarah, and Data was getting one for Travis, so the two Screech Owls captains, one former and the other current, were left alone.

"Are you mad at him?" asked Travis.

"*Nish?*" Sarah said, as if she couldn't quite make the connection. "Mad at him? How can you get mad at Nish?"

"Muck does."

"Muck only does it because he knows Nish expects him to. And he knows Nish won't stop unless someone stops him. But I doubt Muck ever really gets mad at anybody."

"He sure was at Buddy today."

Travis told the story of the incident in the arena parking lot.

"It's guys like Buddy that make people quit hockey," Sarah said.

"I think he's a jerk," Travis offered.

"You heard Roger quit, eh?"

"Roger?"

"The caretaker. Mr. Clifford told us. He said Roger couldn't take working with that idiot Buddy, so he just walked off the job."

"No wonder we haven't seen him around."

"Mr. Clifford told us he'd walk out on Buddy, too – if he could afford to."

"What's he mean? He could get another job at another camp. He's a really nice guy."

"He *owns* the island camp."

"I thought Buddy did."

"Buddy just acts like he owns everything. They're partners. Mr. Clifford's family used to own both camps. It was his idea to set up the hockey school. He says he needed a partner who knew hockey and had the right connections, so he threw in with Buddy."

"I bet he regrets that decision," said Travis.

The others came back with the cookies just as Morley Clifford stood up and rapped a soup spoon against a pie plate to get everyone's attention. He had an announcement to make.

"Boys and girls," he said, "if I can have your attention here a minute before we start the singsong . . ."

Everyone quieted down to listen. It was clear they all liked Mr. Clifford – the girls on the island adored him – and unlike Buddy O'Reilly, he never, ever, raised his voice. As the Screech Owls had learned from Muck, you didn't need to yell to get someone's attention.

RRRRIIIIINNNGGG!

It was a cellular phone – Buddy O'Reilly's, of course. A groan went around the room. Buddy yanked the phone out of the holster on his belt and ducked out the door, seemingly grateful for the excuse to slip away.

Everyone booed.

Morley Clifford waited patiently for quiet to return. ". . . There was an incident today, I understand, at the docks."

A few of the kids snickered. Several of them turned to stare at Nish, who was scrunched down in his seat chewing on his cookie. His face began to turn the shade of the setting sun.

"I've lived all my life on this lake," said Mr. Clifford. "I have never seen, or heard of, a snapping turtle bothering anyone. And I called the Ministry of Natural Resources this afternoon just for confirmation. There has never been an incident recorded – ever – of a snapping turtle biting a swimmer. They are big, beautiful, gentle reptiles. They can't move very fast on land, so they'll sometimes strike back if someone tries to hurt them. But in the water you have nothing, absolutely nothing, to fear. Are we clear on that point?"

Everyone turned toward Nish. As one, they asked: "*NNNII-IIISSHHHH?*"

Nish's face looked like a hot plate. He squirmed, then bit into his cookie, trying to act as if he was just one of the crowd. It wasn't working. Nish would never be just part of the crowd, no matter how hard he tried.

After the marshmallows and singsong they all gathered at the beach. The girls and Mr. Clifford were going to canoe in a convoy back to the island. The stars were out, and they looked magnificent. They had different stars in the country than they did in the city, Travis thought. Just as they have different traffic and different stores.

Mr. Clifford had a circle of campers around him. He was pointing out the North Star to them. "The bright one, there. You see the Big Dipper," he said. Everyone could see it plainly. "Just follow the line. See it now? Good."

He showed them Orion and the Archer and he pointed out the Milky Way.

"There are billions of stars out there," he said. "Not hundreds. Not thousands. Not millions. But thousands and thousands and thousands of millions. Think about it."

Mr. Clifford paused, and everyone thought about all those stars. Travis shuddered. He couldn't help it.

"Our own star is so minor as to be almost completely insignificant," he said. "And yet our star, the sun, has nine planets *that we know of* – and scientists have just learned that there was once life on Mars. Think about *that*.

"Now consider for a moment that it is very, very likely that every one of those billions and billions of stars has its own planets – maybe one big star has thousands of planets, who knows? Somewhere out there there is bound to be another planet our size and our distance from its sun, and maybe it's got a lake and a summer camp where they make huge oatmeal-and-raisin cookies."

Travis could hear gasps all around him. None of them had ever considered such a possibility. You looked up at the stars in the city, or even in a small town, and it was as if you were looking up at a ceiling with the odd tiny light in it. Nothing more. Nothing beyond.

"Or just maybe," Mr. Clifford continued, "life up there is a mirror image of ours. Maybe things developed just a bit differently up there. They say snapping turtles are living dinosaurs, did you know that? Maybe up there the dinosaurs didn't die out. Maybe on this planet we'll call, what . . . well, why not *Algonquin?*" – the girls from the island all cheered – "the turtles are the hockey players . . ."

Everyone laughed. Travis had never heard such an imagination.

". . . and maybe right now they're running like heck to get away from the Snapping Nishikawa that lives under *their* dock!"

A huge shout of delight burst from Mr. Clifford's audience. They turned to look for Nish and howled with laughter. Why couldn't they have Morley Clifford on their side of the bay? Travis thought. Why did they have to have Buddy O'Reilly?

"Come on, now, Screech Owls," Morley Clifford shouted. "Let's help get these canoes in the water."

The Aeros and Screech Owls worked together. They turned the canoes and hoisted them down onto the beach. The girls put on their life-jackets and checked their paddles and began pushing out.

"I'm not afraid of any turtle," Nish said as they waded into the water with Liz's boat.

"Nor is anyone else – now," said Liz. She was still cool to Nish, not yet in a forgiving mood.

But Sarah was her old self. "What's this we hear about the World's Biggest Skinny Dip, Nish?" she asked.

Sarah had broken the ice herself. Grateful, Nish leapt with both feet.

"I'm doing it," he said. "Before the end of camp."

"You haven't got the guts," Sarah laughed.

"Have so," Nish protested.

"You do it," Sarah said, "and produce witnesses to prove it, and I'll get you an Aeros T-shirt."

Sarah knew exactly how to work Nish. He'd been begging for an Aeros shirt since he first saw them.

"You're on," he said.

onight was the night they would fix Buddy O'Reilly. Back at "Osprey" cabin, Andy Higgins cut the blade off a hockey stick, then straightened out a coat hanger and attached it to the end of the stick with hockey tape.

"What on earth is that for?" Data wanted to know.

"That's how we're going to turn on your tape recorder, pal," Andy said.

"I can do it myself, thanks."

"Not in Buddy O'Reilly's cabin you can't."

How did I get myself into this? Travis wondered.

Because he was the smallest, he'd been elected to place the tape recorder in Buddy's cabin, which was just behind the main hall. Nish and Andy had tracked Buddy down – he was drinking beer in the kitchen with the cook while the Blue Jays game played on a little TV in the corner – and they kept up a watch, signalling to Data by the shed, who signalled to Lars at the corner of Buddy's cabin, who kept Travis up to date.

"*Still clear,*" Lars would hiss. "*Still clear.*"

Travis thought his heart was going to rip right through his chest. He couldn't swallow. He couldn't talk. But he was doing it, not because he wanted to do mischief or because he felt any pressure to do it – but because he wanted to. He couldn't stand Buddy O'Reilly, and if Nish was going to get his revenge, then Travis Lindsay wanted a part of it for himself. He was actually enjoying this, even if he was scared half out of his wits.

He found the perfect place for Data's tape recorder: tucked out of sight under the steel frame of Buddy's bed, but close enough for the hockey stick to reach to turn it on. Andy had earlier cut a small flap in the screen with his jackknife, so they wouldn't have to risk opening and closing the screen door once Buddy was inside and asleep.

Travis checked the tape to make sure it had been rewound, then checked the buttons to make sure the *pause* wasn't on. He had scooted out and away with Lars long before the signal came from Nish and Andy that Buddy and the cook had turned off the game. Buddy had drained his last beer and was headed for bed.

By the time Buddy shut the door to his cabin, the boys were completely hidden in the dark cedars that grew between Buddy's cabin and the shed. They had only to wait. The stars were not as bright now as they had been earlier, but they were still out in the eastern half of the sky. To the west, the sky was darkening. Cloud cover was moving in. In the distance, Travis could make out the odd low rumble: the sound of an advancing storm. Perhaps it would pass them by, but even if it didn't, it was still a long way off. They'd have time.

"I wish I had a smoke," said Nish.

"Somebody'd see the light," countered Travis. He hated it when Nish talked this way, trying to be something he wasn't.

"Then a chew," said Nish.

"You'd *chew* tobacco?" said Data, disgusted.

"Yuk!" said Lars.

"*Shhhhhh . . . ,*" said Andy.

Buddy's light had been out for some time. When Andy had got them quiet, they all listened as hard as they could. They could hear an owl in the distance. And every once in a while a distant rumble from the far-away storm.

"He's snoring," said Andy. "Let's go!"

They all waited a moment longer, just to be sure. It was snoring all right. And it was coming from Buddy's cabin. Andy scrambled out of the cedars, followed by Nish. Travis could hear Nish's breathing: excited, a bit frightened.

With the other boys trailing, Andy and Nish made their way to the cabin door. Buddy had shut only the screen door so as to let in the cool air, and they could make out his bed in the moonlight.

Buddy's mouth was open. He was dead to the world. His left hand was over the side of the bed, the palm wide open. Andy gave a hand signal for Nish to bring the stick-and-hanger combination. He was already pulling back the flap of screen that he'd cut earlier.

Nish attached a big soup spoon to the stick and piled it high with shaving cream. The can made a low, quiet *hisssss*. Very slowly, they worked the stick in through the flap. Expertly, Nish dumped the light-as-air cream into Buddy's hand. Buddy didn't even flinch. Working together, silently, Nish and Andy pulled the stick back out and removed the spoon. Leaning low, they could make out the shadow of Data's boom box, so they knew where to aim. With Andy steadying the stick, Nish lined it up and very gently, very carefully, pushed the button.

Quickly, they removed the stick once more. Andy fumbled for the feather to tickle Buddy's nose. He dropped it, and picked it up again. They would have to move fast. He began wrapping the tape around the feather's stem.

RRRRRIIIIINNNGGGGG!

It was Buddy's cellphone. Travis's heart almost flew through the top of his head.

The phone. The phone! The cellphone was ruining everything.

Andy and Nish scrambled away from the door and leapt back into the cedars after the others.

They could hear Buddy swearing through the screen.

"*What the — ?*"

A light went on.

"*Who the hell — ?*"

They could see him shaking his hand. He had grabbed the phone with the hand full of shaving cream, and now it was all over everything. The precious phone slipped and fell, crashing to the floor. Buddy cursed and grabbed it with his other hand.

"*Hang on! Hang on!*" Buddy shouted. "*Just a damned minute, okay? Some kid snuck in here and . . .*"

The Screech Owls didn't have to hear any more. They were already hightailing it back to "Osprey," laughing so hard they could hardly catch their breath.

Maybe it hadn't worked out according to plan. But this way – with shaving cream all over the phone, all over Buddy's ear, all over his hand, all over his room – the result was better than anything they could have imagined.

Whoever had made that telephone call to Buddy at that particular moment, *Thank you, thank you, thank you . . .*

10

"*KKKKK-RRRRRAAAAACKKKKKKKKK!!*"

Travis sat straight up in his bunk, his eyes wide open. The last time he had been in this cabin and heard a crack like that it had been instantly followed by a rush of air and the crash of the falling hemlock. This time, however, there was only the burst of thunder, followed by nothing. He could hear rumbling in the distance; the storm was closer, but still not raining on the camp. The crack that had woken him must have been moving ahead of the pack. Travis lay back down in his bed and was soon fast asleep once again.

The Owls and Aeros practised in the morning. It was, by far, the finest practice so far that week. It was almost exactly as Travis had envisioned hockey camp would be. Muck set up the drills, and Jason and Simon ran them. Morley Clifford was there, and came out during the break with Gatorade and sliced oranges for the players.

The difference, everyone knew, was that Buddy O'Reilly wasn't around. No fancy tracksuit with his name all over it. No shrieking whistle. No chewing out anybody who failed to do exactly as he said. No picking on Nish.

They played a few games – even British Bulldog, which they hadn't played since novice – and then had a wild and crazy scrimmage, defencemen and goaltenders against forwards. The goalies and defence won by about a zillion-to-ten, because Travis's side had no one with the slightest notion of how to make a save.

Nish was the hero of the scrimmage. His puck-carrying abilities were the best of all the defence. He once even set up Jennie Staples, *a goaltender*, for a goal when he went in on the last forward back – poor Dmitri – faked him to the ice, and then sent a perfect Sarah-like pass back between his skates to Jennie, who was driving to the net as fast as her big goalie pads would let her.

After the goal, Nish skated over to Sarah Cuthbertson and went down on both knees, his head bowed. It was Nish's way of finally apologizing for what he'd done to her after she had made the same play the day before. Sarah knew Nish well enough to know how hard this was for him. She wasn't interested in any revenge that might involve hammering Nish head-first into the boards. She laughed, turned her stick around, and tapped him on both shoulders: Sir Nish, Knight of the Between-Your-Skates Pass.

Practice over, the happy Screech Owls and Aeros were on the buses to go back to camp, when Simon and Jason came down the aisle and leaned over the seat Travis was sharing with Nish.

"Good on you, Nishikawa," Simon said.

"Classy act, Nish – proud of you," Jason added.

Nish nodded and looked down. Travis could see that his friend was battling to contain a smile; he was looking straight down into his lap, trying with all his might to remain serious.

Sarah came along, the last player to board the bus. She, too, stopped as she passed.

"You guys ready for adventure?" she asked.

Nish looked up. "Whatdya mean?"

"Muck's given me permission to take you two out in a canoe to the little island this afternoon. We can swim and jump from the rocks."

Travis looked up, unsure. "It's okay?"

"Of course it's okay. I'm a fully qualified Red Cross life-guard, you know. Nish goes down, I can go get him."

Travis smiled. "Would you *have* to?"

"Are you up for it?" Sarah asked.

"Sure," said Travis.

"Nish?"

Nish just nodded. He wasn't even trying to fight the grin any more.

Before they took out the canoe, Travis and Nish had to take care of their wet hockey equipment. They spread it on the ground in front of the cabin so it would dry in the sun. Travis noticed there wasn't even a light dew on the grass, and he remembered the storm during the night. It must have passed right over the camp without raining. He wondered if the lightning with the single clap of thunder had struck anything.

"Let's go!" Nish shouted.

Nish was excited. Before he'd come to camp, he'd never even been in a canoe. Now he thought that, next to Sea-doos – and anything else that had an outboard engine, for that matter – canoes were a terrific way to move about the water. Like the others, he thought the silence was incredible, the way they could sneak up on almost anything: the loons, the ducks, maybe even old Snappy sitting out sunning on a log.

The two boys ran across the main camp grounds and down along the beach to the boathouse. Sarah was already there, waiting for them.

"I thought maybe you'd chickened out," she said.

"You seem to forget you knighted me," said Nish. "I'm ready for anything – even hand-to-hand combat with that stupid turtle."

"*Right*," Sarah laughed.

Nish was anxious to get going. He opened the door to the boathouse and the three friends entered. Inside, the air was musty from woodrot and years of wet life-preservers. But it also smelled neat. The walls had never been painted, and there was the faint odour of cedar, and of oil and gas and outboards – the smells of summer at the lake. They could hear the waves lapping lightly under the boat slip. A swallow left its nest high in the beams and swooped out under the main door.

There were two canoes in the boathouse. One was missing a stern seat, so they moved out the good one and began loading up. Sarah had even brought a small picnic for them.

"I'll get the paddles," offered Travis.

He looked around: old fishing rods, sails, rudders, oars, a fibreglass canoe with a great gaping hole in its side, an auger for drilling holes in the ice on the lake in winter, several old propane lamps that needed cleaning, water-skis, the tube, a new wakeboard.

"Over there!" Sarah called to him.

She was pointing to a jumble of ropes and stacked-up gas tanks on the far side of the slip.

Travis jumped across the slip, took one step, and crashed down onto the rough boards.

"*Walk much?*" Nish shouted. He was laughing.

"You okay, Trav?" Sarah called.

"I slipped on something," Travis answered. He felt okay. He wasn't hurt. He had put his arm down to break his fall, and something had jabbed him near the wrist. "There was something here on the boards," he said, struggling up.

"Yeah," laughed Nish. "Your own shadow!"

Travis bent down to look. It was difficult to see. He rubbed his arm. Whatever it was he'd landed on was hard. A short distance away, something was shining in the dim light of the boathouse. He crept over and picked it up. Without a word he held it out in the palm of his hand for the others to see.

Sarah caught her breath. "*A bullet?*"

It wasn't a live bullet, it was an empty shell. It had been fired. Travis sniffed it: he could smell gunpowder.

Could this have been the crack of thunder that woke him up last night?

"*What's that on your arm?*" said Nish. He was pointing at Travis's other arm, not the one that had landed on the shell. Travis felt it.

Goo!

"What is it?" Sarah asked. She seemed concerned.

"I don't know," Travis said.

"Maybe that bird we scared out left you a present." Nish giggled. He didn't seem in the least concerned.

"It's pitch," said Sarah. "Pitch from the boards."

"I guess," said Travis.

There was a rag near the gas cans. He picked it up and wiped his arm. Whatever the goo was, it was sticky. Probably pitch. He rubbed hard and got most of it off.

"*Let's get going!*" Nish called. "*Day's a-wasting!*"

Travis carried the paddles over to the canoe. Nish was already in, and Sarah handed him the waterproof bag with the sandwiches and drinks.

"We're short two life-preservers," Sarah noted.

"We don't need them," Nish said. He already had one on and was keen to get going.

"We're not going anywhere if we don't all have one," said Sarah.

"Okay, okay – but let's get a move on!" Nish said. "There's probably a couple over there where you found the paddles, Trav."

Travis went around the slip this time, not wanting to jump across and risk another fall. His arm was throbbing a bit. He'd have a bruise.

Everything was piled up in this corner as if it had just been thrown there – and yet everything else in the boathouse had been very neatly stored. It made no sense. He pulled away a couple of the gas cans, some rope, and a pair of old oars. He yanked at a plastic tarp that had been thrown into the mess. It was stuck, but he was sure he could see the faded red of a life-preserver underneath. He yanked again and the tarpaulin gave a little.

There was something sticky on it. It felt the same as what had been on his arm. It couldn't be pitch. What was it?

Blood?

He pulled again, and the tarp came free.

When Travis saw what had been hidden underneath, he gasped. He must be mistaken! The shadows . . . the bad light . . .

He moved so more light could get in. It was an *arm*, the fingers tightened as if trying to hold something. The arm went in under an overturned canoe. And beneath the canoe, presumably, was the rest of the *body*.

"Hurry up!" Nish called.

Travis tried to speak, but he couldn't.

"*Travis!*" Sarah called sharply. "*What's wrong with you?*"

Travis stammered, then spit it out: "*Th-th-there's a b-b-body under here!*"

"*A what!*" Nish laughed.

"*What?*" said Sarah. She wasn't laughing.

Travis felt frozen, unable to move. He could see Sarah coming toward him uneasily. And he could see Nish scrambling to get out of the canoe.

"What do you mean a '*body*'?" Sarah asked.

Travis moved aside slightly so she could see. He heard her breath catch.

"Lemme see!" Nish shouted. He was scrambling across the planking.

"Wh–wh–who is it?" Sarah stammered.

"I don't know," Travis answered. He thought he did, though. He knew the jacket.

"*Move the canoe!*" Nish shouted. He was already pulling at the bow. "Help me!"

Travis moved without thinking. It was as if he was watching a movie of himself, stepping over and reaching down and taking the other side of the bow, and lifting . . .

Most of the body was in dark shadow, but as they raised the canoe higher, some dim light from the side door crept over its chest, and towards the face.

"*Buddy!*" Sarah hissed.

"*Is he dead?*" Nish shouted. He couldn't see as well as the others. The bow of the canoe was in his way, and he wanted to be closer to the action.

"I think so," said Sarah. But there could be no doubt. Buddy was white as a ghost. His face looked as if it had been carved out of candle wax. His eyes were staring past Travis, seeing nothing.

"Let's get out of here," said Travis.

"We better find Muck," said Sarah.

They set the canoe back down, carefully covering the hideous dead face of Buddy O'Reilly.

And then they ran, Nish well out in front of the others.

11

This was no way to picture a summer hockey camp. There were police cars everywhere. There was police crime-site ribbon around the boathouse, Buddy's 4x4, even his sleeping cabin.

"Am I going to get my tape recorder back?" Data wanted to know.

Just like Data, Travis thought – from another planet. Who cared about his stupid tape recorder? He, Travis, had seen a dead body and he couldn't get Buddy O'Reilly's dead, empty stare out of his mind. He and Nish and Sarah were prime witnesses. They had found the body, and the bullet, and the blood. And Data wanted to talk about his tape recorder? *Give me a break*, Travis thought.

Muck and Morley Clifford had taken charge. They had called the police, and the police had brought along an ambulance. Men in white coats removed Buddy's body on a stretcher. It had been covered with a blanket when they carried it from the boathouse to the ambulance, but it was still a body. And everyone watching felt ill thinking that Buddy O'Reilly was dead, no matter what they may have thought of him alive.

"I saw him close up," Nish told the boys in "Osprey." Travis didn't bother disputing Nish's tale. He knew Nish hadn't seen much. Travis and Sarah had seen everything. But he wasn't about to start bragging about it.

Muck had phoned the parents in the morning. Some were already staying at campgrounds and lodges in the area, and they arrived immediately. Others were coming from down south.

Several of the parents had wanted to take their children away immediately, but the police said everyone was to stay where they were for the time being. They wanted to interview everyone who had been in either camp, just in case they knew something or had seen something, perhaps without even realizing it might be important. Some of the parents got angry about this, saying there was still a murderer about. But Sarah's father and Travis's father held a parents' meeting in the main lodge, and at the end of it everyone was agreed, if a bit uneasy, to let the kids stay on. The only condition they asked for was that police be stationed at the camp, and the police were only too happy to comply.

"Who do you think killed him?" Andy asked Nish when the boys in "Osprey" were supposed to be resting.

"I have no idea," said Nish. "Maybe he killed himself, for all we know. He could hardly have liked himself."

Travis shook his head. "There was no gun. Whoever shot him left with the gun."

"But there was a bullet," said Nish.

"Yeah, there was a shell."

"What kind?" asked Lars.

"How should I know?" said Travis. He knew nothing about guns. He didn't want to know anything about guns.

"Do you think you could ask about my tape recorder?" Data asked.

Nish threw his pillow at Data's head.

No one seemed to be organizing any activities, so the boys stood around with everyone else and watched the police at work. Men in suits went into the boathouse and came out carrying dozens of plastic bags, some seeming to hold nothing. There was a police boat drifting over the area between the island and the main camp, and two scuba divers were in the water.

"They're searching for evidence," Nish announced.

Travis shook his head. Anyone who'd ever turned on a TV set would know that, he thought.

One by one, the police were taking everyone who had been at the camp into the camp office and interviewing them. Two police talked to each of them, and another policeman wrote down everything they said.

Travis told the police his story exactly as he remembered it. He had no idea who might have wanted to hurt Buddy O'Reilly.

"Did you see Mr. O'Reilly and anyone arguing or fighting in the past few days?" the older policeman asked.

"No . . ."

Muck! Suddenly the scene outside the arena, when Muck had slapped Buddy's face, flashed through Travis's brain. There had been a fight – well, *almost* a fight – and it had been Muck Munro, the Screech Owls' coach, who'd been arguing with Buddy O'Reilly.

Travis's voice must have given him away. The older police-man looked up from his notes. He cocked an eyebrow over his reading glasses.

"You're sure of that, are you, Travis?"

Travis squirmed. He felt sick to his stomach. He knew Muck hadn't done it, but he also knew he had to tell the truth. He had to tell the policeman every single thing he knew.

"Well . . ."

Travis checked later with Nish. Nish had found himself telling the same story. He seemed almost ashamed, as if he'd let the coach down, but Travis assured him that they had to tell every-thing. It wouldn't matter. The police would soon learn, if they didn't already know, that Buddy O'Reilly was an ass and that all kinds of people had words with Buddy.

"What about Roger?" Travis said suddenly.

"Roger?" Nish asked, puzzled.

"The caretaker who quit. He and Buddy fought over the gun, remember?"

"Yeah . . . *right!*"

They looked at each other, filled with confidence, then instantly filled with dread.

"But Muck took the gun away from Roger," Travis said.

"I know," said Nish. "I just remembered."

Travis decided he had better go and speak to the police again. They had to be told about Roger and the fight with Buddy. And if they had to be told about that, then they had to be told about the gun and where it had gone. But it couldn't possibly have been *that* gun that shot Buddy, could it?

The police already seemed to know everything that Travis could tell them about the incident with the gun.

"The rifle Mr. Munro took is missing," the older policemen told Travis.

Missing?

"Mr. Munro says he put it under the spare mattress in his cabin, but it's gone now. Do you know what kind of rifle it was, Travis?" the older cop asked.

"No."

"It was a .22."

It meant nothing to Travis. What was a .22?

"The shell you found in the boathouse," he continued, staring up at him over his reading glasses, "it was also a .22. Did you know that, Travis?"

"No."

Travis really didn't know what kind of rifle it had been, or what kind of shell he had found, but there was no doubt that the policeman was giving him this information in order to check his reaction. And what exactly was his reaction, Travis wondered, as the police excused him and thanked him for coming back with new information? He knew now that the gun Muck had taken away from Roger was a .22-calibre rifle. And he knew that a .22-calibre shell had been found in the boat-house. And as far as he knew, Muck had the only .22 around.

Travis felt sick to his stomach for about the sixth time in less than a day.

After he got back outside, Travis leaned against the side of the office building, catching his breath and waiting for his stomach to settle. A stand of pine and cedar grew close against the office, and Travis was hidden from the view of anyone approaching the door to the building.

A policeman walked up the path, carrying a long plastic bag. Inside was a rifle!

Travis stayed put. A window above his head was open, and he realized he could hear the voices of the men inside. The policeman carrying the rifle knocked.

"Yes, come in."

"Travers here, sir. The divers found this off the far shoal."

"A .22-calibre?"

"Yes, sir."

"Did you speak to Mr. Munro about this?"

"He just keeps saying he put it under the mattress in his room and that was the last he knew of it."

"What about the box of bullets?"

"Mr. Munro says that he disposed of them."

"*Disposed* of them?"

"He says he took them down to the dump the same day he took them from the caretaker."

"He says that, does he?"

"Yes, sir, he does."

Travis could almost feel the grin grow on the older policeman's face.

"Well, that's very convenient – but he may have forgotten one thing."

"What's that, sir?"

"We have a dozen witnesses who told us he ejected live bullets from that gun and then ground them into the earth with his heel. We find them, we don't need the box of bullets to see if there's a match."

"Yes, sir – I'll put some men on that right away."

"Good work, Travers."

Everything began to move so fast that Travis's head couldn't keep up with his spinning stomach. The police investigative unit set up behind the shed where Roger had fired at the rabid fox, laying out a grid of stakes and string and beginning to dig with small shovels.

Nish and Travis and Andy stayed and watched them search. They were there when the first policeman shouted that he had found something almost at the centre of the grid. With rubber gloves on, he picked up a bullet and dusted it off with a small brush. Another policeman brought a plastic bag over, the bullet was dropped in, and the bag sealed.

"Silver casing on the shell, wasn't it?" said Andy.

"Looked like it," said Travis.

"Same colour as the one we found in the boathouse," said Nish.

"Doesn't mean a thing," countered Travis.

But he knew exactly what it meant. He believed absolutely that Muck had tossed the box of bullets away. That would be just like Muck: they could have the rifle back eventually, but no bullets. He wouldn't have done it to hide anything, because Muck had nothing to hide. But what if the bullet they had just found matched the shell found in the boathouse? Only Muck had had access to those bullets, and now the police would think Muck had hidden the rest on purpose.

The boys watched the policeman dig up two more bullets. Each one was placed in its own plastic bag and carried away to the camp office.

Travis decided to return on his own to his window and see if he could learn anything.

"They're from the same batch."

Travis could make out the voice of the older policeman. He could sense satisfaction in the man's voice.

"The shell casing from the boathouse is an exact match with the three bullets we dug up. We'll need full forensic confirmation, but this is good enough for me. We have a rifle that someone tried to dispose of, a rifle that has been fired recently. We have a match in the bullets now, even though Mr. Munro claims he threw the original box of shells away. And we have the gun hidden in Muck Munro's cabin.

"I think, gentlemen, it is time to pay a call on our Mr. Munro."

12

M uck was in handcuffs.

The Screech Owls – Travis, Nish, Data, Lars, Andy, Gordie, all the others – and most of the Aeros, stood around the parking area as the police led Muck away, in handcuffs. Travis's eyes stung. He looked at his friend Nish, and Nish was staring straight down at the ground, as if he was too embarrassed to look.

It had to be embarrassment, Travis told himself. It couldn't be shame. No one could possibly believe that Muck had shot Buddy O'Reilly, no matter how many clues seemed to point his way.

With a policeman at his elbow, Muck marched straight ahead, chin held high. The policeman tried to ease him into the back-seat of the patrol car, but Muck stopped abruptly and turned.

He scanned the crowd. He stared, sure and steady and confident: it was the look the kids knew from the dressing room just before a very important game. Muck full of confidence. Muck with faith. Muck knowing exactly how things would turn out. It couldn't possibly be a bluff, Travis told himself. *Could it?*

Muck's eyes fell on Travis, and he stared.

Then he smiled, once, very quickly, before getting into the patrol car.

"He didn't do it."

Travis tried to put all the confidence he felt into the statement. He was not talking to the police any more, but to his friends: Nish and Andy and Data and Jesse and Lars. He wanted them to feel what he felt. Muck had stared at Travis because he wanted him to know something. He had smiled because he wanted him to know that they had the wrong person.

"Look," said Andy, "I'm as upset as anybody about this – but it doesn't exactly look good for Muck."

"He *didn't* do it," Travis repeated.

"How can we know that for certain?" Andy asked. "We *think* that – but we don't know it."

Travis had a thought. "But it was Muck who sent us to the boathouse. He wouldn't have sent us if he knew Buddy was lying there, dead."

"Yeah," said Nish, suddenly hopeful. "Right."

Andy shook his head. "Buddy's body was hidden. Whoever did it obviously figured he wouldn't be found so soon."

"He didn't *send* us there, either," added Nish, disheartened. "He just told Sarah she could take out a canoe. It was her idea to meet there."

Travis shook his head. "Muck didn't do it."

"He had the gun," Andy said, ticking off the points on his fingers, "and he knows how to use one. He had a fight with Buddy. He threatened him – there are at least four witnesses to that. And we all know Muck well enough to know that he must have hated Buddy O'Reilly."

"But not enough to kill him," Data said. "Muck wouldn't hurt a fly."

Andy paused. "Well, what would you think if you were a cop?"

"I know what you're getting at," said Travis. "*But he didn't do it.*"

"*Show me some evidence,*" Andy nearly shouted. He sounded exasperated, upset.

"There is none," said a disheartened Nish. "None in Muck's favour, anyway."

The boys fell silent for a while, each thinking his own private thoughts. Then Gordie Griffith, who hadn't said anything, cleared his throat.

". . . There's one thing," he said.

Travis pounced. "*What?*"

Gordie cleared his throat again. ". . . Who was there when Muck took the gun off Roger?"

"We all were," said Nish impatiently. "What's that got to do with anything?"

"Muck took the gun and pumped out the remaining bullets, right?" Gordie said.

"Yeah. *So?*"

"So how many were left?"

The boys all thought about it. Travis could see Muck wrestling the gun away. He remembered being startled at how familiar Muck had seemed with the gun. He remembered how Muck had aimed the barrel down, straight into the ground, before he pumped out the bullets. *One . . . two . . . three . . . four . . . five.*

"Five," said Travis.

"Five," said Data. "Exactly."

"Four or five," said Andy.

"Five," said Lars.

"I don't remember," said Nish.

"Your point?" Andy asked Gordie.

"Well," Gordie answered, "if we all saw five, and the police only found three, what happened to the other two?"

"Maybe the police just missed them," said Nish.

"Maybe they didn't. Maybe someone else came back and dug up two of the bullets."

"We better check," said Travis. He was trying to remain calm, but he couldn't help but feel some excitement rising. No, it wasn't excitement: it was hope. *Finally.*

The police had taken down the grid lines, but it was clear where they had done the digging. The boys got shovels from the shed and Travis found a screen that Roger must have built to sift earth. If they threw the earth they dug into the screen and shook it through, any bullet should quickly show up.

They dug for nearly an hour, but nothing.

"So we now have two missing bullets," said Data.

"The police will just say Muck came back and got them to use on Buddy," said Andy.

"Why would he? He already had the box. But it could have been someone who wanted to make it *look* like Muck had done it," said Gordie.

"What if he threw away the box before he decided he needed a couple of bullets?" countered Andy. "Then he'd come back here."

Everyone looked at Andy.

"Hey," he protested, "I'm not saying he did it. I'm just saying what the police would say to us."

"Look," said Travis, "we have to assume that Muck didn't do it. We have to give him the benefit of the doubt."

"Nobody wants him innocent more than me," said Andy, looking hurt.

"Okay," said Lars, "so what then?"

"Then it means someone else had to come and take the two bullets out of the ground."

"Okay. But who?"

"Who hated Buddy O'Reilly?"

Three of them spoke at once: "*Roger!*"

13

The cook knew where Roger lived: down the road and past the dump, then the first place on the left. A bit run-down, he told them.

"Isn't this something the police should be doing?" Data wanted to know when Travis had suggested they pay Roger a visit.

"The police have already decided who did it."

"They must have talked to Roger by now," said Nish. "What're we going to ask him that they wouldn't already know?"

"I've no idea," said Travis. "I just know for Muck's sake we have to go down there and have a look around."

They took off after the morning practice – a listless, dull affair put on by Simon and Jason simply because there was nothing else to do. Escaping was simple. They just opened a back window in "Osprey" cabin, popped the screen, slipped out, and cut off through the nature trail.

Travis appeared to be the leader. He knew they were all looking to him as captain, but he had no idea what they were seeing. A little boy desperate to prove Muck was innocent at all costs? Or a new Travis Lindsay, sure of himself and where he was going? Probably something in between, Travis thought.

He didn't have a clue where this road was leading them, apart from straight to Roger's place. They passed the dump, the stink rising high, the seagulls loud, and they came to the first turn to the left. It led to an old, run-down home. Out front, the sun was falling on a patch of bright orange irises that had grown up through the open hood of an abandoned Plymouth.

They thought about sneaking up on the place, but it was useless. The bush was too dense, for one thing, but there were also dogs in pens at the side, and already they were barking and jumping against the wire fencing at the scent and sounds of the boys coming along the road.

"We'll knock," Travis decided. He didn't really know why he'd said that. What alternative did they have? Turn and go back to the camp? Forget about the only lead they had?

"You first," said Nish.

"Okay," said Travis. He was captain, after all.

The dogs went crazy as the boys moved slowly up the rough laneway. They walked past an old refrigerator, past two huge truck tires that had once been painted white but were now flaking, past an old pump, and came to a verandah.

"Your idea," Nish said. "We knock or we run?"

Travis steeled himself. He stepped up to a wooden carving of a woodpecker hanging from the door, and saw that if he pulled the bird's tail its beak would hammer on the door. He yanked.

They waited a long time. A curtain moved slightly in the window closest to where they stood, and then the door opened.

It was a girl – a blonde, pretty girl about their own age.

She seemed as nervous as they were. But at least she was smiling.

"Can I help you?" she said.

"We're looking for Mr. . . . " – Travis remembered there had been a name on the mailbox – ". . . Sprott."

"That's my father," she said. "He's out in the work shed. I'll take you out there."

She led them around the corner of the house. The dogs were going frantic, trying to hammer their heads through the wire.

"You must be from the camp," she said.

"We are," said Travis.

"We heard what happened. My dad didn't like Mr. O'Reilly."

"Who did?" said Nish.

The dogs quieted as she approached. Travis realized that they weren't trying to get at them to kill them; they wanted to greet them. The girl ran her hand along the pens as she passed, the dogs lining up to lick at her fingers.

They came to the work shed and she opened the door. Her father, Roger, was sitting inside, painting several more of the woodpecker knockers that Travis had seen on the front door. All around were tiny wooden creations: windmills that looked like flying geese or Sylvester the Cat running on the spot; ducks and ducklings; old men and women who seemed to be bending down so their underwear showed.

"G'day, boys," Roger said. "What brings you down here?"

Roger picked up a cup and spat into it. Travis could almost hear Nish go "*Yuk!*" Travis looked at the girl and she rolled her eyes.

"We're trying to clear our coach," said Travis. He didn't know what else to say.

"There's a hundred people round here might take a shot at Buddy O'Reilly if they thought they could get away with it," said Roger. "I'm one of them."

Roger spat again. "But I didn't do it," he said. He looked at his daughter. "We were up fishing in Algonquin Park. Ain't that right, Myrna?"

Travis couldn't help but turn to Myrna. She was nodding. "We went camping with my cousins," she said.

Travis and the others looked at her. Myrna seemed sure of herself. She didn't sound like she was lying, and she certainly didn't look like a liar.

"The bullets Muck pumped out of the gun when he took it," Travis said. "Do you know what happened to them?"

"Sure," Roger smiled. "Your coach ground them into the dirt with his heel."

"There were five of them. The police found only three."

"Is that right?"

"Somebody must have taken the others and used them on Buddy. That's why the police think it was Muck. The gun he took from you had been fired recently."

"Yah, but at a fox, eh?"

"The police would say it doesn't matter. They can't tell what a gun was aimed at. Just whether or not it was fired."

"Meaning?" Roger said. He didn't seem to follow.

"They think Muck took one of those bullets and put it in the gun and then shot Buddy. And we can't prove he didn't."

Roger took another long spit into the cup. Then he turned and looked suspiciously at Travis.

"What do you know about guns, son?"

Travis was caught off guard. "N–nothing."

"Any of yous?"

"Nope."

"Not me."

"No."

"No, sir."

"Well then, you boys can just relax. If that's what your coach did, they'll soon know for sure. And if he didn't, as you believe, they'll know that, too. The bullets can be exactly the same, and I guess that's what they're going on right now, but even if the bullets *are* exactly the same – same batch, same colour, same weight – and are fired from two different guns, they can tell. They call that 'forensic science.' You ever hear of it?"

They had, on television.

"You give the police time to do the proper experiments," he continued. "They'll sort it out."

Travis could feel new hope. He saw that Nish was giving the thumbs-up. Andy was smiling.

But Travis still had one question: "How come you quit?" he asked. It was obvious that Roger needed the job.

Roger eyed him carefully before he spoke. "I quit because I couldn't live with myself if I stayed on with that man. I know you mustn't speak ill of the dead, but Buddy O'Reilly was an evil, evil man. I seen the way he treated people. Didn't matter if you were a kid or a coach or a business partner, he treated you like dirt. And I won't be treated like dirt."

"Why did you work for him in the first place?"

"I worked for Mr. Morley Clifford, son. The finest man I have ever known. Mr. Clifford built both those camps into what they are. He only took Buddy on as a partner because he needed someone who could run a hockey school. The only way camps around here survive any more is if they specialize. Mr. Clifford decided on hockey, which was a fine idea, but then he took on Buddy, which was a very, very bad idea."

"We thought Buddy owned everything."

"*Buddy* thought Buddy owned everything! He'd already cheated Mr. Clifford out of the main camp – the island camp was just a matter of time, the way I seen it."

"What do you mean, 'cheated'?"

"Mr. Clifford had to take out a bank loan to hire Buddy and get the hockey school going. But I have always believed, and will believe until my dying day, that Buddy O'Reilly deliberately kept the enrolment low at the hockey camp in order to put Mr. Clifford in a position where he couldn't meet his payments on the loan. When it looked like Mr. Clifford was going to lose everything, along comes Buddy with a couple of 'partners' he suddenly discovers – one of them's his brother-in-law, for heaven's sake – and they bail out Mr. Clifford. And who do you think ends up controlling the main camp?"

"Buddy?" said Nish.

"Bingo! You got it."

14

The boys walked back to the camp in the midday heat, their hands in their pockets and their feet kicking up the dust in the road as they went over everything they now knew. The longer they thought about it, the more it became clear that, despite what Roger Sprott had said, it still looked bad for Muck.

They had barely turned into the camp laneway when Simon, half out of breath, came running up to them.

The whole camp had been looking for the boys. There was a big meeting about to get under way at the main building.

Mr. Cuthbertson and Mr. Lindsay were running the meeting. Standing to one side was the older policeman who had twice interviewed Travis. Everyone looked very serious. Travis had never seen his father look so grey and grim.

"Inspector Cox has a brief statement for us all," said Sarah's father, and even before the policeman opened his mouth, Travis knew it was not going to be good news.

Inspector Cox waved a piece of paper above his head. "This is from the forensic office in Toronto, where they've been doing ballistic tests on the rifle we discovered in the lake and the single bullet that killed Mr. O'Reilly. It's a match."

Travis's heart sank. He felt Nish's hand on his arm, tightening.

"In district court this morning," Inspector Cox continued, "a charge of first-degree murder was laid against Mr. Albert Munro."

None of the kids had heard Muck's real first name before. It almost seemed as if it wasn't him. But it was Muck, and it was hard to imagine worse news.

Travis was afraid to look at Nish. He was afraid they would both start crying. He looked, instead, to the far side of the room, where most of the Aeros were gathered with their parents. Sarah had her arms around her mother and was sobbing into her shoulder. Travis felt his own eyes tighten and sting and knew that a hot tear was rolling down his cheek. He didn't care.

Mr. Cuthbertson had something else to say: "Under the circumstances, the Provincial Police have told us we can now do as we wish. We think it best we close down the camp and head back home. You should return to your cabins to pack. Departure time will be six p.m., sharp."

The room emptied without a sound, apart from a few sobs that couldn't be held back. Travis and Nish and the rest of the boys from "Osprey" walked back without a word, their heads down.

They passed by the main equipment shed and then by Buddy's cabin. The police had already taken down the yellow plastic ribbon that had marked it off as a restricted crime site. It seemed the investigation was over.

"I can finally get my tape recorder back!" Data exclaimed when he noticed.

Travis turned on Data, furious.

"*Get a life!*" he shouted. "*Do you ever think of anybody but yourself?*"

But Data was already running toward Buddy's cabin.

"*Jerk!*" Nish called after him.

15

They packed in silence. Travis stuffed everything back in his knapsack – pants, shorts, shirts, sandals, bug spray, sunblock, flashlight – and gathered together his fishing equipment and his hockey bag. The hockey bag was toughest. Every piece of equipment he picked up and stashed away reminded him of Muck.

Travis felt on the verge of tears. And all he could think about was Muck sitting in a jail cell somewhere, his big meaty hands folded in his lap, waiting.

Data came in with his boom box. Travis had to resist the urge to rip it out of his hands and heave it down the steps. Data was thinking not of Muck, but only of his poor tape recorder and how hard it had been used.

"You wrecked my tape machine, you dummy!" Data said to Nish.

Nish turned, shocked. "Whatdya mean, 'wrecked'?"

"You pushed the wrong button with that stupid stick. You hit the *record* button instead of *play*, and now my batteries are run down."

Andy pushed the *eject* button and examined the tape.

"You ruined the mosquito recording," he said to Nish.

"How?"

"Taped right over it. It's gone."

"Damn it!" said Nish. He snatched the tape from Andy and threw it against the wall. It bounced onto Travis's bunk, landing square in the centre of the pillow.

The *record* button? Travis's mind was racing. He leapt for his bunk, grabbing the tape before Nish could pick it up and heave it again.

"What's with you?" Nish demanded.

"*What if the phone call's on this tape?*" Travis yelled, holding it up over his head. "*Maybe it could give us some clues!*"

"Huh?" the others said at once.

"The call that came in to Buddy's cellphone," Travis explained. "It could all be here if Nish accidentally recorded it!"

"*Put it in!*" Gordie shouted.

"Batteries are all dead!" said Data.

"*Empty your flashlights!*" Travis commanded.

The boys rooted frantically in their packed bags and came up with enough batteries to supply the boom box. Travis put the tape back, rewound it, and pushed *play*.

They waited, the room heaving with their tense breathing.

The tape hissed, then they heard Buddy's cellphone:

"*Rrrrriiiiinnnggggg! . . . Rrrrriiiiinnnggggg! . . . What the – Click!* [the light going on] . . . *Who the hell – ? . . .* [a crash, the cellphone dropping, Buddy swearing] . . . *Hang on! Hang on! Just a damned minute, okay? Some kid snuck in here and . . .*"

Buddy's cursing went on for some time. The boys listened, picturing Buddy trying to beat off the shaving cream while keeping up the conversation.

Buddy didn't seem to have much respect for the person he was talking to – but then, Buddy had never shown respect for anyone. The swearing and contempt in his voice reminded the boys how much they had disliked him.

"Now you listen here . . . I thought we were perfectly clear on that matter. You had until midnight tonight to meet those payments, otherwise the island camp is in a default position. . . . Just a damn minute here, mister, I'm talking! . . . You already know that my partners are more than willing to bail you out one last time, but in order for them to forward the funds to your bank account, you'll need to sign those papers I gave you. . . . [a long pause, while Buddy listens] *. . . Morley, please, I don't need any of your whining right now. It comes down to a simple choice for you, the way I see it. You sign the papers, my group assumes control of the entire camp, or the island camp fails completely. Think of it this way, Morley, my friend: you sign the papers, you get to stay on. You don't sign them, you're out of business tomorrow morning. . . .* [another long pause] *. . . Fine, the boathouse at eleven tonight. . . . I'm glad you finally see things my way. This is going to work out just fine . . . Click! . . ."*

The tape continued to hiss quietly, still recording after Buddy had ended the call. They could hear him swearing, still, as he wiped his hand and the cellphone clean. They could hear him moving about the cabin, probably starting to dress, and still cursing the kids who had broken in and filled his hand with shaving cream.

Travis got up and stopped the tape. They had heard enough. He walked over and hugged a startled Data.

"What's *that* for?" said Data.

"For thinking only about your stupid tape recorder."

"What about Nish?" Andy asked. "He's the guy who pushed the wrong button."

"I did it on purpose," Nish claimed. No one, of course, believed him for a moment.

"Who's Morley?" Lars asked.

"Mr. Clifford, dummy," Nish said. "The guy who murdered Buddy."

"The *suspect*," Travis corrected.

"C'mon – we have to get Data's tape to the police."

16

The police brought Muck back in a squad car. No handcuffs – just Muck in his sweatpants and his Screech Owls windbreaker, and the same sure look on his face that he'd had when he left. The parking lot was filled with players and parents, and a great cheer went up when Muck got out of the car. Sarah Cuthbertson broke out of the crowd and raced toward him, hugging him around his big middle. When she broke away, his T-shirt was wet from her tears.

Mr. Cuthbertson made an announcement that the six o'clock deadline had been cancelled. They'd finish out the week. There was still time to practice. And, of course, they still had to have the big tournament, Screech Owls against Aeros.

"What about the World's Biggest Skinny Dip?" Travis whispered to Nish. "Is it still on?"

"Of course – even if the rest of you are so chicken I have to do it alone."

"You haven't the guts," laughed Travis.

Muck was swarmed by the parents, who shook his hand and slapped his back and generally embarrassed him. He seemed relieved to be back, but also anxious to break away from the attention and get back to being nothing but the coach of the Screech Owls.

The boys were headed back to "Osprey" when Muck called to them and came over.

They stood about, not knowing what to say to each other, and then, one by one, they all hugged Muck, and he hugged back. And after that, no one could speak anyway.

Mr. Cuthbertson had found out all the details. Inspector Cox told him that poor old Mr. Clifford had confessed everything the moment they played Data's tape for him.

The police figured that, under pressure from Buddy O'Reilly, the former owner of the camps had finally snapped. Mr. Clifford could no longer take the way Buddy was running things. They disagreed on everything, but particularly on the way Buddy treated the kids. He couldn't stand the idea of Buddy forcing him out and taking full control.

When Morley Clifford witnessed the fight between Muck, Roger, and Buddy over the gun, he saw his opportunity. He took the rifle from Muck's cabin, but he couldn't find the box of bullets and he'd had to dig up two of them from behind the shed. He never meant to leave that empty shell in the boathouse, but he probably couldn't find it in the dark. He panicked then, and decided to dump the rifle in the lake. He had been sure that

Muck would have an alibi in case they found the gun and some-how connected the bullet to it — that way, the police would never figure out who had killed Buddy O'Reilly.

"It's a pretty sad story," said Mr. Cuthbertson. "The desire for revenge makes people do things no one would ever expect of them. But nothing justifies what he did. Nothing."

Mr. Cuthbertson looked at the boys from "Osprey" cabin. "It's a lucky thing for everyone that the police ended up with that tape recording, otherwise we might never have known what was going on."

Nish looked around, smiling, his right hand raised in a royal wave.

"Thank you," he said. "Thank you very much. Thank you very much."

17

The Summer Hockey Camp World Peewee Championship would be a single match, Screech Owls against Aeros, winner take all. Muck Munro would be behind the Owls' bench, and Sarah's father, Mr. Cuthbertson, would handle the Aeros' bench. Simon and Jason would referee. Starting centres: Sarah Cuthbertson for the Aeros, Travis Lindsay for the Screech Owls.

Travis couldn't remember ever feeling quite so alive before the puck had even dropped. It was better than before the championship game in Lake Placid, the big game at the Little Stanley Cup in Toronto, the fantastic final against the Waskaganish Wolverines at the First Nations Pee Wee Hockey Tournament in James Bay. And yet nothing was at stake here. There were no reporters in the stands, no scouts, almost no fans. If you took away the parents, the seats would be completely empty. The game wasn't sanctioned, the officials weren't real, and the score wouldn't count for anything but a bit of good-natured ribbing.

But it felt good. It felt absolutely right when Travis was taping on his shin pads – right one first, then left – and Muck had walked in and scowled at them. It felt perfect when he'd come in after everyone was dressed and Nish had started holding his gut and bouncing lightly so his head kept dipping down toward his knees. Muck had stood there and waited for everyone's attention, Nish's included. He reminded the forwards to keep to the hash marks in their own end, and the defence not to get caught pinching, and told them all to watch their passes.

Muck was right back where he belonged.

Sarah smiled at Travis just before Simon dropped the puck. It was great to be back playing with Sarah – even if she was on the other team. It was great to be reminded what a beautiful skater she was and what a brilliant playmaker. Travis wished she was still with the Owls, but he understood; she said she was headed for the 2002 Olympics in Salt Lake City, and everyone was absolutely sure she would make it.

The puck dropped, and the roar that burst from the parents was as loud and excited as in any real tournament.

Travis used Sarah's own little trick and plucked the puck out of the air before it hit the ice. He pulled it into his skates, turned so his hip blocked Sarah from checking him, and sent a quick pass back to Nish.

He was sure he heard Nish laugh as he picked up the puck.

Nish waited for Sarah's winger to chase him, then slipped the puck neatly between her skates and bounced a pass off the boards to Derek, who hit Travis at centre.

Travis didn't have to think, didn't even have to look. This, he told himself, is when hockey becomes art. He and Dmitri had worked this play so many times, they could do it in their sleep. He lofted the puck up and past the defence, while Dmitri used his astonishing speed to slip around the defence and get instantly clear. The shoulder fake . . . the Aeros goalie went down . . . and Dmitri roofed a backhand.

Owls 1, Aeros 0.

Travis closed his eyes when he got to the bench. He could feel Muck's big hand on his neck. He could feel Nish smack the seat of his pants with his stick. He could feel Dmitri's shoulder against his, the two of them now so used to each other on the ice that they no longer needed words or even looks to communicate. They just *knew* where each other was, and where each other would be.

Sarah's line had stayed out. She was still smiling. And before the face-off, she skated right along the Owls' bench.

"*Hey, Naked Boy!*" she called out.

Naked Boy? Everyone looked around, wondering what she meant. She was looking directly at Nish. He had his head down, but was watching her suspiciously.

"*What about it, Naked Boy?*" Sarah called. "*No skinny dipping so far?*"

"Tonight," Nish said.

"*Sure,*" Sarah laughed. "*We'll believe it when we see it!*"

"You won't see nothin'," Nish said, shaking his head.

"That's 'cause there's nothing to see!" kidded Sarah.

Simon whistled for the centres to come to centre ice for the face-off, and Sarah skated away, still laughing.

Travis leaned back and said to Nish: "What's this about 'Naked Boy'?"

Nish shook his head. "I have no idea – but it's a great improvement over 'Fat Boy.'"

The game went back and forth for more than an hour. Sarah scored; Gordie Griffith scored on a hard shot from high in the circle; an Aeros defence scored on a deflection; Nish scored on a low shot from the point; Travis scored; and Sarah scored again, on a beautiful solo rush in which she simply skated around poor Wilson and drew Jeremy half out of his net before dropping the puck in over the line.

Owls 4, Aeros 3.

"*Last two minutes of play!*" Simon shouted before dropping the puck again.

The Owls and Aeros both pulled off quick line changes. Muck wanted Travis's line out, with Nish and Data back on defence. The Aeros, of course, wanted Sarah out. She had scored twice and set up the third of the Aeros' three goals, and she was clearly fired up for this match against her old team and coach.

The ice was bad. Travis hated ice toward the end of the period and late in games. He loved new ice, so freshly flooded it was as if his skates were writing his name on the smooth surface. He liked quick, smooth ice for passing, hard ice for his fast turns, quick ice for his shots. This ice was chopped up and snowy. He could barely carry the puck in it.

Nish had the puck behind his own net, watching, waiting. If he could kill some time, so much the better. The Owls had the lead, after all. But at the very least, he wanted to get the puck out clean so the Owls could take it into the Aeros' end. Sarah Cuthbertson couldn't score from there.

Travis knew his play. He was to skate back hard and turn sharp right in front of his own net. Heading up ice on a slight angle, Nish would either hit him with a direct pass or else fire it out along the boards for either Derek or Dmitri on the wing to chop out past the defence so Travis could pick the puck up in the neutral zone. Travis could then cross centre ice and dump it in.

Travis dug deep and turned. Nish made a fancy play, firing the puck on his backhand so it hit the boards behind him and bounced out just after the forechecking forward had gone by. Nish had time, and he saw Travis. He went for the up-ice pass. He passed hard, and the puck hit the back of Travis's blade perfectly, right at the blueline.

Travis was already in full flight. He looked up immediately to see one defence charging him, chancing a poke check. He tried to do what Nish had done earlier in the game – just slip the puck between the checker's skates. But that had been on good ice, and the ice was now so thick and slow that the puck stopped dead, and the checker had a chance to drag her skate so it picked up the puck.

The Aero kicked the puck ahead to her stick and then hit Sarah Cuthbertson, who was charging back. Sarah turned instantly, actually passing to herself by leaving a drop pass which she then picked up going the other way. Travis couldn't believe how fast she had been able to change from one direction to the other.

There was only Nish back. He was too smart to be fooled again by Sarah's trick of picking up the puck. He wasn't about to lunge; he was going to wait.

Sarah bent as if to scoop the puck again, but Nish refused to go for it. She scooped snow instead, flicking it in the air at Nish's head. He instinctively ducked, and when he moved slightly, Sarah dropped the puck into her skates, knocked it from one blade to the other and then back up onto her stick, which was already on the other side of Nish.

A quick wrist shot, and all Travis could see was the net bulge behind Jeremy.

Sarah had tied the game: Owls 4, Aeros 4.

The Aeros leapt from the bench and jumped all over Sarah. Simon blew his whistle, and the game was over. A tie. The best result possible. The parents rose in a standing ovation. Muck raced across the ice and shook Mr. Cuthbertson's hand, the two of them laughing at what they had just seen.

The two teams lined up to shake hands. Travis followed Nish, who seemed heartbroken that he had let Sarah slip away.

"C'mon, you owed her one," Travis said.

"I guess."

They came to Sarah, who had her helmet off and was still laughing.

"Now you know why we call you 'Naked Boy,'" she said to Nish.

"I don't get it," he said.

"I just undressed you out there, didn't I?"

18

'm doing it."

Travis had never seen such determination on his friend's face.

"I'm doing it," Nish repeated.

Tomorrow they would be going home. They had just had the big end-of-camp dinner, both teams present, and special awards had been given to Sarah Cuthbertson, for Most Valuable Player, and to Travis, much to his surprise, for Most Valuable Camper. He had a suspicion that Muck had come up with this one on his own. Before Muck could announce the winner, the entire gathering had risen to their feet to honour Muck with long, loud, spontaneous applause.

They would end this extraordinary week at hockey camp with a marshmallow roast and a moonlight swim.

"I'm going to do it."

It was a beautiful night. The parents had built a huge bonfire down by the shore, and it sparked and roared, lighting up the entire beach and halfway out to the diving platform at the end of the dock. The stars were out, big and bright and too many even to begin counting. Someone pointed out Orion. Everyone thought of Mr. Clifford, and how sad it was that such a kind, interesting man could have ended up a murderer.

They toasted marshmallows. Data amazed the entire gathering by burning his marshmallows until they were like pieces of black coal, and then biting them whole off the end of his toasting stick. Nish amazed everyone by eating somewhere between fifty and a hundred of them. Some of them he didn't even wait to toast.

It wasn't Nish showing off, Travis knew. It was nerves.

"I'm still going to do it," he said when they were all gathered around the fire. One of the parents had brought a guitar, and a singsong was starting up.

The Screech Owls and Aeros were starting to swim. Sarah was first off the diving platform, and she swam out in the dark, black water and turned on her back. "*Any Nish sightings?*" she called.

"*None!*"

"*Pssst!*"

Travis turned just as he was about to dive off the end of the dock. He could barely make Nish out in the shadows.

"*Over here! C'm'ere!*"

Travis hurried in under the diving platform, where Nish was huddled with Andy. Even in the dim light, Travis could see Nish was shivering. And it wasn't a cold evening.

"Y-you two are m-my witnesses, okay?" Nish said.

"Okay," Andy said.

"*You're really going to do it?*" said Travis.

"Just watch!"

Quick as a flash, Nish dropped his bathing trunks. He dived off the dock, and swam deep under the water, as far out as he could go.

But when he came up, he was screaming.

"TTTTUUUUUURRTTTTLLLE!!!!!!"

Travis couldn't believe his eyes. The water around Nish was foaming as he flailed away. Still screaming, Nish raced for the dock, his arms thrashing desperately in the water.

Halfway back, he stopped, reached down into the water, and shrieked.

"HHHELLLPPPPPP MMMEEEEE!"

Andy and Travis raced to the end of the dock as Nish approached, his flailing arms splashing them both. He reached up, still screaming.

"HE GRABBED ME!! THE TURTLE GRABBED MY TOE!!!"

Others were screaming now and racing to get out. Travis couldn't believe it. Had Mr. Clifford lied to them about snapping turtles? He'd said they'd never attack.

Nish used his friends' outstretched arms to pull himself up and clear of the water.

He reached under the diving platform for his bathing suit. *It was gone!*

"NNNNNNOOOOOOOOOOOOOO!!!" Nish screamed.

Covering himself with his hands, Nish took off. Stark naked, he ran the length of the dock and onto the shore, past the sing-song, which had come to a sudden halt, and up the path to the cabins, screaming all the way.

"NNNNNNNNNNNOOOOOOOOOOOOOOOOOO!!!"

"*Go, Naked Boy!*"

Sarah was in the water at the end of the dock. She had a scuba mask and snorkel pulled up off her face.

Sarah, the snapping turtle.

She reached out, and someone behind Andy and Travis threw her a pair of dark bathing trunks.

They turned. It was Liz Moscovitz and Jennie Staples. They must have swiped Nish's trunks when Andy and Travis were "witnessing" Nish's skinny dip.

Laughing, Sarah held Nish's bathing suit above her head.

"*This* trophy I'm keeping," she said. "You hit somebody from behind, you're going pay for it!"

In the distance, Travis was sure he heard a screen door slam. And then the inside door.

And even then, he could still make out the call of the Nishikawa.

"NNNNNNNNNNNNOOOOOOOOOOOOOOOOOO!!!"

THE END

THE SCREECH OWLS SERIES

Roy MacGregor has been involved in hockey all his life. Growing up in Huntsville, Ontario, he competed for several years against a kid named Bobby Orr, who was playing in nearby Parry Sound. He later returned to the game when he and his family settled in Ottawa, where he worked for the *Ottawa Citizen* and became the Southam National Sports Columnist. He still plays old-timers hockey and was a minor-hockey coach for more than a decade.

Roy MacGregor is the author of several classics in the literature of hockey. *Home Game* (written with Ken Dryden) and *The Home Team* (nominated for the Governor General's Award for Non-fiction) were both No. 1 national bestsellers. He has also written the game's best-known novel, *The Last Season*. His most recent non-fiction hockey book is *A Loonie for Luck*, the true story of the famous good-luck charm that inspired Canada's men and women to win hockey gold at the Salt Lake City Winter Olympics. His other books include *Road Games*, *The Seven A.M. Practice*, *A Life in the Bush*, and *Escape*.

Roy MacGregor is currently a columnist for the *Globe and Mail*. He lives in Kanata, Ontario, with his wife, Ellen. They have four children, Kerry, Christine, Jocelyn, and Gordon.

You can talk to Roy MacGregor at **www.screechowls.com**